PRAISE for Kathleen Morgan's *Embrace the Dawn*

"In an honest and gripping tale of an American woman taken to Scotland . . . *Embrace the Dawn* unfolds into a glorious story of hope amidst Scotland's green hills."
Marilynn Griffith, author of the Shades of Style series

"Well-written, exciting, and action-packed story."
Library Journal

"Ms. Morgan brings 17th-century Scotland to life with her powerful story. . . . The characters are strong and engaging."
Romantic Times BOOKreviews

"Ms. Morgan deftly weaves a tale of unexpected love with an unsolved murder and the machinations of men who crave power and influence. Her tragic recounting of history horrifies, while her message of faith provides hope during one of Scotland's darkest hours."
Historical Novels Review

"Realistic dialogue, a vibrant setting, and powerful narrative all held me entranced from beginning to end. For a few hours, I was whisked away to the cold, damp Scottish highlands in 1691. . . ."
The Romance Readers Connection

"Morgan has a gift in weaving a story that exposes the soul of its characters, draws the reader in, and wraps them in authentic culture and history. . . . Amazing. A book worth experiencing."
Kay, Amazon.com reader

A NOVEL

Embrace the Dawn

KATHLEEN MORGAN

TYNDALE HOUSE PUBLISHERS, INC.
CAROL STREAM, ILLINOIS

Visit Tyndale's exciting Web site at www.tyndale.com

TYNDALE and Tyndale's quill logo are registered trademarks of Tyndale House Publishers, Inc.

Embrace the Dawn

Cover designed by Beth Sparkman.

Interior designed by Catherine Bergstrom

Edited by Kathryn S. Olson

This novel is a work of fiction. Names, characters, places, and incidents either are the product of the author's imagination or are used fictitiously. Any resemblance to actual events, locales, organizations, or persons living or dead is entirely coincidental and beyond the intent of either the author or publisher.

Library of Congress Cataloging-in-Publication Data

Morgan, Kathleen, date.
  Embrace the dawn / Kathleen Morgan.
    p. cm.
  ISBN 0-8423-4097-1
    1. Scotland—History—17th century—Fiction. 2. Highlands (Scotland)—Fiction. 3. Mothers and sons—Fiction. I. Title.
PS3563.O8647 E48 2002
813′.54—dc21   2002000070

ISBN-13: 978-1-4143-1366-7
ISBN-10: 1-4143-1366-7

Printed in the United States of America

13 12 11 10 09 08 07
 7   6   5   4   3   2   1

To my sister Linda

Delight thyself also in the Lord;
and he shall give thee
the desires of thine heart.

Psalm 37:4, KJV

OUTSIDE the old fortified castle a fierce storm raged.

Sheets of water pelted the long, leaded windows. Flashes of lightning illuminated the curtain of darkness, revealing glimpses of windswept trees and sodden landscape. Blasts of frigid air seeped through crumbling chinks in the ancient edifice, intensifying the stone-damp chill.

A spray of gooseflesh tightened the skin of Killian Campbell's lower arms. She clasped them more tightly to her, crushing the black velvet bodice of her gown, and shivered. Quickening her pace, she drew alongside Adam Campbell.

The laird of Castle Achallader glanced over as he led her up the winding stone staircase, a wry grin teasing the corners of his mouth. "A bit cool for yer blood tonight, is it, lass? Bear with it a moment more and we'll be in the library. The fire burning there will warm ye."

She smiled back at him. Dressed in a fine, white, lace-trimmed shirt and a blue-and-green plaid—which was little more than a length of tartan fabric gathered into a skirt, belted, and the rest slung across his shoulder and fastened with a large, silver brooch—the handsome, raven-haired man had been more than kind this evening. At Killian's express request, he had willingly slipped away from hosting a grand ball to personally escort her to the library.

"You'd think," she said, "after all these months in Scotland I'd have grown used to the dampness."

Adam chuckled. "Ye don't grow so much used to it as learn to ignore it. And even that takes years of living with the wind and rain. A mere six months here, after the warmth of yer home in the Colonies, are but a wee taste of things to come."

Killian gripped the oak balustrade. The time-smoothed wood felt solid, substantial, and even strangely comforting. Far more solid than the seven years of marriage she had worked so hard to save and now realized was beyond salvaging. Far more comforting than this strange, savage land her husband had insisted on dragging her and their son to in the hopes of mending their crumbling marriage. And certainly far more substantial than her self-confidence, battered from years of Alexander's extreme possessiveness, a possessiveness that had gradually disintegrated into constant suspicion and periodic beatings.

She sighed, casting the pointless regrets aside. She was, after all, her husband's property. Few would sympathize, much less care, and especially none of these brutish Highlanders.

"I don't know if I could ever adapt to this climate. Though it *is* similar to where I grew up as a child in Massachusetts, I'm afraid I've long ago come to love the warmth of Alexander's and my home in Virginia."

"Aye, lass." Adam paused at the head of the stairs, swung open the door before them, then motioned her forward. "I can well understand."

Killian stepped inside. The library was dimly lit, the fire blazing in the huge stone fireplace the only source of light. She glanced around, her perception one of shadowy furniture and stale air, tinged with the pungent scent of woodsmoke. Adam closed the door, then strode to two high-backed, heavily scrolled walnut armchairs with red-and-blue-brocaded, upholstered seats set before the hearth.

"Would ye care to sit?" He indicated a chair. "Rest yer bones a bit?"

"No, thank you. I'd rather stand."

Killian walked to one set of tall, dark walnut shelves covering three walls of the room. All were filled with books, many with the thick leather bindings and gilt overlay of volumes dearly bought.

Tentatively, reverently, she touched them, running her fingers down the spines of several finely wrought tomes. The raised leather-

2

work felt opulent; the feel of fine craftsmanship sent ripples of appreciative awareness coursing through her.

She pulled a volume from its niche on the shelf, turning it to cradle the spine in the curve of her palm. She thumbed through the pages, admiring the elegant print, the occasional hand-drawn illustration. Here and there a word caught her eye, then a phrase, a paragraph.

Killian closed the volume and replaced it on the shelf. For one last, lingering moment her fingers traced the line of books, savoring their texture, their haunting promise of secrets untold—and the brief respite they seemed to offer from the brutal reality that was now her life.

Then she turned back to Adam. "I want to thank you for coming up here with me. I know you're Alexander's cousin—however distant—but at this moment you're the closest thing I have to kin." She smiled ruefully. "Especially now, so far from home."

He said nothing, eyeing her with quiet intensity.

"It's . . . it's about Alexander," Killian forced herself to continue. "I think it's best I take Gavin and return home . . . back to Virginia . . . without him."

Adam's brow furrowed in puzzlement. "But Alexander announced this verra night ye all, yer son included, were staying with us until spring. I dinna understand."

She wet her lips, considering then discarding myriad ways in which to broach this delicate subject. How *did* one explain that one's husband—a man she had once adored and would've done anything to please—had become a monster? Indeed, who'd believe it of the affable, generous Alexander Campbell? Only his wife and son ever saw his dark side.

"My marriage to Alexander is over, Adam." As if the failure was all hers, Killian blushed furiously. After the years of insults and degradation, she almost believed it herself. *Almost.*

"This trip to Scotland was Alexander's idea. I'd no say in the matter. But this isn't—and never will be—my home. With or without Alexander, I mean to leave."

"So, ye came all the way to the Highlands because yer husband wished it, did ye? Yet what could ye possibly find here that'd mend it better than yer fine life on yer tobacco plantation in Virginia?"

Though she knew she shouldn't let it, Adam's skeptical query stung. "He claimed a visit back to his home and blood kin would help him set his mind aright."

"And ye, being the devoted wife that ye are, were willing to give him even that." Adam stroked his chin in thought. "What do ye want of me, lass?"

Her pulse quickening, she met his somber gaze. "A loan. A loan to cover the expense of obtaining passage back home."

"And how will ye repay me? Yer husband's tobacco plantation is held in his name, is it not? Do ye mean to hurry home and try to sell it behind his back?"

"No." Fiercely, Killian denied his accusation. "I can legally put claim to my dowry. I'll pay you out of that."

"And then what will ye do?"

She glanced toward the leaded window overlooking the huge forest only yards from Achallader's outer wall. Outside, the heavens continued to weep, the darkness punctuated by abrupt flashes of lightning. Funny how the weather mirrored her life of late. The sky poured out its sorrow, interspersed with bouts of frustrated, if impotent, anger.

"I don't know." The prospects for a divorced woman were dismal. Just not *quite* as dismal as her life as Alexander's wife. "Go home to my aunt and uncle, if they'll have me, I suppose. My uncle's shipping business is thriving. He may well need another clerk."

Killian turned back to Adam. "Before I wed Alexander, I kept all my uncle's books and was quite adept at it. Even after all these years, his letters still assure me he has yet to find another clerk as exacting as I."

Adam rose from his chair and walked over to stare into the fire. After a long moment, he looked up at her. "I feel for yer plight, lass. Truly I do. But Alexander's a fine, braw lad, and what ye ask of me goes against my sense of kinship with him. Mayhap ye don't understand how deeply a Highlander's—"

"I've an inkling, thank you." In spite of her best efforts to hide her disappointment, Killian knew there was an edge to her voice.

As courteously as possible, Adam had just refused to help her. She wasn't surprised. He was Alexander's blood kin, after all. Yet, without Adam's help, what was she to do?

From some place far away, a passing roll of thunder muted the pounding clamor of her heart. In one, dizzying rush all her tightly strung control, all her remaining strength, fled. Killian's knees buckled. She grasped frantically at the chair.

"Are ye all right, lass?" A look of concern tautened Adam's chiseled features. "Ye're white as a ghost. Do ye need to sit for a spell?"

"N-no, that won't be necessary." With an impassioned shake of her head, Killian flung the unsettling sensations aside. "I-I'm fine. All I need is some food. I was so worried and overwrought today, wondering how to approach you about my problem, that I haven't had much appetite." She managed a weak smile. "That's all it is. Just a little light-headedness."

Adam grasped her elbow to steady her. "Then a bit of hearty Scots food is what ye're needing. Ye're such a wee slip of a thing to go without eating all day. It's no surprise ye're so unwell." He tugged gently on her arm. "Come, we both should be returning to the Lion's Hall and the ball."

The big Highlander had been her one chance of help. Killian dragged in a deep, steadying breath. Surely, though, another opportunity would eventually come her way. In the meantime, all she had to do was not provoke her husband's violent temper and avoid him as much as possible whenever he became intoxicated. All she had to do was stay alive.

"Ah, yes, the ball." She met Adam's gaze, her pride refusing to allow her to weep or beg. "I've been selfish keeping you so long from your other guests. I beg pardon."

"Och, it was a pleasure, and no mistake. How often does one get the chance to have a bonny lassie all to oneself?"

"The pleasure was all mine."

A flicker of guilt, regret even, passed across Adam's face. He offered her his arm. "Shall we go?"

"Yes." She accepted his arm, then hesitated. "One thing more, if you please."

"Aye, lass?"

"If I could impose on you not to mention our little talk to my husband . . . well, I'd be most grateful."

Adam nodded. "It's best, I think, I not involve myself in yer marital difficulties. In *any* way, if ye get my meaning?"

She dragged in a relieved breath. "Thank you. Thank you ever so much."

"Come along, then. I wouldn't want ye missing the bagpipes at midnight," he said as he began to lead Killian from the room. "I found some sheet music that must have been hidden away for years. One song's particularly lovely and addresses some daft old prophecy about Glencoe. It's called 'Glen of Weeping,' and the pipers will be playing it. . . ."

The sound of laughter and happy voices engulfed them as they headed down the stairs and entered the lavishly decorated Lion's Hall. In spite of the gaiety, Killian felt removed, distant—as if she were viewing the scene from afar. Adam deposited her at a long table laden with food, filled her a plate, then grinned apologetically, mumbling something about other guests.

She turned numbly to her food. The meat and vegetables swam before her until they resembled a churning mass of color. Killian felt ill.

Quickly setting the plate aside, she hurried to the punch bowl. With trembling hands, she ladled herself a cupful of mulled cider. Its sweet, spice-scented aroma steadied her. She inhaled deeply.

The cup was warm in her hands. Killian clasped it to her. *This* was reality. This room, these people, this drink. The future—a future that held only two choices: continued suffering or escape—didn't matter tonight. On the morrow she'd face the dilemma anew, but not tonight.

She sipped the steaming cider carefully, praying its tart sweetness would soothe her stomach. Try as she might, though, she could barely taste it.

A hand settled suddenly around her arm, squeezing hard. Killian jumped. The cider sloshed over the sides of her cup, drenching her hand with its sticky sweetness.

"And where have *ye* been the past hour?" her husband, bending close, asked. "The dancing has begun—" he made a sharp, sweeping gesture— "and several folk commented on yer conspicuous absence."

Killian followed the direction of Alexander's hand. The hall was jammed with people. Some moved to the gay twanging of fiddle music floating down from the minstrel's gallery overlooking the room. Others stood about in groups, laughing and talking.

Alexander tugged on her arm. "Come along. I've told several of the nobles, the notable Sir John Campbell, Earl of Breadalbane, and Captain Robert Campbell of Glenlyon among them, all about my lovely young wife. If we don't hurry, they'll begin to wonder if ye're not avoiding them."

"No. Please, not now."

Killian dug in her heels. As unwise as it might ultimately be to refuse her husband, to be paraded tonight before strange men like some prize mare was more than she could endure.

"In a little while, perhaps," she pleaded. "I don't feel up to meeting anyone just now."

His eyes narrowed. "Are ye ill, then?"

"No. I'm fine. Just fine."

A muscle began to tick near Alexander's left cheekbone. "Have it yer way. Compose yerself, then come to me. Don't tarry overlong, though, or I won't be happy."

With that he strode off, disappearing in the press of bodies. Besides his voluminous belted plaid, Alexander, like many of the other men there, sported weaponry at even as innocuous an event as a ball. In addition to the ceremonial smallsword, he wore a small dagger known as a *sgian dubh* shoved into his knee-high stockings, and a flintlock pistol slipped in the back of his belt. But then Alexander had always possessed a fascination with weapons—a fascination, Killian now realized, shared by many others of his clan.

It seemed an integral part of the Scottish and, particularly, the Highland heritage. A heritage she had foolishly married into when, as an idealistic, overly romantic girl of seventeen, she had allowed the dashing and already tobacco-wealthy Alexander Campbell to sweep her off her feet.

But then, after the loss of her parents at an early age, and life with her father's dour brother and equally dreary wife, Alexander didn't have to press very hard to win Killian's consent. Killian had long dreamt of a happier life. Alexander Campbell seemed to promise that in every way.

If only she had known then of the fierce emotions and single-minded devotion of the Scots. Of their simple, direct way of dealing with anger and frustration, utilizing savage methods that usually culminated in violence and, frequently, even death.

She'd had more than her fill of Scottish ways just living with her husband. The increasingly brutal tactics he used to control and intimidate had only grown worse over the years.

Yet as hard as it would be for her to walk away from their marriage, as severely as church and society would chastise her for such scandalous behavior, Killian knew now she had little other choice. If she valued her life, and perhaps even that of their son, time had run out. Whether she wished to or not, she *must* begin anew or the choice might permanently—and fatally—be taken from her.

"A toast," Adam Campbell's deep burr reverberated from across the room. "A toast to commemorate this glorious eve!"

Save for the rustle of satin and stiff petticoats, the faint clink of metal swords, the room went quiet. Adam glanced around, then lifted his cup. "Here's to the heath, the hill, and the heather; the bonnet, the plaid, the kilt, and the feather!"

At the beloved Highland toast, all gathered returned the salute, then drank. Once more, Adam lifted high his cup. "Tonight, much will be decided to the mutual benefit of both Scotland and England. Plans will be made, pacts sealed that, thanks to the courage of these brave lads here, will draw Clan Campbell yet closer to the seat of British power. I give ye, lads and lassies, a night that'll grant us all our hearts' desires!"

With that, Adam downed his punch.

"To our hearts' desires!" the gathering cried, following his lead.

Her heart's desires . . .

As she again raised her cup, a shiver rippled down Killian's spine. She had thought she had put such aspirations aside forever, burying them along with all her other shattered dreams.

Yet still, Adam's words as he proposed the toast had touched some chord deep within her. Perhaps it was but a bitter reminder of hopes long dead, crushed beneath the unrelenting brutality of marital life gone awry. Or perhaps it was something more. A pang of envy for what others had always known, and she—miserable failure that she was—never would.

Whatever the source of her sudden, renewed attack of distress, Killian couldn't bear to remain in the Lion's Hall a moment longer. She hurried to the food table, flung down her cup of cider, and fled.

✝

MINUTES later, Killian shut the bedchamber door quietly behind her. Her five-year-old son, Gavin, was sound asleep on his little pallet in the corner near the head of the massive, four-poster tester bed. Killian tiptoed to him.

Not that he'd have heard her approach if she had ridden in clad in full armor on some warhorse, she thought wryly as thunder boomed yet again overhead. Gavin could sleep through anything. She knelt beside him and brushed a wayward lock of blond hair—hair the exact shade as her own tumble of long, pale gold tresses—off his forehead, then kissed him tenderly.

He was her life, the only reality that mattered anymore. He was the reason she had finally made up her mind to leave Alexander, when her husband's violent outbursts had not only escalated to dangerous levels in the past year, but had even begun to involve their son. A son Alexander had once admitted he had never even wanted.

Yet still a sense of sadness engulfed her. She had so wanted to preserve the marriage—their family—hoping against hope she'd eventually be able to help Alexander—to save him. Ah, if only she could've loved him enough!

If it had only been her, despite the personal danger, Killian thought she might have persevered. She was a grown woman. She had sworn before God and man to uphold her marriage vows through good times and bad. And her love of the Lord still remained, even if her love for the man Alexander had become had long ago died. Gavin, however, didn't deserve to live with that decision or its consequences.

Soon now, all she'd have left was her faith in God, her love for her son, and the promise of a fresh start, if only she could return to the relative safety of her aunt and uncle's home in Massachusetts. She had learned a lot in the past seven years of marriage. Learned she couldn't depend on life to be everything she had always thought it should be.

And learned, though it had been the most difficult lesson of all, to follow her head rather than her heart. Some dreams died hard, but die they must. Especially the dream of ever finding her heart's desire in the arms of another man.

Gavin shifted in his sleep, mumbled a few incoherent words, then quieted.

Killian smiled with grim resolve. Whatever it took, she would ensure a safe, stable existence for the both of them. After what they had been through, they deserved a little security, a little peace and happiness. There was no place in her life for anything more, though. The scars, the doubts and fears, ran far, far too deep.

She rose, turned from Gavin's bed, and began to remove her pearl earrings and necklace. Lightning flashed just outside, illuminating the room. Almost instantly, it was followed by a deafening thunderclap.

The building shook; the floor trembled beneath her feet. She jumped, dropping the necklace. With a crack the long strand hit the aged wooden planks and broke, scattering pearls everywhere. Killian barely noticed.

Someone had entered the bedchamber. Someone stood there in the shadows, watching, waiting.

Her heartbeat faltered.

"I told ye to come to me and not tarry," Alexander said, "or I wouldn't be happy."

With a strangled cry, Killian leaped back. She knew that tone of voice. It always precluded a vicious attack. She shuddered, her palms damp, her mouth gone dry. Not now. Not again. God help her, but she couldn't bear it again!

"I-I looked for you." She cast about frantically for something—anything—to appease him. "I just f-felt too ill to be pleasant company, so I decided to r-retire for the eve." Try as she might, Killian couldn't hide the quaver in her voice.

"And did I give ye leave to depart? Do ye realize what a laughingstock ye made of me before my friends? Do ye, wench?" Hands fisted at his sides, Alexander stepped from the shadows and advanced on her. "Ye've been a naughty lass to disappoint me so. Ye must now take yer punishment."

Grim satisfaction mixed with a rising slur in her husband's voice. Terror vibrated through Killian. Alexander was at his most dangerous when drunk.

What am I to do, dear Lord? He's going to beat me.

Her mind raced for a way out of the terrible dilemma she had suddenly been thrust into. Insulated behind these thick, stone walls and muted by the revelry below, no one would hear or come to her aid.

"Why don't you return to your friends and explain that I took ill?" Killian fought to gain control of her rising panic. "Then, on the morrow, I'll personally tender each and every man my abject apology. We can just as easily set everything aright on the morrow."

"On the morrow, ye'll be in no condition to set aught aright." A fist raised, Alexander lurched toward her.

With a gasp, Killian sprang aside. Propelled by the momentum of his greater weight and liquor-dulled reflexes, Alexander couldn't halt his forward momentum. He crashed into a bedpost, slipped, and fell, slamming his head on the wooden floor.

Her breath in her throat, Killian waited for her husband to rise. When he didn't, she gulped in a chestful of air and bent toward him. Was he alive, or had the blow to his head killed him?

Alexander moaned, began to stir. Killian hesitated but an instant longer before running around the bed and waking Gavin. She shoved his shoes on his feet and draped him in the thick plaid that had covered him. Then, grabbing her cloak hanging by the door, Killian all but dragged her son from the bedchamber.

†

"HURRY, SWEETING. We've got to hurry!"

The long corridor leading to the staircase and the castle's entry hall seemed endless. To quicken his pace, Killian pulled a little harder on Gavin's hand.

"M-Mama!"

She glanced back at her son. Gavin's short little legs churned furiously. The plaid and his white nightshirt flapped about him. His big blue eyes were round with fear.

Remorse flooded Killian. Her actions of the past minutes had frightened her child. She forced her steps to slow. "It's all right, sweeting. Mama was just upset and in a hurry to leave. We'll walk slower."

"It's all right, Mama. I l-like to run."

Killian smiled at his childish attempt to support her. Gavin had always been like that—gentle and thoughtful, protective. As if he knew instinctively she needed the nurturance even more than he.

Guilt plucked at her. Once again she had allowed her emotions to cloud what truly mattered—Gavin and his sense of security, his happiness. Her responsibilities as his mother.

She slowed her pace even more. "You know, sweeting, I like to run, too. But I think we've done enough for one night. Are you ready to play a little game?"

Gavin nodded eagerly.

Killian paused at the head of the stairs leading to the entry hall. Just then, a furious curse emanated down the hall from where they had come. She froze.

"Woman, hie yer perfidious self to me! Now, I say. *Now!*" Alexander's voice, hoarse with anger, rose above the din of the storm.

Horror filled Killian. Her husband's mood had escalated to one of his rare, murderous rages. There was no telling what he might do. And if Gavin should inadvertently get in his way . . .

She turned back to the hallway. Already, Alexander's forward progress blocked any hope of escape down the stairs, where they might find refuge in the press of revelers in the Great Hall. The door to the chapel, however, inset in its carved stone arch, lay just a short distance farther down the corridor. If she and Gavin could make it to the chapel, then bolt themselves in for the night, perhaps, on the morrow, Alexander would've forgotten the reason for his fury.

Killian stooped and took her son by his shoulders. "We're going to play a little game with Papa. We're going to run away and hide."

Gavin's eyes brightened with excitement. "What fun, Mama!"

She shot one last, furtive look over her shoulder. Already, Alexander staggered down the corridor toward them. She pulled Gavin up into her arms. "Hold on tight, sweeting. It's time to go."

He nodded, wrapped his arms tightly around her neck, and clenched shut his eyes.

Killian sprinted for the chapel, reached it and, setting Gavin down, shoved open its stout wooden portal. It swung wide at her slightest touch, opening onto a long, dimly lit room.

A blast of chill, turbulent air swirled about her. The rain clattered against the tall, stained-glass panes. The wind howled outside.

Hazy candlelight from the altar at the far end of the room cast shadows that stretched across the floor and ensnared the stone pillars just inside the door. Wooden pews stood aligned in neat rows on either side of the aisle. Off to one side in a stone niche, votive candles flickered in their diminutive, colored-glass containers.

She hesitated. Perhaps it'd be best not to bring her troubles into such a holy place.

Then the sound of Alexander's footsteps sealed her resolve. Killian motioned Gavin in and closed the door. As she began to slide the wooden crossbar in place, however, someone pushed hard from the other side.

Killian toppled backward, striking the last row of pews. She grasped at the wooden bench and righted herself. Arms flailing, Alexander all but sailed into the chapel and plummeted to the stone floor.

For an instant, sheer terror paralyzed her. There was no way to escape her husband now that he had gotten into the chapel. As drunk as he was, Alexander was still capable of moving quickly when he wanted to. Even if she carried Gavin, Killian knew she'd not be able to slip past her husband.

She pressed her hand to her breast, suddenly remembering the bodice knife she kept hidden there. Briefly, Killian considered withdrawing it and using it to defend herself. Then her hand fell away. She could never harm her husband, not even to save her own life.

Ah, how she wished now she had immediately sought out Adam and the ball! It was too late, though, to regret her earlier actions. All she could do was find some way—besides the front door—to flee the chapel.

She spied a smaller wooden portal in the wall to the right of the altar. Killian pointed toward it. "Gavin, the door! Run ahead and open it for us!"

Her son clutched his plaid to himself and hurried down the aisle. "This is fun, Mama," he called from over his shoulder. "I like this game."

He reached the door, grasped the handle, and pulled down. Despite his best efforts, the door wouldn't budge. Killian shot Alexander, who was slowly climbing to his feet, one agonized glance, then sprinted after her son. Reaching him, she jerked down on the door handle and shoved.

The outer door swung open onto a scene of pouring rain, a dark castle courtyard, and a tall stone wall. She choked back a swell of despair. They were trapped. There was nowhere else to run.

Behind Killian, pews clattered together as her husband made his lumbering way up the aisle. "Ye won't . . . ye won't escape yer just punishment," he roared. "Best ye turn back now . . . before ye make it all the worse."

Lightning flashed overhead. Thunder reverberated. And, in that brief instant of illumination, Killian saw another door across the courtyard in the castle wall.

The hairs rose on the back of her neck. An eerie presentiment prickled down her spine. Somehow, Killian knew freedom lay on the other side of that door. Freedom . . . and something more. But could she reach it and make it through in time?

Alexander's hoarse pants drew ever nearer. Killian stooped and pulled her son back into her arms.

"We're going out to play in the rain for a bit, sweeting." She wrapped the plaid snugly around him, then tucked him beneath her cloak.

Gavin looked up at her, trust shining in his eyes. "Yes, Mama."

A pang of remorse shot through her, but she swiftly squelched it. She had no other choice. She was alone and at her husband's mercy.

A quick lifting of her chin, a sharp intake of breath, and Killian raced out into the rain. Only when she reached the little door inset into the wall did she finally glance back. At that moment her husband stumbled from the chapel, slipped, and went sprawling on the slick cobblestones.

Killian set Gavin down, uttered a quick prayer that the iron bolt would slide, then grasped it with both hands and tried to pull it free. It wouldn't budge. Once more she tried with all her might, but to no avail.

Cursing foully, Alexander climbed to his feet and staggered toward them.

A sense of hopeless resignation swamped her. It was over then. She was at his mercy, and no one—not even God now, it seemed—cared.

In that terror-stricken moment, though, the shredded remnants of her pride no longer mattered. Lifting her eyes to the rain-drenched sky, Killian screamed out her frustration and fear. "Save us! Oh, please, sweet Jesus, *save us!*"

Once more Alexander slipped and fell, this time only yards away. Killian turned her back on her husband, unwilling to face the crazed fury she knew burned in his eyes. It didn't matter. Nothing mattered anymore.

She had lost.

Her desperate gaze fell on the iron bolt. That same desperation made her try one last time. Almost of their own accord, her hands rose, gripped the bolt, tugged. Tugged hard, jerking repeatedly over and over and over.

For long, sickening seconds the bolt seemed sealed in place. Then, with a grating sound, it finally slipped free.

With all her strength, Killian shoved at the door. The hinges creaked and groaned. The portal swung open.

She lifted Gavin back into her arms. Clasping him beneath her cloak, she fled into the storm-tossed night. Fled toward the forest.

Toward freedom.

2

THE RAIN sluiced down between the forest's canopy of leaves and thick branches, drenching Ruarc MacDonald to the skin. Still, at that particular moment, it was the least of his worries. Until a short time ago he had made steady progress toward Castle Achallader. Then, somewhere up ahead, a woman had screamed, a woman apparently heading toward him. He hadn't dared move from his hiding place behind a stand of tall bracken. On a night like this and in enemy lands, a man couldn't be too careful.

One way or another, Ruarc meant to reach Achallader and slip inside. One way or another, he intended to discover the reason for this large gathering of Campbell nobles. Clan Campbell's increasing affinity of late for King William and Queen Mary of England, combined with the nearing deadline for all Highland chiefs to sign the pledge of fealty to the two sovereigns, was ample cause for concern. After all, his own chief, Alasdair MacDonald, thanks to his steadfast loyalty to the exiled King James II, was one of the few remaining Highland leaders still left to sign.

Aye, there was much to be done this night and much danger in the doing. He didn't need some daft woman out in a storm to queer things for him. He also didn't, for that matter, need the Campbells discovering his presence.

The sound of footsteps—two pairs, one a woman's followed close behind now by a man's—drew nearer. Ruarc cursed softly. Pulling the excess plaid of his great kilt over his head, he hunkered down behind the large, coarse ferns.

"Oh, G-God! God, help us!" he heard the woman breathlessly cry. She slipped, skidding on the slick leaves and forest decay, then fell to her knees. She set down a blue-and-green plaid bundle and unwrapped it to reveal a small child clad only in shoes and a white nightshirt.

"Run, Gavin," she urged in an accent Ruarc recognized as one not of the Highlands. "Run quickly and hide!"

The lad climbed to his feet, hesitated but a moment, then scampered off. It was too late, however, if he had been meant to escape their pursuer. A tall, dark-haired man clad in Campbell colors raced up.

"Ye're not going anywhere." He grabbed the boy by the back of his nightshirt, lifting him high.

"No! Alexander, put him down!" The woman shoved to her feet and reached toward them. "Don't hurt—!"

With a growl, the man flung the boy aside. The lad hit the ground hard and lay there, unmoving, as the forest muck and mud seeped into and stained his nightshirt.

An anguished cry on her lips, the woman stumbled toward the boy. The man named Alexander was there to meet her, grabbing her by the arm and jerking her to him.

"I told ye to come, but nay, instead ye chose to disobey me," he shouted, his words slurred with drink. "Now ye must suffer the consequences!"

In a swift move Alexander grasped her by the throat, throttling the woman. She fought back. She kicked him, pummeling his face and chest, but to no avail. The man's strength was far superior to her own.

With a snarl that was equal parts disgust and anger, Ruarc flung back his plaid and rose. No honorable Highlander attacked a woman and child. As vital as his mission was to spy on the Campbells this eve, he couldn't in good conscience sit by and watch this woman be murdered.

And that was exactly what this Alexander intended to do, Ruarc realized as he made his stealthy way toward the pair. Even now, the woman had all but stopped fighting. Her choking sounds were weakening, her knees beginning to buckle.

Ruarc reached out, sank his fingers into Alexander's hair, and jerked him back. With a startled yelp the man lost his footing and fell, taking Ruarc with him. Both men struck the ground, then struggled immediately back to their feet. Ruarc was the first to regain his. He hit Alexander squarely in the jaw.

The man's head snapped back. His eyes rolled in their sockets. Then Alexander slumped to the ground.

Fists clenched, legs wide, Ruarc glared down at his opponent. Gradually, though, the sound of sobbing drifted through the soft clatter of rain. He turned away, walked to the woman.

Ever so gently, he took her by the arms and pulled her to her knees. "Are ye all right, lass?"

Aside from the reddened marks on her neck and her sodden, disheveled appearance, she looked unharmed. She was quite bonny, too, Ruarc noted dispassionately as a flash of lightning brightened the forest and their faces.

She gazed up at him, her eyes wide and staring. "My . . . my son." She tried to twist free of his clasp. "I must . . . see to my son."

Ruarc nodded and helped her to her feet. "Aye, that'd be best. It looked as if the lad took a bad fall."

The woman hurried to her child, knelt, and gathered him to her. The little boy lay limply in his mother's arms.

"Gavin." Tenderly, she wiped the bits of leaves and mud from his pale face. "Ah, sweeting, what has your father done? What has he done?"

His father. Freshened anger swelled in Ruarc. The brute! The man had been intent not only on murdering his wife but apparently his son, too. With a low, savage curse Ruarc wheeled about—and came face-to-face with the barrel of a long, black, flintlock pistol.

"Did ye think, then, so easily to best me?" Alexander made a quick, scathing assessment of Ruarc. "Ye're not from these parts, are ye? In fact, ye aren't even a Campbell."

He circled until he stood between Ruarc and his wife and child. Then, with a feral sneer, Alexander cocked his pistol and aimed it at Ruarc's heart.

A wild plan, to unsheathe his dirk and leap at the man before he could fire, filled Ruarc. There was always a chance that, in the rain, the flintlock would misfire. And if it didn't, Ruarc would still be able to use his dirk to deadly efficiency before he died. If for naught else, he could at least save a few lives this night, even if, in the doing, he failed in his primary mission.

In that split second of decision, Alexander's finger moved toward the trigger. Shouting a hoarse battle cry, Ruarc flung himself forward.

Then, with a burst of powder and flame, the pistol fired.

†

"M-MAMA? MAMA, wake up. *P-please* wake up!"

From somewhere on the other side of a deep, dark chasm, a small voice called. A small, sweet, beloved voice quavering against a faint backdrop of bagpipe music.

Killian stirred. She moaned.

"Mama?"

With an effort, she opened her eyes. Gavin, pale of face, blue of lip, and eyes huge with terror, knelt beside her. With a dirt-caked, shaking hand he reached out to her.

"Are you all right, Mama?"

"Y-yes." She shoved awkwardly to one elbow. It was cold, damp, and musty. Her head throbbed and, when she touched her forehead gingerly, Killian felt a tender lump.

"What happened?"

"I woke up and it was still dark. You were asleep, Mama, and I couldn't wake you. Once I heard people, real mad and yelling for us. But then they went away. I was *so* scared."

It all came back with a rush. Alexander . . . their flight from Achallader. His catching them and trying to strangle her. And then, illuminated in the flash of lightning, the man with the jade green eyes!

Killian shivered in remembrance, then froze as she tried to recall what had happened after the green-eyed man had rescued her—and couldn't. Further memory of the events of last night were gone. Totally gone.

Why had she lain unconscious so long? From the bump on her head, Killian surmised she had, at the very least, fallen and hit her head on some rock. But where was everyone? Where was Alexander? And what had happened to the green-eyed man?

She sat up and gathered her son to her. He was crying now, sobbing softly and shivering as hard as she, if for entirely different reasons. Killian clutched him tightly, stroking his head and kissing his cheek, seeking comfort, at least for a moment, in his reassuring physical presence.

"It's . . . it's all right, sweeting. Mama swooned for a time, but I feel fine now."

Even as she spoke, Killian scanned the area. They were in a forest—the same forest, she supposed, they had run into when fleeing the castle. But if so, why were they still here? Why had no one found them?

Glancing up through the dense cover of trees, Killian could barely make out the sun overhead. Midday. Had they been here until almost noon of the next day?

Surely it was safe then to return to Achallader. By now, even if Alexander had chosen to leave them here all night to punish them, he should be recovering nicely from his drunken rage. Still, what if he remembered enough to remain angry at her? And what had happened here last night?

There was no way of knowing until they returned to Achallader.

Killian climbed to her feet, pulling Gavin with her. "We've certainly had quite an adventure, haven't we?" For her son's sake, she forced a brightness she didn't feel. "I suppose the best thing to do, though, is to turn around and head back to the castle. I'm hungry. How about you?"

Gavin stopped his snuffling long enough to bob his head in avid agreement. "Yes, M-Mama. I'm r-real hungry."

They set out then, picking their way through the dense underbrush and across muddy ground. Nothing, however, Killian soon realized, looked at all familiar. Without easy sight of the sun or other landmarks save endless trees with which to orient herself, she soon became lost.

Hours passed, and she never heard or saw any sign of other people. A few wild berries picked along the way and some water from a small stream were all that sustained them. Finally, exhausted, filthy from the mud and damp, low-growing foliage, Killian and Gavin staggered from the forest.

In the distance, mountains overlooked a landscape of sparse forests and a village nestled among rolling hills shadowed by a setting sun.

And still nothing—absolutely nothing—was familiar.

As her bewildered gaze searched the countryside, apprehension snaked through Killian. Where was Castle Achallader? Surely they hadn't walked so far afield they had totally lost sight of the castle? Yet the land now looked so very different, as did the little village that appeared a good three miles' walk away.

For an instant a wild, irrational panic clutched Killian. Then reason returned. No matter where they really were now, once they reached the village it'd be an easy matter to send someone to Achallader to come and fetch them. Besides, she had to be strong for Gavin.

The ground, once they cleared the forest and began to make their way across the hills, was boggy. After the force of last night's rain, that didn't surprise her. Killian regretted, though, not having learned more about the region Achallader served. But then she hadn't planned on visiting so long in the Highlands. Their protracted stay had been her husband's doing—a husband who, by now, was sure to be angry all over again.

She shrugged off the futile worry and slogged on, refusing to deal further with the disturbing thoughts clamoring at the fringes of her mind. There was no need to work herself into a frenzy just yet. Indeed, all that mattered at present was making the village before nightfall.

Twilight blanketed the land before Killian and Gavin limped painfully into the small town. It was a typical little Scots village: drystone houses, squat buildings less than the height of an average man, their roofs covered by divots of earth and thatch held down against the wind by roped stones. There were few windows, and none had glass. The acrid tang of peat smoke tinged the air, stinging Killian's eyes and irritating her throat.

As they entered the village, a scrawny, ill-tempered goat ambled over and butted at Killian's leg. Before the animal had a chance to turn its ire on Gavin, she shooed it away.

"M-Mama, I'm *so* tired."

Killian looked down at her son. His round little face was grimy and tear-streaked; exhaustion dulled his eyes. His nightshirt was soaked all the way to his knees; his feet were in even worse shape. Despite the warm plaid she had wrapped snugly around him, he shivered uncontrollably.

Her firm knock at the nearest door was answered promptly. A rotund old woman peeked out, white kerchief on her head and dressed in a threadbare, long tunic covered by an equally shabby, full-length plaid fastened over her shoulders and gathered at the waist by a belt before falling to her bare feet. Watery blue eyes scanned Killian, taking in the black cloak and glimpse of elegant gown.

The old woman paled. "Och, come in, m'lady." She stepped back and motioned Killian through the door. "Our poor home and hospitality are yers, though we havna much to offer."

Killian hesitated on the threshold, struggling to understand the woman's heavy burr. "Really, all I need is someone to ride to Castle Achallader and inform Adam Campbell that I'm here. He'll soon send an escort to take us back."

An old man wearing a homespun shirt and belted plaid hobbled over. "A friend o' our laird, is she?" He leaned heavily on a gnarled length of wood. "Step aside, wife. I've a wish to see a fine lady so far afield."

The wind whipped up just then, swirling around them, bringing with it a hint of more rain. Desperation flooded Killian. She pulled Gavin to her and stepped closer.

"Please, can you help me?" Her tone of voice was more urgent now. "My name is Killian Campbell. I'm the wife of Alexander Campbell, cousin to Adam Campbell. This—" she glanced down at Gavin—"is my son. We just want to get home."

"And why didna ye say so to begin wi', lassie?" The old man grasped her arm and all but jerked Killian and Gavin into the house. "Highland hospitality being what 'tis, we'd have given ye shelter no matter yer clan, but 'tis a far more pleasant thing to take one o' yer own under yer roof."

"Are you a Campbell?"

Hope at possible kinship welled within Killian; then she caught herself. She truly *was* exhausted, not to mention disoriented, to feel so much excitement over such an unlikely possibility.

"Aye, lassie. Jock Campbell. And m'wife, Enid. Kinsman o' Adam Campbell o' Castle Achallader." He motioned toward the fire. "A hot bowl o' parritch and a good night's sleep is what ye and yer bairn are needin'. The morrow is soon enough to take ye to Achallader."

She had hoped for something more than porridge, Killian thought as she glanced about the one-room cottage. It was sparsely furnished with a rough-hewn table and two rickety chairs. A small bed was shoved against the far wall.

Chickens roosted overhead on the roof tree, and two milk goats were tied in another corner. The air was thick with peat smoke from the small cook fire in the center of the room. The roof hole located directly above, though it sucked up the draught, did little to ease the soot that stung the eyes and blackened the cottage's walls.

Killian's heart sank. This wasn't at all what she envisioned as a suitable place to spend the night.

Enid squinted up at Killian, her eyes all but disappearing in a furrow of sagging brow and chubby cheeks. "'Tisna much, I know, hinny, for such a lady as yerself. But 'tis snug and warm nonetheless."

"It all looks quite fine," Killian hurried to say, knowing if she hesitated much longer, she risked offending the old couple. "I suppose the morrow will be soon enough to send word to Achallader. In the meantime," she added with a dubious glance at the pungently smoking fire, "something to eat, dry clothes, and a bed for the night would be most welcome."

"Right ye are, m'lady." Jock turned to Enid. "Fetch the lassie and her bairn something to wear while their clothes dry. I'll draw fresh water for them to wash up. Then, after a bowl o' parritch, they can take their rest."

As Jock hobbled toward the door to pick up a wooden bucket, Killian turned to Enid. "Really, I don't wish to be trouble—"

"Dinna fash yerself, hinny." The old woman silenced her with an upraised hand. "'Tis an honor, and no mistake, to have a fine lady such as yerself under our roof. Now, come wi' me." She took Killian by the arm. "I've surely an old plaid or two in my kist to wrap ye and the bairn in until yer clothes dry."

It was all Killian could do to follow Enid to her clothes chest. A strange, light-headed sensation had taken hold. Most likely the result of last night's terror, almost nothing to eat, and the exhausting walk all day, she was quick to reassure herself. And, to compound it all, there was also that disturbing loss of memory. . . .

With a fierce wrench of will, Killian shook aside the unnerving sense of disorder and confusion. All she needed was a good night's sleep. Surely by the morrow her memory would return, and everything would be back to normal.

It had to be. She didn't know what she'd do if it wasn't.

†

VOICES, angry voices, woke Killian from a deep slumber. For a moment she lay there, struggling with an elusive reality. A reality, she reflected wryly as her glance snared on a hen roosting on the roof tree directly above her, that wasn't altogether pleasant or reassuring. Her muscles ached, her lungs burned from the smoke still lingering in the air and, in the chill dampness, she felt clammy and uncomfortable.

Shivering in the morning cold, Killian sat up and pulled the thick, warm plaid about her. She glanced around. The stone cottage was empty save for her and Gavin, who slept contentedly on his pallet near the fire. Old Jock and Enid were gone.

The voices moved closer. Excited shouts and enraged curses mingled with the metallic jingle of horse tack and the thud of heavy footsteps.

Killian rose, found the chipped pottery chamber pot Enid had pointed out to her last night, and relieved herself. Then, after a cursory interlude with a basin of icy water, she dressed back in her wrinkled, still slightly damp but much cleaner velvet gown. With one last look to reassure herself Gavin remained asleep, Killian threw her cloak about her shoulders and slipped from the cottage.

It was an hour or so past dawn. A cheery assortment of finches and wrens chirped in some nearby alder trees. The sun's rays barely pierced the mist rising from the land, tinting everything with a hazy, gold-rimmed light.

For an instant, Killian almost imagined this some magical place, some mythical fairyland. Then the din of voices, coming from the road leading into the village, shattered the idyllic setting. To keep from tripping, she gathered up one side of her long ball gown and hurried on, joining others just leaving their own cottages.

A band of heavily armed Highlanders—a few mounted, most on foot—marched down the road, dragging a bound and bleeding prisoner. They prodded the man unmercifully with the stocks of their flintlock muskets. When he stumbled, they jerked him to his feet and struck him hard about his head and shoulders, jamming their fists into his body. The prisoner bore the cruel assaults stoically, enduring as much as he could before sinking once more to his knees.

As if to render the scene even more implausible, a snatch of gay bagpipe music, played by some piper hidden in the mass of bodies, floated to Killian on an errant breeze. It all seemed so unreal she was tempted to laugh. But it *was* real. Stopping short in the middle of the road, Killian faced the Highlanders marching toward her.

The events of the past two nights had been difficult enough to accept, much less comprehend. But now, as she watched the prisoner's inhumane treatment and listened to the bloodthirsty shrieks of the peasants who had gathered to urge the man's captors on, Killian felt as if she were seeing it all from afar—like some make-believe performance.

Last night's dizzying sense of disorientation flooded back with a vengeance. And her memory was no better than it had been then. Perhaps none of this was really happening and she had just finally, and simply, gone mad.

As Killian stood there in indecision, the mob engulfed her, smothering her in the stench of unwashed bodies. Momentarily, the clamor of harsh, angry voices deafened her. Panicked, she dragged in great gulps of air to clear her head, steady her erratically pounding heart.

Then the prisoner stumbled and fell—right at Killian's feet.

For the first time, the people seemed to notice her. A hush settled over the crowd.

"What's amiss here?" an angry but all too familiar voice rose from behind Killian.

She wheeled around. Adam Campbell, who had apparently been riding ahead of the soldiers, turned his big gray horse and trotted it back down the road until he drew up beside Killian.

Today, instead of his belted plaid, he was dressed in brown-and-green tartan trews molded snugly to his long, well-muscled legs, a pair of thin-soled shoes, a brown velvet doublet beneath which peeked a white, full-sleeved shirt, and a black bonnet trimmed with a sprig of bog myrtle set rakishly on the side of his head. A long plaid slung over one shoulder and fastened with a large, silver brooch completed the ensemble. Tall and wide of chest, the big Highlander sat his nervously prancing mount with the ease of an experienced horseman.

With a puzzled glance, he scanned what Killian knew was her bedraggled appearance.

"And what, pray tell, are ye doing here? For that matter, where have ye been? We've been searching for ye for nearly two days now."

Killian's mind went blank. What had Alexander possibly shared with Adam about her and Gavin's disappearance the night of the ball? If she told Adam the truth, and it contradicted her husband's tale, any of Alexander's anger that might have dissipated would flare anew. Better, far better, to pretend ignorance or even—as inspiration suddenly struck her—a loss of memory.

She lifted her hand to her forehead, her fingers glancing off the bruise. Surreptitiously, Killian brushed her hair aside to reveal the tender, swollen spot.

"I-I don't really know where I've been. I fell and hit my head," she mumbled in what she hoped was a dazed-sounding voice. "My memory keeps fading in and out."

Killian glanced up and forced an apologetic smile. "The night before last, I think I wandered from home and ended up there—" she waved vaguely in the direction she had come—"but I can't be certain where my home really lies."

"Mayhap the lady's Alexander Campbell's wife," a young Highlander with flaming red hair offered, riding up to join Adam Campbell. "Ask her if she's Alexander's wife."

"I already know *who* she is, Lachlan." Adam cast Killian a suspicious look.

"Alexander . . ." She seized the opportunity the young Highlander had offered, cocking her head as if deep in thought. "Yes, it *has* a familiar ring."

Her eyes filled with tears, which weren't all that hard to muster what with the peat smoke so thick on the air. "Yes." Killian nodded now with conviction. "Yes, I *am* Alexander's wife."

She sank to her knees, her hands clasped about her. "It's all starting to come back now. Alexander . . . Castle Achallader . . . our home in Virginia. Ah, me. My memory. My poor memory. What else can possibly go wrong?"

Her little act seemed to dispel the last of Adam Campbell's doubts. He swung off his horse. Leaning down, he pulled Killian to her feet.

"Poor lass. Ye've indeed suffered more than any woman should." He paused, eyeing her intently. "Alexander's dead, ye know. The night ye disappeared, we found him sprawled deep in the forest outside Achallader. He had a mortal knife wound to his back."

Killian stared up at him. Surely she hadn't heard Adam correctly. "Alex . . . Alexander's dead?"

"Aye, lass, that he is."

At his simple admission, short, sharp scenes flashed before her. Scenes of a dark forest, of rain and sporadic bursts of lightning. Then, superimposed upon it all, she saw Alexander, his back to her, aiming a pistol at the green-eyed man. A horrifying realization—that he meant to cold-bloodedly kill the dark-haired stranger—filled her.

Rage, long buried, held tightly in check, boiled up within her. And with that rage came the rest of her memory. Killian saw herself flailing at Alexander, all to no avail. Then, as he cocked his pistol, panic seemed to take over.

Her hand slid into her bodice, wrenched free her little dagger. She shoved to her feet, the knife clasped in her hand.

Then everything seemed to happen all at once. With a hoarse cry, the green-eyed man leaped at Alexander. She stabbed wildly, ineffectually, at her husband's back until finally he cried out and staggered backward, falling onto the dagger. At the same time, the pistol fired.

When the smoke had cleared Alexander lay there, facedown in the mud, her knife protruding from his back. Lay there, twitching spasmodically for a few seconds, then went still. The green-eyed man soon squatted beside him, rolled him over, and laid his ear to Alexander's chest. After what seemed an agonizing eternity, he glanced up at her and shook his head.

"He's gone, lass."

Killian recalled little more, save that the trees had begun to spin, and the ground dipped and swayed. Then everything went black.

Only one thing was certain. She had killed her own husband.

"What have I done?" Killian whispered. "What have I done?"

Watching her, a considering light flared in Adam's dark gray eyes. "I'd wanted to save the pleasure of a slow kill for myself. Yer right to demand retribution, though, has precedence over mine. And, since this prisoner is the man who murdered Alexander, it's fitting ye send him to a similar fate."

Withdrawing his dirk, Adam Campbell flipped it over and offered it, hilt first, to Killian. "Ye're a Campbell, if only by marriage. Purge yerself of yer grief. Prove yer loyalty to our clan. Kill Ruarc MacDonald."

Still numb with shock, Killian could only gaze stupidly up at him. Finally, with a disgusted sound, Adam grabbed her hand, forcing her fingers about the dirk.

"Kill him. Kill the MacDonald!" the crowd cried, taking up Adam's command.

At the shouts for his death, the prisoner groaned and shoved to his knees. "Nay! Not like this. Not like some sheep trussed for the slaughter!"

His deep voice wrenched Killian from her appalled preoccupation with the dagger. For the first time, she actually saw him. His face was bruised and filthy, his dark, shoulder-length hair matted with mud and some of his own blood. His once white shirt was torn and gaped open from his belted plaid. Several oozing slashes marred the broad expanse of his heavily muscled, hair-roughened chest.

Pity for the man welled in Killian's breast.

Adam cursed savagely. Leaning over, he ensnared the man's hair and wrenched back his head, baring his throat.

"There. Does that make things simpler for ye? My dirk's razor sharp. Stroke its blade once across his throat and be done with it!"

The man's neck bulged with muscle. Deep within the mass of bronzed, dirty flesh a pulse throbbed, steady and powerful.

Adam was right. One slice of his dirk would end it all.

Killian dragged her gaze to the prisoner's face. He stared back, unblinking, resolute.

He was prepared to die and would face it with courage. He'd

never grovel or beg for his life, never shame the honor of his clan. The surety of this knowledge startled her, stirring a memory of another man, a man whom she had seen only once before. A man with eyes of deepest jade, eyes that pierced to her very soul.

Eyes that now gazed up at her.

Killian stood there, stunned. Was it possible? Was this indeed the man who had come to her rescue in the forest? The man who had then seemingly disappeared as mysteriously as he had first appeared?

The recognition she saw deep in his eyes was her answer.

With a cry she lurched back. The dirk dropped from nerveless fingers. "N-no. No!"

The unnerving sense of disbelief and disorder engulfed her anew. She shook her head in vehement denial.

"Kill him! Kill him!" the crowd shrieked, closing around her. Inexorably, they pushed Killian back toward the man kneeling in the mud. "Kill the MacDonald! Kill him now!"

Killian couldn't tear her eyes from the man before her. His gaze held hers, mesmerizing, incapacitating her. Though his features were bloated from his beatings and his face and body were filthy, she finally permitted herself to admit what she had tried to deny: *Ruarc MacDonald was indeed the man who had come to her aid. He hadn't, though, been the one to kill Alexander.*

She had.

Her throat constricted. A suffocating, gut-wrenching grief engulfed her. Alexander . . . Alexander was dead and somehow, someway, she had killed him. She wanted to run, to hide, and to pretend that none of this had ever happened.

Then Killian remembered Gavin, alone and asleep in Jock and Enid's cottage. Gavin . . . Gavin still needed her, depended on her. Despite what had happened, she *had* to find a way out of this—no matter how mad or desperate—for his sake, if for nothing else!

Perhaps that was the answer to this crazed, waking dream. Perhaps the only way to escape this nightmare was to repay the favor, and save Ruarc MacDonald's life. Then, and only then, might she be permitted to return to reality. Might she gain some sort of redemption for her husband's murder.

But how to do it? She didn't know what to say to placate Adam and the crowd. These weren't her people or her land. Indeed, nothing about this made any sense.

There was no hope of gaining Ruarc MacDonald's freedom, even if she retrieved the dirk and quickly cut his bonds. The guards and enraged villagers would be on him before he could take two steps. But she also couldn't stand there and demand his release by taking him under her protection.

There was but one recourse. She must continue to feign loss of memory and her distraught state, pushing both to their limits. And the craziest plan Killian could think of was the one thing she never, ever wanted to do again.

"I don't wish to demand a widow's right to avenge her husband." Her voice rose, strong and clear, to reach Adam Campbell and the people beyond him. "I wish, instead, a new husband to take the place of the one I lost. I wish—" she gestured toward Ruarc MacDonald— "to wed this man."

At Killian's words, silence settled like a pall over the crowd. Adam Campbell blanched, then purpled with rage.

"Are ye daft, woman?" With a disgusted motion he released his prisoner's hair and turned the full force of his regard on Killian. "Ruarc MacDonald has already ruined one marriage to a Campbell lass, the black-hearted murderer! Would ye sacrifice yer life as well?"

"Lying swine!" Ruarc glared up at him. "I've been exonerated in Sheila's death by no less than the king himself, and well ye know it!"

"Och, and don't we all know how well ye curry King William's favor?" Adam asked softly, leaning close so only Ruarc, his guards, and Killian could hear. "All these years, I've watched ye fill his ears with yer flattery and lies. His turning a blind eye to Sheila's murder but confirms the truth of it."

The guards chuckled derisively. For Ruarc MacDonald, though, Adam's taunts seemed the last straw.

"Ye filthy cur!" He lunged at Adam Campbell.

The Campbell soldiers reacted immediately, wrestling him back from their leader. Ruarc fought them for several minutes, his big body tense with rage. Then, with a shuddering breath, he finally gave up the futile struggle.

Wishing to distract the two men before their personal animosity escalated into a bloodbath, Killian turned quickly to Adam Campbell. "Please, I don't wish to be the cause of a fight. Perhaps I *have* become a bit daft, but I've also just learned I've lost my beloved Alexander. A new husband—even if he *is* a MacDonald—would ease the ache in my heart, and the long, dark nights alone in my bed."

She forced what she hoped was both a seductive and slightly crazed smile. "Or what of you, Adam? If not Ruarc MacDonald, will you be my husband?"

Adam eyed her narrowly, then shook his head. "Poor lass. Ye *are* daft. But, for Alexander's sake, I won't permit yer shame to become the laughingstock of this village." He signaled for the man holding his horse to bring it over, then grasped Killian about the waist and lifted her up to the animal's back.

"Wh-what are you doing? How *dare* you?" Killian feigned a look of outrage.

"I'm taking ye back to Achallader where ye belong," he said, mounting swiftly behind her. "What ye need is rest and some hearty Highland victuals. Later, when ye're feeling more yerself, we can talk further of yer needs."

Adam Campbell glanced down to where his men still held Ruarc MacDonald. "Bring him along. Fate has smiled on him a short while longer. But only," he added grimly, "a verra short while."

Killian could see the impotent anger flare anew in Ruarc's eyes. She opened her mouth to protest Adam Campbell's ominous prediction, then thought better of it.

She had done her best; she had bought Ruarc MacDonald a little more time. In the meanwhile, she had nowhere else to go but back to Achallader. Adam would now be forced to help her obtain passage home. God forgive her, but she had gained her freedom at last, even if in a manner she would've never wished.

Her gaze turned to the prisoner's. His eyes, tormented and bitter, burned into hers. Compassion flooded her.

Around her the crowd surged like waves upon the sea, muttering things she could not, nor really cared to, hear. In but the span of a few seconds, Killian's universe had narrowed to a big, green-eyed Highlander. And, cast adrift in the depths of an uncharted sea, the illusion that this was all some insanely vivid dream fled.

Reality was now the sun on her face, the cool morning breeze ruffling her hair, and a man. A man whom she suddenly feared with every fiber of her being, yet was inexplicably drawn to, just the same.

Terror twisted Killian's gut and set her heart to hammering. A sense of her life spinning out of control, spiraling toward some frightening unknown—an unknown she didn't want to confront, much less examine—filled her. She panicked, turning to hide her face in the thick plaid slung over Adam Campbell's shoulder.

"What is it, lass? What frightens ye so?"

There was a kind concern beneath the softly spoken words. In her misery, Killian grasped at it like one drowning.

"I-I don't know. I'm just so tired, so confused."

"Well, dinna fash yerself. Ye'll soon be safe again within Achallader. Ye needn't fear for aught." With that, Adam Campbell urged his horse forward.

As they rode through the village a goat ran out, spooking the horse. With a snort of surprise, the big animal reared. Muttering a curse, Adam Campbell fought him back to the ground. The distraction, however, was sufficient to pull Killian at last from her tormented haze.

Gavin. She had to get Gavin.

She leaned back and met Adam Campbell's gaze. "My son. I'd forgotten until now. He's in the cottage of Jock and Enid Campbell. Please, allow me to fetch him."

Adam motioned over the young Highlander who had first given Killian the excuse she had so desperately needed. "There's a lad, Lachlan, in Jock Campbell's hut. Bring him along to Achallader, will ye?"

Lachlan nodded his assent and, turning his horse, trotted off.

"Yer son'll be safe with my cousin." Adam smiled down at her. "He has a special way with bairns."

Killian managed a grateful nod in reply. Yet even as Adam set his horse back down the road, her mind roiled once more with a frantic welter of emotions.

She had called upon the Lord to save her from her husband. Her prayers had been answered—though she had never meant for Alexander's death to be part of the bargain—and she was safe at last. Poor Alexander, God rest his soul, would never hurt her or their son again. In his stead, though, had come the obligation for another life—that of the man who had apparently been sent by the Lord to rescue her.

Her head pounded with the effort required to deal with the bewildering contradictions of her situation. Gradually, though, one surety rose from the confusion to stand clear and strong amidst it all. Whatever was transpiring here, she'd find some way through it all—and survive.

She had to. What other choice was there?

That her ultimate freedom, however, had required she kill her husband was a consideration beyond belief. Yes, she must survive, if not for herself, then for Gavin. Would the value of that freedom, that survival, though, ever be worth its purchase price?

3

AS MUCH as Ruarc MacDonald hated to admit it, Adam Campbell had been right. The golden-haired widow was indeed daft. To confront a band of enraged Highlanders and refuse their leader's demand, then manipulate the whole murder-intent group to her bidding, was surely the work of a crazy woman—or one supremely clever.

It all seemed too coincidental, though, he thought as he slogged through the village and down the long, winding road leading to Achallader's lands. The sudden, unexpected appearance of the widow. The seeming ease with which she played Adam to her needs, whatever those needs might ultimately be. Was she, mayhap, even somehow in league with Achallader's laird?

But how, and to what purpose? If the truth be told, it didn't matter at any rate. Survival—and escape from Achallader—must remain uppermost in his mind. Yet, there was just something about her . . .

The lass was either a consummate actress or truly had been revolted at the thought of slitting his throat. And that look she had sent him after Adam had made the decision temporarily to spare his life . . . even now, Ruarc found it difficult to fathom her expression of compassion, understanding and, aye, even one of kinship with him.

He shook his head to clear it of the vision of a sweet, delicately oval face, huge blue eyes, a tender mouth, and a cloud of long, pale gold hair. He must be daft, or at least a wee bit addled in the mind himself, to dwell so long on the seductive attributes of some half-mad widow. His life hung by the weakest of threads. He had no time to spare for a comely lass—*and* a Campbell in the bargain. It was enough he had saved her from her husband that night in the forest.

But one thing was certain in this dangerous muddle he had gotten himself into. His plans—to spy on the gathering of Campbell nobles—had come to naught. No sooner had Alexander Campbell died than Ruarc had had to drag his body away to hide it.

There had been no opportunity, then, to return to the man's widow and child. Somehow, Adam Campbell must have gotten word of Ruarc's whereabouts. A search party, pitch torches blazing, had even then been riding from the castle, their hounds baying before them.

Though he had managed to evade them until late the next eve, his pursuers were a determined lot. Finally, exhausted from two days without sleep, Ruarc had made a fatal error. In trying to snatch a few hours of desperately needed rest, he had failed to hear the hounds in time. If Adam Campbell hadn't led the search party, Ruarc was certain the others would've never called off the dogs. But Adam would never have permitted him such a quick or easy death.

The widow, in sparing his life, had bought him time. Now, no matter the cost, Ruarc *must* discover what the Campbells had been plotting. Too much lay at stake.

By January first, all the Highland chiefs were required to transfer their loyalties from King James to the English monarchs. If the Campbells plotted to thwart the efforts of their ancestral enemies— Clan MacDonald in particular—to sign the oath of fealty, King William must be apprised of that. Knowing William's determination that all comply or be threatened with "the utmost extremity of the law," Ruarc feared proof of a Campbell plot might well be the only way to turn the king from his deadly course.

Aye, he knew King William as well as any man could. Leastwise, as well as he imagined he had once known Adam Campbell.

Ruarc frowned in remembrance. They had all once been the closest of friends, even if the ensuing years had conspired to pull them apart. Now he and Adam were enemies. Looking back, Ruarc realized the rift had begun when he had wed Adam's foster sister, Sheila. Adam had become reserved, distanced himself.

And then, after Sheila's murder . . .

With a shudder, Ruarc shook off the horrific memories. Suffice it to say he now hated Adam as fiercely as Adam hated him. Still, though the rift between Achallader's laird and himself now seemed irreparable, hope remained that he and the king could maintain the trust and easy fellowship they had forged so long ago. Hope remained that something could be done to prevent the imminent clash between the clans and England over the prickly issue of a deposed king with no possibility ever of ruling Scotland—or England—again.

All he had to do was live long enough to reach London, reach the king.

†

AS THE stout wooden gates of Castle Achallader closed firmly behind them, Adam Campbell heaved a sigh of relief. Thanks to the informant in Ruarc MacDonald's own castle, he at last had the murdering dog where he wanted him—under his thumb. A thumb that, once and for all, would crush Ruarc MacDonald like the scurrilous vermin he was.

Three years had passed since Sheila's death. Three years without retribution, without justice for his murdered lassie. He, though, had been a patient man, awaiting the right time and place to take his revenge. And revenge it would be, in her name and memory. It was the least he could do for his wee bonny Sheila.

He swung down from his horse before the doors to the Lion's Hall, handing his reins to the stable boy, who immediately ran up to assist him. Then Adam turned to Alexander's wife.

"Come, lass." He lifted his arms to her. "Come down. Ye're safe now, back amongst yer kin."

She stared at him for a moment, a strange expression in her eyes, then slid off the horse and into his arms. She was a wee slip of a thing, and smelled of sweet grass and heather. She was also, he admitted reluctantly, most attractive.

That realization reminded Adam of the powerful influence, be it good or bad, of a beauteous woman. Releasing her, he stepped back, took Killian by the arm, and swung her around to face the keep.

"Did I ever tell ye of Achallader's glorious history?" After the questionable circumstances surrounding his cousin's death, he had decided it might be wisest to keep his distance until he learned more of that night. "Were ye aware Campbell ownership of Achallader dates back three hundred years, when we first received a license from the king to build it?"

"No, I didn't know that."

"Well, I suppose it's naught that'd interest ye, especially after just learning of yer husband's death." He offered her his arm. "Come along then. Janet can assist ye as always with a bath, clean clothes, and any victuals ye might desire. Later, I'll come for ye and we can talk."

She managed a halfhearted smile. "That'd be wonderful. I can't thank you enough for your continued hospitality." She glanced around and found her son, escorted by Lachlan Campbell.

Catching sight of his mother, the lad twisted free of the young Highlander's grip and ran the last few feet to throw himself into her arms. They embraced. Killian lifted him to hold him close.

"If you've nothing further to say to me—" she looked back up at Adam— "I'd appreciate your leave to adjourn to my chambers. This has been such an—"

Ruarc MacDonald, firmly imprisoned in the midst of his armed guard, strode past them. He shot Adam a rancorous look before riveting a fleeting glance on Alexander's widow. Then he was gone, dragged up the steps to the Hall, his eventual destination Achallader's dungeons.

His passing look at the woman, however, pricked at some cautionary instinct in Adam. What was the basis for Ruarc's interest in Killian? It was exceedingly strange that, not long after Killian had revealed to him she wished to leave her husband, both she and Alexander had disappeared, and that only a short time before Adam had received the message informing him Ruarc MacDonald was in the area. Then later to find Alexander dead, and Killian and her son missing . . . yet the most disturbing event of all was Killian's refusal to avenge herself on her husband's murderer, instead pleading and bargaining for his life.

"Is yer memory beginning to recover?" Adam inquired as he led her up the steps to the Lion's Hall. "Since ye've returned to Achallader, I mean?"

"Somewhat." Her gaze swung to her son, snuggled against her, and back to the keep's front entrance. "I remember this building. You've a huge fireplace in the Great Hall, haven't you?" Killian smiled, and the effect was both radiant and breathtaking. "Does this mean I'm getting better?"

"Och, and for sure." Adam chuckled. "Give ye a few more days and ye'll be as right as rain."

"I hope so."

A few more days and he'd have all the information he needed. Just as soon as he escorted Killian Campbell and her son to their room, Adam intended to send a rider out posthaste to confer with his informant. He'd discover soon enough if this woman was already known in Ruarc MacDonald's lands, or if the circumstances surrounding her husband's death and his enemy's arrival were only coincidental.

Just a few more days . . . time enough to watch her closely and, meanwhile, see to Ruarc MacDonald's long overdue punishment. To be sure, it'd be an interesting, if not entertaining, next few days.

Adam forced an encouraging smile. "Och, I'm most certainly right, lass. Just ye wait and see."

†

"NO, I CAN'T. I'm sorry, Adam, but I just can't."

Killian turned from her bedchamber's roaring hearth fire and faced Adam Campbell. As she did, her glance snared on the small pendulum clock perched on the carved oak mantel. Seven-thirty. How many more hours would it take before the castle was at last in bed? How many more hours before she could finally seek out Ruarc MacDonald?

"Come, come, lass," Adam chided from the room's open doorway. "I know the news of Alexander's death was difficult for ye, but ye've had the entire day to rest and compose yerself. Surely ye can find the courage to come down for the supper meal."

"No." She shook her head firmly. "Perhaps on the morrow I'll be able to face everyone, but not tonight."

"But Cook has prepared a special meal in honor of yer safe return. We'll be having roast mutton, boiled pigeons in dill sauce, baked salmon, and a fine mess of cooked vegetables. For dessert—" he cast a conspiratorial glance at Gavin sitting before the fire, playing with one of the castle's cats—"there'll be shortbread, French cake with icing, and crumpets filled with jam."

"Oh, Mama." Suddenly Gavin was all ears and boyish enthusiasm. "Can we go down to eat? It sounds *so* good."

Guilt swelled within Killian. For all his surprising and most unnerving hatred of Ruarc MacDonald, Adam Campbell had treated, and continued to treat, them with the utmost kindness.

Yet, despite Adam's generosity, she didn't dare risk inadvertently exposing her active involvement in Alexander's death. Already, Adam had shown little interest in knowing why she had wished to leave her husband. And, though he seemed correctly to assume she was still too much in shock over Alexander yet to properly mourn him, that small favor wouldn't last long.

There was no hope, however, that he'd spare her any sympathy for killing his cousin to save his enemy. No, too much—Ruarc MacDonald's life notwithstanding—hung in the balance to risk speaking prematurely with Adam.

With a weary sigh, Killian lowered herself onto a wooden chair made lavish by its deep, intricate carvings, metal inlays, and gilt. "No, sweeting, we can't go down to eat. Or at least not tonight anyway." She smiled at her son, then turned back to Adam. "Please try and understand. I just can't."

He eyed her for a long moment, then nodded. "Have it yer way, lass. It won't change things in the end, yer having finally to face yer kin, but the morrow's time enough, I suppose. Now that Alexander's gone, this *is* ye and yer son's home."

Killian went very quiet. "And why would you think that?" she asked finally. "We may still need that loan I spoke of to get back to Virginia, but once we're there, I'll now have more than adequate funds to repay you."

"I wasn't thinking of the loan, lass. Gavin's a true Campbell. His father would have wanted him to remain in the Highlands."

"How do you know this? Indeed, who are you to presume to say what Alexander wanted?" In spite of her best efforts to control her anger, Killian could feel it rising, threatening to spiral out of control.

Calmly, Adam met her gaze. "Because the verra night he died,

Alexander confided that not only would he and his family be staying until spring, but upon his return to Virginia he planned on selling the plantation, then taking up permanent residence back in the Highlands."

He leaned against the doorjamb and folded his arms across his chest. "Considering the circumstances, ye'd be well advised now not only to discard yer plans of returning to the Colonies, but to give serious thought to selling yer lands. The money raised would provide ye a handsome dowry when ye eventually remarry here. And Campbell wealth would remain in the clan."

Killian felt as if a fist had slammed into her gut. It was bad enough Alexander had at last seized on the perfect plan to gain total control by isolating her not only from her family but from her own country and people. But now, less than two days after his death, another man had stepped in to take over her life and force her to his needs. She had been a fool to have imagined she had won her freedom.

Her husband might yet have his victory, even if he were no longer alive to savor it.

"All . . . all I have is your word that Alexander planned to sell the plantation and move permanently back here." Her voice went hoarse, quavered. "A-Alexander never mentioned any . . . any such plan to me."

Adam shrugged, his mouth quirking in apology. "Mayhap not, lass. For that I'm verra sorry. But I wouldn't lie to ye about this."

Wouldn't you? Killian countered silently. Still, there was no point in arguing the matter. Just as she had been at her husband's mercy all these years, she was now—at least temporarily—at Adam's. But only temporarily.

"We can talk more about this another time." She rose and walked over to him. "Tonight's not the night for either of us to make any rash decisions."

"Aye, I suppose ye're right, lass." He straightened, turned to go, then hesitated. "About Ruarc MacDonald."

She froze. Did Adam Campbell suspect something after all? "Yes? What of him?"

"Ye don't still have yer heart set on wedding him, do ye?"

"I don't know." Killian's mind raced, searching for some plausible reason to give Adam. She knew she couldn't tell him the truth—that Ruarc MacDonald was increasingly becoming her only possible chance of escape from the Highlands. Still, if she wasn't careful, he'd easily catch her in an inconsistency.

"I wasn't thinking too clearly at the time." She managed a shaky laugh. "I feel like a fool now, wanting Ruarc MacDonald one moment, then in the next asking you to wed me. But it all seemed so right not so very long ago.

"One thing I am certain of, though, is that I don't want to see him dead." Killian shook her head. "Alexander's death is almost more than I can comprehend. I couldn't bear the thought of yet another man dying."

"Even a MacDonald who cold-bloodedly backstabbed yer husband? Have ye so quickly forgotten that scurvy knave was responsible for Alexander's death?"

"No, I haven't forgotten." Killian fixed him with an unrelenting gaze. "Did you actually see this man kill Alexander? Or has he admitted to it?"

His glance narrowed. "Nay, I didn't see him, and he hasn't confessed. He's the most likely suspect, however."

"Well, senseless revenge won't bring back my Alexander. And, more to the point, how far has the endless feuding and insatiable hunger for retribution gotten the Highlands or its clans? Answer me that, Adam Campbell."

Anger flashed in the Highlander's eyes, appeared to wage a brief battle with his will, then was gone. "Well, as ye said, tonight's not the night for such things. Just don't attempt such a ploy again. I don't care much for being used—and especially not to Ruarc MacDonald's advantage."

"I'll try, Adam. Truly I will."

Killian lowered her eyes in mute apology. After all, she wasn't lying this time. She *wouldn't* try such a ploy again. She wouldn't have to, once she had freed Ruarc MacDonald.

"Ye're a strange one, and no mistake." Her host shook his head in bemusement. "But I like yer spirit and yer honesty." A scowl wended its way across his forehead. "Ye must believe me, though, when I tell ye Ruarc MacDonald's an evil, hard-hearted man who thinks only of himself. Ye weren't here when his wife died. Talk has it he killed her in a jealous rage for cuckolding him."

"Is that what you think?"

A look of pain, guilt and, finally, fierce resolve flared in Adam's eyes. Then it was gone. "Aye, Ruarc killed my bonny Sheila. In the end, that's all that matters."

There was something hovering at the edge of his words, something that gave Killian pause. Briefly she considered probing further, then thought better of it. She had no right, or reason, to pry. Indeed, the sooner she put this man and his clan behind her and returned to Virginia, the better.

"She was your sister, then?" Killian chose to ask instead.

"My foster sister. It's a common Highland custom, ye know, to foster children with other families. It's meant to strengthen clan bonds. The fosterlings grow up as equal and loved as any of the other children in the family. So it was with Sheila, who was given to us as a wee bairn."

"I didn't know. I'm sorry. You were close then?"

"Aye, verra close."

There was nothing she could say to that. Whatever had happened to Ruarc MacDonald's wife, Killian now knew Adam Campbell believed in the truth of his claims. And believed, as well, in the righteousness of his intent to see Ruarc dead.

On a wild impulse, she almost asked Adam what he planned to do with his prisoner. That idea, however, was quickly discarded. If she showed too much interest in his prisoner's welfare, he might begin to suspect her motives, keep her from her plan to repay the big MacDonald by setting him free. Indeed, for all his continued hospitality and courtesy, Killian sensed Adam didn't quite trust her story of temporary memory loss. Which was all the more reason to seek out Ruarc MacDonald this very night.

But Killian also knew she was treading in dangerous waters to even dare to contemplate such a preposterous idea. She knew hardly anything about Ruarc MacDonald. True, he had saved her from Alexander, but then had callously left her and Gavin in the forest. That didn't bode well for his being a man of compassion or consideration, a better man than either Alexander or Adam.

Even more importantly, how in heaven's name was she supposed to rescue a man from a castle dungeon? And if she helped him escape, then remained behind, what would be the consequences to her and Gavin?

Yes, it *was* a preposterous idea, but the longer Killian considered it, the more convinced she became that was exactly what she must do. At the very least, she knew she couldn't live with herself if she didn't repay the debt she owed the big Highlander. Ruarc MacDonald had just better be able to supplement where she was lacking.

As for what she might do once he was free, there was still time to think on that.

†

SOMETHING scrabbled, then squeaked in a far corner. Ruarc grimaced.

Rats.

He wasn't surprised. They were common denizens of dungeons.

There were fates far worse, though, than sharing his cell with them. As unpalatable as the idea was, if Adam chose not to feed him, sooner or later he might even be forced into killing and eating the big rodents to survive.

It was indeed a most heartwarming of considerations, but an act he'd still perform if he had to. Above all else, he must maintain his strength. Knowing Adam, part of the torture would be to weaken him in body as well as in spirit. Yet if he were ultimately to prevail, Ruarc knew he must anticipate and stay one step ahead of the man.

A fetid gust of air rushed by. Ruarc choked back a surge of nausea. The deep pit was dark, dank, and filthy. He could only imagine how many men had met their ends in here, wasting away amidst the dripping, slime-coated walls and excrement-filled straw as hope died and, eventually, they lost even their sanity.

Only one question remained—Adam's plan for him. Torture and death, Ruarc well knew, were his ultimate fate, but whether it would be one of slow degradation or a more painful but quicker repose on the rack was yet to be seen. There was always the possibility that Adam meant to leave him in this pit without food or water, never giving him another thought. Not that he'd be consulted in the matter, but he'd rather be tortured to death than languish here alone, inexorably transforming into a crazed, slavering animal before he finally died.

It was the not knowing, the waiting, that grated on him. It was the doubts and uncertainty that would eventually undermine his strength and resolve. He had little else left to sustain him.

His clan would never succeed in rescuing him. His religious faith had long ago ceased to provide him comfort, much less a reason to meekly bear all the pain and brutality in life. Still, it was more a case of God's finally turning from him than Ruarc's first rejecting the Lord. His mouth quirked grimly. One way or another, the reality remained the same. He was alone now, whether he wished it or not.

There was nothing left him but the primal instinct to survive— that, and his deep-seated sense of responsibility to his clan. But would even those motives be enough to save him this time?

One thing, and one thing alone, was certain. Adam's hatred ran deep. He'd never be freed.

Something rustled near Ruarc's left foot. He kicked at it, striking something soft and alive that squealed and scurried away. He choked back yet another bitter swell of despair. He didn't dare sleep. The rats would have him for their next meal.

He hadn't slept since just before his capture late yestreen, and then he had been forced to march all through the night. Yet by his calculations, it was barely past midnight. He didn't know how much longer he could stay—

Overhead, a door creaked open. Ruarc guessed it must be the one opening onto the small room where his pit lay. Outside, in the large antechamber, sat his guard. Mayhap the man had decided it was time to check on him.

The approaching footsteps, however, were light and tentative, not at all the sounds made by an overweight, lumbering, barrel- chested man. Ruarc shoved to his feet, gazing up at the metal grate high above that imprisoned him in the pit.

A face, hazily lit by the flickering flames of a torch, moved into view. After total darkness, the sudden glare of light blinded Ruarc. He shielded his eyes with an upraised hand until they adjusted. Then he saw her.

Ruarc sucked in a startled breath. It was the woman from the road—Alexander's wife.

"What are ye doing here, lass?" he croaked out the query. "Are ye daft, to wander about this castle so late at night?"

She smiled uncertainly. "Well, *daft* might indeed be the correct word, considering what I mean to do."

Ruarc frowned. "And what might that be?"

"I've come to get you out of there." She glanced down at the grate, wrinkled her nose in apparent distaste at its filthy condition, then stooped and began gingerly to drag it aside.

After considerable effort, she managed to clear the opening to the pit. Shoving the torch into a crack in the stone floor, she lowered herself to her stomach and leaned down, extending her hand.

"Come on. Take it."

He shook his head. "Ye haven't the strength to pull me out, lass. Look about the room. There should be a ladder or a stout length of rope ye can use instead."

As if considering his words, the woman cocked her head. "You're right. I probably wouldn't have the strength to pull out a big oaf like you." In a flurry of skirt and petticoats she rose, took up the torch, and walked away.

"A big oaf, indeed," Ruarc muttered, not certain if he should be amused or offended by her unflattering assessment.

Then, save for a faint light high above, the pit once more was swallowed in darkness. Ruarc stood there, his heart pounding. Did this woman truly mean to help him, or was she playing some strange game in that crazed mind of hers? He had no way of knowing.

The seconds ticked by. Nothing happened. Then something scraped across the floor, something large and unwieldy.

"I . . . found . . . it. A ladder . . . I mean." The woman paused then, the end of a rickety wooden ladder perched at the edge of the hole. "We have to strike a bargain, though, before I help you out."

Tendrils of suspicion entwined with disappointment, twisting Ruarc's gut painfully. He should've known it was all a game.

"Aye, and what might that bargain be?"

She must have heard the tinge of sarcasm in his voice. "Nothing as horrible as your firstborn child or anything like that. I just want you to take my son and me away with you."

Ruarc frowned. "Why would ye wish to go away with me? Ye're a Campbell, after all. Adam's yer kin."

She bit her lip and looked away. "It's a long story. Suffice it to say, I don't mean you or yours any harm. Now, is it a bargain or not?"

"Aye." Ruarc nodded his assent. Indeed, what other choice had he?

"I want your word on it."

His eyes narrowed. "Do ye doubt me, then? Didn't I already tell ye it was a bargain?"

"But your word of honor holds even more weight. You Highlanders place great store on your word, don't you?"

"Aye, that we do." He shot her a furious look. "Ye've my word on it then. I'll take ye and yer son with me to Rannoch."

Apparently satisfied at last, she shoved the ladder into the pit's opening and began to angle it downward. Ruarc stepped aside, knowing the ladder would come tumbling down as soon as she cleared the hole.

"Hold tight to the end," he called up to her, still not daring to allow his hopes to soar. "Ye don't want to drop the whole thing into the pit, do ye?"

"I think I've gotten *that* part of this figured out."

In spite of himself, Ruarc grinned. The lass had spunk, if naught else.

With a harsh, grating sound the ladder entered the hole and came plummeting down, settling into the sodden straw with a resounding squish. In the next instant, Ruarc grasped it and climbed its length, nearly bumping heads with the woman as he shot from the hole.

"Have a care, will you?" She scooted back. "It's not polite to brain your rescuer."

He crawled clear of the pit, then stood. "Is that what ye truly are? My rescuer?"

"What else would I be?" She stared up at him from her spot on the floor. "How many people do you know who skulk around a castle in the middle of the night?"

"Verra few, to be sure." Ruarc offered her his hand which, after a moment's hesitation, she accepted. "I just didn't expect help from the likes of ye."

"You probably," she said, rising to her feet and quickly releasing his hand, "didn't expect help from anyone in Achallader. But I owe you a debt for coming to my aid, and I always pay my debts."

Ruarc knew, free at last of the pit, he should be hieing himself from the castle as quickly as possible. But this strange, beautiful woman had risked much to liberate him. He owed her some show of gratitude.

"I beg pardon," he said, "if I seemed unwilling to take ye with me earlier. Ye're more than welcome to come with me to Rannoch Castle. I'm its laird. Ye'll be treated well there."

In that moment of decision, Killian's courage suddenly fled. Was she mad then, to run away with a man she hardly knew? Though Adam would most likely guess she had been the one to free Ruarc MacDonald, the odds were in her favor he'd never suspect her of killing her own husband. He'd demand to know, though, why she had felt it necessary to free his avowed enemy. Would he accept the truth, that Ruarc had come to her aid when Alexander was attempting to strangle her, and not probe any further?

Even if he did, Adam had already intimated he might not permit her and Gavin to return to Virginia. In his anger at her for robbing him of his revenge against Ruarc MacDonald, what was to prevent him from forcing her to remarry and remain here in the Highlands? Her plantation, if she even still possessed it by then, would belong to the next man who wed her. Adam might deem it a just punishment for cheating him of a vengeance he seemed so dearly to desire.

Still, Adam was a known entity, and this man standing before her was little more than a stranger. At the realization of her rapidly worsening situation, frustration filled her. Dear God, what had she done? What had she done?

"We need to be going, lass," Ruarc MacDonald said gently, as if sensing her distress. "If ye're still of a mind to come?"

Was this where God intended her to go next? To Rannoch Castle with Ruarc MacDonald? Though she still found it hard to believe God had actually answered her prayers and saved her from her husband, He surely hadn't intended her to become a murderess. Nonetheless, clearly a savior had arrived.

It was just so hard to be sure of anything, with Alexander dead, her life in such turmoil, and her mind so confused. Still, she could leave for Virginia much easier from Rannoch than Achallader without Adam to stop her. And Ruarc MacDonald wasn't aware of the Virginia plantation. Once in his lands, at least there'd be no knowl-

edge of her potential wealth to sway him to more selfish considerations.

Killian released a shaky breath. "It'd be best if I went with you."

He grinned then and she thought his lopsided, endearing smile
must be a sign from heaven. It transformed his face, as bruised and
battered as it was, into something breathtakingly beautiful.

To hide her sudden discomfiture, she glanced around, found the
torch, and picked it up. "Shall we be on our way?"

"Wait a moment." Ruarc grabbed her by the arm. "The guard.
What of him?"

"He's unconscious. Did you think I could get to you without first
rendering him senseless?"

Ruarc eyed her, the realization that she truly did mean to help
him filling him with a wild, if strangely unsettling, elation. "Nay, I
suppose not. Ye seem to have planned for that well enough. Now,
how do ye propose getting us clear of the castle?"

"Well, there's a door in the castle wall not far from the chapel.
We'd have to cross an open courtyard, though, and there's the danger
of sentries seeing us."

"Och, aye, that'd greatly increase our chances of a successful
escape." Ruarc pondered the dilemma for a long moment, then
sighed. "The sally port off the guards' quarters is a better route. It's
a good drop from the door to the ground, but less conspicuous than
walking out across an open courtyard."

"And you know how to find this . . . this sally port?"

"Aye." He shot her an enigmatic look. "In earlier days when
Adam and I were still friends, I spent some time in this castle." He
tugged on her arm. "Come. We must leave this place before the castle
wakens."

She followed him into the main guardroom. True to her word, the
single night watchman lay sprawled across the table, his scraggly
locks slowly absorbing the spilled remains of the bowl of soup he had
been eating.

Ruarc chuckled wryly at the mess, then walked to the table and
picked up the small knife the guard had used to cut the loaf of bread
he had apparently been eating with his soup. He tested it, found the
blade sharp, and shoved the weapon beneath his belt.

"His neep bree will be cold by the time he wakens." He gestured to the bits of turnip scattered amidst the pool of broth. "Well, it most likely wasna verra tasty. The cook here leaves much to be desired."

"Considering our present circumstances," the woman said with a twist of her mouth, "your assessment of the castle cook seems a tad ill timed." She turned to a shadowed alcove in the far wall. "Gavin. Come here, sweeting."

A small, blond-haired boy scampered out. When he saw Ruarc and the guard sprawled facedown upon the table, he hesitated, casting his mother an uncertain look.

"It's all right, sweeting." His mother pulled him to her, then guided him over to Ruarc. "His name is Ruarc MacDonald and he's our friend."

Gavin eyed him from the haven of his mother's skirts. Ruarc managed a crooked smile, his split lip and swollen face preventing anything more.

"He looks nasty, Mama." His small nose wrinkled. "And he smells, too."

The woman flushed and smiled at Ruarc in apology. "I'm sorry. Children can be so blunt at times."

"I imagine I do smell verra rank. I haven't had a bath in over two days and, besides my mud-drenched journey here, I've just spent the greater part of a day in a filth-encrusted pit." He paused. "Ye said yer son's name is Gavin. What's yers?"

She smirked at what he belatedly realized was his own equally blunt manner. "I'm Killian Campbell."

"Well, Killian, ye and yer son need to keep yer mouths shut, walk softly, and be prepared to obey me at a moment's notice. It's the only way we'll have a chance of escaping this castle. Do ye understand?"

"Yes, I understand."

He could tell by the suddenly subdued tone of her voice and flash of hurt in her eyes that he had offended her. Ruarc cursed his lack of tact. For all his fine education, he continued to be a blundering boor when it came to women.

Ruarc sighed and shoved the tangled mess of his hair from his face. "I beg pardon if I caused ye offense, but ye seemed verra confused earlier today. And now our lives hang on ye following closely everything I say."

"I know." Killian glanced down. Ruarc had the distinct impression she was purposely avoiding his gaze. "To a certain extent I *was* confused earlier, but I'm feeling a lot better now."

He scowled. "Then ye're not daft?"

"No."

Ruarc made a frustrated sound. "Then why did ye—"

"That isn't important right now. Getting out of here is."

"Aye, ye're right." He didn't like being put off, but this wasn't the time or place for a quarrel. "Follow close behind me then and don't make a sound."

"I think I understand that part of the instructions."

Ruarc shot her a hard-eyed stare that would've silenced a howling dog. By mountain and sea, one minute she was meek and compliant, and the next . . . she indeed had spunk, but he couldn't say he cared much for her mouthy ways.

He didn't like being burdened with the responsibility of her and her son, either. But he had given his word. And, if the truth be told, he did harbor a wee curiosity to discover what she was about.

With the utmost stealth, they climbed the stairs leading from the dungeon. The hall angling off in the direction of the soldiers' quarters was dimly lit and chilly. From time to time, an errant breeze found its way through the myriad chinks in the ancient stone, setting the torches to fluttering wildly. The castle was deserted, though, which suited Ruarc's purposes.

He loosened his shoulder plaid, slinging its warm, tightly woven weight over his shoulders and back. Beside him, Killian shivered, slipped the hood of her cloak over her head, then stooped briefly to ensure her son was equally bundled up in his little breeches, shirt, and thick, knee-length coat. They continued on.

If Ruarc's memory served him, the sally port was located at the far end of the armory. A short journey more, if no one discovered them, and they'd be well free of Achallader.

Luck was with them. Only one soldier stirred, no doubt on a nocturnal visit to the latrine. Ruarc dispatched him with a quick blow to the jaw. After dragging the now limp body into a dark corner, Ruarc returned to Killian. Her face had gone pale and she gazed back at him with a wide-eyed, uncertain look. He managed a taut smile of encouragement, then turned and forged on.

They passed through an armory bristling with basket-handled

claymores, pikes, flintlock muskets, pistols, and the traditional Scottish shields called targes. After shoving two loaded pistols in his belt, handing Killian a particularly lethal-looking dagger, and taking up a claymore, Ruarc skirted the wooden racks of weapons, leading Killian and her son to a small door at the far end of the room. He slipped the rusted iron bolt and pried open the aging wooden portal.

An easily defensible entry and exit route during war, the sally port opened about ten feet above ground. From the doorway, Ruarc studied the drop for a long moment before turning to Killian.

"We'll have to jump. I'll go first. Then ye can lower the lad down to me."

"And then what? I can't jump that far. I'll break my leg—or worse!"

This time, there was real fear in her voice. Ruarc understood its source. There was scant time, however, to spare in cajoling her into a more adventurous mood.

"Dinna fash yerself, lass," he said, hoping his tone of voice, if not his words, was of some comfort. "I'm strong. I can catch ye before ye hurt yerself."

She eyed him dubiously. "But *will* you? Catch me, I mean?"

He cocked his head in puzzlement. "And why wouldn't I catch ye? Ye talk verra strange. Are ye certain ye're not still a wee bit addled?"

"From where I come from, you talk strange too!"

"True enough," he agreed in an attempt to calm what he guessed was her rising fear. His conciliatory gesture, however, only seemed to unsettle her the more.

"Fine . . . all right." Killian motioned to the sally port. "Let's get this over with before I change my mind."

"Suit yerself." Ruarc lowered himself to sit at the edge of the opening. He tossed down the claymore. After a careful survey of the ground below, he jumped.

The landing was jarring, but he managed to keep his balance. Turning, Ruarc glanced up at the faint glow of the doorway. "Hand the lad down now," he called to Killian in as low a voice as still would carry to her.

She did as told. The boy dropped only a few feet before Ruarc caught him.

"Stay close by, lad," he ordered the child, "but out of my way. Yer mither won't be as easy a load to catch as ye were."

Gavin moved even farther aside. Ruarc called once more. "Jump down now, lass. I'll catch ye."

She moved to the edge of the door, lowered herself to the floor, and nodded once. Ruarc was grateful for the dim light. He could almost imagine her look of terror.

Killian pushed off, nonetheless, and came plummeting down.

Caught off guard by his momentary inattention in considering her fear, Ruarc was barely able to break her fall. As it was, they both slammed to the ground, her atop him.

"Mmmph," she grunted from beneath a tumble of hair and long skirts. "I thought you said you'd catch me."

He shoved her back until she sat on her heels. "I *did* catch ye. With my body, no less. And ye don't look any too worse the wear for it, either."

"No, I suppose not." Killian struggled to her feet, hastily smoothing back her tousled hair and skirts into some semblance of order. She glanced down at him. "How did you fare?"

It was the second time today she had shown interest in his welfare. As brief and brusque as both had been, it was also strangely pleasing.

"I'll do." He pushed to his elbows. "I think I bruised my shoulder on a stone, but amongst so many other injuries, it hardly matters."

"Well then, shouldn't we be on our way?" She offered her hand.

Ruarc stared up at it, suddenly reluctant to touch her again. The feel of her pressed against him just a few seconds ago was still too fresh, too stirring. It'd be better, indeed, if he hied himself as fast and far from her as he could.

But he couldn't. Or, leastwise, not until they reached Rannoch. Then, to add further complications to his already complicated life, he must determine what next to do with her.

Like it or not, the strange lass was his for a time more.

4

AFTER an arduous trek through dense forest and soggy moor, with
only the thinnest sliver of light to illuminate the way, Killian and
Ruarc found the MacDonald search party early the next morning.
Their rescue came none too soon. Exhausted, cold from the morning
damp, Killian could barely walk. Indeed, there was but one consolation in the midst of her suffering. Her son slept, dry and warm,
wrapped in Ruarc MacDonald's plaid and cradled in his arms.

Two hours' journey out from Castle Achallader, the big Highlander had offered to carry the boy when Gavin began stumbling in
the darkness. He had also made Killian grasp the back of the belt
fastening his plaid, soon sensing that she, too, was having difficulty
finding her way.

It was a strange sensation, being led as if almost blind. She didn't
like the implied helplessness and dependence the act engendered in
her. She didn't like the faith and trust it demanded, either.

In the blackness and silence of that difficult night, second
thoughts assailed her. Though the man had saved her life, Killian still
wondered if she could truly rely on Ruarc MacDonald. Indeed, what
did she really know about him, save that he was a Campbell enemy,
and Adam Campbell thought him a wife killer? A wife killer . . . just
like Alexander had almost become.

At the admission, a shiver coursed through Killian. In her escape
from Castle Achallader, had she but run from one brutal man into the

arms of another? Surely the Lord hadn't answered her prayers only to allow her to fall into yet another equally cruel fate. Surely she could trust in Ruarc MacDonald's promise to take them back with him to Rannoch, to protect them.

Throughout the long night, Killian had clung to that pledge as tightly as she had clung to Ruarc MacDonald's belt. There was, after all, no other choice now.

The reunion of the MacDonalds was joyful and boisterous, Ruarc's men leaping from their horses to clap him resoundingly on the back. Killian bit back a sympathetic grin as Ruarc winced repeatedly from the good-hearted poundings, knowing he must still be exquisitely tender. And then, as suddenly as the camaraderie had begun, it was over. Ruarc was handed the reins of a huge chestnut gelding, and his clansmen remounted.

Despite his injuries—or was it sheer, stubborn pride and force of will? —after passing Gavin to one of his men, Ruarc swung lithely up onto his horse, then turned it and rode to Killian.

He leaned down, offering his hand. "Are ye ready for a fine gallop to Rannoch Moor?"

"Most certainly, if it gets us to your castle." Killian placed her hand in his. An upward jerk of a powerful arm quickly deposited her squarely before Ruarc MacDonald. "Er," she muttered, suddenly uneasy at their close proximity now that the tension-fraught escape seemed over, "perhaps it'd be better if I rode behind you."

"Nay." Ruarc gave a firm shake of his head. "It wouldn't. It isn't proper for a lady to ride astride, and ye'd surely fall off if I let ye ride sideways behind me."

He had a point. About the falling-off part, at any rate, if she rode sidesaddle behind him.

"As you wish, then. It wouldn't do to offend anyone's sense of propriety, now, would it?" Nonetheless, though she dared not look up at him again, Killian shifted surreptitiously to put a bit of distance between them.

The attempt, however, either to visually or physically shut out a man like Ruarc MacDonald, did little good. The rough rasp of his calloused palm upon her arm, the gentle yet firm pressure of his fingers, sent repeated jolts of awareness shooting to Killian's befuddled brain. The heat of his big body, only inches from hers, and the scent of damp wool and unwashed man—albeit a tad strong—only reinforced the intense perception of the proud, forceful Highlander who held her. Killian swallowed hard and closed her eyes, already dreading the ride ahead.

"Of course I'm right," Ruarc replied with a matter-of-fact arrogance Killian found rather irritating. "I haven't lived in the Highlands these thirty-five years without learning a few things."

"No, I'd imagine not," she agreed beneath her breath, then turned her attention to Gavin, now snugly ensconced in the arms of another MacDonald warrior. She looked at Ruarc. "My son. If you wouldn't mind, could he ride with us? I'll hold him close. You'll hardly notice he's there."

He studied her in thoughtful silence, then nodded. "As ye wish, lass. Yer bairn will add scant weight for my horse." With that, Ruarc motioned to the clansman carrying Gavin.

The boy was handed over and quickly settled within the warm folds of his mother's cloak. Without another word, Ruarc signaled his mount. The horse bounded forward, unseating the unsuspecting Killian and throwing her back hard into Ruarc MacDonald's chest. If not for the strong restraint of his arms about her, she would have immediately slid from the animal.

"Not so keen a rider, are ye? I suspected as much."

"Actually, I'm quite a good rider." Once again, Killian adjusted Gavin's position more comfortably against her. "I'm just accustomed to handling my own horse by myself."

Ruarc glanced down at her. "Ye Colonists are an independent lot, aren't ye?"

"Yes, we are, and proud of it. Suffice it to say, under the proper circumstances I could hold my own against many of your men."

"Well, that sets my mind at ease. I can't abide an addle-brained, helpless female."

Fully expecting a teasing smile to accompany that statement, she turned more fully to eye him. Ruarc MacDonald's gaze, however, was fixed straight ahead, his expression quite serious.

Killian rolled her eyes. What a humorless, self-absorbed man. Didn't anyone in this dank, dismal country have a sense of humor? But then, why would they, as immersed as they all were in daily life-and-death struggles, ancient blood feuds, and the almost perpetually gloomy, rain-soaked weather?

She hugged Gavin close and settled back against Ruarc's solid form. One way or another, it didn't matter anyway. Whatever the basis for the dreary Scottish temperament, it was hardly of concern to her. Soon enough, she'd return to Virginia and be rid of them all. Soon enough, she'd never again have to give the Highlands another thought.

But she mustn't think about that right now. Too much had happened in the past few days to fathom, much less deal with in any kind of clearheaded manner. Only one thing mattered, and that was making it to Rannoch Castle, getting a hot meal and bath for her and Gavin, and then a good night's sleep. The morning was soon enough to plan for the future.

Killian glanced down at her son. His eyes were bright, his cheeks flushed with excitement, and his small hands clutched the gelding's red mane. Her heart warmed with motherly affection. Gavin so loved animals, loved this horseback ride.

The realization eased a little of Killian's inner turmoil. There was some consolation in this awful situation, if only she could protect Gavin from its harsh reality until they were able to get back home. It was a blessing he had still been unconscious when she had killed his father. And she could only assume, since Gavin hadn't mentioned it, that he hadn't woken in time to see Alexander dragged away, either.

As long as he wasn't scarred by the experience, Killian thought she could endure almost anything. After all, she had already endured so much so many times before. Murder, however, she thought with a shudder before firmly thrusting the horrific memory aside, had never been part of the plan. But she couldn't think about that just now. She didn't dare.

Killian eyed the terrain, making careful note of the direction they were heading. Sooner or later she might need to head back this very way on her journey to the nearest seaport. If all went as she hoped, next time she'd have an escort of armed MacDonalds at her side. Still, Killian knew better than to depend on the honor or kindness of strangers. After all, if her own husband could betray her so foully, she hardly dared depend on a man she barely knew.

The ride to Rannoch took almost two hours, their progress slowed by the hilly terrain and the fording of myriad small streams. Ruarc seldom spoke, his face riveted ahead, his expression shuttered. Killian, though, was kept more than occupied with Gavin's delighted observations of the landscape and the horseback ride.

Though an unsettled day, damp and somberly lit, the land was still a pleasing palette of golds, rusts, and browns. As they headed northwest into what was apparently MacDonald territory, eagles and kites soared in the distance, swimming high in the currents above the jagged cliffs that Ruarc pointed out as Aonach Eagach. Linnet and thrush sang in the trees. Occasionally, a fox or badger darted by.

An unspoiled land, this Glencoe region, an enclosed garden apparently as fertile and plenteous in summer as it was said to be harsh and unforgiving in winter. Indeed, the land was just like its people. Bound by a Highland code of honor that demanded they share everything with any who requested their hospitality, they were also held to a merciless retribution if that same honor demanded it. Though good, simple people in many ways, in their superstitious ignorance the Highlanders could also be vicious and quite merciless. She'd be glad to be gone from here.

Unbidden, Adam Campbell's words filtered through Killian's mind. *"Ruarc MacDonald is an evil, hard-hearted man who thinks only of himself. . . . Ye weren't here . . . he killed her in a jealous rage . . ."* His words filled her with renewed foreboding. There was something strange going on, something that involved both Ruarc MacDonald and Adam Campbell. Something that spanned more than mere clan feuding.

Killian hesitated but an instant. In her current situation, knowledge was essential for survival. Moreover, for both her own and Gavin's sake she needed not only to survive right now, but to prevail.

"Adam told me something yesterday evening," Killian said, choosing her words with care. "Something about your murdering your wife, and that you were a cruel man."

Behind her, already hard, masculine muscles tensed even harder. "Aye, and what of it? If ye haven't pieced it together yet, Adam and I are hardly the closest of friends."

Killian swallowed convulsively and forged on. "I-I didn't for a moment believe that of you, of course. You saved my life, after all. And I appreciate your willingness to take me into your home. I just want to know what you expect of me."

"Expect? Verra little, actually. Stay out of trouble and play no games with me."

"Play games!" Killian flushed in anger. Were all men, then, possessed of the same suspicious minds? "Do those conditions apply to you as well?"

He reined his horse to an abrupt halt. "What did ye say?"

Her heart leaped to her throat. Ah, curse her waspish tongue! Now she had gone and done it! "I meant," she began again, this time taking pains to use the utmost tact, "I find it difficult to begin our friendship with such mistrust and conflict between us. I would prefer if you gave me a chance before passing judgment."

"That isn't what ye said at all. Truly, ye speak in the strangest way, even for a Colonial!"

Killian glanced back, struggling for a plausible explanation to soothe him. "And how many Colonials have you known? Like you Scots, there are different speech patterns in the Colonies, depending upon where you live. I'm sure the British would say you Highlanders speak just as strangely."

Surprisingly, his anger faded as quickly as it had risen. He managed a taut smile. "It doesn't matter, lass. I was being overhard on ye." Ruarc nudged the gelding back into a rocking canter. "It isn't yer fault ye're saddled with the likes of me. And I'm grateful to ye not only for helping me escape Achallader, but for not slitting my throat when ye had the chance."

He swung his glance back to the land before them. "Though it might've been better for ye if ye had," he then added cryptically. "Campbell lasses haven't done well with me."

"Why do you say that?"

The big Highlander gave a mirthless laugh. "There are opinions aplenty on that particular topic. Take my word. Ye'll hear all of them soon enough."

As he spoke, they cleared the last hill and paused to gaze down at a long, wide, boggy plain. Though the sun broke fleetingly through the clouds to gild the land, there was something haunting about the place—a lonely, almost tragic feel to this land of ochre-colored grass, of moss and browned heather, and empty, leaden lochs.

"Rannoch Moor," Ruarc murmured softly. "Few know or love it save the people of Glencoe. But it's my home."

Killian's gaze turned westward. In the distance stood a castle, surrounded by a scattering of croft houses and farm holdings. Situated on higher ground at the edge of an ancient oak forest, all four stories of the two-towered house, with its fairy-tale skyline of turrets and jagged battlements, were smooth-walled and clean-lined. The grounds and buildings surrounding it were well kept, the close-cropped grass lush and green, the long road leading up to it graveled and bordered by stones.

In spite of her determination not to like the Highlands, Killian found Rannoch beautiful. For some reason, the sight of it filled her with a bittersweet longing—a longing for home, security, heritage. That unexpected admission, however, frightened her. Angrily, she flung the unsettling emotion aside.

"I know you don't care for, or even necessarily trust, me," she said, turning to Ruarc MacDonald, "but I still wanted you to know I'm honored to be taken into your home. Truly, if I say or do anything to offend you, please tell me, and I'll try my best to make amends."

He eyed her quizzically. "One moment ye cannot wait to hie yerself as fast and far from me as ye can get, and the next, ye wish to be my most loving friend. Is this yet another Campbell trick?"

Though she knew she shouldn't let it, for some reason his question hurt. There was, Killian realized, a chasm of wariness and pain between them that might never be breached.

"No trick, m'lord," she said with a sigh. "I was just trying to make peace between us."

"Are we at war then?" Ruarc's dark brows knit in a scowl. "Is that the way of it?"

"No, certainly not." Killian shook her head. The man was beyond hope. "Please forget what I said. It was of no import."

"Aye, that it wasn't." Ruarc MacDonald nudged his horse down the hill. "Just have a care, I say. That sharp tongue of yers will win ye no friends in Rannoch."

"Aye, m'lord," was the sweet, albeit grudgingly rendered, reply.

†

A SHOUT from the tower sentry signaled their approach. By the time they drew near the castle, a small party had gathered to await them.

Ruarc experienced a momentary surge of irritation. There'd be expectations of an explanation, not only for the woman and child he carried with him but also for his sudden disappearance the evening before and the signs of the beating he now bore. Fact was, Ruarc felt in no mood to appease anyone's curiosity.

Father Kenneth stood at the head of the castle's welcoming party. At least the priest's interest in what had transpired would be sincere, his concern for Ruarc heartfelt. As heartfelt as the paternal tongue-lashing Ruarc would then next receive for his "carelessness" in being captured.

Still, at the consideration, something in the big Highlander softened. He almost smiled.

A regally clad woman and a younger man moved to stand beside the little priest. Ruarc's gut tightened. Lady Glynnis—his *dear, loving* stepmother—and her sly, scheming son, Thomas. They, he well knew, would be eager to hear all the sordid details, then hurry off to gloat over his misfortune. Gloat, then, as always, set to work turning it to their advantage.

But it didn't matter. Not any of it. As he did others who hated him, Ruarc refused to succumb to their devious machinations no matter the obstacles thrown into his path. He'd never admit defeat or let the lies and accusations, the greed and envy, drag him down. He was Rannoch's laird. He knew what he must do, no matter how badly Glynnis and others wished it otherwise. Her petty plottings to the contrary, that lady hadn't the wherewithal to effect anything of consequence. And Thomas . . .

His half brother was a weak, preening peacock, unworthy of the MacDonald name. If not for the vow he had made his father, he'd have turned Thomas out long ago for his avarice and immoral, self-serving ways. And if Glynnis hadn't been a woman . . .

Aye, women. Ruarc glanced down at Killian. As if he didn't have enough problems, now he had gone and brought yet another one into his life. In all truth, though, she was a bonny lass.

Her hair was the color of sunshine streaming through the morning mist. Her skin was soft and smooth, the continued chill of the day caus-ing it to glow with a healthy pink color. And her eyes, fringed with thick, brown lashes, were a gloriously clear blue green. A man could lose his bearing in eyes like those . . . and never find his way out.

But she was a Campbell. He must never forget that. A Campbell who bore him no affection or loyalty, despite all her fine words to the contrary. A Campbell with a mysterious and suspicious past.

A sudden exasperation filled Ruarc. Didn't he have enough to concern him without now being burdened with an unwanted woman and her child?

Well, there was nothing to be done for it. He'd muddle through this night as best he could. Then, on the morrow, he'd relegate her to some corner in the back of his mind . . . just as he had done with the Lady Glynnis, Thomas, and the rest of them.

As harsh as that might seem, Ruarc knew he had little other choice. Not, at any rate, if he wished to keep not only his sanity but his head fastened firmly to his neck and shoulders.

†

AS THEY drew near the castle, Killian was startled to see a sleek, dark blue-gray form dart from the crowd and speed toward them. The beast was large, with small, folded ears, a long, curved tail, and a harsh, wiry, ragged-looking coat. Only when a joyous barking ensued did Killian belatedly realize it was a dog.

"Fionn!" Ruarc slid his mount to a halt. He vaulted off, leaving Killian still clasping Gavin atop the horse, and ran to meet the dog.

The animal was nearly three feet tall at the shoulders and easily weighed a hundred pounds. The impact of master and hound meeting nearly toppled Ruarc over. He sank to the ground and began to tussle with the dog. For a heart-stopping moment, Killian thought he was fending off an attack.

Then Ruarc broke into laughter, a rich, vibrant sound that skit-tered pleasantly across her nerve endings. She relaxed, realizing this was all some ritualistic greeting between the very best of friends.

"Mama," Gavin whispered in awe, "he sure has a big dog."

"Yes, sweeting, he does."

Someone stepped up to help the two of them dismount. "Maybe he'll let you make friends with his dog sometime."

Before Killian could stop him, Gavin ran toward the animal. "Now! I want to make friends now!"

The huge dog stiffened at Gavin's approach. A growl of warning rumbled in his throat. Even from the distance still separating them, Killian could see the hackles rise, the lean muscles tense for attack.

"Gavin!" She gathered her skirts and raced after him.

"Fionn. Down!" Ruarc commanded in a low voice, rising to his feet.

The dog immediately sank to the ground and looked up at his master, his long tongue lolling from the side of his mouth. Adoration gleamed in his big, black eyes.

"Good dog." Ruarc turned to await Gavin's approach.

The little boy halted a few feet from Fionn. He gazed up at Ruarc. "Sure is a big dog."

"Aye, that he is, lad."

"Sure is a pretty dog, too."

The dark-haired man chuckled. "Aye, but I'd wager few aside from us would think so."

Serious blue eyes studied Fionn for a long moment. "What kind of dog *is* it?"

"A deerhound, lad."

Gavin inched closer. "Can I pet your dog?"

"He doesn't trust strangers, lad. Mayhap in time, when he's had a chance to know ye."

"All right." Before Killian could shout a warning, Gavin plopped down beside the huge animal. "I won't pet him. We'll just get started on knowing each other."

Simultaneously, Killian and Ruarc made a move toward the pair, then halted. The dog just sat there, gazing at Gavin with mild interest. The boy grinned back, pleased as punch with his newfound friend.

Killian's eyes lifted to Ruarc's and saw the alarm dying there. He hadn't known what the dog's reaction would be any more than she. She managed a weak smile. "He's always had a way with animals."

"So it appears." Ruarc bent down and pulled Gavin up into his arms. "Let's see how well he does with people."

They were greeted by a host of stares, from the mildly curious to the outright suspicious, and all were centered on Killian.

Ruarc immediately broke the heavy silence. "This is the Lady Killian Campbell. And this lad," he said, hefting the little boy more securely in his arms, "is her son, Gavin."

Ruarc's steely gaze met Glynnis's. "Killian, this is my step-mither, the Lady Glynnis MacDonald. She'll see to yer comforts, a suitable room, and a bath."

Killian turned to greet a tall, coldly beautiful woman who looked to be in her early forties. Her ebony-colored hair was dressed in a short, curly fringe on her forehead, the sides done in longer curls and ringlets, the back drawn up tightly in a bun. She was elegantly garbed in an emerald green wool gown, cut low to set off her voluptuously ample bosom. Realizing that, before her arrival, Ruarc's stepmother had been the sole lady of the house, Killian thought it wisest to start out on the right foot by enlisting her aid. She gave her a friendly smile. "I'm very happy to meet you, Lady Glynnis."

The woman smiled thinly in return. "And I, ye, m'lady."

"And will ye not introduce me to the bonny lassie as well, Brother?" A tall, brown-haired man in his early twenties, plain of face with a long, thin nose and petulant twist to his mouth, stepped forward. He was impeccably garbed in a white shirt, tartan trews, and a pair of brass-buckled leather shoes. Across his chest he wore a plaid, fastened with what seemed to be the requisite silver brooch. He smiled at Killian, an appraising light gleaming in his pale brown eyes.

"Madam," Ruarc said, a surprising edge to his voice, "this is my half brother and Glynnis's son, Thomas MacDonald. Thomas, the Lady Killian."

The man bowed low. "I am honored, m'lady."

"And I as well, Thomas," Killian replied, unsettled by the almost palpable hostility arcing between the three MacDonalds. She glanced uncertainly at Ruarc.

A little priest, white of hair, thick of beard, and blessed with the roundest, most ruddy cheeks, stepped forward.

The big Highlander inclined his head from Killian to the priest. "This is Father Kenneth, comforter of souls and bestower of the most abundant and creative penances ye'll ever hope to receive. He's far older than he appears and wise to every game."

"M'lady, it's my greatest pleasure to make yer acquaintance." The priest graced Killian with an elegant bow before turning to Ruarc. "And what, pray tell, happened to ye, laddie?" he next demanded, his frowning gaze encompassing the younger man's filthy, battered form. "Did the lass truly demand such a rough wooing?"

Ruarc shot the priest a quelling glance. "Nay. It's a long story, but suffice it to say, there wasn't any wooing. Now, I've a wish for a bath and my wounds tended, then a short rest before dealing further with any questions. I'm certain the lady has personal needs as well."

"A wooing?" Glynnis's delicate brows lifted as she stepped forward and entered tardily into the conversation. "Have ye brought back yet another Campbell lass to take as wife, then?"

Ruarc expelled a weary breath. "The lady's but a friend. See to her welfare, Glynnis, and ask naught more. Time enough later for yer inquisition."

A mutinous light flared in the older woman's eyes, then was quickly tamped down. "Aye, m'lord."

Ruarc turned to Killian, offering his arm. "Come then, madam. It's past time ye were taken to yer room."

He was such a darkly brooding, enigmatic man, Killian thought as she accepted his arm and walked with him into Rannoch Castle. Ill tempered and short of patience, he suffered fools poorly—and anyone else, for that matter.

Yet, inexplicably, in spite of all caution and common sense, she found herself drawn to him. The admission disturbed her. The last thing she needed in her life was another potentially unstable, domineering, righteous man. One had been more than enough! Indeed, she doubted she'd survive another such man.

As they entered the front door of Rannoch Castle, Killian shoved the unsettling thoughts into some distant corner of her mind, forcing her attention to the dwelling before her. The first-floor entry was little more than an access point to the household work areas on one side and the Great Hall on the other. A broad set of stone stairs wound upward to floors holding what were likely the more formal rooms and bedchambers.

What immediately stopped her short, though, was the general

condition of the house. The entry wall hangings were little more than shabby rags. The meager furniture and floors seemed buried under years of dust. A stale, musty odor permeated the air.

Killian shuddered to think what the upper levels were like. She refused to consider the kitchen.

She glanced at Ruarc as he led them up the stairs. He appeared neither concerned nor embarrassed by the filth. *Just like a man,* Killian thought in disgust. Too busy with "more important" matters to spare time worrying about the upkeep of his house. Her glance swung to Glynnis's.

Ruarc's stepmother noted her look of horror. She shrugged, as if to say, "Aye, I know it's shameful, but what am I to do?"

After leading the way up two flights of stairs and down a long corridor, Ruarc halted outside a thick oaken door. "I'll return for the lady at suppertime," he informed his stepmother, surrendering Killian and Gavin to her custody. "Have her ready."

With that, he nodded to Killian, then turned on his heel and strode away, the gaunt form of Fionn trotting at his side. Both women watched until Ruarc disappeared down the dimly lit hallway, then faced each other.

"I don't wish to be any trouble—"

Glynnis held up a silencing hand. "Dinna fash yerself, my dear. I won't hold Ruarc's boorish behavior against ye."

She laid a gentle hand on Killian's arm, her brown eyes warming with friendship. For the first time in the past two days, Killian felt herself relax. Perhaps here was someone she could eventually trust and confide in, someone who might help her. She returned Glynnis's smile, then followed her into the bedchamber.

†

THE ROOM, though as untidy as the rest of the castle, was soon warm from the fire hastily started in the hearth. Dominated as any great house's bedchamber was by its four-poster bed, the carved fir bedstead was hung with curtains of heavily embroidered bright blue velvet in sore need of a washing. A quilt, made of the same, now dingy fabric, covered the bed. An embroidered footstool standing beside the bed, a tall chest of drawers, a full-length looking glass, and a small stand set with a porcelain ewer and basin completed the chamber's décor.

After seeing to Gavin's hunger and a quick bath, Killian tucked the exhausted child in for a nap in the small, adjoining room. She had little appetite for her own lunch of cold roast chicken, brown bread, and cheese. The hot bath, however, was a welcome balm to the ache in her saddle-sore muscles. Afterward, as she sat before the fire dressed in a spare gown Glynnis had loaned her, a young maidservant named Finola brushed out her wet, lavender-scented hair.

Lulled by the soothing, rhythmic brush strokes, Killian soon set aside the memory of the unsettling day and the uncertainties of her current situation. She eased back in the little low-slung leather chair. In time, her lids began to droop, then slowly closed.

An insistent and most irritating rapping on the bedchamber door roused Killian. She jerked awake, glancing around in confusion at the unfamiliar surroundings as an equally unfamiliar girl hurried across the room.

Finola . . . Killian recognized the maidservant at last. Rannoch Castle . . . she was now in Rannoch Castle. She pushed herself from the chair and stood, hastily tugging up the sagging neckline of Glynnis's generously cut dress.

A lock of pale hair, fully dry now, tumbled down onto her breast. How long had she been sleeping? Then there was no time left to ponder anything, as Finola swung open the thick door.

"Ah, lassie." Father Kenneth, a book of some sort clasped to his barrel-shaped chest, caught sight of her and hurried into the bedchamber. "I see ye're clean and rested at last. All the better, for what I plan to propose to ye wouldn't set well on a weary mind. Nay, it wouldn't set well at all."

Killian eyed the old priest, wondering whatever gave him the idea she was fully rested after a long day and night without sleep. Well, no matter. She could surely deal with the man, whatever the purpose of his visit.

"Please, come in, Father," she said, offering him a welcoming smile. "Sit with me by the fire."

Finola's sandy-colored brows arched, and she cocked her head inquisitively, but silently closed the door behind the priest. Then, as quietly as she had first made her way to the door, she slipped back to her post across the room.

Father Kenneth soon took his seat by the fire. Killian settled herself, tugged yet again at the gaping neckline of the lace-trimmed, blue woolen gown, then met the priest's gaze. "And to what do I owe the honor of your visit, Father? As new an arrival as I am to Rannoch, I hardly expected anyone to call so soon."

"Och, and aren't ye the modest one?" the priest responded with a hearty laugh. "But since ye asked, my visit is twofold." He offered her the book he held. "First and foremost, I saw that ye came to Rannoch with nary a possession save the clothes on yer back. I thought ye might find renewed inspiration and comfort in having yer own Bible."

Killian's heart couldn't help but warm toward the little cleric. She took the Bible. "Thank you, Father. This will indeed bring me much comfort and inspiration." She paused. "And what of your other reason for coming to visit?"

He chuckled. "Well, that reason concerns both ye and Ruarc, lass. Why, already the tongues are wagging fast and furious over yer mysterious ties to Rannoch's laird." He chuckled again. "A friend, indeed, or so Ruarc tried to claim. Even I could see the bond ye two already share. That's the other reason I came to ye this eve, lass. It's imperative this bond between ye be strengthened as soon as possible. For yer sake as well as for that of Ruarc's."

Unease twined about Killian's heart. She gripped the Bible. "Truly, Father, I don't understand. Ruarc and I share no bond, save that he saved my life and then I saved his. But there's no need—"

"Aye, there is indeed, lass." The little cleric raised his hand to silence her. "I've been praying over this verra matter for a long while now, and our Lord has finally seen fit to answer me. His will is clear, and no mistake. Before this night passes, ye and Rannoch's laird must make yer vows as man and wife."

5

"SOMETHING'S afoot, Thomas," Glynnis MacDonald muttered a short time after the midday meal. "Something foul and furtive. I can feel it in my bones."

"Indeed, Mither?" Her son lifted a crystal goblet of claret to the light streaming through the library windows. "And would ye, mayhap, be speaking of my dear stepbrother's surprising—and most disappointingly safe—return?"

For a distracted instant, Glynnis was caught up in the beauty of the crimson shards sparkling through the prismlike cut of the glass. Then she angrily shook the diversion aside. "Ye know quite well of whom I speak," she ground out through clenched teeth.

Though Glynnis dearly loved her only child, there were times when his attempts at a clever cynicism grated on her. Times like now, when carefully laid plans had gone dreadfully awry, and even greater threats now loomed on the horizon.

Thomas took a deep, leisurely swallow to empty his cup, then lowered it and shrugged. "There'll be other opportunities. There always are."

"Och, aye." Glynnis laughed shrilly. "But only until Ruarc finds himself a new and far more fertile wife. Only until he finally breeds an heir. Then where will we be, my fair son? Where will *ye* be?"

He frowned, set down his goblet, and turned to her. "Ye heard

Ruarc. The woman he brought back is only a friend. They aren't wed, and most likely never will be."

"Mayhap not, but there's something between them nonetheless. Something that fills me with unease."

"Ye worry overmuch, Mither."

Her frustration rising, Glynnis watched her son pour out yet another cupful of claret. He turned to the bottle far too frequently of late, as if the liquor held some magical quality. Did he, mayhap, hope to find answers in it, or just escape?

"And ye, my fine son, drink overmuch." Without care for the mess she made, Glynnis snatched away the goblet. "This," she said, lifting the cup, "will never win ye Rannoch. For such work, ye need a clear head. And much is the work still before us if we're yet to prevail against the likes of Ruarc MacDonald."

Thomas sighed and shook his head. "As ye wish, Mither. But first a wee drink more. Then we'll put our heads together and plot anew."

"Nay." Glynnis poured what was left of the claret back into its flagon. "By the looks of ye, ye've already had far too many 'wee drinks' before I arrived." She gestured toward several high-backed chairs placed along a massive, mahogany table inlaid with myriad bits of ebony. "Sit. We must talk while we've yet the time. I've a plan."

She always knew how to engage her son in some endeavor, and that was to pique his curiosity. This time was no different. Thomas quickly settled into the nearest chair, his attitude now expectant, his gaze avid.

Glynnis smiled grimly. Ruarc MacDonald only thought he had the better of them. He only imagined he deserved Rannoch more than they.

But she was his father's lawful and last wife, and Thomas was as much a MacDonald as he. They were just as entitled to Rannoch as Ruarc MacDonald believed he was. Indeed, if having to endure the last years of a miserably cruel, half-mad old man's life meant aught, they deserved it the more.

Ruarc MacDonald hadn't even been in Scotland when his father died. He had no idea what they'd had to endure. Not that he would've cared, at any rate. He was, after all, cut from the same ruthlessly contemptible cloth as his father.

†

KILLIAN didn't know whether to laugh out loud or explode in anger. Was this priest mad, or just equally as puffed up with his lofty status as was Rannoch's laird? One way or another, he overstepped himself in suggesting she wed Ruarc MacDonald—and wed him this very night, no less.

Little good was served, however, in antagonizing the cleric unnecessarily. It was obvious, even from the short time spent earlier observing Ruarc and him, that the two men were very close. But how to gracefully deflect such an absurd demand?

"Your affection for your laird is most commendable," Killian said, picking her way as cautiously as possible. "However, I can assure you neither Ruarc nor I wishes to wed, and especially not to each other."

"Och, dinna fash yerself." The old man brushed aside her statement with a casual wave of his hand. "Many a marriage has been made where neither bride nor groom even knew each other, much less were in love. In time, though, true love can grow between a man and a woman, as I'm certain it will with ye and Ruarc. All that matters now is that ye wed before it's too late."

"Not that I'm giving your proposal serious consideration, but what exactly *is* the reason for such haste? Your laird only returned a few hours ago, and I'm but a widow of two days."

The priest eyed her a moment. "As long as Ruarc produces no heirs, his life's in danger. Do ye think his capture was an accident? Nay, on the contrary," he said, tugging at his beard now in apparent agitation, "his mission to spy on the Campbell nobles that night was betrayed. Otherwise, Ruarc would've never been captured."

"Well, as luck would have it, our paths crossed. Ruarc saved my life, and I, his. Then, after it became apparent I needed to leave Achallader and Ruarc required rescuing from the dungeon, I freed him and we escaped."

"So ye think that fulfills yer mission, do ye? That the Lord has no further need of ye?"

Father Kenneth's query took Killian momentarily aback. What did God have to do with this? "Well, no, Father, I don't think that. I'm sure God has further need of me. He's endlessly expecting something from each of us, isn't He? I don't see why He'd ever mean for me to wed Ruarc MacDonald, though, much less be the one to bear his children."

"Our Savior's will is clear enough to me, leastwise. And He has every right to expect everything of ye." The priest's shaggy thatch bobbed with the insistent nodding of his head. "Didn't He come to yer aid that night ye escaped Achallader? Didn't He answer yer prayers when ye asked Him to save ye and yer son? Didn't He?"

A reply lodged in Killian's throat. Her chest grew tight. How was it possible Father Kenneth could've known what her prayer had been, as she stood that storm-tossed night at the chapel's door looking out onto Achallader's courtyard? Had God truly spoken to him? Or was the wily little man but making a lucky guess?

"Whether our Lord did or didn't answer my prayers remains to be seen," Killian replied hotly. "I've still to survive my stay at Rannoch, it seems. And survive your devious matchmaking attempts in the bargain."

"Och, now, lassie. I mean ye no harm." Father Kenneth smiled sadly and shook his head. "Truly I don't."

"Then please, speak no more of my wedding Ruarc MacDonald. It isn't proper to talk of marriage when my husband's only two days dead." She clasped her arms protectively about herself. "Why, even to broach the subject of remarriage is not only hard-hearted and self-serving, but downright evil!"

"And do ye mourn yer late husband so deeply then, that ye can't abide the thought of wedding another?" the priest asked, tilting his head to study her. "Or rather do ye fear wedding again at all? Nay, lassie," he continued with a sigh. "Rather, I say, what I'm proposing isn't evil at all. On the contrary, saving someone's life—and immortal soul—is of the highest good."

"Good, perhaps, for you and Ruarc MacDonald," Killian cried, her anger finally breaking free of all control, "but not good for me or my son!"

"Yet sooner or later ye must render our Lord His due. Well, ye know He paid the purchase price for our souls that fateful Holy Friday. Surely it's not too much for Him to ask now for yer help, in exchange for the favor ye begged of Him." Father Kenneth leaned forward, impaling Killian with a steady but gentle stare. "In the meanwhile, ye're free to leave anytime, to return to Adam Campbell and his ilk. If, that is, ye feel ye'd be safer at Achallader than Rannoch?"

Did the priest, too, know she had killed her own husband? If he did, Killian wagered Ruarc MacDonald, rather than God, had been the one to tell him. Indeed, was Rannoch's laird somehow behind the priest's little ploy to get her to marry? If so, her problems had just doubled.

"So, you've discussed all this with Ruarc, have you?" She decided a frontal attack was long overdue. "It was his idea to send you to me with this proposal, wasn't it?"

Father Kenneth sighed. "Nay, lassie, it wasn't. I've yet to talk with Ruarc. As I gave ye time to rest and compose yerself, so I'm doing the same for him."

"Then how did you know—?"

Before she incriminated herself further, Killian bit off her words. No matter what he might protest to the contrary, he knew she had killed Alexander. She could see it in his eyes. Yet if he hadn't spoken privately with Ruarc, how could he?

The priest lied. That was the truth of it, and all that really mattered. But he wouldn't manipulate her, no matter what he said or did. She could play his game and beat him at it in the bargain.

Ruarc MacDonald owed her a debt of gratitude. After all, she had twice saved his life. Surely she could put an end to this ridiculous plan if she only talked with the big Highlander face-to-face. Surely, even if he had fleetingly considered the priest's idea of wedding her, she could convince him otherwise. At the very least, Ruarc MacDonald seemed a sensible man.

"This is getting us nowhere," Killian said at last. "A very important third party is being left out of this conversation. We can hardly proceed further until we pay your laird a visit."

"Och, to be sure, lassie." Father Kenneth pushed awkwardly from his chair. "But what'll ye say if, after we present our plan to him, he accepts? Will ye wed him, then?"

Once more, anger boiled up within Killian. Like a fly caught in a spider's web, the more she fought back against the priest, the more entangled she seemed to become. This newest challenge, though gently couched, only drew her in the further.

The priest knew more than he let on. He knew she was trapped here until she could make an escape. He knew she didn't dare return to Achallader. And he knew, as well, she was now alone and defenseless in a foreign land, at the mercy of strangers, and that not only her welfare but her son's depended on what she did.

He wouldn't win, though. Alexander, in the end, hadn't won, nor had Adam Campbell. If Ruarc MacDonald truly was in league with the little cleric, he wouldn't win either.

Her mind was made. Killian would get Gavin and herself back to Virginia. The plantation was theirs now. No matter what little she had really left behind there, now she had the chance to make it better.

"I hardly think he'll accept your plan in the end," she said finally. "Still, one way or another, no, I won't agree to such a travesty. I'd be lying if I said I would, and I won't lie."

"Well, then mayhap ye'll be free of us all sooner than ye think." Father Kenneth's already round cheeks swelled with a smile. "Ruarc will indeed be difficult to convince—mayhap even more so than ye." He turned toward the door and when Killian didn't follow, he paused. "Well, are ye coming with me or not, lassie?"

Killian laid aside her Bible and rose. "And where would we be going?"

"Why, where else?" A wry chuckle rumbled in the stocky little priest's chest. "To pay Rannoch's laird a wee visit, of course."

†

WITH A sigh of pure contentment, Ruarc slid into the bathing tub until the warm water lapped over his shoulders. He closed his eyes, rested his head on the tub's metal rim, and gave himself up to the glorious sensations inundating his body.

This luxuriating soak was long overdue. Though he had planned it otherwise, Ruarc had barely sent the Widow Campbell off with Glynnis before Francis, his young clerk, had hurried up with several matters demanding Ruarc's immediate attention. Before he even realized it, several hours had passed, as had the midday meal. Ruarc would now have to curtail the long nap he had intended on taking. What little sleep he did get, he decided as he reached for the soap and began to lather his hair, would at least be enhanced by this hot bath.

The mud- and blood-encrusted locks needed not one, but two, good scrubbings before Ruarc felt his hair sufficiently clean again. Just as he began to sink beneath the water for a final rinse, a knock sounded at the door.

"Enter," he shouted, leaning back to glance briefly around the screen the ever proper Seamus, his manservant, insisted on placing between his master and any female servant who might happen by. When no one immediately walked in, Ruarc assumed it was probably Seamus, pausing to juggle another pitcher of hot water for his bath before opening the door.

With that Ruarc slipped into the water, thoroughly rinsed the soap from his hair, then resurfaced. Instead of Seamus's, however, his gaze met Father Kenneth's.

"Well, Father—" Ruarc flung the water from his eyes and propped his arms on either side of the tub edges—"what brings ye here? Naught of any import, I hope. I intend my long overdue nap to follow swiftly on the heels of this bath."

Just then a sharp, and decidedly feminine, intake of breath from the other side of the screen alerted Ruarc to the fact that they weren't alone. Once more, he leaned back to glance around the screen. There stood a red-faced Killian Campbell.

"Obviously, this isn't a g-good time to importune—," she began haltingly.

"It's as good a time as any." Father Kenneth appropriated the folded sheet of linen toweling draped over one corner of the screen and tucked it beneath his arm. "A nice long soak'll do our laird's bruised and battered body good. In the bargain—" he patted the folded toweling he now held and grinned down at Ruarc—"he can't walk out on us until he's heard all we've come to say."

"Indeed." Ruarc sent the priest a narrow look. "And, pray, what've ye come to say that'd make me want to walk out before ye're finished?"

Instead of immediately answering, the priest disappeared on the other side of the screen and, by the sound of wood scraping across the stone floor, pulled over two chairs. "Come, lass," Ruarc then heard Father Kenneth say. "Come and have a seat."

If the sudden silence was any indication, the lady in question seemed most unwilling to do so.

Ruarc chuckled. "I assure you, madam, I'm quite decently covered by this screen. Father Kenneth would never permit even the slightest impropriety between an unmarried man and woman."

"Aye," the little cleric urged, "come, lassie, and take yer seat. We can't get down to the business at hand until ye do."

"Fine," Killian muttered. A rustle of stiff petticoats told Ruarc she had complied with the priest's request. "Why should I expect anything different, considering how outlandishly this whole escapade has begun? Get on with it, if you please, Father."

"Aye, get on with it, if ye will, Father." Ruarc grinned wolfishly to himself. This was getting to be quite amusing. "Already, I fear the lady's imagination is running amok, and I cannot vouch for where it may soon lead."

For his efforts, he received yet another outraged gasp. "And you, boorish lout that you are, are most impertinent, not to mention quite mistaken," Killian cried. "Why, you're the last man I'd ever—"

"Well, since ye both asked," Father Kenneth chose that moment to join the conversation, "I'm thinking it's a fine idea that ye wed, and wed this verra night. The lassie here," he apparently indicated Killian even as Ruarc's mouth slowly fell open, "is verra against the idea, but with yer approval, I feel certain we can sway her."

"W-wed?" Ruarc barely managed to choke out the word. "To her, or did ye have separate victims already picked out for the two of us?"

"Why, of course I meant to the lassie," the priest replied. "Ye're perfect for each other. What better way to start afresh, than with a lass who's not tainted by those rumors about ye and Sheila?"

In his indignation, Ruarc made a move to climb from the tub before he remembered he was in the presence of a lady. He ground his teeth in frustration. His clothes were across the room, Father Kenneth had his toweling, and there was only the screen to shield him. As planned, the wily old priest had trapped him. There was no hope of ending this ludicrous conversation by beating a hasty retreat.

"Aye, who else would dare have me?" Ruarc leaned around the screen to shoot Father Kenneth a frigid glare before settling back in the tub. "Still, well ye know I've no wish to marry again. Not now, and not ever!"

"Then ye'll leave Rannoch without an heir, and it'll all someday fall into Glynnis's and Thomas's scheming hands," the priest countered in exasperation. "Is that, then, what ye want, laddie? Is it?"

Ruarc dragged in an unsteady breath. "Nay, ye know it isn't."

"Three years have passed since Sheila's death. It's past time ye remarried and well ye know it. This lass—" once more, he apparently indicated Killian—"is young, bonny, and doesn't come to the marriage bed a virgin nor without proof of her fertility. Besides, she's alone now and needs a protector."

"I don't need anyone's protection," Killian was quick to protest. "I'm quite capable of taking care of myself!"

"Aye," Ruarc agreed with sour emphasis. "She's also a Campbell to boot."

"And what better way to mend the feud between MacDonald and Campbell alike," the cleric asked, "than by joining again with another Campbell?"

"Like I did with Sheila?" Before Ruarc could marshal his defenses, the old pain and memories flooded back. "Much good *that* did me!"

"Och, laddie, laddie. Sheila was a lost soul, ill fated from the day she was born. This woman, on the other hand, has always been meant for ye."

Ruarc turned and stretched to peer around the screen, his gaze slamming into Killian's. Her eyes were wide. Her lips moved but no words came forth. She wanted this no more than he did.

Yet Ruarc also knew Father Kenneth was a true Christian, one of the Lord's holiest and most devoted of servants. If any man knew God's will, it was the little priest. And he was intensely loyal to the MacDonalds of Rannoch. All Father Kenneth ever did was for their greater good.

And Ruarc *did* need an heir. If it was the last thing he ever did, he intended to find some way to keep Rannoch for those of his blood, a bloodline untainted by that of Glynnis and her worthless son. To do that, though, he must have another wife—a wife capable of bearing him healthy sons. Sons like Killian's.

That, in the end, was all that really mattered, indeed all he could hope for after the mockery that was his first marriage. Children . . . heirs. Rannoch and its people expected—nay, deserved—at least that from him. And, since he had little hope—or even deserved—a love match or any semblance of a happy family, any wife was as good as another. Aye, any wife, just as long as she bore him strong, healthy children.

But to wed another Campbell . . . the very thought turned his blood cold. Still, Killian wasn't actually a Campbell, save by marriage. In that sense, at least, she'd not defile the MacDonalds' proud heritage.

Ruarc threw back his head and closed his eyes. Why not, then? Father Kenneth was right. Fearing him a wife killer, few women would have him. What did he have to lose?

"If the lady agrees," Ruarc acquiesced finally, "then so be it. As ye said, Father. I need heirs, and she's evidently fertile."

"*Evidently* fertile? *If* I agree?" Killian leaped to her feet. Had the man lost his mind, to agree to such a ludicrous proposition? She had counted on his possessing at least a shred more sense than the priest. But apparently he didn't, and now she must battle two men instead of one.

She refused, however, to be manipulated and used yet again by men. It seemed, though, she'd never be safe until she reached the safety of Virginia and her plantation. A plantation, thanks be to God, about which Ruarc and the priest apparently had yet to learn.

"Ye've reservations, do ye?" By the sudden slapping of water, it sounded as if the big Highlander was shoving up in his tub. "Well, then spit them out. It's a far better remedy to yer distress than working yerself into some apoplectic fit."

Killian inhaled a steadying breath. He was right. Hysterics wouldn't sway them. She forced herself to take her seat.

"Of course I have reservations," she said. "You hardly know me or my temperament. Marriage isn't to be entered into lightly. And there are troublesome things that've happened of late in my life. . . ."

He twisted to peer around the screen at her. The knowing light in his eyes sparked a surge of anguish.

Killian looked away. "Indeed, considering what I've done," she said, her voice now little more than a harsh whisper, "I'm hardly a more worthy candidate as wife than you may be as husband."

"Ye've naught to worry over in that matter," Ruarc replied softly. "I was there, if ye recall."

"That doesn't condone what I did!" Killian dragged her now tear-filled gaze back to his.

"It does for me."

This was getting them nowhere. She swiped away her tears. "Nonetheless, I cannot remarry so soon. Alexander was my husband and Gavin's father. He deserves a proper time of mourning."

Ruarc gave a snort of disgust. His head disappeared back behind the screen. "Och, aye. Every man deserves that, he does, especially a wife and child beater."

"The lass has a point." Father Kenneth chose that moment to add his agreement. "Whatever sort of man her husband may have been, she deserves a time to mourn as she sees fit."

"Indeed? And weren't ye, just a few minutes earlier, urging us to wed, and wed this verra night?"

"Aye, that I was. But, thinking on it now, I allowed my eagerness to get the better of me. The lass is right. She deserves a proper mourning time, as well as a courtship."

"*A courtship?*" The Highlander nearly bellowed in outrage. "I haven't the time—or inclination—for such foolishness!"

"Och, dinna fash yerself, laddie. Considering this'll be a second marriage for the both of ye, and in light of yer situation, dispensations can be made." With disconcerting alacrity, the priest dismissed Ruarc's remaining protests. "Six weeks is adequate time both to mourn and court. I'll read the first banns this Sunday."

He rose, took Killian by the hand, and tugged her to her feet. "Best for all if we don't tarry. It's past time for m'lord's long overdue nap."

Flabbergasted at the sudden turn of events, it was all Killian could do to dig in her heels. "Wait! I didn't agree—"

The priest halted and turned to her. "Would ye prefer we sent ye and yer son back to Achallader on the morrow? As I told ye before, ye're free to leave anytime."

He had trapped her. Killian looked to Ruarc, who had once again peered around the screen. He watched them both with no small amount of amusement. Anger filled her. Curse the man. The priest had won him over, and there'd be no further hope of aid from him.

And why should there be? All Ruarc MacDonald seemed to care about was heirs. He'd use her whenever it suited him, then toss her aside until he needed her *fertile* body again. He was a man, after all. When it came to fulfilling their own selfish desires, all of them were alike.

But the priest had bought her six weeks. Six weeks. Surely time enough to discover allies within Rannoch and plot her escape. And she'd make no promises she couldn't keep. After all, agreeing to a courtship was by no means an acceptance of a proposal of marriage.

"No, I don't wish to return to Achallader," Killian said finally through gritted teeth. "A period of courtship is acceptable, though."

"Och, what a braw lass ye are!" the priest exclaimed heartily, then turned and began to lead her toward the door.

"Wait up! Wait up, I say!" From behind the screen, water sloshed wildly as Ruarc hastily stood in the tub and glared over the screen at them. "I haven't—"

"Dinna fash yerself, laddie," Father Kenneth called back as he opened the door. "Best ye take that long overdue nap. Ye'll need all yer strength for the days to come. Aye, that ye will."

Before Ruarc could utter another word, the priest hustled Killian from the room and closed the door. A colorful string of expletives, however, followed them as they made their way down the hall.

6

THE REMAINDER of the day went surprisingly fast. Killian chose to keep to her room, rather than have to deal further with Ruarc MacDonald. Pleading a sick headache, she asked Finola to bring supper to her. Finola, however, was apparently detained, and a young man, tray in hand, appeared at the door.

"Well, hello," she said in surprise, eyeing him.

He was about her height, slightly built, dark blond and pale, as if he spent most of his time indoors. His features were delicate for a man, exquisitely wrought, possessing a kind of masculine beauty usually seen only in those Italian paintings of angels.

Angelic. Yes, that's exactly what he looked like. An angel. Killian gave him a tentative smile.

He smiled back, serene and beautiful, but there was something flat and hard behind it. "M'lady." He held out the tray. "Yer victuals as ye requested."

Killian accepted the tray. "Thank you . . ." When no introduction was proffered, she tilted her head. "And who might you be?"

"Francis MacLean, m'lord's clerk." The young man said nothing more.

"I'm pleased to make your acquaintance, Francis. And thank you again. For this tray, I mean."

"Ye're verra welcome." He bowed, turned, and without further comment, walked away.

She watched him briefly, then with a shrug reentered the bedchamber. Gavin and she quickly devoured the generous but rather poorly prepared meal. After a time spent entertaining her son, Killian tucked the heavy-lidded youngster into his bed in the adjoining room.

Thanks to her nap earlier, however, she wasn't sleepy. Finola finally returned. Her bustling about with a feather duster, putting the finishing touches on the bedchamber, would've made sleep difficult, at any rate. And then there were all the thoughts and ideas bombarding Killian, keeping her head spinning—too soon to think of rest.

As she sat before the hearth fire for the next few hours, Killian gave her situation intense consideration. Reality being what it was, an inescapable truth remained: she and Gavin were now at Ruarc MacDonald's mercy.

Killian reproached herself for failing to press her one advantage, in reminding him he owed her an even bigger debt of gratitude than she owed him. Yet, perhaps it had been wisest to hold her tongue on that matter. What if she broached it, demanding he help her return to Virginia, and her ploy failed? Ruarc would be sure to watch her every move after that. Her chances of escape might then be next to impossible.

But what other choice had she but escape? Even God, it seemed, had all but deserted her. But then, He now had every right to.

The admission sickened her, tore at her heart, but the truth nonetheless remained. She was a murderer. She had killed her husband. She had sinned, and sinned grievously.

If God had ever been on her side, He had surely now turned His back on her. It wasn't what she wanted, what her religious upbringing had led her to, but it was grim fact nonetheless. She had no one left to depend on but herself.

A knock sounded on the door. Killian wrenched herself from her morose thoughts and, from the corner of her eye, watched Finola hurry over to it.

Apprehension filled her. She glanced at the mantel clock. Half past ten. Who might want to speak with her at this late hour?

Surely not the priest. He had accomplished his mission. He had set the marital noose about her neck. Now he had only to sit back and watch, as the days ticked by and the rope tightened, hemming her in, choking off, bit by bit, all her options.

Finola paused before the door, then opened it a crack. As she seemed to recognize the visitor, her whole attitude changed. She swept back, her free hand hastily tugging her already low-cut bodice a tad lower, and pasted a seductive smile on her face.

A tall, broad-shouldered man strode into the room.

Killian almost jumped out of her skin. She couldn't help it. Ruarc MacDonald—so large, so overpowering, so threatening—was the last person she wished to see this night.

She recognized the feeling for what it was—her justifiable fear of big, potentially violent men. Men who were stubborn and fiercely possessive. Men like . . . Alexander.

Alexander . . .

A sharp pain thrust through her heart. When had it all gone so wrong? When had the adoration and attention he had lavished on her during their courtship and early years of marriage transformed into unreasonable jealousy and blame? In time, it had gotten so bad she dreaded even leaving their house.

She lived in fear of being caught conversing with one of the male servants and accused of all sorts of shameful things. In time they had stopped entertaining, until Killian was cut off from friends, if she indeed had ever had any to begin with in that tightly knit community. And, to add even more to her sense of growing isolation, the female house servants, she eventually discovered, reported everything she did to her husband.

In her heart of hearts, Killian had always known Alexander would never, ever let her leave him. She was his—had always been and always would be. In her heart of hearts, she had known that only death could ever free her.

As Ruarc's long, forceful strides carried him across the room, Killian stood. An impulse to flee—similar to the one she had felt that night at Achallader—filled her. She fought past the ludicrous urge.

Fool, this man isn't Alexander, she scolded herself. *He won't hurt you. And where would you go just now, at any rate? There's nowhere to run, leastwise not yet. But soon . . . very soon . . .*

He drew up and rendered her a small bow. "Madam."

Her heart pounding in her chest, Killian barely managed a curtsey in reply. "M'lord."

The Highlander straightened. In the brighter light of the hearth fire, Killian was finally able to get a closer look at him. He still sported a nasty cut over his right brow. His eye was slightly swollen and purple red bruises darkened his left cheekbone and jaw, but Ruarc MacDonald had cleaned up surprisingly well.

With the grime and blood gone from his now dry hair, Killian saw it was actually a rich chestnut brown, tumbling down to graze his shoulders in soft waves. Hair that'd tempt any woman to run her fingers through it or lightly brush that recalcitrant lock off his high, intelligent forehead.

The snowy white shirt flattered him as well. Full-sleeved with a lace-edged silk neck cloth at the throat, it clung to his impossibly wide shoulders before tapering to a narrow waist. He, too, now wore tartan trews that hugged his slim hips and muscled legs, and a plaid was fastened over his shoulder.

He was a fine specimen of manhood, of that there was no doubt. But the man himself, his heart and soul, remained a mystery. A mystery only a woman's love could ever hope to fathom . . .

With a jerk, Killian pulled back from her fanciful musings. This was insane, dreaming about someone she'd soon be leaving forever. And good riddance to him, too! From what little she had already discovered about Ruarc MacDonald, he promised to be nothing but trouble.

"Your eye," she said, fixing on something solid and real to ground herself in the present moment. "Your right eye had swollen shut by the time we'd reached Achallader. Now, it's almost back to normal."

He shot her a quizzical look. "Don't Campbells use leeches? Father Kenneth, amongst all his other healing skills, is particularly adept with the leeches."

"Leeches?"

"Aye, to suck off the old blood and lessen the swelling."

Killian stared at him for a long moment, her train of thought once again fleeing her. "W-why, of course," she replied at last. "Yes. There was an old midwife not far from our plantation who . . ." At the realization she had already revealed too much, her voice faded.

His gaze narrowed.

Sudden terror filled her. "What? What's wrong?"

"By all the saints, but ye're acting most strange," Ruarc muttered. "Do I look that poorly, that ye must gape at me so?"

Hot blood flushed her cheeks. Was it possible? *Had* she been gaping at him? She forced a lighthearted laugh. "No, you don't look all that poorly, considering what you've been through of late. I suppose I'm just . . . just a little unsettled . . . and nervous."

A smile twisted Ruarc's lips. "It's understandable, I suppose. In the past few days, ye've been through more than anyone should have to bear, and now ye find yerself in some stranger's castle, agreeing to his courtship."

He leaned close and picked up a lock of her hair that had tumbled onto her shoulder. "Ye needn't be so fearful of me, though," he said huskily. "I mean ye no harm."

With her face only a breath away from his hand, Killian couldn't help but feel the heat emanating from him, inhale the scent of clean male skin. She scanned Ruarc's ruggedly etched features. The memory of the cruel treatment he had suffered, his courage in the face of certain death, filled her with a strange mix of compassion and admiration.

Her throat constricted. An inexplicable urge to reach out and smooth away the bruises marring his face swept through her.

Just then, Ruarc's gaze lifted from the flaxen lock he had been holding. The look there was suddenly hard, as if he had read her thoughts and didn't like them.

"Does it hurt much? Your face, I mean?" Killian whispered.

"Nay. Don't concern yerself over me. I've borne far worse and need no one's pity."

His words were like a blow to the belly. Killian tensed, then stepped back, almost grateful his sudden harshness had broken the heady spell. Almost . . . and that frightened her.

"I assure you, you're hardly the kind of man who engenders pity. And you're also," she added, all thoughts of compassion vanished, "not worth anyone's concern, either."

Ruarc cocked his head, a warning light gleaming in his eyes. "What did ye say, madam? I didn't quite catch that last remark."

"Never mind." It took all of Killian's willpower not to respond with a tart rejoinder. "Believe me, it's not worth repeating."

He took her arm, pulled her to him, then paused as if suddenly recalling Finola's presence. "The night is fine, now that the rain has passed. Let us take a wee stroll, if ye will, up onto the battlements." He glanced over his shoulder at the maidservant. "Stay, Finola, and keep an ear open for the lad lest he wake and find himself alone. The Lady Campbell and I desire some fresh air."

Intermittently bowing and curtseying, Finola signaled her acquiescence. "As ye wish, m'lord. I'm at yer service as always, *whenever* ye may need me."

†

THEY WALKED for a time in silence, Killian following him down the long corridor to a door that led up a narrow, winding flight of stone stairs. When they finally reached the top, the cool caress of the evening breeze, the silver moonlight and twinkling stars, seemed well worth the effort.

Ruarc watched as Killian walked to the crenellated parapet wall and gazed out onto a vast expanse of night-blanketed, open moor. The scent of it, of damp peat and rich, fertile earth, wafted to him. The woman must have noticed too, for she inhaled deeply, seeming to savor its pungently familiar aroma.

She turned then, as if suddenly remembering him. He had drawn up beside her.

"Ye look quite fetching, madam." Ruarc broke the silence with a compliment that he hoped would prepare the way for the suggestion he was about to make. "Though I know we spoke earlier of a time of courtship, I'm thinking no purpose is served in prolonging the inevitable. What say ye we adjourn shortly to my bedchamber?"

A progression of emotions played across her face . . . melancholy, shock, then anger. "I'll do no such thing! Just because I consented to a courtship doesn't mean I intend to warm your bed before we're wed!"

Ruarc sighed and shook his head. Was this lass, then, determined to play the same role Sheila had performed so expertly—sending him enticing looks, running her gaze thoroughly over his face, then his body, and yet pretending innocent outrage when he responded to her unspoken offer? Unfortunately for the Campbell widow, he was in no mood to tolerate much of that anymore.

He turned his glance back out toward the darkness. "So it's to be more of yer games again, is it? Well, I tired of them long ago. I know when a woman wants a man. The looks ye sent me in yer bedchamber were proof enough of yer desire."

"M-my desire! Why, you—you're truly in the grip of some delusion, you are!" she said with an outraged sputter. "It was pity for your injuries that made me look at you as I did. Pity, I say, and nothing more!"

For one crazed moment, Ruarc could only recall his soul-deep anguish over another Campbell woman. Sheila had also played games with him, manipulating his mind and heart. Angrily, he wheeled about and pulled Killian to him.

At her soft gasp, Ruarc cocked his head. "Well, madam," he said, dropping his voice, "is this more to yer liking then?"

As he spoke, his free hand moved to the back of her head. His mouth lowered to hers.

"No! Wait!" Killian lifted her hands and pressed against his chest. "Perhaps this is all going too fast. Perhaps—" she pushed harder against him—"it'd be best if we talk more about this on the morrow."

Ruarc went very still. "And what would postponing the inevitable accomplish? Courtship or no, we'll wed in six weeks' time. To my mind, the sooner I get ye with child, the better."

Killian twisted free of his hold and stepped away, backing toward the stairs.

"And where, madam, do ye think ye're going? I'm still laird of Rannoch. I don't recall giving ye leave to depart."

"We've all the time in the world to . . . to conceive an heir," she choked out finally. She slowly met his gaze, and he saw once again her pretense of rejection. "That is, after all, your only reason for wanting to wed me, isn't it?"

"It is. Did I fail to make that clear to ye?"

She gave a shaky laugh. "Oh, not at all. I understood you well enough."

"Then don't play the shy maiden with me. We've both been wed before, and I'm verra weary."

"All the more reason to put this off for a few days or so," Killian insisted. "You'll be rested and I'll have had time to—"

At the end of his patience, Ruarc closed the distance between them, determined to teach her a lesson. The lass needed to realize that, just as he had always kept his promises, he expected her to do the same.

Killian cried out and leaped backward. Her heel caught in the hem of her cloak. She tripped, losing her balance, and slammed into the wall beside the door.

He came to her, standing close, making it difficult for her to avoid him. "Ye don't need time to adjust, madam. Ye just need to stop yer foolish, seductive little games!"

Killian exploded with surprising fury. "Stay away from me, you animal! I won't let you treat me this way. I won't!"

What was wrong with the woman? Ruarc hesitated, then took a step back. Surely his advances hadn't terrorized her that thoroughly. Something odd was going on here, of that much, he was certain.

"Don't hurt me . . . don't hit me. I'll be good. I promise."

He stared down at her, unable to believe his eyes. Her anger had dissipated as quickly as it had risen, and now she was crying, tears flowing down her cheeks.

"Just pl-please . . . don't . . . hurt me!" Killian begged, sobbing hysterically. "Oh, dear God, please don't let him h-hurt me!" Her weeping turned to great, gulping breaths.

"By mountain and sea, madam!" He backed slowly away from her. The woman wasn't playing games. She truly was panic-stricken.

And he was responsible.

It was evident her late husband had terrorized her, both mentally and physically. Now he had gone and done the same. He had done the unthinkable; he had dishonored not only a helpless woman, but himself, too.

What must Killian think of him now? Could he ever make amends?

Bit by anguished bit, her breathing slowed, became deeper. With a groan, she shoved the hair from her face and glanced groggily around.

For a long, anguished moment more Ruarc stared at Killian,

appalled at what he had brought her to. Then, unable to bear his guilt an instant longer, Rannoch's laird wheeled about and stalked away.

†

HE WAS no better than Alexander. Indeed, Killian thought as she paced the confines of the ample bedchamber, he was worse. It had taken years for Alexander's violence to evolve into the fearsome thing it had become. Yet tonight, in but the span of minutes—and in only days of knowing her—Ruarc MacDonald had transformed into a crazed animal.

Ruarc's deep voice reverberated in her mind: *"No purpose is served in prolonging the inevitable . . . adjourn shortly to my bedchamber . . ."* What did he take her for, a trollop? Killian's initial shock had swelled to anger, effectively scorching away her poignant, melancholy mood. Her anger quickly turned to terror, though, at the daunting and formidable appearance of the Scotsman looming over her.

Her mouth went dry again, remembering. With his height, which she guessed to be an inch or two over six feet, and his bruised and battered form, Rannoch's laird looked more some primordial man than the highborn Scotsman he truly was.

Even her frantic, fervent prayers for help had not saved her from his advances. Her stomach had roiled in panic as Ruarc MacDonald's face had been replaced in her mind's eye by that of another man . . . Alexander.

Alexander . . . leaning over her . . . slapping her. Twisting her arm so painfully she thought he'd break it. Pushing her face into the softness of their bed until he almost smothered her, shouting at her all the while, calling her vile, degrading, hurtful names.

The present blurred with the past, and Killian was no longer certain where reality bled into old nightmares. Once again the tears welled, flowing down her cheeks.

Ruarc seemed as wild and savage a Scotsman as all the rest. The only hope for her now lay in putting him off long enough to make her escape. But how to do that after the violent way he had attacked her this night?

She was fairly certain Father Kenneth could be convinced to persuade Ruarc to abstain from taking carnal favors before the marriage. But after they were wed, she could hardly count on him. After all, it served his purpose for them to produce heirs. Heirs indeed!

There was also Glynnis as a possible ally. At the consideration, an ember of hope flared in Killian's breast.

Ruarc MacDonald's stepmother didn't seem to bear him any great affection, nor he for her. Perhaps Glynnis could advise her how to deal with her volatile stepson.

Killian sighed and shook her head. All she could hope for was a truce between her and Ruarc MacDonald—a truce whose terms included not only a full six-week courtship, but no further demands to bed her before a legal marriage took place. It was worth a try, as slender a chance as it might be.

Anything was worth a try if it'd keep her out of Ruarc Mac-Donald's bed.

†

NUMBLY, Ruarc stared down at the Great Hall's pitted and grooved dining table. A family heirloom dating back over four hundred years, the long, walnut, plank-topped board had survived the abuse of countless generations of MacDonalds. It'd survive, as well, he thought glumly, the ever widening pool of blood dripping from the cut Killian, in her frenzied thrashing, had broken anew over his right brow.

He watched in morbid fascination as yet another dark drop fell, plummeting to splat messily into the middle of the little puddle. He supposed he should staunch the bleeding. Somehow, though, Ruarc not only didn't care but couldn't quite find the energy necessary to move his limbs to the task.

Nothing, for that matter, seemed to possess much importance. Nothing seemed to hold his attention save the vivid memory of what had so recently transpired outside on the battlements.

She had thought him a monster. That was the truth of it, and no mistake. Her eyes had been full of stark, vivid fear and loathing. She had fought him wildly, in panic-stricken self-defense. She had thought him intent on ravishing her.

He had only himself to blame. He *had* initially imagined she desired him. Recalling, however, her panic-stricken gaze and piteous pleas, Ruarc now admitted his poorly conceived plan had miscarried.

Ruarc grabbed at a used table napkin left on the unwashed table-top and applied it gingerly to his now oozing eyebrow. Even the gentlest touch hurt, so he pressed the harder. It was the least he should suffer for what he had done this night. If only the pain could truly and fully atone for it.

On the morrow, he'd tender Killian his sincerest apology.

It rankled that he must do so—he desperately hated asking anyone's pardon—but the lass deserved that and more. As proud a man as he was, this was hardly the time to lay blame on anyone but himself.

Indeed, Father Kenneth would be the first to chide him, quoting him chapter and verse that claimed a man's pride always brought him low. But then the old priest was always poking away at some failing of his, seemingly intent on luring his lost lamb back into the fold.

Not that any of that mattered at present. His only concern, if he wished ever to salvage a relationship in or out of bed, was what to say to the Campbell widow, how to mend the bridge already crumbling between them.

Ruarc groaned aloud and clenched shut his eyes. Och, *why* had he ever let Father Kenneth talk him into such a daft undertaking? And with another Campbell lass no less!

"M'lord?" A soft, familiar voice rose from behind him. "Are ye all right?"

"Nay, Francis." Ruarc removed the bloodstained napkin and glanced over his shoulder. "It's late, though. Hie yerself to bed. All will be well enough in the morn."

The young clerk stepped to the head of the table and pulled out a chair instead. "Ye aren't yerself, m'lord." He sat. "If ye wish to talk about it, I'm willing to listen."

The lad was as loyal as they came. As loyal as his dear, departed father had been before him. There'd be no carrying of tales to Glynnis or to the other servants.

Nonetheless, Ruarc was reluctant to confide such personal matters to anyone save, mayhap, Father Kenneth. And, though the temptation was strong to pay the old priest a visit and shake him from a sound sleep to hear how sadly awry this marriage plan of his had already gone, Ruarc hadn't the heart for that just now, either.

Gazing, however, into Francis's open, adoring eyes, he was sorely tempted to tell his side to someone Ruarc knew would have a sympathetic ear. As hard as he tried not to encourage it, Francis had always viewed him as far more than just Rannoch's lord. Ruarc imagined he was, at the very least, seen as the big brother Francis had never had. Indeed, he might even have become, thanks to a sire frequently too involved in Rannoch's affairs to have much time for his motherless child, almost a paternal figure.

As sincere as Francis's wish was to render comfort, though, at all of two and twenty he was hardly experienced in the ways of women. Still, it'd be unkind to cast aside the lad's offer without some effort made at easing the rejection.

"There isn't much worth talking about," Ruarc said, then sighed. "Lady Campbell still requires a period of adjustment. But it'll all work itself out in time."

"She toys with ye, doesn't she?" The tone of utter contempt in the young man's voice took Ruarc aback. "Just like the Lady Sheila did in the end. They're two of a kind, those two are. Och, have a care, m'lord, or this one will betray ye just as Sheila did!"

Ruarc's gaze narrowed. Well meant as Francis's words were in his master's defense, Ruarc still couldn't permit a servant to think he could involve himself in his lord's private affairs. "Ye forget yerself, lad," he said softly, "to speak ill of a noblewoman. Whatever our differences, she must be treated with all respect."

Hot color flooded the younger man's face. "I beg pardon, m'lord. In my concern for ye, I forgot myself. Yet yer wife's dying nearly destroyed ye in so verra many ways. If something like that were to happen again . . ."

"This lady and Sheila are too verra different women." Ruarc firmly countered the clerk's protests, even as he wondered if Francis didn't speak true. "And ye're making far too much of this, for but her first day at Rannoch. Dinna fash yerself. It'll all work out. It always does."

Francis's mouth opened, then clamped shut again. "Aye, m'lord, I suppose it will. Once again, I beg yer pardon for my thoughtless words."

Rannoch's laird motioned his apology aside. "It's forgotten." He paused, dragged in a deep breath, then shoved back his chair. "Well, I think it's past time I see to my own bed. As should ye, lad, to yers."

Francis rose. "Aye, m'lord. Sleep well then."

"Aye, Francis."

Ruarc watched the clerk depart, a bone-deep wave of exhaustion swamping him. It was indeed time he took his rest. The morrow was soon enough to deal with this night's unpleasantness. As he had told Francis, it would all work out. It always did, one way or another.

†

FAR PREFERRING the risk of starvation to that of prematurely confronting Rannoch's laird, Killian was tempted to hide for the rest of the next day. Two things, however, forestalled that plan. Gavin soon lost interest in playing indoors and begged for a walk outside. And, Finola, barely disguising her curiosity about what had transpired last night to bring Killian back to her room in such a state of distress, drove her to such distraction that Killian soon decided escape was far preferable to a nosy maidservant.

So, just before the midday meal, Killian ventured from the relative seclusion of her bedchamber. As she made her cautious way down the stone corridor, fully expecting Ruarc MacDonald to step from some dark niche at any second, Gavin skipped happily ahead.

"Do you think Fionn's about, Mama?" He bounded back to grab her hand and gaze up at her. "I need to make friends."

Even the mention of the huge, ghostly dog sent shivers down Killian's spine. Despite his seemingly gentle acceptance of Gavin yesterday, she still wasn't so certain of the beast's true nature. Like his master, it seemed best to avoid him.

"There'll be ample opportunity to make friends with that dog," Killian said, barely able to give her son's hand an affectionate squeeze before he pulled free and romped ahead again. "First things first. You need a good run about outside before the midday meal."

She paused at the head of the stairs and glanced through the open entry doors. Unlike the soggy, overcast pall that had accompanied them all the way to Rannoch yesterday, today was bright, sunny, and dry.

In spite of the unease still nibbling at her, Killian's spirits gave a leap of joy. In the short time she had been in Scotland, she had already learned to cherish each and every sunny day. Ruarc Mac-Donald or no, she vowed as she grabbed Gavin's hand to slow his perilous pace down the stairs, she intended to savor this day as well.

To her delight, Rannoch possessed a most pleasing garden. Located on the back side of the castle, Killian and Gavin had first to pass the stables, a bakehouse, brewhouse, dairy, washhouse, and herb-and-kitchen garden before reaching a charming—and surprisingly well cared for—walled garden.

A painted sundial stood at its center. In the sunny portions of the sections separated by stone paths grew tall hollyhocks, snapdragons, Scabiosa, African marigolds, and myriad rosebushes. In the shady spots beneath sporadic stands of alder and birch trees, the greenery of ferns and spent lupines and sweet william could be seen. Tucked here and there were small statues of children dressed as shepherds.

A flight of steps led down from the back of the flower garden to another level and what appeared to be a water garden, replete with fountains and several fishponds of varying sizes. Here, too, stands of trees dotted the area, affording cooling shade or shelter from an unexpected rain shower. It was down to the fishponds that Killian took Gavin.

At their approach to the first pond's edge, several dark fish swam toward them. "Oooh, look, Mama," Gavin exclaimed in delight. "They've come to greet us."

"More likely," his mother observed dryly, "they think we've come to feed them." With a quick motion, Killian grabbed her son's collar and pulled him back before he leaned forward far enough to fall into the pond.

"So, m'lady," a feminine voice unexpectedly drew Killian from her preoccupation with her son, "I see ye're no worse for yer rough experiences of the past few days."

Still grasping Gavin by his collar, she spun around.

Glynnis, garbed this morn in a brilliant crimson wool gown trimmed with silver lace, stood there, a friendly smile on her face.

With anticipation fluttering in her chest, Killian returned the smile. "Thank you for your concern, Lady Glynnis, but you need not have worried about me. I'm more resilient than you might first imagine."

The ebony-haired woman's mouth quirked wryly. "More's the power to ye, then. My stepson isn't known for his gentle ways."

No, Killian thought, *and he amply demonstrated that last eve.* She turned to Gavin. "If you promise to stay back from the ponds, you can walk around a bit and look at all the fish."

"I promise, Mama." With that, he wrenched free of her clasp and scampered off.

Killian watched him scurry from pond to pond, suddenly at a loss as to how to broach the subject of enlisting the other woman's aid, when Glynnis solved her problem.

"Ye're a brave lass, that ye are," the older woman said. "I well know, though, Ruarc treated ye harshly last eve."

Startled, Killian turned back to her. "And how would you . . . ?"

Finola. Of course. The maidservant had seen enough last night—Killian's return without Ruarc's escort, her disheveled appearance, not to mention her heightened emotional state.

Color flooded her cheeks. Though she dearly wished a friend to confide in, Killian couldn't be certain that anything she told Glynnis might not eventually get back to Ruarc. And it wasn't as if she felt settled enough in her own mind about what had transpired last eve to discuss it coherently even if she dared. So, instead of an admission of an attempted coupling gone awry, she shook her head and sighed. "Ruarc is a good man, and I'm sure—"

"He has a foul and vicious temper!" Glynnis's eyes blazed with high emotion. "I'm only hoping he didn't choose to display it last night. He at least managed to keep his sorry moods from Sheila for several years. He owes ye the same courtesy, I'd say."

Killian bit her lip. *A foul and vicious temper?* Suddenly, her empty stomach felt sour, queasy. "His first wife . . . Sheila . . . ," Killian began, choosing her words with care. "Surely the tales about his having murdered her are false. A man wouldn't kill his own . . ."

Once more her voice faded, as a memory of Alexander filled her mind. One blustery, glorious day aboard ship as they had traveled to Scotland, they stood together out on deck, Alexander behind her, clasping her firmly to him about the waist. He bent down, whispered in her ear, as his hold tightened even more. "Ye'll see, lass," he said. "Things'll be better once we reach the Highlands. Then ye'll finally understand me, who I really am, and why I love ye as I do."

Killian had moved restlessly in his embrace, feeling smothered, her fear—all too frequently with her whenever she was near her husband—rising anew. "I know you love me," she replied, forcing out the words she knew he wanted to hear. "And I love you. But you needn't hold me so close all the time or mistrust me. I won't—"

"I don't know what I'd do if ye ever left me, lass. I couldn't live without ye, and the thought of any other man having ye . . ."

Without his even finishing the sentence, the warning was given. If she ever attempted to sever their marital ties he would kill her. And most likely kill himself, too.

That fear was the last and strongest glue binding them, when all other bonds had gradually disintegrated, rotted away by the increasingly frequent bouts of violence, the threats, the insults, the accusations. And that fear bound them until the night of the storm, when even that final and most tenuous of attachments had broken.

On that night, Killian finally realized the risk to her life was worth any escape from Alexander. As was also the risk to his life. A part of her wondered if his death hadn't been a blessing for him, a release from the personal hell that had become his life.

But that was perhaps a coward's way out—that attempt to absolve herself for what she had done in killing Alexander. Ah, if only she hadn't panicked when he had pointed his pistol at Ruarc MacDonald. If only she hadn't reached for her bodice knife instead of continuing to use her hands—her fists—to stop him. If only he had been wounded just enough to be distracted from his deadly intent and not fallen back on her dagger so hard or unexpectedly.

She had but meant to stop Alexander, to save the man who had saved her. She had only meant to temporarily incapacitate her husband so as to make good her escape.

"Och, this isn't the time or place to be speaking of such things, m'lady." Glynnis's voice, at that moment, wrenched Killian back to the present. "There's many a tale about that sad night, and ye'll surely hear them all sooner or later, but it isn't my place—"

"It is if I ask you." Killian took her by the arm, impaling her with a desperate glance. "And I'm asking you. What do *you* think happened? Did or didn't Ruarc kill Sheila?"

Glynnis's bright red lips pursed. She glanced nervously about. Finally, though, she met Killian's gaze. "Aye, he killed Sheila. Who else would've done it, after learning she'd cuckolded him yet again? Only this time, the blow to his pride was more than he could bear."

"And why was that?" Killian dreaded the answer but, perversely, needed to know. "What was so different about that last time?"

"That last time," the older woman replied, her gaze gone flat and expressionless, "Ruarc finally learned Sheila had lain with a man who had been forbidden her. She had lain with Adam Campbell, her foster brother."

7

IT WAS all Killian could do not to gasp aloud. Was there no end to the complex tapestry binding Campbell and MacDonald alike, the threads of which now seemed inexorably to be entwining about her?

But Adam?

Glynnis's revelation explained so much. Why Adam and Ruarc bore such a deadly and long-standing enmity. Why, if Glynnis's words were indeed true, Ruarc might've been driven to such fury as to kill his wife in a moment of blinding pain and passion. And why he had truly meant what he had said last night when he informed Father Kenneth he wished never again to wed.

Two men, one woman, and an ill-fated triangle. Had their bond gone only as deep as lust, or had far, far more lain below that deceptively simple surface? Killian wondered now, as well, about a woman who had lived such a tragic, destructive life—a life spanning more than just her own in the impact it continued to have on others—and what sort of woman she really had been.

"I assume Ruarc discovered his wife's unfaithfulness sooner or later?"

"It wasn't hard to do so. Sheila all but flaunted it in his face in order to convince Ruarc to divorce her." Glynnis sighed. "I suspect that's why he killed her in a fit of jealous rage."

"Then why wasn't Ruarc ever punished for it?"

"Och, he was bound over for judgment but spent only a short

while in Edinburgh's Canongate Tollbooth. The king, an old friend of Ruarc's since their days together in Holland, heard of our laird's imprisonment and took a personal interest in the proceedings. It wasn't long before Ruarc was freed on a technicality of law." Glynnis shook her head. "To this day, though, everyone still suspects Ruarc of the foul deed."

Killian stared at the older woman in horror.

She reached out and laid a hand on Killian's arm. "Och, m'lady, I don't tell ye this to trouble ye. It's best, though, ye know from the start the manner of man ye may wed. Why, isn't it apparent Ruarc holds women in disdain, if only in the way he has always treated me? Me, who tried for so many years to be a mother to him. Yet never once since I wed his father have I received aught but cold indifference in return. What else is one to think of such a man?"

One could think many things, Killian thought to herself, *and not necessarily that Ruarc MacDonald hates women. Still, recalling last night . . .*

But none of that mattered if she didn't let it matter. Indeed, nothing was served in allowing herself to be caught up in this sad and increasingly sordid mess. She had problems enough of her own, one of which was not only to extricate herself from an unwanted marriage but from Scotland itself.

Distractedly, Killian turned to where Gavin sat in sunlight-dappled shade beneath some birches, stroking a big, gray mass. She blinked in surprise, and the mound of gray became a dog. Fionn!

At that identical moment, Glynnis must have comprehended the same fact. Unless he couldn't help it, Fionn was never far from his master. Ruarc was surely nearby.

As one, the two women swung about. A dark scowl on his face, Rannoch's laird stood at the head of the stone steps leading down to the ponds. Guilt swamped Killian, then fear. How long had he been standing there? How much had he heard?

Ruarc's gaze fixed on Glynnis. "I've a wish to speak privately with Lady Campbell, madam, before we take the midday meal. See to the lad. We'll join ye shortly."

"Aye, m'lord." His stepmother gathered her skirts and headed promptly to where Gavin sat with Fionn.

Killian watched as she approached and carefully circled the big deerhound. "Come, lad," she heard Glynnis say, holding out her hand. "Ye must go with me. Yer midday meal awaits ye."

Gavin lifted his gaze to his mother.

Killian nodded. "Go with Glynnis. I'll come for you later, after you eat and have your afternoon nap."

"But Mama, I want to play with Fionn. Can't I? Please? Can't I?"

"Do as yer mither says, lad." Ruarc drew up at Killian's side. "Ye can play with Fionn later. I promise."

With a long-suffering sigh, Gavin gave the dog a final pat, then climbed to his feet. "All right. Just don't forget. My papa used to forget all the time, and that made me sad."

Her son's words stabbed at Killian's heart. She looked to Ruarc, trying to gauge his reaction.

For a fleeting moment the big Highlander's tight-lipped expression softened. A smile tugged at the corner of his mouth. "I won't forget, lad."

With that, Glynnis took Gavin's hand and led him away. Both Killian and Ruarc MacDonald stared after them until they finally disappeared around the side of the castle.

Then Ruarc turned to Killian. "Ye've managed to make yerself conspicuously absent for almost half the day," he said, eyeing her with an appraising glance. "Were ye mayhap hiding from me?"

As accurate as his assessment of the situation was, it rankled nonetheless. Did Ruarc MacDonald actually take some perverse pleasure in intimidating and manipulating others to his purposes? If so, he managed to do it very well.

"After our less than romantic interlude last eve, why would I care to see you anytime soon?" Killian demanded, refusing to cede him the advantage. "But no, I wasn't hiding from you in your own castle. Avoiding you, perhaps, but not hiding. That would've been pointless, don't you think?"

"Aye, I suppose it would've." He extended his hand. "Come. There's a bench beneath those birches where Fionn lies. I've a wish to speak with ye, out of earshot and view of the castle, if ye please."

After a moment's hesitation, Killian took his hand. It was big, warm, and callused, but not altogether unpleasant, even considering the unsettling enigma this man seemed to be.

"You don't like people spying on you, do you?"

"Nay, I don't," he said as they walked along. "I prefer to keep my personal affairs personal. There are some in the castle, however, who feed on every morsel they can scrape together about me. I urge ye, madam. Have a care who ye take into yer confidences, and what ye say to them."

She knew he warned her of Glynnis. Problem was, Killian didn't know which one of them to trust or befriend. Of the two, Glynnis seemed more forthcoming with valuable information. She also appeared a better chance of help in Killian's plan to leave Rannoch and return to Virginia.

"I thank you for your advice." She knew she had to make some reply, and that seemed the most innocuous response. "Everything's yet so strange and new here, and I've so much to learn."

"After we dine, I'll have Francis take ye on a tour of the castle. Ye can trust whatever he tells ye is truth."

Or at least the truth as you *wish me to hear it,* Killian countered silently. From what she had gathered in just meeting Francis last night, it was easy to surmise the young clerk cared as little for women as did his master. Most likely any tales that fell from Francis's lips would be fashioned to Ruarc MacDonald's favor. Yet how more balanced were his words than what Glynnis and others might tell?

"I'll look forward to that with great anticipation, m'lord," Killian said, rendering her apparent acquiescence.

They reached the stone bench, paused, and took a seat. The bench, however, wasn't all that large. Killian found herself sitting far closer to Ruarc MacDonald than she preferred. There was no escape, no hiding now from his sharp perusal. She swallowed hard, then lifted her gaze to his.

"Ye're a strange one, ye are," he said in his rich, deep burr. "Yer moods change as quickly as a reflection in turbulent water or clouds passing before the sun. Try as I might, I can't quite figure ye out."

And she couldn't figure him out either. After the terror of last night, once more they seemed to have resumed their earlier, needling banter. Killian arched a brow. "And is that meant to be an insult or a compliment, m'lord?"

He grinned. "Och, and aren't ye the prickly one? Most lasses would take that as a compliment and savor the feeling of power it gave them over a man."

His attempt at lighthearted repartee fell suddenly flat. He was just as unnerving, after all, as he claimed she was.

"Is that why you asked to talk to me? To make some mindless chatter in the hopes of smoothing over what happened last night? Well, if so, I can't say I'm much in the mood. I can't say I much like or trust you, either, after what you did last night."

His smile faded. "Och, lass, I didn't mean any harm by what I said. I just didn't know how to begin to beg pardon for last night."

"Well, perhaps you should just spit it out then, what you really meant to say."

Ruarc looked away. "Aye, mayhap I should." He turned back to her. "I'm so verra sorry for how I treated ye last eve. Ye must think me some slavering lecher or heartless brute. I assure ye I'm neither. Never in my life have I treated a woman like that, and never again will I do so."

Killian wasn't sure she believed him. Especially now, after just having heard about Sheila's transgressions. Still, he seemed so sincere. . . .

"Why did you force yourself on me like you did then?"

"Why?" Rannoch's laird appeared to ponder that for a moment, then shrugged. "Ye angered me. One moment ye were sending me all sorts of invitations with those bonny eyes of yers, and in the next . . . well, ye seemed to play me for some fool." His mouth went taut. "As I told ye before. I'd my fill of games with Sheila. I didn't wish to play any more with ye."

She *had* been playing a game with him. Indeed, she did so still. Guilt rose once again, but Killian firmly quashed it.

What other choice had she but to use him to further her plans? She was in this too deeply now to blithely inform Ruarc there'd be no wedding, that her agreement to allow him to court her was but a ruse. If he had become so enraged because she refused to bed him before their marriage, what might he do if he learned she had no intention of long remaining in Scotland or of becoming his wife?

If only that scheming little priest hadn't pushed so hard at the both of them. If only Adam Campbell had agreed to help her return to Virginia. And if only Alexander had never convinced her to come to Scotland in the first place.

Men . . . all of them sought to use her in some way to serve their purposes. Ruarc MacDonald meant to use her to his own purposes as well. She must never forget that. Never.

Why, oh why, though, was it necessary she surrender her humanity and sense of decency, indeed the essence of what made her who she was, in order to survive? What must God think of her right now? Was there no honorable, moral, *Christian* way out of this?

"Asking that you grant me time to adjust to you and this life, that you court me in a more gentlemanly fashion, is hardly playing games, m'lord," she said softly. "And, Campbell though I may be, as was your first wife, I resent being compared to her. I'm my own woman. I expect you to pay me the courtesy of respecting that."

"Ye're right, of course. It isn't fair to compare ye to Sheila."

Taken by surprise at Ruarc MacDonald's easy agreement, Killian stared up at him. Was this some new game *he* played? Indeed, was that all there'd ever be between them—a constant give-and-take of self-serving strategies? Well, whatever it was, best to seize any advantage offered her while it was still possible. Surely her heavenly Father understood she did this only in order to protect herself and her son. Ah, if there was any other way . . .

"And what about your word that there'll be no more incidents like last night until we're wed? Does that seem fair as well?"

Ruarc's brows dipped in a frown. "I already told ye it'll never happen again."

Killian knew she was pressing the limits of her luck here and daren't press too far, but she needed adequate time to plan, then make her escape with Gavin. She needed Ruarc MacDonald's word.

"Give me your word, then," she said. "Give me your word you'll never force yourself on me again."

Rannoch's laird's frown deepened into a thunderous scowl. "Ye insult me, madam, ye do. But if it's my word ye're needing to calm yer fears, then ye have it."

"On your honor as a Scotsman, a Highlander."

Ruarc MacDonald glared at her so long and balefully, Killian felt certain she had finally overstepped her bounds. Then, with a harsh laugh, the big Highlander nodded. "Aye, on my honor as a Scotsman and Highlander. And ye, madam, are not only the strangest lass I've met in a long while, but ye're also the most stubborn and conniving one as well. I know, though, it's harder for a woman in such circumstances than it is for a man."

Relief filled her. Killian leaped to her feet. "Thank you, m'lord! Oh, thank you!" She whirled around, setting her hair flying and her gown fluttering.

A bemused expression on his face, Ruarc MacDonald stood. "Ye needn't act so happy over it. It's not as if ye're saddled with some ignorant boor, with no inkling of what it takes to please a woman."

She stopped short. "Oh, I didn't mean it that way. I just . . . I just . . ." Her voice trailed off as she struggled for some plausible explanation . . . and found none.

"Six weeks, madam," he said, cutting her short. "And then ye give *yer* word there'll be no further hysterics or protest from ye? Six weeks more, and then ye promise to become my wife in every way?"

His wife in every way . . .

Killian's throat went dry. She didn't want to meet that direct, searching gaze but knew she must. She looked him straight in the eye.

"Six weeks, m'lord," she forced out the reply, knowing she'd be gone from Scotland before any marriage occurred. "Six more weeks. I promise. That's all I'll need."

†

THEY STARTED in the Great Hall, Francis stalking about the large chamber as servants haphazardly cleaned away the noon meal's remnants. With not much in the room save the long trestle table, a few "forest work" wall hangings depicting elaborate designs of fruit, flowers, and foliage—all of which had seen better days—the dark, wainscoted wooden walls, and an impressive stone fireplace, the tour there soon ended. At the far end of the room, they entered a short hallway and, across from that, another room that proved to be a combination drawing room and library.

"M'lord frequently likes to retire here after the supper meal," Francis said, casting her a quick glance over his shoulder. "Ye'd do well to see a fire is always lit on cold days and the draperies drawn each eve. The servants can oft be amiss in such duties, as most of them are with their other responsibilities."

Killian almost snapped back that she wasn't yet Ruarc

MacDonald's wife and not to be ordered about, then thought better of it. No harm was done in appearing to accept her fate. Indeed, more the better if it lulled them all into a false sense of security.

She glanced around the room. Two walls were filled with bookcases. Another large stone fireplace occupied the other wall, and the fourth held a glass-paned door and two windows that overlooked the gardens. A painted screen filled one corner, and before it was a small table and four chairs. Near the bookcases, another trestle table stood, set with additional chairs.

Her gaze lifted to the large painting above the fireplace. A man dressed in a belted plaid stood behind a woman seated on a stone bench in a garden Killian quickly realized was the very garden outside. The man closely resembled Ruarc, and the woman, who was tiny and auburn-haired, gazed up at the man with such adoration it was evident the couple were wed.

"M'lord's mither and father," Francis supplied without being asked, walking up to stand behind her. "Even after he wed the Lady Glynnis, Lord Robert refused to have that painting removed. Naught, he told her, would be touched in this room, and naught ever was. She didn't like it, the Lady Glynnis didn't, but she could never do aught about it. And, after Lord Robert's death, m'lord refused to allow Glynnis to touch this room, either."

There was a note of grim satisfaction in the young man's voice. His opinion of Glynnis, Killian surmised, was apparently no higher than that of his master's. She was beginning to see how the lines of battle were drawn in this house, and who served which side. The knowledge could well be invaluable.

"Unfortunately," she said, noting the shabby curtains and fabrics, the filthy floors, the thick coating of dust and mote-laden air where the sunlight streamed in from the windows, "someone should long ago have touched this room, if only to clean it."

She turned just in time to see fury flash in the young man's eyes before being quickly extinguished. "Aye, mayhap ye're correct, m'lady," Francis muttered, averting his gaze. "And mayhap ye'll see fit to remedy that failing. It'd be a most pleasant change from the slovenly way the Lady Glynnis has always discharged her duties."

"And did the Lady Sheila, before Glynnis, see to her duties more properly?" Killian demanded, already growing weary of Francis's snidely derogatory tone. "Or did she, too, fall short of your expectations?"

Francis paled and, for a moment, said nothing. Then his mouth narrowed to a thin, white line. "The Lady Sheila tried, for a time, to attend to her duties. In the last years of her life, however, her interests turned to other than wifely charges. That sad tale, though, isn't mine to tell."

No, it isn't, even if you'd dearly love to spill the venom you most evidently harbor for Sheila in your heart. Killian sensed it was a rancor even stronger than that which he seemed to hold for Glynnis. The realization disturbed her. What was it about Sheila that stirred all who knew her to such strong emotions, be they good or bad?

"Your loyalty to your master is most commendable," Killian chose to say instead. "Have you been in his employ long, Francis?"

"All my life, m'lady."

She arched a brow. "Indeed? That long, and you all of twenty or so?"

Francis scowled. "My father was the MacDonald family clerk. I helped him from the time I could read and cipher. And now, since my father's death, I've been in m'lord's employ as family clerk."

"I used to do the books for my uncle. You'll have to show me Rannoch's accounts some time."

"Overseeing the castle accounts is hardly what Rannoch and m'lord need from ye, m'lady, but if ye insist, with m'lord's permission, I'd be happy to show ye some time. I assure ye, though, they are well kept."

"Oh, I suspect they must be." Killian laughed. "I was just curious, that's all. I didn't mean to imply anything else."

He shot her a suspicious look. "Mayhap ye didn't. Still, ye'll have to ask m'lord's permission first. He refused ever to allow Lady Glynnis access—or her son, for that matter."

"Well, I suppose it's of little import just now anyway." Killian glanced around the room one final time. "Is there anything more you wish to share about this room, or should we move on?"

"Aye, we should be getting along. We've still the kitchen, larder, bakehouse, and washhouse to visit."

"Lead on, then." She motioned toward the door. "I wouldn't want my education to be lacking in any way."

The kitchen was quickly toured. A huge hearth filled one wall of the high-ceilinged room, equipped with metal hooks and chains from which pots and pans were suspended. There were also three spits, on which a pig and two hens had already begun to roast in preparation for the supper meal. On the long worktable sat a mortar and pestle, a grater, a colander, and several chopping knives. Hanging over the table was an additional assortment of brass, copper, and iron pots and pans.

A thin woman, garbed in a food-grimed apron, appeared to be in charge of the three girls working about the room. Francis led Killian over to meet the woman.

"M'lady, this is Bessie, the head cook," he said without preamble. "Bessie, this is m'lord's, er, betrothed, the Lady Killian Campbell."

The head cook eyed her critically for a moment, then executed a flawless curtsey. "I'm verra happy to make yer acquaintance, m'lady. Is there aught ye'd be wishing of me? Any special victuals ye'd like for the table?"

Killian opened her mouth to reply she'd first and foremost like more attention paid to cleanliness, taking note of the refuse piling up on the floors and the food-encrusted worktable, not to mention the poorly cleared and cleaned dining table in the Great Hall. Then she thought better of it.

What purpose was served playing the castle lady, she asked herself, even as she surreptitiously lifted the hem of her skirt higher, when she had no intention of ever being one? Better to leave things as they were and would be again once she made her escape. It was surely the kinder thing to do.

"No." Killian shook her head. "There's nothing I can think of at the moment. "There'll be plenty of time to talk and sort things through later, once I've had a chance to get to know everyone better." She smiled, glancing at Bessie, then at each of the kitchen maids. "I bid you all good day."

Amid murmured farewells and more curtseys, Killian and Francis left the kitchen. "So, what's it to be next?" she asked her companion. "The larder, perhaps?"

"If ye wish, m'lady." He halted and gestured down the corridor to their right. "We must take the stairs at the end of this hall. Ye may not like what ye find down there, though. The larder's dark and dank, and there are rats about."

Killian repressed a shudder. It was bad enough to venture down into such a place, but to also be accompanied by such a continually dreary, unfriendly person . . . besides, what was the point? The dismal state of this place would soon be far from her thoughts, as would the castle and all its inhabitants. There was really no need to submit herself to such an unpleasant experience.

"It's such a lovely day," she said. "Would you mind terribly if we left the larder for some other time and visited the bakehouse and washhouse instead?"

"Suit yerself. It doesn't matter to me."

Nearing the end of her patience with Francis MacLean, Killian ground her teeth in frustration. What, in the short time she had been at Rannoch, could she have possibly done to antagonize this young man? He was acting insufferably and she was past weary of it. Better they both part company now and save each other further misery.

"Well then," she began sweetly, "since it doesn't matter to you, and I'm quite capable of finding the bakehouse and washhouse all on my own, why don't you go on about what I've so selfishly kept you from? There's no sense ruining the rest of both our days."

He stared at her, bewildered, as if he were trying to fathom the true intent behind her words. Then, ever so slowly, as if he had finally comprehended her unhappiness with him, Francis's face reddened. "Of t-truth, m'lady. I-I didn't m-mean that the w-way ye might h-have imagined. I-I'm at y-yer disposal—"

"Och, Francis, there ye are! I've been looking all over Rannoch for ye." Father Kenneth's voice, booming down the corridor behind them, took them both by surprise. Killian and Francis turned to find the little cleric hurrying in their direction.

Watching his approach, though, only Killian stiffened. She had nothing good to say to the priest. Best to make her escape now rather than risk offending him. She turned to the clerk. "I'll leave you to Father Kenneth. I've better things to do—"

"Och, nay, lass," the priest exclaimed that moment as he drew up before them. "Don't leave. I've been looking for ye as well. Stay a moment, I pray, while I deliver a message to Francis. Then we must talk, ye and I. Aye." He nodded vehemently. "We must most definitely have a talk."

8

WITH A low oath, Adam Campbell crushed the letter in his hand, then flung it into the fire. "So, she's gone over to the MacDonalds now, has she?" An impotent fury filled him. "My cousin's wife has chosen to betray us!"

"So 'twould seem, m'lord."

Reminded of the messenger still standing there, Adam whirled about. "I thank ye for yer diligence in delivering this letter." He motioned over his manservant, Archie Campbell, who had circumspectly adjourned to guard the library door. "Archie will see ye get a hot meal in yer belly before ye return to Rannoch."

"And will ye be sending m'lady back a reply, m'lord?"

Adam hesitated. What, indeed, would they do now, Glynnis and he, with this new turn of events? How could they twist this cursed situation to their advantage?

"Aye." Already, his mind raced with new plans. "Most likely there will be. I'll send for ye before ye depart."

"Very good, m'lord." The messenger bowed, turned, and followed Archie from the room.

Adam watched them leave, then, with yet another curse, stalked to one of the two high-backed chairs set before the fire and flung himself into it. Killian . . . run away with Ruarc MacDonald and planning on wedding him in six weeks' time. . . . It'd be too preposterous to believe if he hadn't just learned of it from Glynnis

MacDonald's own hand. But why? Why would Killian do such a foolhardy thing?

There were too many unanswered, disturbing questions, and all of them stemmed from the night of Alexander's death. Why had Killian and her son disappeared at nearly the same time Alexander had? Why hadn't she been found again until more than a day and a half later, miles from Achallader? Then there was her strange rapport with Ruarc MacDonald, a bond seemingly present from the first moment she had encountered him as a prisoner on the road.

Adam's gut instincts *had* been correct. Somehow, some way, Killian had always been in league with Ruarc MacDonald. Had she been a spy, feeding Adam's enemy information about the Campbell nobles' meeting at Achallader? And had Alexander mayhap lost his life when he had come upon the two that night, plotting their next move?

With a weary sigh, Adam lowered his head and massaged his aching eyes. Whatever Killian's motivation, it was more than he cared to deal with just now. In the end, only two things really mattered. Alexander's murderer must be apprehended, and Ruarc MacDonald must pay for Sheila's death. Mayhap, just mayhap, the death of Rannoch's lord could now solve both problems.

He leaned back in the brocaded, walnut armchair and closed his eyes. Sheila . . . even now Adam couldn't think of her without experiencing a deep, searing pain. Even now the longing ache in his chest swelled at the slightest consideration of her. His wee, bonny Sheila. Och, how he had loved her, and loved her still!

But Ruarc MacDonald had taken her from him, just as he had taken Killian. Not that Adam had begun seriously to consider Killian as a potential wife. She had been Alexander's. So soon after a kinsman's death, Adam was hardly the sort normally to covet his wife.

It had been different, though, with Sheila. Sheila had yet to become any man's that summer he had met her again. Since he was the second-born son with no prospects of inheriting Achallader or its estates, his father had sent him away at age ten to be educated in Holland. When Adam had left, Sheila was but a wee lass of five. When he returned on an extended holiday at the strapping age of twenty, his foster sister was fifteen and had blossomed into a gloriously beautiful and innocently beguiling young woman.

From the first moment they set eyes on each other that warm summer day in Achallader's gardens, there had never been another love for either of them. It didn't matter that Sheila's fosterage joined them almost as closely as brother and sister. In their eyes, at any rate, the old customs served little barrier to the feelings burgeoning between them.

That summer, they had come alive to each other. Everything seemed fresh, new, and so very wonderful. In their youthful naïveté, they refused to mar the heady experience with morbid worries or stultifying strictures.

Sheila looked up to him, needed him, clung to him with all the fervor of a girl whose emotions had been finally awakened. And Adam, lonely and alienated from his native land after what had seemed ten years of exile, imagined he had at last come home.

He should've taken Sheila with him, back to Holland, when the summer ended. Not a day passed even now when he didn't curse himself for that. She'd have been his forever if he had. She might well still be alive, too.

With a despairing groan, Adam shoved from his chair and strode to the fireplace. There, encased in a huge, gilt frame, hung a portrait of Sheila. It had been painted that summer they had spent together, commissioned by Sheila's true father who was even then dying of some liver ailment, no doubt brought on by the copious amounts of fine claret he constantly imbibed.

Garbed in a pale blue satin gown, her auburn hair a wild tumult of curls tied up with a matching blue satin ribbon, Sheila had sat in a formal pose. Mature beyond her years, she was a bemusing yet totally irresistible combination of angel and seductress.

Gripping the oak mantel mounted below the portrait, Adam stared up at the painting. Thanks to Ruarc MacDonald, this was all he had left of his beloved Sheila. Once Ruarc had offered for Sheila's hand, there seemed nothing, absolutely nothing, that could sway her from her chosen path. Though he railed against, pleaded, and reasoned with her every way he knew how, eventually Adam had had to admit defeat. Sheila had been strangely adamant in her conviction that Ruarc MacDonald was the man for her.

Their love was doomed, Sheila tearfully assured Adam the night before her wedding to Ruarc. Far better they part now, once and forever. Far better for the both of them.

A sour taste in his mouth, Adam turned at last from the portrait. It didn't matter *he* had been willing to risk even hell, and forfeit heaven, for Sheila. The choice, that morning she and Ruarc Mac-Donald had pronounced their marriage vows, had been irrevocably taken from him.

And now, nothing was left him but vengeance. Vengeance and the wound that would never heal—until death severed his body and spirit for all eternity.

†

WITH A sinking heart Killian watched Francis walk away, sent on some apparently urgent mission for his master. Then, with a sigh, she turned to the priest.

"I was about to pay the bakehouse and washhouse a visit," she said, hoping to hurry Father Kenneth along in what he had come to say. "If you please, you can either tell me now what you mean to tell me, or we can talk along the way."

"Och, it's such a lovely day, I'd imagine we can talk as we go," the old cleric replied with a laugh. He offered her his arm. "If ye will, m'lady."

Eyeing his black serge–clad arm, Killian struggled for some plausible excuse not to accept it. She hardly felt in a friendly mood right now, especially toward the man who had all but browbeaten her into a possible marriage she hadn't wanted. Still, there seemed no way to avoid offense if she refused.

Killian took his arm and strode out down the corridor. "So, Father, what was it you wished to talk about?"

"Och, I was but wondering how ye're managing. I've a special interest in yer welfare, ye know."

"I'm managing as well as can be expected." With an effort, she maintained a tight rein on her temper. "This isn't at all, though, how I imagined things would turn out."

"Ye must have patience, lass. The answers ye're seeking will all come in time. Mark my words, they'll all come—in our Lord's own good time."

"And how can you be so certain of that?" Killian demanded as they entered the Great Hall and headed across it. "You say it's God's will Ruarc and I wed. Are you so sure, though, it isn't your own desires but muddying your interpretation?"

"One must always be vigilant that one's own desires never take precedence over our Savior's. But I pray constantly to know His will. That doesn't mean I always hear Him correctly, but it *has* helped attune me a wee bit better to His voice. Still, I'm but a weak vessel and I do make mistakes.

"I'll tell ye this, though, lass. Of all the times I've thought I knew our Lord's will, this time I've never felt more certain of it. Mayhap I was wrong in the way I presented it to ye and Ruarc, but weren't all of my reasons valid? Weren't all of them for both of yer own good?"

"Perhaps for Ruarc." Killian slid to a halt, extracted her arm from the priest's, and glared at him. "But how can you possibly imagine that coercing me to marry a man I hardly know and forcing me to stay in a country I don't even like is for my own good? I've a beautiful home in Virginia where I'm far nearer my own family than I am here, halfway across the world. How can you possibly think I'd ever be happier in Scotland?"

"And were ye happy in Virginia then, wed to yer first husband? Did ye ever feel loved there, like ye truly belonged?"

His quietly posed question took Killian aback. How could he possibly know—? She cut off the question abruptly. It didn't matter *what* the priest thought he knew.

Still, his words had stirred memories. Of aching loneliness. Of the local landowners' wives who always seemed to look down their elegant, aristocratic noses at the girl who had worked as a shipping clerk before wedding Alexander. Even now, those memories filled her with pain and despair.

No, she had never belonged in Virginia any more than she had belonged anywhere else. Perhaps she had once belonged with her parents, but they had died far too young for her to remember much of them. Nonetheless, Killian knew she didn't belong here.

"Things have changed," she replied finally. "I know I'd be happy there now."

"Mayhap." Father Kenneth shrugged. "But mayhap not, if yer heart's desires lie in Scotland."

Her heart's desires . . .

A shiver rippled through her. Once again, the priest seemed to possess an uncanny ability to recall words and events about which he should've had no reason to know. If he wasn't so obviously a man of God, Killian could have almost imagined him some practitioner of the black arts.

To say the very least, his continued pronouncements were unnerving. What if he *did* speak for Christ in this? What chance did she have then of ever returning to Virginia?

As quickly as the doubts surfaced, Killian quashed them.

There was only one way to know if her upcoming marriage to Ruarc MacDonald was truly God's will, and that was to test it. If she and Gavin made it safely back to Virginia, then the answer was obvious.

"Please, Father." She forced a smile. "Your interest in me is appreciated, but you and I may never view this in the same light. Perhaps it's best we agree not to speak of this matter again."

"As ye wish, lass. Only know ye cannot open yerself to yer new life until ye let go of the old. Aye, mayhap not until ye cast it forcibly aside. It's that way with all things, in dying to ourselves so that we may be reborn, ye know."

Killian gave an unsteady laugh. If this priest thought now to manipulate her by clever use of Scripture, he was sadly mistaken. "Well, one has first to want the new life over the old, doesn't one?"

"Aye, that one does. And if ever ye feel called to do so, know I'm here for ye whenever ye need me. Ye're soon to be a MacDonald, and my calling is to serve the clan." With that he stepped back, rendered her a little bow, then turned and walked away.

From her spot below the upstairs gallery that overlooked the Great Hall, Killian watched him depart. A deep frustration welled within. *If ever ye feel called to do so . . .*

Why, oh why, must the priest constantly drag God into this?

She wanted to serve the Lord in all she did, but everything she tried to do seemed to end in failure. Indeed, not just in failure, but in tragedy. Surely God didn't mean for her finally to discover His true will here, far from home and in the midst of savage, unfathomable strangers. Why, it was past ridiculous; it was incomprehensible.

With a deep, shuddering breath, Killian banished the unsettling thoughts and wheeled about in the opposite direction. As she did, from the corner of her eye she caught a movement overhead. Glancing up, Killian saw Glynnis standing there.

A look of concern furrowing her brow, the other woman, as if ascertaining that no one had seen them, looked hurriedly about. Then she gripped the railing and leaned forward. "Meet me in the library," she mouthed the words. "We must talk."

There was something in Glynnis's expression that sent a flash of hope through Killian. She nodded, gathered her skirts, then turned and made her way back across the Great Hall to the library.

†

FROM HER vantage in the gallery, Glynnis watched Killian go. Excitement thrummed through her veins. Bless the good fortune that had brought her past the gallery hallway at just the right moment! The opportunity to overhear Killian's conversation with Father Kenneth had been priceless. Now she knew what Killian wanted most. She wanted to return home to Virginia.

But how could that serve her and Adam's purpose in destroying Ruarc? One way or another, if Killian left Rannoch, it'd ruin Ruarc's new hopes of wedding and siring an heir by her.

Meanwhile, even more time would elapse in finding another willing woman to marry him. That might take months, if he indeed ever found anyone. Months she and Adam could use to further their plans.

Her excitement rising, Glynnis headed down to meet Killian in the library. If the new Lady MacDonald wished to leave Rannoch, she must be helped to accomplish that in every and any way. There was plenty of time left to do so. In the right hands, six weeks could be as much as a lifetime.

†

SOMETIME deep in the night, Killian awoke with a start. Save for a few embers glowing in the hearth, the room was dark. For a long moment she lay there, disoriented, her heart racing.

She was alone. She wasn't being attacked. Alexander was dead, and she was safe in Rannoch Castle.

Strange that such a realization should be the cause of such relief. Strange that a man who was still little more than a stranger should comfort her like Alexander's presence never had. A man who might ultimately be just as dangerous and violent.

Tears welled, spilling down Killian's cheeks. She was so confused. She didn't know what to think, whom to trust anymore. Indeed, even her own judgment was rapidly becoming suspect.

Only today she had confessed all to Glynnis, how she wanted to leave Rannoch and return to Virginia. Only today she had begged the woman to help her. And only today, Glynnis, seeming to understand her yearning for her own land, had agreed to find some way to get Killian out of Rannoch.

The nearest seaport with ships sailing to America, the older woman informed her, was on an inlet on Loch Linnhe. To reach it, though, Killian would have to travel back through Campbell lands. Did she wish to enlist the aid of her late husband's kinsmen to get her safely to the seaport, once she was again among Campbells?

"No," Killian had swiftly informed her. "I didn't leave on good terms with Adam Campbell, after helping Ruarc escape. I'd rather take my chances traveling on my own."

"That'll be dangerous, m'lady." Glynnis frowned. "There are reivers and broken men abounding these days. If any of those should come upon ye . . ."

"Nonetheless, I'll take my chances." Killian's resolve hardened. Despite the threat of lawless cattle thieves and men with no allegiance to clan or family, she meant to see this through. She was tired of being used by and dependent on men. It was past time she stood on her own, prove she could.

"All I need are directions, a horse, and money for the sea journey. I can offer you this in return." She removed the ruby-and-emerald wedding ring Alexander had given her now so many years ago and presented it to Glynnis. "Surely this will be a goodly down payment for the trip. When I reach my home in Virginia, I'll send you what-ever else is still lacking."

Glynnis waved aside the ring. "Keep it, m'lady. Ye may need it later to see ye safely home. I've sufficient funds of my own and will pay yer ticket. Ye can send me the entire amount later."

At the other woman's generosity, gratitude welled in Killian.

"Thank you. I can't tell you how much this means to me. You're a kind, wonderful person."

"And ye, m'lady, deserve better than the likes of my stepson." Her eyes darkened with anger. "Nay, if I've aught to say about it, Ruarc won't have the opportunity to ruin yet another fair lass's life."

With that, the two women had parted, Glynnis promising to confer again once all the preparations had been made. A few more weeks, Killian thought, lying there in her bed. A few more weeks and she'd be on her way home. There were times in the past months when she had despaired of ever seeing Virginia again. She had always feared that Alexander's ploy to bring them to Scotland for a visit hadn't been just for the summer. And when Adam had confirmed that, Killian's hopes had been cruelly dashed.

But now, at long last, she had found someone who'd help her. Someone she could trust, who had her best interests at heart. On the morrow, Killian planned to pen a letter to their plantation overseer, apprising him of Alexander's death and her imminent return. She'd then ask Glynnis to see to its posting.

If all went as planned, she'd soon be free of Scotland and the encumbrances of men forever.

Killian's thoughts snagged once more on Ruarc MacDonald. She wished she could've trusted him. She wished he had been an honorable man, or at least as honorable as any Highlander could truly be. She didn't like leading him to think he'd soon take her to wife. Even a man like Ruarc MacDonald had his hopes and dreams.

But she had her dreams, too. Dreams that had been battered and sullied by life with Alexander—from living with almost constant fear for years, from all the denial, compromise, guilt, and loneliness. More than anything she had ever wanted, Killian wanted finally to be whole again, to put the pieces of her life back together and feel clean. More than anything, she wanted someday to have a good, strong, loving family.

That family, it seemed, would now have to consist only of her and Gavin. She was past weary of what every man who had ever played some part of consequence in her life had tried to do to her. Her uncle, then Alexander, Adam Campbell, the priest, and finally Ruarc MacDonald.

Still, even now, the thought of betraying Rannoch's laird filled Killian with remorse. What of the pain she might cause him? Strange as it was even to admit, Killian found such a consideration increasingly difficult to bear.

9

SHE HADN'T always been like this, so manipulative, so perfidious, so deliberately cruel. Nay, Glynnis thought two weeks later as she glanced one last time at Adam's newest letter before tossing it into the fire to burn, once she had held high hopes, possessed romantic ideals about making a difference. But that was before she had wed Ruarc MacDonald's father. That was before his cold indifference had slowly but surely sapped all the joy and kindness from her.

Now she did what she could to survive, all the while fighting to pry her and her son's rightful inheritance from the greedy, clutching grip of Robert MacDonald's eldest son. Ruarc well deserved what he got, for his own sake as well as for that of his father. But Killian . . . Killian was fast becoming an innocent pawn in the battle for Rannoch.

A long time ago, Glynnis would never have used another person as she planned to use Killian. But a long time ago she had still possessed a heart. These days, however, only one thing mattered—her stepson's downfall and loss of control of Rannoch Castle.

Even more than for his despicable treatment of her all these years, Ruarc must pay for what he had done to Sheila. Adam and she were united in this. Rannoch's laird must not get away with this brutal murder. If the king wouldn't punish him, then they must.

With a heart-deep sigh, Glynnis walked from the hearth to stare out her bedchamber window. The deep, stone-cut opening in the castle walls looked down on the gardens. Och, a sudden bittersweet remembrance filling her, how Sheila had loved these gardens! It was where her body had been found that morning, after she and Ruarc had been seen engaged in heated argument the night before. Sheila, beauteous Sheila, stabbed through the heart and left to die in the darkness, alone and helpless to save herself.

Glynnis watched now as Killian and her son walked among the autumn foliage, the lad frolicking with Ruarc's monstrous dog. If she hadn't heard it otherwise from Killian's own lips, Glynnis might have thought the young Colonial was beginning to settle into life at Rannoch.

But Glynnis knew better. Killian was homesick for her own land, still felt uneasy with Ruarc, whom she admitted she really didn't wish to wed, and desperately wanted to leave. Listening to her anguished pleas for help, Glynnis's heart had gone out to the young woman. All the while, though, she had also considered what she could gain in helping Killian, how this might be used to Ruarc's detriment.

In the past days since she had first informed him of Ruarc and Killian's wedding plans, Adam must also have been thinking along these same lines. The plan he had outlined in his letter dovetailed nicely with Glynnis's needs. Indeed, though he had yet to be informed that Killian had requested her help in escaping Rannoch, Adam had already suggested a similar plan. Get Killian back to him without Ruarc knowing how, he had urged Glynnis. In the meantime, he'd set a trap to capture Rannoch's laird when he came after her.

Problem was, Killian had been quite adamant about not returning to Achallader when Glynnis had suggested it. All she wanted was to leave Scotland forever. Yet to help her accomplish only that wouldn't address the bigger and far more important problem—how to destroy Ruarc.

Nay, Adam's plan was best. Once she was safely back at Achallader, Killian would just have to bargain with Adam for a way home.

It was passing strange, though, that Killian seemed so resistant to returning to the safety of her kinsman's castle. From what she knew of Adam Campbell, Glynnis far preferred him to her stepson. In his visits to Rannoch when Sheila was still alive, she had always found him courteous and charming. As unseemly as their secret affection had been for each other, she could well understand why Sheila had always loved him.

In the end, Glynnis knew what was better for Killian than Killian did herself. She was safer with Adam Campbell than she'd ever be with Sheila's murderer.

Still, Glynnis regretted purposely losing Killian's company. There were few in Rannoch with whom she dared confide or even spend time. Thomas always seemed busy with his own endeavors. Most of the servants were either loyal to their laird or were too lazy and ignorant to care about anyone but themselves. Even Finola, who was Glynnis's spy, was flighty and shallow. And it wasn't as if the dour Ruarc MacDonald ever entertained anymore, save when the clan chief paid an occasional visit.

Glynnis sighed and stepped back from the window. Things had been different when Sheila was alive. There had been parties, banquets, and myriad visitors coming and going. Ruarc, madly in love with his wife, had been far more hospitable in those days.

She and Sheila had been the closest of friends. Though Ruarc had been far from happy about it, Sheila had confided many things to her, even, eventually, her secret and lifelong love for Adam Campbell. Glynnis had shared in her joys and her sorrows, especially the heartbreaking loss by miscarriage of all the bairns her friend had conceived. Four wee babes . . . all dead early in each of Sheila's pregnancies.

In the end, though, it must have been God's will. Sheila, for all her desire to give Ruarc an heir, would've never survived childbirth. She was too tiny, too frail. And Ruarc, if the truth were told, would've made a poor father. He was too much like his own sire. Too cold. Too distant and unforgiving.

Nay, Glynnis reassured herself, in the end Ruarc MacDonald would finally pay for his cruelty to her and, through him, so would his father. There'd be no children of his inheriting Rannoch. Not by Sheila and now, not by Killian, either.

This time she and Adam would succeed in putting an end to him. They had the perfect bait in Killian. Aye, this time they were sure to succeed, and no amount of pity or concern for anyone—Killian included—could be allowed to get in the way.

†

"SO, MADAM," Ruarc asked several days later at the noon meal, "ye've had a few weeks to survey Rannoch. What do ye think of yer new home?"

Killian paused in the cutting of her overcooked roast chicken with oatmeal stuffing and glanced at him. What did he wish to hear? Surely not the truth.

She looked down at her pewter plate. The dry, tasteless dish lying there would've made most men gag, yet Ruarc ate his as if it were quite palatable, if not absolutely delicious. And the first course, of barley broth, had been even worse, served cold with big globs of rancid chicken grease floating on its murky surface.

"I find it all very interesting," Killian ventured the most tactful reply she could imagine. "I've never lived in a castle before, you know, so I'm still rather overwhelmed by it all."

Ruarc's mouth twisted in wry amusement. "Nonetheless, there must be something ye find that needs improving. Few women coming into a new home don't want to change at least a few aspects of that home."

Apparently her evasiveness wasn't going to work on him. "Well, of course that's true." She turned her gaze back to her meat. "I just didn't think it fair to start making changes, leastwise not until I'd had a bit more time to understand how everything worked here."

"But if ye *were* to make a change, what would the first be?"

With a sigh, Killian laid down her knife and fork and looked him squarely in the eye. "First and foremost, I'd improve the cleanliness of the kitchen. The worktable is always filthy. The pots and pans are barely scrubbed and most times are reused with the last meal's leavings still coating the insides. And then there's the produce. It's poorly washed, and the—"

Ruarc gave a bark of laughter and held up his hand. "Ye needn't say more. I think I've a verra clear picture of yer displeasure with the kitchen. By all means, have a go arranging that the cleanliness of the place is improved. Then, when ye're done with those corrections, I wouldn't mind if ye saw to bettering the taste of the food. If ye think ye've the expertise to do so, that is."

"Food is food, no matter where it's served. It might take me a time to learn the nuances of Scots' cooking, but I'm sure a bit more attention to detail would immeasurably enhance the taste of the meals."

"Well, ye won't hear any complaints from me from that quarter, madam." Ruarc picked up a goblet and took a deep swallow. "I assure ye, if ye take charge of the meals, ye'll endear yerself to the castle's inhabitants almost immediately."

Suddenly perturbed, Killian turned back to her own plate. Whatever had possessed her to launch into such a diatribe against the kitchen? She'd be gone from here soon. It wasn't fair to make Ruarc think she was settling into life at Rannoch or that she even cared what became of him and his cold, drafty, dirty castle.

Still, no harm was done leaving him with a cleaner kitchen and better-tasting meals. It'd surely pass the time a lot more quickly. It wasn't as if she could spend the entire day in the garden or sequestered in her bedchamber. Well, she *supposed* she could, but that'd soon bore her to tears.

No, both she and Ruarc would profit by her efforts in reforming the kitchen. It'd be her legacy, however small it was, of her time here at Rannoch, and hopefully—

David MacDonald, Ruarc's cousin and captain of the guard, strode into the Great Hall and headed directly for their table.

Ruarc laid down his knife. "Aye, Davie?" he called out to the other man. "What's amiss?"

"Naught ye should hasten yer meal for, m'lord," the muscular, auburn-haired man of medium height said, drawing up before him. "Ye'll be pleased to hear, though, we've apprehended Ewen MacPhail at long last. He's in the guardhouse even as we speak, and none too keen about it, either."

Immediately Ruarc pushed back his chair and rose. Killian glanced up at him. A savage, scorching fury darkened his features.

"M'lord? What's wrong?"

"A bit of unfinished business and naught more." Even as he spoke, Ruarc strode around the table to join David. "Finish yer meal. This won't take long."

Rannoch's laird stalked from the Hall, David at his side. Killian stared after him in dismay. Save for his encounter with Adam Campbell at Achallader, she had never seen him angrier.

Glynnis hurried to her. "M'lady." She bent close so no one else could hear. "Pretend ye're done with yer victuals and come with me. It's important ye see and fully understand the manner of man ye're to wed."

Killian was tempted to protest that Ruarc had told her to stay and finish her meal, but she really was interested in discovering what had made him so furious. "Go on ahead," she whispered back. "I'll join you at the main door in a few minutes."

Glynnis nodded and hurried off.

After a making a show of trying to saw through her chicken, Killian sighed loudly and laid down her cutlery. "I think that's enough for me," she said, smiling at Francis and Thomas, who sat at the other end of the table, still eating. "If you'll excuse me, I believe I'll adjourn now for a short walk outside."

As Killian rose, both men hurriedly scraped back their chairs and climbed to their feet. She nodded at them as she passed, then swept from the room.

Glynnis awaited her at the front door. "Come, m'lady." She took her by the arm, then turned and headed from the Hall in the direction of the stables.

Before they were far from the castle, the sound of angry male voices rose in the air. There, outside the stable's main entrance, stood Ruarc and David facing a bound, burly, disheveled man being held by two other men. Killian drew to a halt about fifty feet from them.

"So, Ewen, ye filthy scum," she could hear Ruarc snarl as he grabbed the front of the burly man's plaid and jerked him to himself, "did ye think ye'd get away with what ye did? Did ye?"

"I-I didna do it, m'lord," the man named Ewen babbled, his grime-coated, sweaty face gone white. "I-I swear it, m'lord!"

"And what of the witnesses, then?" At the man's stunned expression, Ruarc nodded grimly. "Aye, ye didn't know that Sarah Menzies and little Johnie Cameron saw ye, did ye?"

"Th-they're lyin'! 'Twas someone else, mayhap some broken man or reiver! 'Twasn't me. 'Twasn't me!"

Ruarc slapped him across the face. "Stop yer blathering, man! It'll do ye no good. I won't abide a man of yer sort on Rannoch lands. Ye're to be handed over to the constable for trial, but first I intend to send ye on yer way with a little less skin on yer back than what ye returned to us with."

He looked to David. "Tie Ewen to that pole —" he indicated a log about nine feet in length with a heavy metal ring inserted in it—"and strip the shirt from his back." Ruarc then walked into the barn and soon returned with a long, black whip.

Ewen, his hands now bound to the ring over his head, his back bared, awaited him. Ruarc wasted no time or further niceties on the man.

As the thin leather cut into Ewen's back for the first time, the man howled in pain. "Nay, nay, m'lord! 'Twasn't me! 'Twasn't me!"

His protests were lost on Ruarc, who proceeded to lay the whip again and again across the unfortunate man's back.

Watching Ruarc and the coldly methodical way he beat his clansman, Killian's blood ran cold. Whatever could poor Ewen have done to merit such torture? Between ever increasing shrieks, he began to writhe and shudder. The blood welled, then trickled down Ewen's back. She turned away, unable to watch.

"I knew ye wouldn't like what ye saw, m'lady," Glynnis said. "But ye had to know."

"Yes, I did," Killian whispered, sickened by Ruarc's unfeeling brutality. "I had to know."

"And now, at long last, do ye believe me when I tell ye Ruarc MacDonald's a heartless wretch? Do ye?"

"Yes." She barely breathed out the word. "Yes, I suppose I do."

Glynnis took her by the arm and began to lead her away. "Come along then, m'lady. Thank the Lord ye won't have to endure him much longer."

"When, Glynnis?" Killian looked to the other woman. "When will all be ready for me to leave for home?"

"Soon, m'lady," Glynnis assured her. "There are but a few more details I must iron out, and then we'll await the right moment."

"And when will that be? I don't know how much longer I can stand this."

"I'll know when the proper time comes. Ye must trust me in this, m'lady. Trust me and no other."

†

"BY MOUNTAIN and sea!" Ruarc muttered in exasperation a week later. "Alasdair MacDonald is bound and determined to risk all for the sake of a deposed king who'll never again be Scotland's ruler! The old fool! The fatally loyal, old fool!"

Francis glanced up from the letter Ruarc had only minutes ago tossed down onto his desk. "So it'd seem, m'lord. Our clan chief may well wait until it's too late to sign King William's oath of fealty, if he waits until King James frees him to do so."

"Well, he can't wait too much longer. The deadline's a scant nine weeks away." Rannoch's laird walked to where Francis sat, snatched up the document with the royal seal, and scanned it yet again. "William, solely out of friendship, has taken it upon himself to warn me yet again of the dire consequences if my chief refuses his fealty."

Ruarc sighed and shook his head. "With the Campbells all but breathing down our necks, I fear, Francis, those consequences might warrant not only our lands, but mayhap our verra lives."

"What will ye do, m'lord?" The young clerk gazed up at him with concern. "Ye've already urged and warned Alasdair several times since the proclamation was read. But, as clan chief, if he still chooses not to sign . . ."

"Then the whole clan risks extermination." Ruarc frowned and rubbed his jaw thoughtfully. "Mayhap a trip to London is in order."

"To speak with the king, m'lord?" Francis leaned forward eagerly. "If ye go, m'lord, I beg that ye take me with ye. To visit Court has always been my dearest desire."

Ruarc cast an affectionate glance in the young man's direction. He couldn't blame Francis' hunger for a taste of the world outside the Highlands. He had hungered just as avidly all those years ago, importuning his father to send him to Holland to further his education, as was the custom for noble youths then.

But, in the doing, Ruarc had also seen enough of the corruption, self-seeking greed, and empty allure of such a life to satisfy him forever. Indeed, he had seen and lived enough of it to sicken him to the marrow of his bones.

Life in the Highlands might be simple and sometimes even brutal, but it was also honest and real. You always knew who your friends—and your enemies—were. You could always count on a roof over your head and a hot meal in your belly, no matter where you went.

The air was clean, the water fresh and sweet, the living earned by dint of good, hard work. There was little of the dry rot of hearts corrupted and dying. There was no need to choke on the stale, disease-laden vapors of overcrowded living and filthy, refuse-filled streets. There was still honor, hope, and valor to be found in the Highlands, and that was more than enough for him.

"*If* I go, lad, I'll give yer request serious consideration," Ruarc replied finally. "A trip to Court, however, will only be taken as a last resort. Even for the chance to renew old acquaintances with the king, I don't fancy spending any more time in London."

Disappointment darkened Francis' eyes. "But what other choice do ye have, m'lord? As intractable as Alasdair is known to be, I'd wager convincing King William to show us mercy would be far easier than changing our chief's mind. He entered into that bond to support James over two years ago now. As far as I can tell, his resolve to uphold it hasn't wavered."

"Nay, it hasn't. Still, I have hope . . ."

Mayhap, Ruarc thought, as the time grew nearer for the deadline, Alasdair might begin to weaken. And there was always the chance James might yet release the Jacobite chiefs still loyal to him from their bond.

A request had been sent to the exiled king asking that very thing. The possibility was strong that the MacDonald chief would take the oath to William if James allowed it. That field must be continually plowed, however, to keep such an eventuality foremost in Alasdair's mind.

"I'm thinking, lad," Ruarc said, turning back to Francis, "it's past time I pay our chief yet another visit. Best not to let him long forget the grave state of things."

"Aye, m'lord. But have a care. There are those in the clan who think ye a traitor to the cause, in yer persistence over taking the oath of fealty. I've heard it said ye cling overhard to the English king, and English ways."

Ruarc gave a harsh laugh. "Och, and would they rather all be put to the sword, their houses burned, their fields laid to waste, and their cattle confiscated? We cannot beat the English, leastwise not anymore. William will give us leave, though, to live the life we all cherish, if we but assuage his fears that we won't turn against him. He has enough troubles of his own in dealing with James and France, not to mention handling Parliament and that court of his. The sooner our clansmen see the truth of that, the sooner we can all go back to living without further interference."

"When will ye leave for Carnoch then?"

"This afternoon, I'm thinking. Mayhap a wee overnight visit will be enough to stir Alasdair's thoughts back to the problem at hand. I should be home again early on the morrow."

"Do ye wish for me to accompany ye, m'lord?"

He considered that query for a moment, then shook his head. "Nay. The Lady Killian isn't all that comfortable with Rannoch as yet. I'd prefer she come to ye for assistance rather than Glynnis."

"Aye, ye've a point, m'lord. I've my hands full as it is, repairing all the damage the Lady Glynnis contrives to wreak each day."

"Ye're a good and faithful man, Francis." Ruarc walked over and clasped him on the shoulder. "I don't know what I'd do without ye."

Francis beamed. "I'd do aught for ye, m'lord. Aught. Ye've only to ask."

†

JUST BEFORE midnight of that same day, Glynnis came to Killian, woke her, and informed her it was time for her and Gavin to leave. It didn't take long to prepare. Killian had already packed a small satchel for herself and Gavin. Some bread, cheese, and a flask of cider were soon added.

Accompanied by Thomas, who intended to ride with them for part of the way, Killian paused only long enough to bid Glynnis a tender farewell. "I can never repay what you've done for me, my friend," she said. "Have a care Ruarc doesn't discover what you've done, though, or I fear for your safety."

"He can't prove aught, no matter what or whom he suspects. I planned too carefully for that." Glynnis took Killian's hand and pressed a small leather bag into it. "Here, I want ye to take this. Ye'll need it for the journey ahead."

Killian opened the bag to find it full of additional coins and several pieces of jewelry. She looked up. "I-I can't take this, Glynnis." Emotion choked her voice. "You've already done enough in loaning me the money necessary for our sea passage." She tried to give the little bag back.

"Nay, take it." The older woman pushed her hand away. "The journey will be hard enough as it is. I want to do this for ye. Just hide it away and keep it safe for later."

Blinking back tears, Killian clasped the bag to her. "Thank you."

The two women stared at each other for the space of a breath; then Glynnis stepped back. "Get on with ye, then. Every minute ye tarry here is a minute longer to reaching yer destination."

Killian nodded. "Yes, you're right of course." She turned and put the bag into the small leather purse hanging from her waist. With Thomas's help, she mounted her horse and took Gavin from his arms.

For one last time her gaze lingered on Ruarc's stepmother, standing there in the darkness, a silent, solitary figure. "Farewell, my dear friend. I'll never forget the favor you did me this night."

"Nor will I, m'lady," came the soft and strangely sardonic reply. "Nor will I."

10

KILLIAN was nowhere to be found. Ruarc had returned late that morning and it was now well past midday. Not only hadn't Killian and Gavin come to table for the noon meal, but try as they might, neither Francis nor Finola could seem to locate either of the pair inside Rannoch or its immediate environs. To add to Ruarc's unease, Fionn paced the castle, alternately whining and growling like some pup that had lost his favorite bone—or his best little friend.

Something was wrong—very wrong. Had something untoward happened to Killian and her son while he had been gone? Or had she run off, back to Adam Campbell?

If that were so, he was certain Glynnis had had a hand in that escape. To confront her, however, was pointless. She'd but smirk at him, then deny any knowledge, all the while her eyes flashing delight that he had failed yet again to find another woman to wed him.

What did it matter anyway? he thought, even as his legs carried him from Rannoch toward the chapel. Most likely Killian had left willingly, intent on seeking sanctuary with her Campbell kinsmen. The first month of the six-week deadline was almost over. She seemed no more eager now to wed him than she had that first night at Rannoch.

Problem was, he realized he couldn't blame her. Though he had initially imagined himself capable of marrying for the sake of potential heirs, he knew now he needed more from a wife than grim acquiescence.

Perhaps he could've tolerated such behavior from some other women, but Ruarc wanted more than that from Killian. True, she inflamed his desires—what red-blooded man wouldn't want her?—but it was more, indeed had always been more, than just that.

From that stormy night in the forest outside Achallader when he had first looked into Killian's terrified eyes, Ruarc had been drawn, however unwillingly, to her. Perhaps it was an air of vulnerability about her that appealed to his protective instincts. Perhaps it was the challenge she constantly presented, in the canny but expert dance she executed about his heart and mind. Or perhaps, just perhaps, though Ruarc abhorred even the consideration, it was the gut-deep feeling they were kindred spirits, born from a pain, disillusionment, and need not so very different from each other's.

That admission, more than anything else, made the possibility that Killian had willingly chosen to leave him hurt the most. It also angered him.

Fool, he berated himself silently. *When will ye learn that any woman with Adam Campbell's taint upon her is not for ye? She has betrayed ye. Let her go. Forget her, and be thankful she left when she did.*

Ruarc shoved open the chapel doors and stalked inside. Father Kenneth was at his prayers, kneeling in a pew near the front of the church. At Ruarc's less than quiet entrance, however, he glanced over his shoulder, took one look at him, then quickly closed his Psalter and rose.

"What is it, lad?" He hurried down the aisle toward Ruarc. "Ye look like a thundercloud about to unleash its fury."

"Killian's gone." Ruarc slid to a halt before him. "So's her son. I fear all yer fine plans for procuring an heir for Rannoch have come to naught."

"Then ye must go after her, bring her back."

"To what purpose?" He gave a harsh laugh. "So I can force myself on the lass? If she doesn't want me, any chance of a marriage is over. I won't beg her. And I refuse to allow her to manipulate me by dangling the hope of an heir over my head. Rannoch's welfare or no, I have my pride."

"Aye, and well do I know that." The little priest nodded sadly. "Haven't I always warned ye yer pride might someday be yer undoing?"

"Killian's departure has naught to do with my pride!" Ruarc's frustration blazed into anger. "She couldn't know about that. She never gave me a chance to teach her aught about me."

"Aye, that may well be true. But yer pride will yet be yer undoing if it keeps ye from going after her."

Ruarc made a sound of disgust. "The ungrateful wench went back to Adam Campbell. Do ye wish me to risk my life yet again riding into that lion's den, and all for a woman who must surely despise me? I think not, Father."

"I'm not so certain she went back to Adam." The priest frowned and scratched his beard. "What sense would that have made? Ye told me she killed her husband to save ye. Then she not only refused to slit yer throat at Adam's insistence, but helped ye escape Achallader. Do ye seriously imagine she thinks Adam would welcome her back?"

A ray of hope pierced Ruarc's heart. "Mayhap not. *He* might, though, if he thought in the doing he could lure me into a trap."

"Aye, I suppose he might, but would the lass take such a risk? Nay—" Father Kenneth shook his head firmly— "rather, I think she means to take her son and hie herself back to the Colonies. She all but told me one day she longed to return to her home there."

"But that's daft. She'd need money, supplies, and aid finding her way to the nearest seaport."

"Yer lady's hardly the helpless kind. I'd wager she found some way to procure all those things."

"Aye." Ruarc's anger swelled anew. "And I'll wager Glynnis was most happily involved in helping Killian do so. I may yet have to wring the truth from that despicable woman."

"Och, Glynnis won't tell ye the truth. She'll but send ye off in the opposite direction."

"The closest seaport is on Loch Linnhe." Swiftly, Ruarc sorted through all the options. "But to reach it, Killian would have to ride back into Campbell lands. Would she risk that, do ye think?"

Father Kenneth pursed his lips in thought. "It'd seem likely. The route is straightforward and can be reached with a good day's hard travel." He paused to eye him. "Will ye go after her then?"

The priest's question drew Ruarc up short. *Would* he go after her? He suddenly didn't know. "Whether Killian chose to return to Adam or the Colonies, what would be the point of going after her?

Either way, she doesn't wish to stay with me. Would ye have me drag her back kicking and screaming?"

"Nay, I wouldn't have ye abuse the lass in any way. But think on this, lad." The cleric laid his hand on Ruarc's arm. "She needs ye as much as ye need her. Like ye, though, she just doesn't realize it yet."

"And how do you expect me to apprise her of that fact? I can't say I even believe it myself!"

"Rather, I'd say ye're afraid to believe it." The priest's grip tightened on Ruarc's arm. He stepped close to gaze up at him with a fierce intensity. "Afraid, deathly afraid, to let yerself hope there's yet a woman who'll love ye as ye've always wished to be loved. It's that fear that throws up the barriers between ye and the lass. That, and yer overweening pride."

"It isn't pride making me hesitate to ride into what yet may be a trap!" Though he knew Father Kenneth meant well, Ruarc was getting mightily weary of the endless harping about his pride. "Have ye already forgotten Glynnis most likely had a hand in Killian's escape? Why, to see me dead, I wouldn't put it past her to enlist Adam Campbell's aid in this."

Father Kenneth appeared to consider that for a moment, then sighed. "Aye, this may well be more complicated than what first meets the eye."

"Yet ye still think I should go after her? Ye still think there's hope she might willingly come back with me?"

"Aye, I do. Go to her. Open yer heart to her. Ye may well be surprised at what ye find."

Open his heart to her? Even the slightest consideration of baring his emotions to this mysteriously compelling woman terrified him. Father Kenneth could never fully understand what it was like to love and trust someone, then have all one's illusions ripped asunder to discover you had always been naught more than a love-besotted, misguided fool.

"Sheila never loved me, ye know," Ruarc whispered, looking away.

"She loved ye, lad, as best she could. She but loved Adam better."

He gave a short, sharp bark of laughter. "Well, I never liked being second-best."

"Ye've never liked being wrong, either. Sadly, few men do, especially when it comes to things of the heart. Have ye the courage it may require, though, to fight on until ye attain what ye so avidly seek? Have ye, lad?"

If only he knew for certain Killian was the one true love he had always sought. But he didn't. There was no surety even in that, and Ruarc had always been a man who liked surety. He might well risk his life to bring back a woman who'd never thank him, much less love him. It seemed a foolhardy gamble.

Ruarc exhaled a deep breath. "I've the courage, if the cause is sufficient. I'm just not convinced it is." With that, he turned and stalked from the chapel.

†

KILLIAN peered from her hiding place behind a mass of bracken and ferns. She and Gavin had been here now over three hours, watching and hoping the men would finally give up and leave. They were Campbells, no doubt about it, from the clan plant badges of bog myrtle they wore in their bonnets to their occasional comments as they sat guard on the tree-covered bluff overlooking the road.

Thank the Lord, Gavin had insisted on relieving himself when he had. And, thank the Lord, they had ventured far enough from the main road to halt before a small burn flowing through the forest. The sound of the chuckling stream and the thick stand of trees provided sufficient cover. The Campbell band passed without seeing or hearing them, before turning off the road to hide and wait.

It was obvious they expected someone. Killian left Gavin behind with their horse and carefully made her way closer in hope of overhearing the men. And overhear them she did. They had been sent to waylay her and Ruarc MacDonald as well, when he came after her. Their orders, however, appeared none too specific about taking Ruarc alive or not.

Fury surged through Killian as she made her stealthy way back to Gavin and their horse. Someone knew of her intent to travel this road. Someone also had guessed Ruarc might follow and try to bring her back. Though she couldn't be sure of her ultimate fate in being captured, she was very certain where Ruarc would be taken and what would happen to him.

Glynnis had surely betrayed her—and Ruarc MacDonald—to Adam Campbell. For a long moment, bewilderment at the woman's motives—a woman Killian had thought was her only real friend in Rannoch Castle, all but immobilized her. Then the grim reality of the situation flooded her.

As angry and frustrated as it made her to have to do it, she had no choice but to retrace her steps and try to warn Ruarc of the trap. She already had Alexander's blood on her hands. She'd not knowingly add another's, no matter how badly Killian resented what she must now do.

It'd be just her luck, though, that Ruarc wasn't even on the way to rescue her, and her sacrifice would be in vain. More likely he had discovered her disappearance and decided he was well rid of her. More likely he was still holed up safely in Rannoch, with no intention of leaving it for the likes of her.

"Come along, Gavin," Killian whispered when she finally reached her son. "Those bad men up ahead don't seem to be leaving, so we're going to sneak away. We've got to be very quiet, though, so they don't hear us. You can be very, very quiet, can't you?"

His eyes grew wide. His head bobbed. "Yes, Mama. I won't make a sound."

She gave him a quick kiss on the cheek, then lifted him to the horse's back. "Hold on tightly now, all right?" With that Killian untied the horse's reins and began cautiously to lead the animal back through the forest in the direction they had first come.

For the next hour they skirted the road, making their way through thick underbrush and trees. The going was slow, but Killian didn't dare risk being seen or overheard. Besides, she wasn't certain how wide and far a vantage the bluff provided the Highlanders. Finally, she felt it safe to return to the main road. Remounting behind Gavin, she urged her horse to a slow canter.

The sun began to dip behind them, toward the great knuckle that was Bidean nam Bian, the Pinnacle of Peaks. Annoyance filled her. She had wasted the lead she had gained, a lead that would've taken them all the way to Loch Linnhe by nightfall.

She had Glynnis to thank for that. Glynnis, who had managed, in her self-serving conniving most likely to destroy Killian's last hope of returning to Virginia.

It seemed that as hard as she tried to avoid it, her life repeatedly swung, like the arrow of a compass, back to intersect with that of Ruarc MacDonald's. Killian didn't understand it. She was convinced neither of them really wished it to be so, yet the constant entwining of their lives was fast becoming fact nonetheless.

The thought, however, was far from comforting. Indeed, it deeply disturbed and frightened her. She didn't belong here with him, any more than she belonged anywhere else.

Still, Killian refused to let the twisted circumstances that had, of late, become her life defeat her. Somehow, she'd find a way through it all. She had survived Alexander. She would survive Ruarc MacDonald, too.

Sunset gradually gilded the land in an intricate melding of muted colors. Lost in her morose thoughts, Killian rode on. Too late came the warning that they were no longer alone.

A guttural snarl, a cacophony of snapping twigs as feet pounded through the bracken, and then hands were reaching out seemingly from everywhere. Grabbing at her horse's head. Capturing her hands. Tearing at her cloak and legs.

"Mama!" Gavin shrieked in terror.

With an anguished cry, Killian pulled back on the reins, trying frantically to spin the animal around and urge it through the throng of unkempt, wild-eyed men groping at her, trying to pull her down. The frenzied beast half reared, lashing out at one man foolish enough to stand too close. He screamed once, then fell.

Killian kicked hard at another ruffian who had taken hold of her leg and was hanging on with all his might, trying to unseat her. Her knee connected with his face, breaking his nose. As blood spurted everywhere, he grunted in pain. Still, though his knees buckled and he fell, he continued to grip her leg.

She was no match for his greater weight. Killian lost her balance and tumbled sideways off her horse. At the last minute, she released her hold on Gavin, leaving him still in the saddle.

Three more men were on her before she could even struggle to her knees. A brawny arm slipped about her waist, dragging her to her feet. Her hands were pinned at her sides.

"Look, will ye, Walter, what a prize we've gone and caught fer ourselves?" the bearded, hook-nosed Scotsman holding her shouted. "If I dinna miss my guess, we've got us here a verra fine lady."

"Nay, ye must be dreamin', Georgie," another man behind Killian cried. "No fine lady'd be out alone at this time o' day, or any day fer that matter."

"Then what's all this gold doin' in her satchel?" Yet another man held aloft a handful of coins. With his free hand, he now controlled Killian's horse and the terrified little boy still seated upon it.

"Unless the lassie's gone and robbed some rich man, I'd say Georgie's called this one true."

"Well, be that as it may, this eve we've struck it rich in more ways than one." Georgie's hot, tainted breath wafted across Killian's cheek. "Come along, lassie," he said, dragging her toward the trees from whence the men had first come. "Be a good girl, and we promise not to hurt ye. "Or leastwise," he added with a lewd chuckle, "we willna hurt ye more than ye can bear."

Panic swept through Killian. These weren't Campbell men backtracking to find her. These were some band of outlaws, roaming the land for unsuspecting travelers. She'd be lucky to escape with her life.

"Let me go, I say!" She kicked out, twisting in his grip, struggling to break free. "Ruarc MacDonald will kill you all if I come to any harm!"

"Och, and will he now?" Georgie grabbed her face and pulled it around to his. "Then why are ye all alone wi' all this money?" The sight of his scarred, feral face chilled Killian to the bone. "Rather, I'd wager ye're one of MacDonald's servin' women runnin' off wi' his money. Money ye can now share wi' us, canna ye?"

With a painful rotation of her arm, Killian jerked a hand free and struck him full across the face. "You big oaf! You won't have me *or* my money!"

To add further emphasis to her pronouncement, she stomped down hard on his soft-shoed instep.

Roaring in pain, Georgie momentarily let her go. Killian dashed to where her horse stood, pulled Gavin down, and ran. She had barely taken five steps, however, when fingers snagged in her hair and cruelly wrenched her backward.

"Not so fast wi' ye." Walter slammed her hard to him. He jerked Gavin from her and flung him to the ground.

"Take the lad, Robbie, tie him to some tree, and bind his eyes so he canna see. No sense in the lad knowing what we mean to do to his—"

Robbie never had a chance to touch Gavin. Snarling like some hound from hell, a sleek, gray animal streaked from the trees across the road and launched itself at Robbie, knocking him to the ground. Then, as man and dog writhed in a horrendous melee, a pistol exploded. Georgie cried out then fell, a blackened hole in the middle of his forehead.

As the man with the broken nose climbed to his feet, Walter, clasping Killian before him as a shield, spun about in the direction of the pistol blast. Even as he did, Ruarc strode from the trees, tossed his spent pistol aside, and unsheathed his basket-hilted sword.

Walter made a gurgling sound of terror. He thrust Killian at Ruarc and sprinted for the trees, his compatriot following swiftly on his heels.

Moving Killian out of the way, Ruarc watched the two men for the space of a deep breath, then sheathed his sword and pulled yet another pistol from the back of his belt. Ever so calmly, he took aim.

"No! Don't!" Killian slapped at his hand.

The shot missed. With a scowl, Ruarc turned on her. "Are ye daft, madam? Those men were about to ravish ye, mayhap even leave ye for dead, and ye just prevented me from punishing them. Now there's yet two more outlaws left free to roam the Highlands!"

"No matter how bad they might be, it isn't right to back shoot them. It isn't . . . isn't honorable."

"And I say it's best to save honor for those deserving of it." Ruarc shoved his pistol back in his belt, then paused to look her up and down. "Did they harm ye in any way?"

Killian touched her scalp where Walter had tugged so roughly on her hair. "A little bruised, I suppose, but not harmed."

She suddenly remembered Gavin. Wheeling about, she looked for her son in the ever-deepening twilight.

Gavin stood not far away, his arms flung around Fionn's neck. The dog's mouth and chest were flecked with red. Nearby lay Robbie's inert and bloodied body.

"Gavin!" Killian ran to her son and gathered him into her arms. "Are you all right? Tell Mama. Are you all right?"

The boy squirmed in her clasp. "Did you see what Fionn did, Mama? He made that man let me go. He really *is* my friend, isn't he?"

Killian's glance strayed to the deerhound, which gazed back at her with calm, liquid eyes. "Yes, I suppose he really is."

She rose, clutching Gavin to her. Her gaze locked with Ruarc MacDonald's glittering one. Her throat went dry, but she forced out the words of explanation she knew she owed him.

"I came back to warn you of the Campbells awaiting you down the road. They meant to capture you or kill you if you resisted."

"Indeed, madam?" he replied silkily, his expression shuttered. "And here I was thinking ye'd turned back because ye regretted yer decision to leave me."

"Mama," her son protested at that moment, "you're holding too tight. Let me down. I want to play with Fionn."

Killian did as Gavin asked. Then she straightened. "I didn't turn back because I wanted to. I came back because I feared for your life if you came after me."

Ruarc drew in a ragged breath, then released it. "Well, if for naught else, I commend ye for yer honesty."

There was something heart-wrenching in the way he said those words. "I didn't leave to hurt you. I just don't belong here, and never will."

His mouth tightened. "Well, mayhap ye're right, but this isn't the proper time or place to discuss that. We daren't linger here. Those men ye allowed to go free might, even now, be seeking out others of their ilk. And the Campbells may have finally realized they've been thwarted and soon head out in this direction, searching for the both of us."

"Then I suggest you return to Rannoch." Killian lifted her chin defiantly. "Now that I know you'll be safe, I can continue on my journey."

"Where? To the seaport?" Ruarc laughed. "Are ye daft, woman?" He glanced about him. "And on what? Yer horse is gone. With it, I'd wager, went all of yer supplies and money."

Horror filled her. Frantically, Killian scanned the area. Her horse had disappeared, most likely bolting when Ruarc fired his pistol. Her hopes plummeted. Where indeed could she go without a horse and money?

"It doesn't matter." Killian blinked back tears of frustration. She stepped out toward Gavin, who sat there still hugging Fionn. "We'll find some way to get back home. I won't let this stop me."

"Well, if ye haven't the sense to see how foolish ye are, I do, and *I'll* stop ye." Ruarc moved to block her way.

Killian tried to dodge him, but to no avail. Unencumbered by a long cloak and skirts, Ruarc was far too agile for her. Finally, in exasperation, she struck out at him, hitting Ruarc squarely on the chest.

"Get out of my way, you big oaf! I didn't let those other men stop me, and I won't let you, either!"

Behind them Fionn growled, but didn't move.

"Lass, ye aren't thinking clearly." Ruarc took her hands and held them at her sides. "Do ye despise me so deeply ye'd risk yer and yer wee son's life, rather than come back with me to Rannoch?" When she said nothing and averted her gaze, Ruarc pressed her yet again. "Well, do ye?"

She clamped shut her eyes and shook her head. "I don't despise you, but this agreement of ours is a farce, and well you know it. And I'm just . . . just so tired of fighting everyone. I just . . . just want to g-go home!"

With that, Killian broke into tears. She tried to pull away, but he wouldn't release his hold. "Pl-please. I don't m-mean to be cruel to you, or t-to anyone, but I don't b-belong here. I just d-don't belong!"

Uttering a low groan, Ruarc pulled her to him. Though she resisted, stiffening her body, he didn't seem to care. And bit by bit the warmth of him, the sense of sanctuary she discovered in his arms, began to soothe her. Killian pressed into Ruarc; her hands lifted to clutch at the thick wool of his plaid, and she cried until she could cry no more.

"Come back to Rannoch with me, lass," Ruarc said at last. "Give us a wee bit more time to see if we can work things out. Then, if we can't, I give ye my word I'll personally see ye on a ship bound for the Colonies."

Overwhelmed by all that had transpired today, for a long moment Killian wasn't certain she fully understood him. Then, as the meaning of his words filtered through her exhausted mind, she reared back to search his face. Ruarc gazed down at her, a solemn look in his green eyes.

"Truly?" she whispered. "You'll let me go home?"

"If it comes to that, aye, I will."

"You know, you needn't go to so much trouble. We haven't married. You're free to wed someone better suited for you."

"I'd like to see first if we aren't well suited ourselves." He managed a wan smile. "If we're both truthful, I'd wager we'd admit we haven't tried verra hard to discern that."

Killian nodded in reluctant agreement. "I know I haven't. I wasn't particularly flattered that all you seemed to want me for is a broodmare."

He inhaled a deep breath, then expelled it slowly. "I hid behind that excuse. It seemed far safer than risking yer rejection."

She searched his face. There was no guile here, no false bravado masking truth. For the first time since Killian had met him, Ruarc had stripped away all the shields, offering her a simple honesty that bared his heart.

Alexander had never wanted children. From the start he had always seen Gavin as a competitor for Killian's affection. But even in the short time she had been at Rannoch, she had seen Ruarc's natural affinity for children. Already, he and Gavin were fast friends.

A surprising joy welled in her breast. A part of the wall about her heart crumbled. Perhaps, just perhaps, she *could* make a family with him. Killian touched his face, tracing her fingers along his unshaven jaw. Then her hand fell away. "Come. As you said before, it isn't safe to linger here. We can talk further at Rannoch."

"Aye, that we can." Ruarc turned then to Gavin and his dog. "Stay with Fionn and yer mither, lad, while I fetch my horse. Then we'll have a braw ride back to Rannoch."

The boy grinned up at him. "That'll be fun. Yes, it will."

Killian watched Ruarc stride off to retrieve his horse from its hiding place in the trees, a crazed mix of emotions roiling within her. Was she a fool to agree to return to Rannoch, and a greater fool still to hope they could finally work out their differences? Yet when Ruarc had held her to him but a few minutes ago, she had almost begun to believe they just might. Was she but allowing her unsettling physical attraction, her heart-deep need for love and family, to take hold yet again and sway her?

There were just so many unanswered questions, and she was too weary to sort through them this day. Indeed, she didn't need to. Ruarc MacDonald had given her his word. He'd die rather than forswear it.

Ruarc walked from the trees with his horse. The sun's fading rays touched his face, bathing it in light. For a fleeting instant, his features were wrought with a savage beauty. Then the sun dipped below the mountains. Shadow shrouded him.

"Come, Gavin." Killian turned to her son. "It's time to leave."

The boy pushed to his feet, paused to pet the big deerhound once more on the head, then joined her. "We're going home then, Mama?"

Home.

The word pierced clear through to her heart. "Maybe, Gavin," Killian said, turning the thought over and over in her mind. "Maybe we finally are."

11

KILLIAN awoke with a start. For a disoriented instant, she couldn't fathom where she was. Then the faint wash of dawn on the horizon, the cool breeze wafting across her cheek, and the swaying movement of a horse brought it all back.

She and Gavin were with Ruarc MacDonald. They were returning to Rannoch Castle. At the belated realization that all her fine plans to sail for Virginia had come to naught, an aching sadness filled her. Yet what choice had she, once she had discovered those Campbells waiting on the road?

Perhaps they had only been waiting for her, but Killian knew she couldn't take the chance she might be wrong. Perhaps she should've gone some other way and let fate run its course when it came to Ruarc MacDonald. Killian wished she could have, but she couldn't.

She rubbed her face against the rough wool of Ruarc's plaid and sighed. He had been silent for most of the trip, never demanding an explanation or berating her even though he had every right to do so. Killian was grateful for that. Her head was in such a muddle, she wouldn't have known how to respond.

Right now, all she wanted was to lay her head on Ruarc's chest, hide in the warm sanctuary of his arms, and listen to the reassuring beat of his heart. There she could forget, if only for a short while, all the contradictions and questions, all the uncertainties and fears. And maybe, just maybe, when she finally came back into the light, everything would be as it should be.

"Ye slept for a long while." Ruarc's voice rumbled pleasantly against her ear. "Ye must have been exhausted."

Killian leaned back to stare up into his face. Shadows smudged beneath his eyes. His face was beard-stubbled, and deep lines of weariness and strain etched his features.

Remorse filled her. While she had selfishly taken her fill of sleep, Ruarc had ridden on all night. "I was no more tired than you," she said. "I wish I was strong enough to have held you on your horse while you slept. It would've been only fair."

Ruarc chuckled softly. "Och, dinna fash yerself, madam. I've endured far worse than a wee night ride many a time. I'll be all right."

Killian frowned, opened her mouth to speak, then thought better of it.

"Whatever is the matter now?" he was quick to inquire, obviously having noticed her sudden change of mood. "Spit it out and be done with it. Ye're hardly of a temperament to let things fester at any rate."

"Why do you persist in calling me 'madam,' rather than my given name?" she blurted at last. "Do you know how that makes me feel? Do you?"

He eyed her quizzically. "Nay, I don't, but I'm willing to hear what ye think about it."

"Well, it makes me feel like . . . like some old warhorse. It distances you from me, and it isn't at all warm or friendly."

"Ye don't use my given name, either, ye know." As if in deep thought, Ruarc tilted his head. "Correct me if I'm wrong, but I believe all I've ever heard ye address me as is 'm'lord.'"

She expelled an exasperated breath. "True enough. I just never thought you wished me to call you anything more. You *can* get a bit stuffy and off-putting at times, you know."

"I've learned not to allow many to get too close to me. And, though ye may call me stuffy and off-putting, I prefer to think of myself as formal."

There she went again, leaping to the offense and angering him for what was really but a minor matter. "Well, perhaps I was being a bit harsh there. I've been told I do that to cover what I truly mean to say."

"And what do ye truly mean to say, then, lass?"

She grinned. "Just that. I like *lass* ever so much better than *madam*. And could you please call me Killian, too, from time to time?"

A smile twitched at the corner of the big Highlander's mouth. "Agreed, but only if ye call me Ruarc or sometimes even *my braw, bonny lord.*"

For the longest moment, Killian wasn't sure if Ruarc was serious or teasing her. Then, as he suddenly grinned like some impish lad, she had her answer. She laughed. "Why, miracle of miracles! You really *do* have a lighthearted streak after all, don't you?"

Ruarc shrugged. "I suppose I do. It's just a wee rusty from disuse." Killian eyed him. "That's sad, you know. Very sad."

"Be that as it may, that's the way it's been for a long while now."

"Since Sheila died?"

A look of pain flashed across his features, then was gone. "Aye, since Sheila died and even before. The last year or two of her life weren't all that pleasant for either of us."

She wanted to ask him why that was so but didn't feel the time was right. Someday, though, *if* she decided to stay, she meant to know. There was more than just Sheila's side to this tale. And Killian was beginning to suspect Ruarc wasn't the complete brute Glynnis painted him to be.

Still, there was that incident with Ewen MacPhail . . . at the recollection of the man's vicious flogging, Killian shuddered. Taking care not to disturb Gavin, who slumbered in her arms, she twisted back around to look at Ruarc. "May I ask a question about something you did that really disturbed me? And will you promise not to get angry about it?"

He arched a dark brow. "Ye set some verra stringent requirements before I even know the question. I can't say I find that particularly fair."

"It's something you did that frightened me. It helped seal my decision to leave you."

Ruarc pulled her close, his lips moving to her ear. "Then I give ye my word I won't get angry with ye," he said huskily. "Whatever it was, I wish ye'd come to me and asked me about it. I wouldn't intentionally frighten ye. Leastwise, not if I could help it."

The feel of his warm breath against her ear sent a tremor through Killian. Instead of pulling away, though, as she might have done days earlier, she leaned against him. He felt solid, reassuring, and finally, blessedly, safe.

"Why did you whip that poor man so viciously? What could he have possibly done to warrant such brutal treatment?"

"Whip what man?" Bewilderment roughened Ruarc's voice. "Och, do ye mean Ewen MacPhail? Is that who ye're talking about?"

"Of course. Who else would it be?" She reared back to look up at him. "Or have there been others since him who I'm not aware of?"

His mouth twisted. "Nay, I don't think so. I'm not in the habit of beating my clansmen, no matter what ye may have been led to believe. Ewen, though, performed a foul, brutal act upon a wee lass. He caught her one day on the moor, dragged her off to a place where no one could hear her, and viciously and repeatedly ravished her. Then, to finish the deed, he strangled her.

"Wee Mary was but thirteen. There were witnesses to the act, though—two children who hid in fear—not to mention a bag of tools belonging to Ewen that were found near Mary's body."

Ruarc's voice hardened. "The man was fortunate to have received but a whipping from me. I was sorely tempted to strangle him on the spot, just as he had done wee Mary. But that would've been far too kind for the likes of him. Better he languish in some foul jail for months on end than be tried and finally hanged. Better he have time to regret what he did and regret it over and over and over."

"I . . . I didn't know," Killian said. "I thought the man had but displeased you, and you were—"

"Overhard and cruel, as Glynnis would have ye believe? I saw ye both walk away that day. I knew she was filling yer mind with all sorts of lies about me."

"Then why didn't you find me later and explain?" she cried in anguish. "Why did you let me go on thinking the worst about you?"

"Ye'd only to ask me, lass." Ruarc sighed. "If ye'd truly cared to know the truth, ye could've come to me and asked. But I think yer mind was already made. I think ye were but looking for yet another excuse to justify leaving me."

It was true. She *had* been looking for every excuse she could find to warrant returning to Virginia. Glynnis hadn't had to do much to poison Killian's mind against Ruarc.

"I didn't want to like you." She laid her head on his shoulder and closed her eyes. "I fought in every way I could to find fault in you, to see you as just some other brute like my poor Alexander had been. Yet the harder that became to do, the harder I fought. In many ways, I fight it still."

When Ruarc didn't reply, Killian feared she had said too much, perhaps even forced him into the uncomfortable position of having to admit similar feelings he didn't feel. "It's all right, you know," she hurried to explain. "You don't have to say anything. I just wanted you to understand, if even only a little. . . ."

Ruarc groaned suddenly from behind her. "Och, lass. I understand more than ye may think. Ye're not the only one who finds all this difficult. After Sheila died, I swore I'd never again give my heart to another. Indeed, a part of me was almost glad that if I wed ye, I'd do so cold-bloodedly. I thought if I could keep the marriage strictly a business proposition . . ." He sighed and shook his head. "That wasn't fair to ye, though, nor to me, either."

"Are you saying, then, you wish to cancel our marriage plans?" Strange that now, when it seemed like it might all be over, Killian was no longer certain she wanted it so. "After what I've put you through, I can't say I'd blame you."

"Is that what ye'd wish?"

She expelled a long, thoughtful breath. "No, leastwise not yet. You asked for a time more to see if we could work things out between us. The more I think about it, the more I'd truly like to have that time."

Once again, Ruarc went silent. Killian waited, willing to give him all the time he needed. Both of them had come to the agreement under compulsion. She refused, however, to remain in it that way.

Gradually, the sun's rays fingered across the land, stroking it with a gentle hand. Light gilded the autumn-browned grass and trees, bathing them in a glorious radiance. Birds chirped their bright songs, and the horse's measured cadence on the dirt road only added to a sense of life's predictable, precious pattern. A life that would, surprisingly, seem a little less complete now if Ruarc MacDonald chose to leave it.

"Ye'll have that time, lass," he, of a sudden, spoke up. "Do ye wish to set yet another deadline as to when we must make up our minds?"

"No." Killian shook her head with a firm resolve. "I think we'll know, one way or another, soon enough, don't you?"

"Aye, I suppose so," Ruarc agreed softly, a smile once again brightening his features. "I suppose so."

†

TWO HOURS later, Killian watched as Ruarc gave instructions to the stableboy holding his horse. Then, as the lad led the animal away, he turned to Father Kenneth. "I want to see Glynnis and Thomas in the library. Would ye have Davie send one of his men to fetch them one by one, then ask a servant to bring a flagon of claret and some goblets to the library?"

The priest arched a shaggy brow. "And what do ye mean to do, lad? Ye won't be extracting confessions from those two, no matter how hard ye press."

"Mayhap not." Rannoch's laird shrugged. "It doesn't matter if they confess or not. It's enough I know they played no small part in all this. Didn't they, lass?"

Suddenly, two pairs of eyes riveted on her. Killian's heartbeat faltered, then resumed at an increasingly faster rate. "I-I don't recall us discussing that," she said, frantically casting about for some way to avoid giving Ruarc the answer he sought.

Though she was furious with Glynnis, Killian didn't care to be responsible for the woman's banishment from Rannoch. And some sixth sense warned her that was exactly what Ruarc meant to do.

"Nay, we didn't discuss it," he admitted, "but unless ye sent some sort of correspondence to Adam Campbell, who else would've contacted him but Glynnis? Who else stood to profit from my recapture by the Campbells?"

Adam and Glynnis in league against Ruarc. The consideration was too horrible to consider, but the evidence against them was all but incontrovertible. And what did she really know about Ruarc's stepmother? How much of anything the woman had ever told her was truth, and how much was lies?

"I give you my word I haven't contacted Adam since I've come to Rannoch," she said, lifting her gaze to Ruarc's. "What possible purpose would it serve me to return to him? If he ever found out what really happened that night I ran away . . ."

She didn't need to say more. The look in Ruarc's eyes told her he understood.

"Still, though Glynnis *did* help me leave Rannoch," Killian then continued, "that doesn't mean someone else might not have overheard our plans and informed Adam. It *is* possible, isn't it, another besides Glynnis might well be in league with Adam?"

"Aught is possible, but Glynnis and that prissy son of hers are the most likely suspects." He paused to eye her closely. "Why are ye defending her? Ye all but rode into a trap yerself. Then, when ye turned back because of that trap, ye were set upon and nearly ravished by outlaws."

"I hardly think Glynnis planned for that to happen."

"Truly, madam, whose side are ye on?" Ruarc, evidently at the end of his patience, glared at her. "I'd begun to hope ye were on mine but now, once again, I wonder."

Killian glared back at him. "There you go again."

He frowned in puzzlement. "Whatever do ye mean, 'there I go again'?"

"What else? Calling me madam!"

"Calling ye . . ." He stopped, then scowled at her. "By mountain and sea! We've more important things to discuss here than how I address ye!"

"Indeed we do, but I've found when you begin addressing me as madam, you tend to cease giving me credence. So I thought it best to put a stop to that right now."

He stared down at her in speechless amazement. Finally, however, Ruarc managed to find his tongue. "Well then, *Killian,* I ask again. Whose side are ye on?"

"I'm on your side, of course. Why else would I have come back to warn you like I did? But there's more than enough hurt feelings and misunderstanding in this castle to keep everyone at everyone's throats for years to come. I can't say I relish the thought of getting in the middle of it."

"Well, ye *are* in the middle. I cannot help it if Glynnis insists on using ye to get to me."

"Still, lad," Father Kenneth chose that moment to interject, "we're called to love everyone, and part of that loving is a willingness to forgive. Don't ye think Glynnis is needful of yer love, even after what she tried to do?"

"I never gave it much thought. And I can't say, at this particular moment, I want to, either."

"Nay, I'd imagine ye don't, lad." The priest sighed. "But ye must someday, ye know."

Ruarc gave a harsh laugh. "Aye, mayhap someday. But not now, and not anytime soon."

†

GLYNNIS couldn't believe the sight that greeted her as she glanced out her bedchamber window that morning. It was more like some nightmare than reality. If the sting of the cold, stone floor on her bare feet and the chill breeze seeping through a chink near the window hadn't reminded her she was uncomfortably awake, she might have hoped this was indeed some terrible dream.

But it wasn't, and the horror of her plight increased with each moment she stared down at Killian and Ruarc, standing outside Rannoch speaking with Father Kenneth. Obviously, the plan to entrap Ruarc had failed. Killian had returned. With her returned the truth of Glynnis's involvement in her escape. She could only hope the young Colonial had been forced back against her will by her stepson and hadn't told Ruarc anything.

But if she *had* come back willingly and *had* talked . . .

Shivers wracked Glynnis's body. If Killian had told Ruarc everything, Glynnis feared what would happen next. As it was, Rannoch's laird bore her little affection. He well knew the sentiment was returned in kind. Most likely he had been but awaiting the perfect excuse to banish both her and Thomas. At long last, she may have inadvertently given it to him.

"Finola." Glynnis waved the maidservant over. "Help me dress and make it quick. Then fetch Thomas. I must speak with him posthaste."

The girl immediately set to work, all the while babbling about all sorts of things until Glynnis wanted to scream.

"Hush, will ye?" she cried at last. "I cannot think with all yer chattering."

"As ye wish, m'lady." Her servant's mouth flattened.

"That one will do." As Finola finished fastening the bustle in place over her petticoats, Glynnis indicated a burgundy wool gown trimmed with lace. "This morn I must look my finest."

Aye, she did indeed need every bit of confidence a grand appearance could muster this morn. There was no turning back now from the course she had embarked upon when she had agreed to this fatally flawed plot. Problem was, though Adam Campbell might find his desire to avenge himself on Ruarc MacDonald thwarted yet again, she'd be the one to pay the price. While he sat safe and sound in Achallader, she must soon walk into the lion's den.

Best to present a concerned but innocent front. Best to deny knowledge or involvement in the trap Adam had set. Her only motive must be Killian's welfare and a need to help her in her misery. Besides, Killian *had* been miserable and afraid. Best to remind her of that and, in the doing, hopefully win the young Colonial again to her side.

Finola was soon done and hastening from the bedchamber to fetch Thomas. Glynnis spent the ensuing minutes pacing the room, mentally countering every possible accusation Ruarc might toss her way. At long last, the door reopened and footsteps sounded on the stone floor.

"Och, at last ye've come, Thomas." Glynnis wheeled about to face her son. To her dismay, only Finola stood there.

"M-m'lady." The girl's face was white. "I-I couldn't fetch him as ye asked. Even as I neared his door, a guard came up and informed Thomas his immediate presence was desired in the library."

Glynnis stared in shock. Then, with a determined lift of her chin, she gathered her skirts and headed for the door. "This sounds verra serious," she said. "I must see what the problem is."

As Glynnis hurried from her room, her hands clenched in frustration. With each passing moment, her and Thomas's plight worsened. And now, to make matters even more disconcerting, they were being kept apart so Ruarc could likely question them separately.

Please, Lord Jesus, she silently prayed, lifting a fervent entreaty to a deity she seldom thought of nowadays. *Calm my son's mind and guide his tongue. Don't let him say aught that'll later contradict what I may say.*

And, please, please protect us from Ruarc's wrath, or everything will surely be lost.

12

RUARC waited quietly as Thomas entered the library. His half brother was wary and frightened. More the better. Thomas had never been able to hide his emotions well. He wasn't doing so today, either.

"Come, Thomas." Ruarc indicated the long table, whereupon was set some cups and a flagon of claret. "Share a toast with me on this fine October morn."

His half brother hesitated, suspicion now gleaming in his eyes. Then, as if deciding he required the liquid courage more than he needed to proceed cautiously, Thomas strode over and took up the fine, pewter goblet Ruarc had just finished pouring for him.

"To yer health, brother dear," the younger man said, lifting his cup in a salute that was half bravado and half defiance.

"And to yers," Ruarc replied quietly.

From the corner of his eye as he sipped his claret, Ruarc saw Killian watching them. There was a certain taut expectation in her, a wary dread, as if she feared some physical outburst on one or the other of their parts.

But then, he couldn't really blame her. She didn't yet know him all that well. She didn't realize this wasn't the sort of situation requiring violence. All it demanded was a cold, careful attention to detail.

"So, brother," Ruarc said as he finally lowered his cup, "what can ye tell me about yer involvement with Killian's sudden and unexplained departure from Rannoch yestreen?" Noting that

Thomas had drained his goblet, Ruarc took up the flagon and carefully refilled it. "What did ye hope to accomplish in aiding her?"

Thomas's eyes widened. The hand clasping his cup began to shake so violently some of the sweet liquor sloshed over its sides. "I . . . I don't know what ye're talking about." His glance swung to Killian, frantically searching her face for any hint as to what she had told Ruarc, and how to respond.

Ruarc shot a quelling look at her over his shoulder.

She glared back. "Stop tormenting him, will you?" She turned to Thomas. "I told Ruarc about you and Glynnis. He knows how you both helped me in my attempt to leave."

"Ye . . . ye told him?" The young man's jaw worked furiously. "But . . . but why? Are ye daft, woman? Now ye've gone and ruined everything! Everything!"

"Have a civil tongue when ye speak to the lady, Thomas," Ruarc warned. "Besides, there's no need to dither here. It won't do ye any good at any rate. The damage has been done. Best ye own up to it like a man, *if* ye think ye can muster the courage."

Thomas paled, opened his mouth to speak, then clamped it shut again.

Just then the library door opened. Despite the guard's efforts to keep her from entering, Glynnis slipped in around him. Her sharp, assessing glance quickly took in the situation. "Ye summoned me, m'lord?" She drew to a halt before him.

Ruarc's mouth twisted wryly. "Aye, that I did, but ye were to wait outside until ye were called, madam."

"And what purpose would that serve, m'lord? Best we get to the problem and work it through before it has time to sour."

"It'd serve *my* purpose, madam, and that's all that matters. Leastwise, as long as I'm still laird of Rannoch." He smiled thinly. "But stay. I already know all I need to know at any rate."

It was Glynnis's turn to look first to Thomas, then to Killian. This time, however, Killian said nothing, returning the other woman's questioning look with a shuttered one of her own.

"Killian claims she told Ruarc we helped her to leave Rannoch," Thomas spoke up just then in an apparent effort to warn his mother.

"Well, that's true enough." Once more she faced Ruarc, her chin lifted, her hands fisted at her sides. "The poor lass was beside herself with fear of ye, terrified she might become the next victim of yer uncontrollable rages. Who wouldn't have been willing to help her?"

"The same person, mayhap, who first filled Killian's mind with false tales about me?" His gaze hardening, Ruarc studied her. "Och, ye don't fool me, Glynnis. I'm well aware how wonderfully aiding Killian's escape served yer plans."

For a long moment his stepmother glared up at him, her animosity a searing, virulent force. Then she turned back to Killian. "Ye know I only did it because I cared about ye, didn't ye, m'lady?" she asked softly. "Ye, yer happiness, were all that mattered to me."

"Perhaps it was, Glynnis," Killian replied, "but that ambush set to capture Ruarc seemed to have been so well timed to coincide with my journey that I have to wonder if you didn't also have a hand in that, too." She paused to eye her closely. "Did you, Glynnis? Have a hand in planning that ambush?"

Puzzlement furrowed the older woman's brow. "An ambush? Whatever are ye talking about, m'lady? I know naught of such a thing."

"A-aye," Thomas chose that moment finally to chime in. "What ambush?"

"Ye're wasting yer time, lass," Ruarc interjected angrily, looking to Killian, "if ye think to get either of them to confess plotting to turn me over to Adam Campbell. It doesn't matter at any rate. I cannot risk traitors at Rannoch. They must be sent away."

"Och, nay!" Glynnis wailed, reaching out to Thomas. He came to her, taking her into his arms. "Nay, ye can't send us from Rannoch! This castle is as much our home as yers. Ye've no right—"

"I've all the right I need." His fury getting the best of him, Ruarc advanced on them. It was past time he put an end to this sorry mess.

"Ye're fortunate I've tolerated ye as long as I have, what with yer petty scheming and backstabbing ways. But, between the strange circumstances surrounding my first capture by Adam and now this second attempt, well, this time, ye've gone too far."

"Ruarc, don't." Killian hurried to take his arm and halt him. "Don't say things you cannot ever take back and may someday regret."

He wheeled about to face her. "Stay out of this, lass. This feud goes back for a long, long while and doesn't concern ye. Indeed, ye're just another of a long series of pawns Glynnis has used to torment and prick at me. Kin or no, I won't have them poisoning what we may someday have, as they poisoned my marriage to Sheila."

"Och, ye blind, misguided fool!" The tone of Glynnis's voice verged now on hysteria. "Ye and Sheila never had a chance, not even from the start, and well ye know it. She never loved ye. Never! All I ever did was try to be a friend to the wee lassie and offer comfort that ye couldn't—and wouldn't—give her."

"Did ye now?" Ever so slowly, Ruarc turned back to face her. All the pain, all the bitter disillusionment, bubbled up again like some acrid bile. "Well, ye've yer view of that, and I've mine. I don't, however, care to hear yer shrill harping again. On the morrow, ye and yer son will be escorted from Rannoch to wherever ye choose to go. And, the good Lord willing, I can only hope ye and I never cross paths again."

†

FOR HOURS afterwards, Killian couldn't forget the expressions on Glynnis's and Thomas's faces as Ruarc pronounced the words of banishment. They looked as if they had been struck some horrendous blow, as if the foundation that was their whole existence had just crumbled beneath them. As it had. All Glynnis's and Thomas's hopes had been entwined with Rannoch.

In the end, though, the decision had to rest with Ruarc. Only he could truly know the extent of their transgressions. Still, the severity of his punishment disturbed her. It presaged a ruthless side of him she didn't care ever again to encounter.

But then, there was so much she had yet to learn about Ruarc MacDonald. This time, though, Killian was determined to know it all. She had to if she was ever to make an informed decision about whether to remain with him or not.

After the meeting in the library and a quickly eaten breakfast, Ruarc declined her urging to take even a few hours' rest. The last of the haying must be finished, he informed her, and they were short several clansmen who had driven the cattle to market earlier this year.

Shaking her head at the proud, headstrong Highlander, Killian watched Ruarc eventually ride off with the other men before turning and reentering the castle.

Finola awaited her just inside the door. "M'lady," the maidservant immediately said, "if ye will, the Lady Glynnis would like verra much to speak with ye."

Killian drew up short. She could well imagine what Glynnis wanted to speak with her about. The woman quite understandably was desperate and most likely thought to implore her assistance with Ruarc. Killian, however, no longer trusted Glynnis. She also didn't care to be seen aligning herself with her in any way.

"Tell your mistress I haven't the time just now. I must see to a bath for Gavin and then one for myself."

"Och, I'd be most happy to bathe the wee lad for ye, m'lady," Finola offered eagerly. "Ye could have yer talk with Lady Glynnis while I do so. Then, when ye're finished, I'd be sure to have yer bath ready for ye, that I would."

Killian gave a sigh and shake of her head. "Finola, your offer is most kind. But the truth is, I don't care to speak with Glynnis just now. Tell her—"

"Lady Glynnis is beside herself, m'lady," the girl cut in, a worried look on her face. "I've never seen her in such a state. I fear . . . I fear if ye don't talk with her, well, I don't know what she might do."

Finola truly did look concerned for Glynnis.

Killian sighed again. "Fine. Tell your mistress I'll come to her in an hour's time. In the meanwhile, considering the arduous events of the past day, I intend to take a short respite for myself. Where did you say she was?"

"I didn't, m'lady, but she's in her bedchamber. I'll go there posthaste and inform the Lady Glynnis of yer plans."

"See that you do." Killian gathered her skirts and, without another word, headed for the stairs.

"M'lady?"

"Yes?" Killian halted and glanced over her shoulder. "What is it?"

"Thank ye, m'lady, for yer kindness to Lady Glynnis. The good Lord will bless ye for it."

Killian shot her a tight smile and turned back to the stairs. She needed more than a blessing, she thought as she ascended the steps leading to her bedchamber. What she really needed was the presence of mind to deal with a woman most likely near hysteria. Indeed, what possible comfort could she offer when she still felt so angry at Glynnis's betrayal? When the hurt was still so fresh?

"We are called to love everyone, and part of that loving is a willingness to forgive."

Unbidden—and most definitely unwanted—Father Kenneth's words to Ruarc earlier this morning seeped into her mind. Killian ground her teeth in frustration. Though the priest's words, for once, were truth, she hated to give them credence. To do so was to admit he might also be right about other things, things about her and Ruarc that, even now, filled her with unease. To do so would also require her to treat Glynnis with a compassion Killian wasn't so certain the woman deserved.

But then, when had following the Lord's will ever been easy? Certainly, not in the last years of her marriage to Alexander, and not in the past days since his death, either. Running from the hard things in life, though, wasn't the answer. She certainly couldn't run from this.

For a time, as Killian set about bathing Gavin, then putting him down for a nap and seeing to her own bath, she managed to banish further thoughts of what to do about Ruarc's stepmother from her mind. Even afterwards, as she settled in one of the chairs before the fire, she imagined she had found a blessed refuge in a hot cup of tea and the Bible Father Kenneth had given her. Her reading, however, soon seemed to draw her inexorably back to the issue at hand.

For some reason, the Bible had fallen open of itself at St. Paul's epistle to the Romans. As she read chapter 12, it didn't take Killian long to be caught up in the eloquent words of that apostle to the Gentiles. All had gifts, Paul had written, though each one differing according to the grace given him. What was Glynnis's special gift? she wondered. If only she could discover it and turn it to Ruarc's advantage . . .

But then, Killian wondered, what was her own gift? It certainly wasn't that of prophecy or ministry. Killian read on, searching now for her own special gift. Was it the gift of mercy, perhaps? Was that what she was meant to teach Ruarc, especially in regard to his own family?

"Recompense to no man evil for evil. . . . Avenge not yourselves. . . . Be not overcome of evil, but overcome evil with good." Killian sighed and, one hand still keeping her place on the page, lay her head back against the chair and shut her eyes.

God's truths were in this book. Sometimes, though, they were very hard to accept, much less fulfill. And Glynnis most likely had tried to set that trap for Ruarc. How could she possibly find some merciful way through this terrible dilemma? A way both merciful for Glynnis and her son, and for Ruarc, too?

"Overcome evil with good . . ."

The mantel clock struck the hour. With an exasperated sound, Killian opened her eyes. It was time to see to Glynnis. She closed the Bible and set it aside.

"Help me, Lord," she muttered as she climbed to her feet. "Help me do Your will and begin by showing Glynnis the mercy You seem to think I should. But, if You would, help me along the way, for I really don't know how to go about this. Especially to not betray Ruarc at the same time."

Though she prayed all the while she walked to Glynnis's bedchamber, still it took Killian a moment standing outside the other woman's door to fortify her resolve. Then, with a firm setting of her shoulders and a resolute lift of her chin, she knocked.

There was a long pause—long enough that Killian began to hope Glynnis wasn't there and the meeting could be put off a while longer—and then the door swung open. Glynnis, with red eyes and swollen face, stood there. At sight of Killian, her gaze widened in surprise. Then she smiled.

"Och, m'lady." She took Killian's hand. "Come in. Come in. I wanted so desperately to talk with ye, but didn't dare hope ye'd come."

Reluctantly, Killian allowed herself to be dragged into the room. It, like its occupant, was in a state of total disarray. The window was flung open; a stiff breeze kept the bed curtains fluttering, and various gowns and petticoats were strewn everywhere. The bed itself, though evidently once made, was wrinkled, with pillows bent and twisted. Several necklaces dangled from various unlikely spots in the room, and one half of a pair of ruby-and-pearl earrings glittered on the stone hearth.

Glynnis, Killian surmised dryly, had indeed been having hysterics.

"Please, if ye will, m'lady," the older woman urged as she closed the door, "have a seat by the hearth. I'll just be a moment while I shut the window." Glynnis hurried to the window and closed it against the sharp breeze.

She joined Killian at the two chairs and small, round table situated before the stone fireplace. After a time nervously smoothing the skirt of her gown and trying to pat her hair into place, Ruarc's stepmother finally settled. She clasped her hands in her lap and earnestly met Killian's inquiring gaze.

"First," Glynnis said, "let me tell ye that, though I thought I was doing the best by ye in helping ye leave Rannoch, I can honestly say I'm verra glad ye returned. I'd imagine ye don't feel all that kindly toward me just now, but I truly mean that."

That was most definitely an understatement of the facts, but Killian knew she couldn't say that. *"Overcome evil with good,"* she repeated silently to herself. "After what you tried to do to Ruarc," she said aloud, "in arranging that ambush to capture him, can you blame me if I doubt anything you say or do anymore is worthy of trust?"

"I never admitted to being involved in that unfortunate turn of events." Glynnis's mouth went tight. "Someone else must have—"

Killian held up a silencing hand. "Say what you will. It won't matter much one way or another after tomorrow."

At the reminder, all the blood drained from Glynnis's face. "I can't leave Rannoch, m'lady. It's my home, the only home I have!"

"Surely you can return to your parents' house. And Ruarc said he'd send an escort with you."

"Both my parents are dead. My elder brother now holds control of their estates. He and I have never gotten on. He won't take me and Thomas in, ye can be certain of that."

"Then perhaps you and Thomas should seek out your coconspirator, Adam Campbell," Killian said, beginning to lose patience. Mercy and forgiveness aside, this was really none of her business. "Let him take responsibility for his part in that contemptible plot and any others you three may have concocted."

"There were no other plots. I swear it!" The ebony-haired woman frowned in sudden speculation. "All Thomas and I did was help ye as ye asked and now suddenly ye're acting the loving, loyal friend to my stepson? Would ye kindly explain what happened between last night and today to change yer opinion of Ruarc? He's most assuredly the same man he was yesterday, as are Thomas and I but ye . . . ye've changed completely."

Killian's guard rose. *Help me, Lord,* she thought, offering up a quick little prayer. *Despite what she has done, she is still beloved by You. Help me to keep that foremost in my mind.*

"I may have changed my original opinion of Ruarc," Killian replied as gently as she could, "but that doesn't mean I owe you an explanation of anything."

"Nay, ye don't, m'lady," Glynnis agreed with a sigh. "But I'd still like verra much to understand why ye've had such a radical change of heart. Or were ye and Ruarc, instead, but meaning to set a trap for Thomas and me all along?"

"It won't work, Glynnis." Killian waved away her accusation. "Don't try to turn this around on Ruarc and me. You were the one who tried to play the games, and they all failed."

Glynnis looked away. "Then ye won't help us, Thomas and me? Though ye bore a part in all that transpired, ye won't lift a finger to speak to Ruarc on our behalf?"

The confirmation hovered on the tip of her tongue, but Killian couldn't find the heart to utter it. Perhaps she was but a naïve fool, but her Bible reading and prayers earlier had left a lasting impression on her. She didn't want to see Glynnis and Thomas gone. In some strange way their departure would seem a failure, not only for Ruarc but for her as well. A failure in loving . . . a failure in mercy. A failure for yet another family.

"Ruarc's my friend," she finally, softly said. "We came to an understanding yesterday. Neither of us had given the other a fair chance. We vowed henceforth to try to do so."

Glynnis turned back to her, disbelief in her eyes. "Ye . . . ye wish now to stay, to wed my stepson?"

"Yes, perhaps I do." Killian drew in a deep breath. "I'm not saying we'll be able to work out our differences in the end, but I'm committed to making a far greater effort than I had before. In the doing, though, I owe him my utmost loyalty. I won't be part, in any way, to something that might harm him."

"And that means supporting him in his decision to banish us, does it?"

Killian smiled and shook her head. "Not at all. You're the only family Ruarc has left. I'd see your banishment as a terrible tragedy."

A desperate hope flared in Glynnis's eyes. "Then ye'll talk to him? Ask him to reconsider?"

"Ask him to *forgive* you?" Killian nodded. "Yes, I will, but the forgiveness must come equally from you and Thomas, too. This pitiful feuding must end. It's past time you and Ruarc made peace with each other."

"Och, aye." Glynnis gave a disparaging laugh. "Ye obviously don't know him as well as ye might imagine. Ruarc MacDonald doesn't know how to forgive—or forget."

Perhaps he didn't. Perhaps none of them did, and they'd carry that soul-rotting defect with them to their graves. But perhaps, just perhaps, there was yet a way, if only they could find the love to lead them through it all. The only Love that could heal all wounds.

"He can learn, Glynnis," she said, struggling to summon the same conviction she meant to convey in her words. "With God's help, he can learn and so can we."

†

AS MUCH as Killian hated doing it, she was going to have to ask the priest for help. Time was short if there was to be any hope of obtaining a reprieve, if not a pardon, for Glynnis and her son. Killian needed an ally when she went to Ruarc. Not only did Father Kenneth know Rannoch's laird far better than she did but, at least on this matter, they both also even agreed.

She found him in the garden, reading his breviary. At her approach, the old priest closed his book of psalms, prayers, and readings that he said at certain prescribed hours of the day and glanced up with a smile.

"Och, lass, it's a pleasure to see ye. Are ye certain, though, ye've rested and refreshed yerself adequately after the harrowing events of yestreen?"

Ruarc must have told him about the outlaws. Was there nothing about which the two men didn't confide?

"I'm quite fine, Father." She indicated the spot beside him on the bench. "Could you spare me a few minutes of your time? There's something I'd like to talk with you about."

"I can spare ye more than a few minutes, lass," Father Kenneth said, scooting over to make room for her. "Ye've been in my thoughts and prayers many a time since ye first arrived at Rannoch. I'm verra pleased ye've finally come to talk with me."

Killian sat down beside him. "I suppose, if there's to be any hope of me remaining here, you and I need to come to some sort of truce. It's apparent you and Ruarc are very close."

"Aye," the priest replied slowly, "I suppose we are. I've known him since he was a lad and am honored he thinks enough of me to come to me with his problems."

"Has he spoken to you, then, of the reasons why he refuses to pardon Glynnis and Thomas? Can you give me any insights that might help me convince him not to banish them?"

"And why would ye care what happens to them?"

Killian hesitated but a moment. "Earlier, Glynnis asked to see me. She begged me to intercede for them with Ruarc. Though I know I'm hardly the one to judge the situation, I can't see how Ruarc's casting out part of his family will solve anything. Leastwise, not in any positive way."

"True enough." Father Kenneth studied her intently. "Ye heard me caution Ruarc about the verra same thing. But I ask ye again. Why do ye care?"

Why indeed? Though she pitied Glynnis, who had nowhere else to go, those were definitely not the emotions she felt when it came to Ruarc MacDonald. No, her feelings for him were far, far more complex.

"I care," she finally replied, "because I believe God wouldn't want this—or any—family destroyed. I care because Jesus asks us to forgive others their trespasses against us. And I care because I care what happens to Ruarc. Because I don't think this is the right way to solve this. Because you can't run forever. That's why, after all, I agreed to come back with Ruarc. Because we both needed another chance to try to work out our differences."

"Just as he needs another chance to try and work out his problems with Glynnis and Thomas?"

"Yes." Killian nodded. "I know this isn't a simple problem. I know it goes back many years. And I know Glynnis's and Thomas's enmity is a potentially deadly thing. Perhaps, though, there's still hope for them all."

"I pray that there is, lass."

"I know you do. That's why I came to you today. I need help. I need to know the right words to say."

"Show him that ye care, lass."

Frustration filled her. What possible help would that be in convincing Ruarc to pardon his stepmother and brother? "Are you saying, then, that you won't help me? Is that it?"

"Nay, I'm not saying that at all. I'm telling ye that, more than aught else, Ruarc needs to know ye care about him. His heart is so bound up and guarded now—because he fears being hurt—that he lashes out first rather than give anyone a chance to gain the advantage.

"He needs to learn how to forgive, to trust, to love again. Ye must teach him all that, lass. Ye must help Ruarc rediscover his long-abandoned faith and the God who has always been there for him. It's why ye were brought here, why ye were meant to wed him."

"And do *you* know how weary I am of hearing you talk as if you have some special relationship with God?" She gave a strident laugh. "Why is it *I* must be everything to Ruarc? What about me and what *I* need?

"We learn to forgive by forgiving. We learn to trust by trusting. And we learn to love again by loving." The priest smiled sadly. "Truly, lass, don't ye need all that as much as Ruarc?"

Had her marriage to Alexander wounded her even more deeply than she realized? Was that what this canny old priest was implying? Was she as dearly in need of the gifts of forgiveness, trust, and love as was Ruarc?

Most likely she was, Killian admitted reluctantly, her despair rising to mix crazily with her angry confusion. At this precise moment, she couldn't sort out if she hated herself more than she hated Alexander, despised her failings more than his, or was just too afraid to face it all.

"I don't know how to teach anyone anything," she whispered miserably. "Don't you see that? Don't you understand that's why I came to you?"

"Och, lass, lass. Ye understand more than ye might imagine."

The priest laid a hand on hers. "It's all there, buried in yer heart, where the Lord Jesus placed it from the day ye were born. Ye've only to trust yer own good sense. Ye've only to turn to Him who is Love Incarnate and hearken to His voice. Acknowledge that apart from Him, ye can do nothing. Aye, do all that, and all that ye learn will pour forth to drench those ye care most about with those same truths. It's yer calling, ye know, has always been, as it is for the rest of us."

Tears stung Killian's eyes. "You speak wonderful words, but I don't know where or how to begin. Sometimes I feel so lost and alone. My life's in such a shambles. And I feel so . . . so unclean for what I've allowed my life to become and for what I did . . . did to Alexander."

"Do ye truly wish to learn what to do, lass? Do ye?"

"Yes." With her fierce, fervent nod, tears flowed down Killian's cheeks. "I think I've always wanted that, even when I didn't know what I wanted."

"Then begin by summoning yer courage and going to Ruarc. Plead Glynnis's cause, but do so with all honesty about what is truly in yer heart. And do not fear. Trust in the Lord for guidance. Surrender to Him, and He will surely help ye."

Courage and honesty. Trust and surrender. Such simple words, yet so fraught with potentially dire consequences. She had withheld them from Ruarc, and the consequences had indeed been dire. She had withheld them from herself, too, and it had nearly destroyed her. She had almost lost her life, honor, and perhaps even her soul, in the process.

What more could she possibly lose?

Pulling her hand from his, Killian climbed to her feet. "Pray for me, then, Father. I'll need all the help I can get."

"Aye, lass, that I will," the old priest said. "That I will."

13

THAT EVENING a storm blew in. The winds began to howl; the
temperature dropped rapidly, and rain turned quickly to sleet. Even
as the castle servants scurried about shutting windows and pulling the
heavy draperies, Killian watched Ruarc, exhausted and soaked to the
skin, ride in.

Before she could even make it down the stairs, Francis was at
Ruarc's side, throwing a blanket about his shoulders. Rannoch's laird
shot the young clerk a grateful look. "Ye always know what I'm needing before I even realize it myself," he said. "My thanks, Francis."

Just then Killian drew up before them. The clerk sent her a
triumphant little smile before bowing and walking away. She stared
after him a moment, puzzled at his strange behavior, before turning
back to Ruarc.

"He's verra protective of those he loves, lass," the big Highlander
explained, apparently noting the interchange. "And, right now, Francis cannot help but place ye with all the other women who have
touched my life."

"So, of course, as far as Francis is concerned I'm the arch villain-
ess, as were Sheila and Glynnis," Killian muttered. "You haven't, you
know, the most warm, welcoming people in Rannoch."

"I'm sure it must seem so to ye." He drew the blanket more
closely to him. "Indeed, now that I think on it, things *have* been
rather dismal here for quite a while." He arched a dark brow.

KATHLEEN MORGAN

"Mayhap ye'd like to do something about that wee problem. A woman's touch has been said to work wonders."

Killian gave a disparaging snort. "I'd hardly know where to begin."

"Begin with me." He grinned down at her. "I could use a hot bath and some dry clothes. A steaming tankard of mulled cider would do a lot for warming me, too."

She grinned back. "I'd anticipated your return. The bathing tub is ready in your bedchamber, and the water is steaming on the kitchen hearth. Hie yourself upstairs. I'll see that the water's brought to you posthaste, as well as something warm to drink."

"Indeed, lass?" Ruarc eyed her with surprise. "Ye've truly done all that for me?"

"It was a simple courtesy."

He reached out and touched her face. "Aye, but it isn't something I've had done for me in a long while. I thank ye."

The look in Ruarc's eyes was warm, the gratitude gleaming there frank and unabashed. A queer little joy exploded in Killian. It felt so good to have her efforts, even if for such a small thing as preparing a bath, appreciated. Until this instant, she hadn't fully comprehended how long it had been since a man had spoken such words to her.

"You're most welcome," she said, smiling shyly as his hand fell away. "Now, why don't you head upstairs before you catch cold? Get out of those wet clothes and wrap something dry around you until the water arrives." Killian gathered her skirts but, before she could step out, Ruarc took her arm.

She glanced back. "Is there something else you were needing?"

"Aye, but one thing more, lass, if ye will."

"And what's that?"

"Would ye stay and visit a time with me?" His voice was husky and tinged with hope. "Just to talk, mind ye, and naught else, of course."

Killian chuckled. "Well, yes, I suppose I could, but only for a moment or two, while the servants ready your bath. Later, though, could you join me in the library? There *is* something I need to talk with you about."

"Agreed." He released her. "Be off with ye, then. I dearly need that bath."

She wrinkled her nose and laughed out loud. "Oh, don't I know it. Don't I know it!"

†

THIS WAS surely a foretaste of heaven if ever there was one, Ruarc thought as the soothing warmth of his bath seeped into his bones. And, best of all, a yellow-haired angel had prepared it for him. His lids grew heavy; his eyes closed.

Then, unexpectedly from around the screen, a hand poked him. He opened his eyes. The hand now held a pewter mug filled with something hot and steaming.

"Here, drink this," Killian said. "It'll chase the chill from your bones."

Ruarc accepted the mug and took a deep draught of the liquid. It was mulled cider, fragrant with cloves and other spices, and sweetly flavored. It tasted wonderful.

He finished the mug, then handed it back to her. "Have ye aught more? That was delicious."

"I think one is enough for now. As tired as you are, if you drink any more, you're sure to fall asleep and drown."

"But that's why ye're here, aren't ye?" He cocked his head. "To save me if I mayhap need saving?"

She laughed. "The servants are ready to leave, and so am I. I'm afraid you'll just have to save yourself, if any saving's needed."

Ruarc smiled. "Ever the proper matron, are ye?"

"Unfortunately for you, yes, I am." Killian paused. "Is an hour sufficient for you to bathe, dress, and join me in the library?"

"For ye, lass, a half hour's sufficient. If ye're quite certain ye cannot stay and visit a while longer, that is?"

Killian's answer was to laugh, then turn and walk away.

†

NO SOONER had Killian and the servants departed than Ruarc set to scrubbing himself. True to his word, a half hour later he joined her in the library.

"And what, fair lady, would ye like to talk about?" he asked, taking a seat beside her at the table. The bath had warmed him quickly, and in the heady presence of a beautiful woman Ruarc was now feeling a wee bit mellow.

No answer was immediately forthcoming. He glanced at her. Killian's smile had faded, and a look of grim intent now tightened her pretty features.

Ruarc frowned. "What is it, lass? What's wrong?"

"It's about . . . about Glynnis and Thomas," she finally blurted. "I know I've no right to ask this of you, but could you please reconsider sending them away?"

The warm, pleasant mood that had carried him through this evening vanished. He fixed Killian with a piercing stare. "And why would ye suddenly care what happens to them? Ye didn't seem of a mind to protest earlier today."

"I didn't say anything earlier because I didn't feel I knew enough about what had happened between you and Glynnis all these years."

A mixture of rising anger and disappointment welled within Ruarc. Had all of Killian's tender care this eve been but a ruse to soften him for this moment? "Then why now?" he demanded. "What has changed?"

She flinched, and Ruarc knew the tone of his voice had sharpened, gone hard. He didn't care. Let her understand, if only a little, what her request meant to him. Let her understand this was no easy thing she asked.

"I . . . I had time to think about . . . about what it'd do to all of you if you carried out your plan to send them away. That's no way to treat your family, Ruarc."

"My family?" He gave an incredulous laugh. "Are ye daft, lass? My *family*, as ye call them, nearly saw me captured twice now. In case ye haven't noticed, there's been no love lost between us for a verra long while."

"They're your closest living kin, Ruarc. Thomas is your brother, Glynnis, your father's wife. Don't turn your back on them."

"I thank ye for at least not naming her my mither. She has never been a mither to me."

"And is that all her fault?" Killian leaned forward. "Glynnis and I've had a lot of time to talk in the past weeks. She told me how you received her when she first came to Rannoch. She told me about your father, and how cold a husband he was to her. Such treatment would soon wither any woman's heart!"

"So, ye're taking her side once again, are ye?" Ruarc glared at her. "Truly, madam, I can't say I care much for all the games ye play."

"I'm not playing games, you silly, pigheaded man!" Killian glared back at him. "I just don't want you someday to regret banishing Glynnis, or what it might ultimately do to you, in having to perform such a hard-hearted act. Your family's the most precious possession you'll ever have!"

"Precious to ye, mayhap, though I'm thinking that husband of yers was hardly worthy of ye. But I long ago gave up on that myth of a happy family."

"It's never too late, Ruarc."

"Isn't it?" He sighed and shook his head. "Well, leastwise, it is for Glynnis and me. She only has herself to blame. Twice the woman has tried to see me dead. Twice, Killian!"

"Yes, perhaps she has, but what happened to bring her to this? And what part did you play in it?"

He turned away. How could he make her understand? He hadn't wanted another mother and, at age thirteen, didn't need another one, either. Then, without warning, his father had returned home one day with a new wife, a girl only six years older than himself. It had taken a long while to forgive his father for trying to replace his beloved mother with that . . . that brazen strumpet. And he had never been able to stomach her awkward, maudlin attempts to mother him.

It had been a difficult time for all. Ruarc knew he had been an unhappy, confused boy on the brink of manhood. His father, still deeply grieving his first wife, had soon realized his mistake in taking such a young and totally unsuitable wife. And Glynnis . . . well, Glynnis had finally withdrawn into herself in hurt and anger, seizing every opportunity to strike out and wound in any way she could.

If Thomas hadn't been born nine months later, Ruarc wondered what might have become of the beautiful, ebony-haired girl who had been chosen as his stepmother. But with Thomas, Glynnis seemed finally to have found someone to love and who loved her. It became increasingly easier to ignore her. For the most part, life settled back into its usual pattern.

"Most likely I played a part in Glynnis's hatred toward me," he admitted, meeting Killian's gaze at last. "Still, I did my best to allow her to live her life, and I led mine. But that was never enough for her.

She always wanted more—she wanted Rannoch for her own; she wanted to destroy my marriage to Sheila, and she wanted me dead."

"So much hurt, so much hatred," Killian said softly. "But it must stop somewhere, before one or all of you are destroyed by it. Can't the forgiveness, the healing, begin here?"

"Let the healing begin when they're gone. Once I put Glynnis and that sniveling son of hers out, they'll be gone from my mind, too. Then I'll be healed."

Her hands fisted on the tabletop until they were knuckle white. "That's no way to heal, Ruarc." Killian's voice went low, fervent with intense emotion. "The only way to be truly healed is to forgive. Please, Ruarc. For yourself. For us. Forgive them. Don't send Glynnis and Thomas away!"

He met her imploring gaze. She seemed deeply concerned not only for Glynnis and Thomas but for him as well. But did he dare trust her in this? Indeed, why should she care so much for any of them? It didn't make sense.

"Ye don't understand, lass," he whispered, shaking his head and closing his eyes. "What ye ask requires more than I can give. I can't trust—"

"And do you think it was easy for me to trust, to come back with you? Do you? But I thought the chance of a life together, the chance to build a good and true family, was worth the risk. I thought *you* were worth the risk!"

Ruarc's eyes snapped open. What he saw sent a wild stab of joy through him. Killian's eyes blazed. Her face was alight with the fervor of her conviction. She looked so much like a warrior queen, or a saint on fire with some call from God, that it made his throat go dry.

"I don't want to begin our marriage with some cruel, tragic act." Killian drew in an anguished breath. "Though I know both you and Glynnis have carried a terrible animosity for each other long before I came here, I can't bear to be the cause of this final break between you. And I was the cause," she hastened to add when Ruarc opened his mouth to protest. "I begged her to help me leave you, and she did."

"So it doesn't matter she used ye to plan some sort of trap for me, does it?" he asked, suddenly weary beyond bearing. "All that matters is that I forgive her and allow her to stay on at Rannoch?"

Killian reached out and tenderly ran a finger down his cheek.

"For now, all that matters is you forgive her and allow her to stay on. Make the overture. The next step is up to her. All the rest will come in time."

"Will it, lass?" Ruarc searched her face, desperately seeking an assurance he knew wasn't truly possible. There were no guarantees in this life, and especially none when it came to other people. Yet still, if only for another short, sweet time he could know love and trust and joy . . .

"Yes, it will," she promised. "If we help each other. If we seek the Lord's help, it may well be enough."

Ruarc closed his eyes, wrestled a fleeting moment more with his doubts and fears, then opened them. "This one time more then, I'll give Glynnis another chance. But only because ye ask me, lass. Have a care, however, what ye do with that trust, for I can't say I'll give it again if ye misuse it."

He smiled ruefully. "Indeed, I can't say I even know why I do so now."

†

ADAM CAMPBELL held the letter from Glynnis MacDonald in his hand, cursing savagely all the while. He hadn't needed her letter, full of apologies and accusations, to tell him what he had easily ascertained by the end of the day of the ambush. Once again, Ruarc MacDonald had slipped from his grip.

It was past time he stopped relying on happenstance to give him what he so avidly sought. It was past time he took the matter to higher authorities. If all went as he hoped, in but another two months, Ruarc MacDonald and his ilk, by order of the king, would be fair game.

Not that many would mourn the well-deserved downfall of the arrogant MacDonalds. Clan Campbell, whose lands they had raided for years, had been but their most formidable of enemies. Finally, though, many in the English government were also beginning to look increasingly askance at them.

The last straw was MacDonald of Glencoe's failure to sign the Treaty of Achallader this past June, which his uncle, Sir John Campbell, Earl of Breadalbane, had cleverly engineered in order to win favor with King William and bring some semblance of peace to the restless Highland chiefs. Then, the very next month, one of MacDonald's sons and his men had raided British supply boats on Loch Linnhe. Though these men were soon captured and imprisoned at Fort William, Queen Mary, in King William's absence, had eventually pardoned the scurvy lot.

It was past time the MacDonalds pay, and pay dearly. Though his uncle was far too cunning and slippery to be trusted save to serve his own interests, mayhap, this time, what served Breadalbane's interests might also serve Adam's. After all, the Earl stood to lose a great deal if his prized Treaty fell by the wayside. What little favor he had managed to curry with the king because of it would soon wither and fade.

Indeed, Adam decided as he crumpled Glynnis's letter of pitiful excuses and tossed it into the fire, there might be much gained by paying his uncle a wee visit. The Earl, after all, was a confidant of Sir John Dalrymple, Master of Stair and Secretary of State for Scotland. As a member of the Privy Council, the Master of Stair had the king's ear in all matters pertaining to certain recalcitrant Highland clans.

Meanwhile, Adam could also work on yet another front. In her diatribe of pointless comments, Glynnis had hit on one potentially useful idea. As of yet, Adam had made no attempt to approach Killian and offer his continued friendship. Though a physical visit with his cousin by marriage was no longer feasible, there was nothing stopping him, with Glynnis's assistance, from writing the young Colonial. Any and every avenue of attack that might get him within striking distance of Ruarc MacDonald was worth a try.

All he needed was to discover the proper means to inveigle himself back into Killian's confidences.

†

"I'D LIKE, if ye're willing," Ruarc said a few days later just after the midday meal, "to take Gavin with me this afternoon. There are several crofters I need to visit, and one of them has a litter of wee pups Fionn sired."

His blue eyes sparkling with anticipation, Gavin peeked out from behind Ruarc. "Could I, Mama? I promise to be careful and mind Ruarc. I want to see the puppies."

Killian looked from Gavin to Ruarc. The big Highlander's gaze was almost as eagerly expectant as was her son's. She didn't have the heart to refuse. "Well, I suppose that would be all right." She glanced out one of the Great Hall's windows. It was still sunny and calm, if a bit chilly.

"Be sure to keep warm, and always stay near Ruarc." Killian looked to Rannoch's laird. "How long do you plan to be gone?"

He shrugged. "Two or three hours at the most. We'll be back well before the supper meal."

"I can have Gavin ready in about fifteen minutes. I just need to get him cleaned up from dinner, then dressed for the ride."

"That'll do. Meet me outside the castle then."

Not long thereafter, Killian saw the two off. Watching Gavin settle snugly before Ruarc on his big horse, Fionn loping along beside them, something tugged deep within her.

It was evident Rannoch's laird adored Gavin, and he, Ruarc. Ruarc was always so gentle and solicitous, going out of his way to seek out the small boy every chance he had. Of course, Killian thought with a smile, it was rarely hard to find her son, who had all but attached himself to Ruarc's big deerhound.

With each passing day since her return to Rannoch, her own relationship with Ruarc MacDonald had improved as well. Some symbolic barrier had been breached the night he had finally agreed to allow Glynnis and Thomas to remain at Rannoch. They seemed to be settling into a comfortable congeniality.

The time was fast approaching, however, when their six-week pact would end. Yet, even still, her emotions remained all in a jumble.

She was still afraid, but now not because she feared the kind of man Ruarc truly was. No, now she feared her own needs and desires. She feared how swiftly she had grown attached to Rannoch's laird. She feared she might even be falling in love with him.

In any other circumstances, Killian would've laughed away her silly fears. But Alexander had been dead barely five weeks, and she had killed him. It didn't matter that he had cruelly abused her for years. It didn't matter that he had nearly strangled her to death before Ruarc had rescued her. And it didn't matter that she had not meant to kill Alexander in her attempt to save Ruarc's life.

No, none of that mattered. What mattered now was how could

Ruarc want to marry her, a husband killer? Whether or not he had killed Sheila—which she no longer even believed—she *had* killed Alexander, and right before Ruarc's eyes. How could *he* want such a woman to bear his children, mother them?

And how could *she* be lusting after another man—however wonderful and physically attractive he seemed—so soon after Alexander's death? Was that the measure of her love, that she could so quickly, and even eagerly, forget Alexander? Dear Lord, was that the measure of herself as a human being as well?

"Something's troubling ye, isn't it, lass?"

With a start, Killian swung around. Father Kenneth stood there, a warm, knowing look in his eyes. She blushed. Had he guessed what she was thinking? She fervently prayed he hadn't.

"It . . . it's nothing, Father." Killian forced a wan smile. "I just have many things to sort out in my head."

"And in yer heart, lass?" His glance moved to where Ruarc and Gavin's forms were even now disappearing over a hill. "It must surely pluck at ye, how well those two lads are striking up a friendship."

"I'm glad for it, not sad or afraid. Gavin's father wasn't one to spend much time with him. And when he did, he quickly lost patience."

The priest turned back to her. "It has always been Ruarc's dearest, if closely kept wish, to be a father. In yer son, he's finally begun to fulfill that wish."

"I didn't realize it was such a secret." Killian frowned in puzzlement. "He's made it more than evident he greatly desires an heir for Rannoch."

"Desiring an heir out of duty and desiring one out of the yearnings of yer heart are two different matters altogether," the little priest said. "To spare Sheila's feelings, since she couldn't long carry a child, Ruarc was forced to pretend it didn't matter much to him."

Touched by yet another facet of Ruarc's complex personality, Killian smiled. "I didn't know. It explains a lot about his friendship with Gavin, though."

"And why any child of yer union will mean far, far more than just an heir for Rannoch?"

Killian chuckled. "You push and prod all the time, don't you, to ensure Ruarc gets everything he desires?"

"I want the best for the both of ye, lass. Still, I want ye to give Ruarc a fair chance. For ye to do that, the more ye understand about the man, the easier it'll be for ye to do so, will it not?"

"Every day, every moment I'm with him, he reveals yet another part of himself, of his heart," she replied softly. "He truly is a good man, isn't he?"

"Aye, the verra finest. And he deserves the finest in his wife. Hence, why I so strongly pushed for ye two to wed."

Killian blinked in surprise. The old priest had just paid her the highest of compliments.

"Well, I don't particularly feel so fine just now," she admitted, remembering her earlier thoughts about Alexander. "I wasn't the best of wives in my first marriage. Indeed, even now I find it truly hard to mourn my husband."

"And ye think that makes ye an evil, coldhearted woman, don't ye?"

"Doesn't it?" Hot tears stung her eyes.

"What would it have taken to assuage yer guilt, lass? Yer or Ruarc's death rather than his? Would ye rather yer son have had only his father to raise him?"

"No, I wouldn't have wanted any of that!" Killian looked away. "But if I'd done things differently. If I hadn't run from Achallader that night, but stayed and tried to work things out with Alexander . . ."

"But didn't ye run *because* ye knew all was lost, that yer marriage was dead, and all ye'd left were yer son and his welfare?" Father Kenneth shook his head and sighed. "Truly, lass, the only person who'd any choice left was yer husband, in choosing to let ye be. And he made the wrong choice for the last time."

The tears welled, trickled down her cheeks. "All that you say makes perfect sense. But in my heart it still hurts. I still wonder."

"And ye will for a time more," he assured her gently. "Ye've suffered a grievous wound to yer soul. It won't heal soon or easily. Being the woman ye are, ye can't help but care, even for the poor wretch that was yer husband."

"Y-yet I'll soon wed another man, and my first husband's barely cold in his gr-grave."

"Aye, that ye will, because ye have to and because ye need to." Father Kenneth took her hand and squeezed it. "And then where will ye go, what will ye do, with the life the Lord has led ye to?"

"I-I don't know. I truly d-don't know what to do."

"Why not begin by forgiving and loving yerself?" he suggested, his voice falling like the soft murmur of a gentle rain. "That in itself will free ye like naught ye may have ever experienced. And once ye're freed, mayhap then ye can truly begin to seek out yer heart's desires. Desires that encompass not only yerself and all those ye love but, above all, the good Lord Himself."

14

"M'LADY? May I have a word with ye?"

Killian looked up from her inspection of the myriad piles of dust and other indescribable objects lying beneath one of the beds in an unused bedchamber to see Glynnis standing there. Nearly a week had passed since Ruarc had given her and her son leave to remain at Rannoch. Save for an emotional thank you and the most minimal interaction at mealtimes, Ruarc's stepmother had so far kept well out of everyone's way. Whatever Glynnis now wanted, it must be important.

"As you wish." Killian climbed to her feet. "Just give me a moment, if you will."

Turning to one of the maidservants, a girl named Doiranne, Killian indicated the wheat straw broom, rags, brushes, and bucket of hot water sitting just inside the door. "Start under this bed. Sweep it well, then scrub the floor. Once you've finished beneath the bed, begin cleaning the rest of the floor. I should be back soon to help you."

Doiranne curtsied. "Aye, m'lady."

Killian next glanced at Glynnis. "Now, what can I do for you?"

The ebony-haired woman shot Doiranne a sidling look. "Mayhap it'd be best if we speak of this outside. It doesn't concern the servants."

"Then come, let's take a walk." With that, Killian gathered her skirts and headed for the bedchamber door. When they were a sufficient distance down the corridor, she drew up and turned to Glynnis. "Whatever is the matter?"

"Cook came to me a short while ago and informed me the larder is almost empty. When I asked her why that was so, she said Master Francis MacLean told her she must be wasting the provisions. By his calculations, there should be enough to last for another month. He then, of course, refused to pay for any more food."

Killian frowned. "So is Bessie known for wastefulness? You'll have to tell me, Glynnis, for I haven't been here long enough to know."

"Nay, m'lady. Truly, she may not be the best of cooks, or the cleanest, but I've always known her to be most thrifty."

"Well, then, there's no other alternative. Francis will just have to advance more money. We can't all starve for the next month just so the accounts balance."

Glynnis gave a small, skeptical snort. "I suggest then either ye or Ruarc broach that subject with Francis. He's verra protective of the castle accounts and doesn't particularly like being questioned about them."

"I suppose it'd be best if Ruarc spoke with Francis," Killian said. "Unfortunately, Ruarc will be gone a few days with business in Edinburgh. I don't think, however, this is a problem that can wait for his return."

"Nay, m'lady, neither do I." Glynnis's mouth tightened in irritation. "Have a care with Francis, though. He's a strange one, that he is, and has always been unnaturally hostile to me as well as to poor Sheila. I don't doubt he'll treat ye the same way."

Harking back to the day Francis had given her a tour of Rannoch and his sly, cutting looks since then whenever they met, Killian didn't doubt the chilly reception the young clerk would give her. Nonetheless, the issue must be addressed.

Killian managed a grateful smile. "My thanks for your concern, Glynnis. And for relaying the problems in the kitchen. I appreciate your taking an interest in the castle."

"It was my duty before ye came, m'lady," the older woman said. "And now that it's soon to be yers, I'd be happy to aid ye in any way I can."

Glynnis's words gave Killian pause. As time passed, she supposed everyone presumed she'd be Rannoch's next lady. And it *was* past time she and Ruarc come to some decision. Perhaps when he returned . . .

"I'd like that very much," Killian said at last. "Your experience and knowledge would be a godsend."

"Yer dedication to Ruarc is most apparent, m'lady. And, for yer sake, if not as much for my stepson's, I'll help ye. I'm verra grateful for what ye did for Thomas and me. Ruarc would've never pardoned us if ye hadn't intervened."

"But he did. He took the first step, Glynnis. Now you must try to meet him halfway. That's the only way all this feuding between you will ever end."

Glynnis's eyes glittered with barely contained anger. "I'm not so certain the rift between us can ever be repaired. There's been so much pain, so many cruel deeds done and words spoken . . ."

"Please try, Glynnis." Frustration welled in Killian. *Dear Lord, help me help her understand.* "Don't lose heart. It's not too late."

The older woman's face softened. She laid a hand on Killian's arm. "Ye're far too good for the likes of my stepson. I've said that before, and I'll say it again. And, that said, I'll try to make amends with Ruarc. I doubt it'll help much, but I'll try."

"That's all anyone can do." Killian took her hand and gave it a quick squeeze. "Now I must be off to Master MacLean's workroom. The sooner I get this problem with our food supplies settled, the better it'll be for all of us."

"Aye, m'lady," Glynnis agreed with a laugh. "Empty stomachs make for a verra peevish castle."

†

DRAWING up at the door to Francis's workroom, Killian knocked and then waited. When no response was forthcoming, she knocked again. Finally, she grasped the handle and tried the door. It opened easily.

Francis was nowhere to be seen. Killian hesitated. Should she come back later when Francis was about? Then the sight of a large, leather-bound book lying open atop a sea of papers on the desk caught her eye. If these were the castle accounts, it'd be a simple and quick enough task—what with her bookkeeping experience—to discern where the problems with the kitchen supplies might lie.

And it wasn't as if she weren't entitled to peruse the accounts.

Ruarc had already given her leave to improve the living conditions, not to mention the quality of the food served. Both required knowledge of the castle budget and an expenditure of money. Still, her current relationship with Francis was, at best, tenuous. If the young clerk really was touchy about his accounts, this might not be the best way to win his trust.

Even as she considered her options, however, Killian's feet carried her across the musty, cobweb-strewn room to the desk. A brief glance, no more, she told herself. If an answer didn't offer itself quickly, she'd wait until Francis' return, then ask to see the accounts with him present. In the meanwhile, no one need be the wiser.

The numbers and notes on the open pages, however, were the most confusing, disorganized jumble Killian had ever encountered. Even after several attempts to make sense of them, she couldn't tell which of the numbers in the ledger were debits and which were credits.

The expenses were haphazardly posted to the most unlikely places: straw bales that should've gone to the stables were expensed to the house; the price of a rug had been added to the farm's account; kitchen vegetables were debited to the stables. There were loose bills stuffed between pages. One apothecary bill with five items had only one posted. The mathematical errors were egregious, and frequently numbers were written backwards or even upside down. None of the columns, when there *were* columns, balanced.

How the castle had run as well as it had—and that wasn't saying all that much—for as long as it had was a mystery to her. Ruarc must have been very frugal and the castle very self-sufficient. One way or another, though, he had to be made aware, and soon, of the sorry state—

"What are ye doing in my room? How dare ye come in uninvited?"

Killian whirled around. The fury in Francis's voice was mirrored in his face and stance. Instinctively, she took a step back, before she remembered she had every right to be here.

"I came to speak to you about some problems with food supplies." Killian tried to keep her voice calm. "I knocked several times. When I found you weren't here but your door was unlocked, I thought perhaps I could take a look at the castle accounts and determine myself where the problem lay."

He gave a harsh laugh. "And what do ye know of reading a ledger?"

Killian couldn't help but bristle at his sarcastic tone. Still, she cautioned herself, this was no time to resort to anger. "Actually, Francis, I know quite a bit about accounts. Before I married, I worked for my uncle in his shipping business, keeping his books."

The blood drained from the young clerk's face. "So, mayhap ye do know more than most folk then. Still, there was no need to be spying on my work."

"I wasn't spying. I've every right to know how money is spent and what it buys."

"M'lord hasn't informed me ye were to oversee the accounts."

"M'lord, as you must have ascertained by now," Killian countered dryly, "also doesn't seem to care to oversee these books, either." She gestured toward the volume still lying open on the desk. "If he had, he'd be very disturbed by what he'd find."

With an oath, Francis strode across the room, skirted her, and slipped behind the desk. Grabbing up the ledger, he snapped it shut, then clutched it to himself. "M'lord has never had a moment of complaint over how I manage the accounts!"

"Perhaps so, Francis, but he rarely, if ever, sees them, does he?"

When no answer was forthcoming, she prodded him again. "Does he, Francis?"

Tears sprang suddenly to the young man's eyes. "Nay, he doesn't."

"And that's because he trusts you."

"Aye." His chin raised a notch in defiance. "That he does."

Killian considered him a long moment. "Tell me true. Has anyone ever taught you how to keep accounts?"

He looked away. "Not really. My father never had time for me, and when he did, he soon lost patience with my slowness. He thought me stupid."

"I don't think you're stupid, Francis," she said softly. "To have kept everything running as well as it has when you didn't really even know what to do says a lot for your resourcefulness."

His eyes narrowed. "Ye're going to tell m'lord, aren't ye?"

"Not necessarily, and certainly not right away." Killian motioned toward the ledger book. "Ruarc has more than enough burdens without adding this. It may take a while to straighten out the accounts and set up a better system, but together, I think we can do it. If you'll allow me to help you, that is." She smiled. "You know, if the truth be

189

told, I'd love to try my hand at bookkeeping again. I truly enjoyed doing it all those years ago."

The first vestiges of hope flared in Francis's eyes. "Ye'd help me and not tell m'lord?"

"Yes, I would. After all, we both want to help Ruarc. Why not work together?"

Once more, Francis's gaze narrowed. "And what would it cost me, this 'working together'?"

Killian laughed. "Well, nothing as precious as your clerking job. Your friendship would be deeply appreciated, though, if you think that's possible."

"It's possible, I suppose, but I'll tell ye now. I can't abide anyone who tries to hurt or betray m'lord."

"Well, then we're in agreement on yet another thing, aren't we? I feel exactly the same way."

He shrugged. "Mayhap ye do and mayhap ye don't. We'll just have to see about that, won't we?"

"Yes, I suppose we will," she agreed with a nod. "In the meanwhile, why don't we sit down and start looking over that book. Ruarc won't be back for another few days. If we put our heads together, we can accomplish a lot in that time."

"Aye, mayhap we can." Ever so slowly, Francis lowered the ledger back to the desk and opened it.

†

FROM THE vantage of a windswept catwalk high up on Rannoch Castle, Glynnis watched as, three days later, Ruarc returned. If it wasn't bad enough to see him again, it grated on her even worse when Killian and her son, accompanied by his new deerhound puppy, ran out to greet him so warmly; one would've thought Ruarc had just returned victorious from some battle.

It seemed all her fine plans had come to naught. Nay, worse than naught, Glynnis amended bitterly. What had initially appeared a farce of a betrothal seemed rapidly to be becoming a true love match.

Yet, just as he had never deserved Sheila, Ruarc didn't deserve Killian, either. For the life of her, Glynnis couldn't understand what the young Colonial saw in her stepson.

She must tread very, very carefully. Killian could no longer be trusted to cooperate, much less be counted upon. Despite the increased risks, Ruarc must still be eliminated. It was only a matter of time before he overcame his passing fancy for his new wife and her life became endangered. It was also only a matter of time, Glynnis well knew, before Ruarc found some other excuse to banish her and Thomas from Rannoch.

Time, Glynnis resolved as she turned and made her way from the catwalk and back down the stairs, most certainly wasn't on her side. Now, though, there was even more at stake than there had been before. Now she must also see to the tenderhearted if naïve young Colonial as well as to Thomas's and her own welfare. Just as Glynnis had tried to look out for Sheila, she must now protect Killian. She owed her that much, for what the young woman had done for her.

It had been far, far easier with Sheila, though. *She* had soon seen Ruarc for the man he truly was.

†

THAT NIGHT, as a torrential rain clattered overhead, Killian found Ruarc waiting in her bedchamber when she returned from tucking Gavin into bed; he was slouched in one of the hearthside chairs, a cup of some liquid in his hand.

He looked up as she entered. "The lad's asleep at last, is he?" he asked, a smile of welcome on his lips.

"Yes." Killian sighed and shook her head. "I'd more trouble settling that puppy down, than I had Gavin. You realize, don't you, the box you had built for her will soon be outgrown?"

Ruarc chuckled softly as she came to stand beside him. "Then we'll build yet a bigger one, until the wee Eilidh can mind her manners. It won't take long, I promise ye. Deerhounds are the most amenable of dogs."

"I'm sure they are. And even if they weren't, the joy you gave Gavin in allowing him a puppy would be worth it at any rate. It was very kind of you."

She laid a hand on his shoulder. His shirt was damp, as was his hair. He hadn't made it home before the rain.

He covered her hand with his. "Every lad needs his own dog.

Besides, it was getting so I hardly saw my own dog anymore, what with all the time Gavin was spending with Fionn."

Killian laughed. "I suspected that was part of your motivation. Every *man,* I suppose, needs his own dog, too."

"Aye, he does."

"So, did your trip to Edinburgh go well?"

"Aye. Come spring, Rannoch's cattle herds will grow by a third."

She smiled. "You've plans to become a wealthy man someday, do you?"

"Rather, I hope to make Rannoch and its people wealthy."

They fell silent then, warmed by the fire burning merrily in the hearth, content in each other's company. Finally, though, Killian pulled back on her hand, only to find Ruarc's grip tighten.

"It's been six weeks, lass," he said, his voice dropping to a husky rumble. "We need to decide what we're next to do."

Killian's throat went dry. So, he, too, had kept close track of the waning days of their agreement, and knew exactly when it had ended. She let her hand relax on his shoulder.

"There's nothing to decide," she said finally, her voice sounding curiously strained. "We had an agreement. You held to your part. Now I'll hold to mine."

Ruarc released her hand. "Come, sit." He motioned to the chair opposite him. "There's more to this than each of us keeping our word, and well ye know it."

In a swish of crisp overskirt and petticoats, Killian took her seat. "And pray, what more is there?" She folded her hands in her lap and met his piercing gaze. "Or have you changed your mind and no longer wish to wed me?"

"Och, aye, now there's a thought." Ruarc gave a bark of laughter. "Ye're the only lass in all of Glencoe who'd dare marry me, and I no longer want ye? Hardly!"

"I'd prefer you wanted me for myself rather than for my singular availability."

"Och, lass," he said, "I was but making a poor jest. Even if I'd dozens to choose from, I'd still choose ye."

Killian eyed him wryly. "Well, if that's not the reason, what is it? You seemed more eager that first day I came to Rannoch than you seem now."

"More importantly than my inclinations—which, by the way haven't changed a whit—what about yers?" He leaned toward her, an intent look on his face. "Do *ye* wish to wed *me?*"

So, it did matter to him whether or not she desired him. Killian couldn't help a tiny frisson of excitement. Perhaps, just perhaps, she was beginning to mean something more to Ruarc than just a chatelaine of his castle and mother of his future children. She definitely wanted more than that from him.

The admission was frightening, fraught as it was with expectations that could well be disappointed. In his own way, Alexander had loved and wanted her, but his love had ultimately been sick and destructive. What if she let herself fall in love with Ruarc, and he disappointed her too? What if he was but playing some game to ensure her cooperation, or was just taken with her now but would soon lose interest?

She was *so* weary of being used.

"I gather by yer long silence," Ruarc interjected just then, "that ye're reluctant to answer for fear of offending me. Well, ye needn't be. I understand."

Killian frowned. "And what exactly do you understand? Have you suddenly the ability to read minds?"

"What else?" He shrugged, his face now impassive. "Ye don't find me desirable."

His reply was so ludicrous, if charmingly unpretentious, that Killian couldn't keep from laughing.

It apparently wasn't quite the response Ruarc had been expecting, however. He scowled. "I hardly see what's so amusing. Have a care for my feelings, if ye will."

"Oh, no, no." Killian fought to stifle her laughter. "It isn't like that at all. I just find it hard to believe you think you aren't desirable."

"If ye must know, I've never given it much thought."

She smiled tenderly. "You really are quite charmingly modest. I think I like that most about you." Killian paused, an impish glint in her eyes. "Along with, of course, your big, braw body and handsome countenance. And then there's your kindness to my son and patience with me and your endless concern for your people."

"All well and good, lass," Ruarc agreed, locking gazes with her, "but I ask ye again. Are ye finally willing to wed me?"

She hesitated for the space of a heartbeat, then nodded. "Yes, I'm willing to wed you, Ruarc MacDonald."

A fierce joy exploded in his eyes. He smiled in a gentle, wondering uplifting of lips that grew until it became a wide grin. He stood, gazed at her for a long moment, then reached down and took her hands, tugging her to her feet.

"Then we'll wed, and soon," he said. "Within the week, if it's acceptable to ye."

He was close. Too close to draw a decent breath, much less think clearly. Killian took a step back. "When you make up your mind, you don't waste much time, do you?"

Ruarc pulled her back to him. "Am I rushing things again too fast for yer liking?"

His gaze dropped to hers. For the space of a sharply inhaled breath, they stared at each other.

Killian's senses vibrated with awareness. She became acutely conscious of the blood coursing through her veins, of the gentle caress of the heated air billowing from the fireplace. Her nostrils filled with the aromatic tang of woodsmoke, of damp skin and hair. And, all the while, the silence pressed down, strumming around her like a harp string too harshly plucked.

Never in her life had she felt so alive, so intensely mindful of this moment and place—of this man.

Then, finally, with a tender glance, Killian shook her head. "No, you're not rushing things too fast. Not this time."

15

He HADN'T thought he'd ever feel so good again. Ruarc sat close to the bed, watching as Killian—his wife—slept peacefully. They had wed just yesterday, barely a week after she had given her consent. And now, as the first tender rays of dawn peeped through the curtain opening, Ruarc brushed a long, pale strand of hair from his new wife's cheek and bent to kiss her.

At the gentle brush of his lips on her forehead, Killian stirred and mumbled something incoherent in her sleep. Ruarc smiled. She was like a child in the unguarded abandon of her slumber—innocent, guileless, trusting.

She was so beautiful. Even more beautiful than his fiery, tragically unbalanced Sheila. Yet, in a quieter, deeper, more honest way, Killian had touched his heart last night. Touched it as Sheila had never touched it, nor ever could. That was an admission, though, that both thrilled and terrified him.

He could easily fall in love with Killian if, indeed, he wasn't already falling in love with her. But that was daft. Ruarc knew he wasn't the kind of man so easily to succumb to purely physical feminine attributes. If he had, there were more than a few of his clanswomen who would've gladly joined him for a rousing night. But he had always wanted more, wanted what his father and mother had shared.

There was also Rannoch to consider. He didn't need a mistress and illegitimate children. He needed legal heirs. To protect Rannoch, Ruarc needed a wife.

But, he wondered, glancing down once more at Killian, soundly asleep, her head on his pillow, would he finally find all he sought with her? Indeed, did he dare even hope for such a wildly improbable thing?

He'd be wiser to keep Killian at arm's length. It had taken him a long while to relinquish his dreams of a loving wife, a happy family complete with children. The shield he had learned to carry always before his heart now felt safe, comfortable, and would be hard to lay aside. Especially for some illusory specter of happiness that might open him once more to the threat of betrayal.

Yet if he didn't, what chance was there for the future? Did he truly wish to remain as he was—fixed, suspended, going around and around in circles? Going nowhere?

It was bad enough his once vibrant and devoted relationship with God had withered to such a state. But the trials of life, the pain and despair and sense of failure—and most especially the betrayals of those close to him—had ground down all his hope of ever finding happiness and, consequently, in a merciful, loving God. In the end, weren't all the Lord's promises but empty illusions if, indeed, a Divine Being of any sort even existed?

Better, instead, to face life in all its godless but honest reality and live out one's allotted time on this earth the best, the most honorable way, one could.

With a deep, heartsick sigh, Ruarc gently took Killian's hand and closed his eyes. The best . . . way one could . . . time enough to face what lay ahead, be it happiness or yet another betrayal. For now, it was enough to savor the sweet warmth of his wife and pretend that all would turn out well.

†

IT WAS strange, yet curiously comforting at the same time, to be sharing a bedchamber again, Killian mused dreamily as she slowly brushed her hair later that morn. Though she and Alexander had ceased to share the same bed years ago, the remembrance of the happier times had included pleasant interludes, snuggling close on a cold morn, or waking together to birdsong and sunshine and gentle summer breezes.

But her new husband was strikingly different from Alexander.

This man was bigger, more muscled, and definitely hairier. He smelled different too. More like fresh, crisp air and wool and misty moors than the cloying scents Alexander was wont to wear. And he was so warm and strong.

She could get to like this very much. Very, very much.

"Are ye finally awake then, lass?" Ruarc's deep voice reverberated in the large bedchamber as he entered.

Killian smiled. "I could be, if given a good enough reason."

"And would this be good enough a reason?" Crossing to where she sat, he leaned down and playfully kissed her nose.

She shrugged, her eyes closed. "Perhaps. I'll have to think on—"

With a throaty growl Ruarc grasped her arms, leaned even further over, and kissed her, this time on the lips. As his mouth claimed hers with the most exquisite tenderness, a fierce joy swelled within her. Surely, she thought, slipping her arms around his neck, this was how it was meant to be between a man and woman. This playful, gentle, ardent loving.

At long last, Ruarc pulled back to gaze down at her. "Ye look most assuredly awake now, lass." His self-satisfied grin was completely masculine in its intent. Killian laughed. "Well, I wouldn't take all the credit if I were you. I was awake, you know, before you kissed me."

"Och," Ruarc said with a chuckle as he released her and took a seat in the room's other chair, "and here I was thinking my consummate skill had roused ye." He sighed. "Ye're a hard-hearted lass, that ye are, Killian MacDonald."

At the sound of his name joined with hers, she cocked her head and grinned. "I like that. *Killian MacDonald*. It has a nice ring to it, don't you think?"

Ruarc eyed her tenderly. "Aye, I think it has a verra nice ring."

"I think I'm going to very much like being married to you, Ruarc MacDonald."

"Truly, lass?" He looked thoughtful. "Then ye've no regrets, no second thoughts? No wish ever to return to Virginia?"

"Now that we're married, do you still doubt my commitment?"

He leaned toward her, eyeing her intently. "Mayhap we can even begin to look forward to the arrival of a wee bairn. Would that disturb ye, lass, if it were true?"

A baby . . . Killian hadn't considered that. Still, according to

Glynnis, Ruarc had fathered several babes with Sheila. Sooner or later, the odds were good she'd bear him a child.

She wasn't surprised to discover she rather liked the idea. She had always wanted more children, although not with Alexander.

And Ruarc would be a good father. That much she knew from watching him with Gavin. There was more to it, though, than even that. In the gifting of a child, Killian sensed Ruarc would finally find some of the completion he still seemed to need.

"No." Smiling, Killian shook her head. "It wouldn't disturb me to discover I was carrying your child. I've always wanted Gavin to have a little brother or sister." She laughed. "Even two or three more little brothers or sisters, if the truth be told. I was the youngest in my family and even now fondly recall all the attention I received as the baby."

"And I would've liked to have been a brother to more brothers and sisters," Ruarc said, smiling back at her.

A sudden, sad realization struck her. "Well, you *are* a brother to at least one other brother. Perhaps it's still not too late—"

"There was never any chance," Ruarc cut her off with a surprising bitterness, "of Thomas and I ever feeling any brotherly affection for each other. Glynnis took care of that, filling his head with all sorts of lies and his heart full of her venom even before the lad had a chance to sort anything through himself."

She sighed. "Oh, Ruarc, how sad. How sad for all of you."

"Aye, I suppose it is, but it's past now, and naught can be done about it."

It was the perfect opportunity to learn more about the circumstances of this tragic family feud and perhaps even how to mediate it. Killian shoved to one elbow.

"Are you certain it's too late? You're still all alive, of sound mind, and under one roof. And surely Father Kenneth would be willing to help."

"Nay. There's been too much pain, too much rancor, and too many cruel words spoken on both sides. There are just some things that can't be taken back or forgiven."

"Like what?" She poked him in the ribs. "What have *you* done that can't be forgiven?"

He arched a dark brow. "Och, why would ye be thinking I'm the one who has done all the unforgivable things? And here I was hoping ye were beginning to like me."

"I *do* like you, you silly man!" Once again, Killian jabbed him playfully in the ribs. "I just got the impression, by the way you spoke of all the pain and cruelty on both sides, you felt you were at fault, too. Besides, since you can't possibly know Glynnis's view of things, I was hoping to understand your side a bit better."

"And what, in the end, do ye hope to gain by all this 'understanding'? Isn't it enough ye got what ye asked for, in obtaining my pardon for Glynnis and Thomas?"

Killian met his frowning gaze with a steady one of her own. "No, it's not enough."

He gave a snort of amusement. "Well, it's hard to refuse ye aught when ye look so prettily at me. Still, I must say I'm not at all inclined to put forth the effort this wild plan of yers would require. I've far more pressing matters of late to deal with than the issue of my vexatious stepmither."

A sense of excitement swelled in her. "At present, you need do nothing more than share with me your view of why things went so awry between you and Glynnis. Let me be the conciliator. Just tell me what happened."

He sighed his acquiescence. "Come then." Ruarc opened his arms to her. "Come close and let me hold ye. The tale will be far easier to tell with ye close by."

She rose and went to him, standing beside his chair as he circled her hips with a possessive arm. Bit by bit Ruarc was opening his heart to her, trusting her. It felt good.

"My mither and father were verra much in love," he began, his deep voice rumbling gently against her belly. "Indeed, my father, hardly a demonstrative or outgoing man, seemed entirely changed whenever he was near my mither. He brought her flowers; they seemed constantly to be touching each other, even if it was just a hand lightly cupping a waist or a tender stroke of a cheek. And I gloried in their love. It all but killed the two of us when my mither died."

"How old were you when it happened?"

"I was barely thirteen. Neither of us knew how to deal with our grief, and we shut the other out. The crowning blow, however, was the sudden return of my father one day with a new wife."

"Did you ever ask him why he remarried so quickly?"

"Nay." Savagely, Ruarc shook his head. "I was so furious with him that, for a long while, I couldn't bear even to be near my father, much less talk to him. And Glynnis didn't help matters any. She was either lording it over me as my new stepmither and Rannoch's lady or attempting to shower me with hugs and kisses like I was some wee bairn.

"The last thing I needed was a new mither, especially from the likes of her. I rejected all her overtures of friendship. I was quite harsh with her about it too. In time, I suppose Glynnis gave up on me."

"Can you blame her?" Compassion for the young woman Glynnis had been then, trying so hard to be a mother to the grieving boy, filled Killian. "She'd come to a strange place, married to a much older, still heartsick man whom she most likely hardly knew, and then had also to deal with a boy who resented her. It seems, though, she at least tried."

"Aye, I suppose she did. It did her no good, however, neither with me and soon enough, not with my father, either. They never suited each other. And, once Thomas was born, she devoted all her energies to her son."

"And all the love she had to give, as well," Killian added softly.

"Most likely. My father and I certainly had never wanted aught of it from her."

So much pain, so much cruelty, Killian mused. Yet, in the beginning at least, none of them had been able to see past their own confusion and need to discern the damage they were wreaking, the hearts that were breaking. One thing had built on another until now the walls were so high and strong no one seemed able to break them down. It had become easier, safer even, to do battle than to face the mistakes and forgive.

She, too, Killian admitted, had built walls about her heart after years of Alexander's mistreatment. Finally, the only solution left was escape. But life never let you run for long. For that matter, neither did God.

Yet, though Alexander's problems had been past healing or leastwise beyond her ability to heal, at any rate, that wasn't so with Ruarc. He was still capable of understanding, compassion, and forgiveness.

And perhaps, just perhaps, Killian thought with a sudden flash of insight, she, too, could find her own rebirth in helping him find his.

Just like Ruarc, her spirit had been violated. Her self-confidence in herself was still in tatters. Her dreams were but melancholy phantoms of what they had once been.

"You asked me before," Killian said finally, her surety growing with each word she uttered, "what I hoped to gain in understanding what was between you and Glynnis. At the time, I thought my motives were quite evident, and your reluctance angered me. But now . . . now I see there's far more here than what first seemed so apparent. We all—myself included—stand to gain in this attempt to reconcile you with Glynnis and Thomas. We're all in pain in some form or another. We all need love and forgiveness, a renewed sense of kinship and family. And we all, it seems, need to let the Lord back into our lives to guide us through it all."

"Well, I'll tell ye now, lass, that I gave up on God a long while ago." Ruarc looked up at her. "But what of ye? What terrible sins could ye have possibly committed that require forgiveness?"

She made a sad little sound. "What sins indeed? There were many days—and nights—after Alexander had beaten me yet again, when I silently cursed my husband and wished him dead. I think on that often now, and wonder if perhaps that night in the forest was but a final fulfillment of my evil desires. Perhaps I truly meant to drive my dirk harder than I thought. Perhaps—" she paused for a moment as tears filled her eyes—"in the end, it mattered more that I killed Alexander than even that I saved you."

"Nay." Ruarc shook his head, a fierce, determined look on his face. "I don't believe that. Ye're not that kind of a woman, sweet lass. Ye stayed with that monster far longer than he deserved. And ye didn't kill him out of hatred. It was an accident, perpetrated in the heat of the moment, in yer fear he meant to shoot me."

"You can't know that." She averted her gaze. "You can't truly know what was in my heart."

"Can't I? Then why didn't ye use yer dirk on him after he hit Gavin, then proceeded to strangle ye? Yer hands were free. Ye could've easily reached it."

No, I couldn't have, Killian silently contradicted him.

The terror that had seized her as Alexander's hands closed about her neck had rendered her all but immobile. But there *had* been a moment in the chapel, just after Alexander had staggered in and knocked her to the floor, when she had remembered her bodice knife.

In that frantic instant, Killian *had* considered using it to defend herself. But then her hand had just as quickly fallen away. No matter the threat to her own life, no matter the anguished, desperate nights spent sometimes wishing for Alexander to be gone from her life, Ruarc was right. She didn't willingly—or purposely—kill Alexander.

As if plucked away by the hand of God, a heavy weight lifted from her. *Thank you, Lord Jesus,* she thought. *Thank you.*

"When Adam captured you and accused you of killing Alexander," Killian said after a moment more, recalling herself back to the man who was holding her, "why didn't you tell him the truth? He intended to execute you for Alexander's murder."

Ruarc grunted in disgust. "Do ye seriously think Adam would've let me go, even if I'd pointed a finger at ye? Nay, Alexander's murder was but the excuse he hid behind. Adam has hated me since the day I wed Sheila. When she died, my own death was a foregone conclusion."

"Because he thinks you killed her?"

He shrugged. "At the verra least."

Killian slowly, mournfully shook her head. "Oh, Ruarc, what a complex, dangerous muddle your life has become. Your wife is dead, murdered by some unknown assailant. Your stepmother and brother scheme to take Rannoch from you. Adam Campbell hates you and seeks to end your life. And then, it even seems you've forfeited the comfort and guidance of your faith. Is there anything more you still hide from me, or do I at long last know it all?"

"Well," he said, his voice dropping to a husky whisper as he reached up to tenderly stroke her face, "I do also have a fine, bonny new wife who pleases me greatly. And that, I think, matters far, far more than all the other things ye've just mentioned."

She smiled then, eyeing him with wry amusement. "I'm glad I please you, but I should never matter more to you than God."

Ruarc sighed and shook his head. "Well, ye do matter more, lass. And let that be the end of this talk about God. Let us, instead, rejoice in what we do have, right now, together. It's enough for me."

There was a deep sadness, a longing no other human being could ever fill, behind those words, but Killian knew the time wasn't right for Ruarc to face that. "Well, I want to do more than just be a fine, bonny new wife," she said, deciding, for the present, it was best to take another tack. "I want to help you heal the terrible wounds these events have wrought on you and others. I want there to be peace in your life and in mine. I want to raise our children in happiness and harmony."

"As do I, lass. Still, I don't know if aught can be so neatly solved as ye wish it. Life doesn't always go the way we want it to go."

"No, it doesn't, but we must still try nonetheless. I'm beginning to see that God has given us a work to do in this life, and that work is to reach out in love to Him and to one another. Therein lie all the answers we'll ever need, Ruarc; therein we find all the grace and forgiveness and happiness this life can bring."

He chuckled and his eyes warmed with emotion. "I can see Father Kenneth has gained a most eloquent ally in his quest to bring me back to a more righteous path. And, indeed, ye do speak strange but wonderful words. Ye stir a hope within me that has long been dead. But I'll tell ye true, sweet lass, ye and yer fine dreams also frighten me. I fear I'm not man enough for the task."

"Sometimes, sweet husband, I feel the same," Killian whispered, her heart swelling with such joy it seemed suddenly too large for her chest. "But, oh, the satisfaction found in the striving. And the comfort of having a helpmate on the journey!"

16

THE NEXT day dawned cold but surprisingly cloudless for mid-
November. Immediately after breakfast Killian donned a kerchief
and apron, then entered the kitchen. Her mission was twofold—
a thorough cleaning of the pantry and, at the same time, questions to
Cook and some of the other kitchen staff about the night of Sheila's
death. Now that she had committed to Ruarc and Rannoch, it seemed
imperative, at the very least, that some sort of peace be made between
him and Adam. And, as convinced as she now was that Ruarc hadn't
killed his wife, she was equally certain Adam hadn't either.

Somehow, though, the investigation into Sheila's murder seemed
to have stalled at Ruarc and Adam. Each certain the other had killed
her, no other suspect had seemingly ever been considered. Killian,
however, didn't intend to leave it at that.

"Good morrow, Bessie," she said as she briskly moved to the
older woman's side. Though breakfast was barely over, already the
kitchen staff was busy preparing for the noon meal.

Cook looked up from the head of cabbage she was chopping.
"Och, good morrow, m'lady." She took notice of Killian's garb and
grinned. "Come to help us, have ye?"

"I thought the pantry might do us today." Killian glanced
around. "Where do you keep the mops, brooms, and rags?"

"In the closet over there." With the tip of her knife Bessie indicated a small door in the farthest corner. She laid down her knife.

"Jane, come here and finish up with this, will ye? I'm needed by m'lady."

Killian followed Bessie to the closet, extracted the necessary cleaning supplies, and headed for the pantry. They worked for a time in silence, first removing all the remaining bags of beans, flour, salt, and sugar, before returning to wash down all the shelves.

Finally, though, as the heavier work eased, Killian turned to Cook. "How long have you been at Rannoch now, Bessie?" She shot her an inquiring glance before turning back to rinse a dirty cloth in the bucket of water.

"Nigh onto fifteen years now, m'lady. And, for the most part, 'tis been a verra happy labor."

"So you were here the night Ruarc's first wife, the Lady Sheila, died, were you?"

"Aye, that I was, m'lady. 'Twas horrible, me finding her lying out there that morn, all covered in dew, cold and still as she was."

Killian straightened, the rag now forgotten. "*You* found Sheila? I hadn't heard that."

"I'm thinking most folk here dinna care to talk about it. 'Twas so sad and all."

"Who was present at Rannoch that night? Were there any guests?"

Bessie paused to scratch her head. "Nay, not as I recall. We'd no extra lasses in the kitchen that night, which we always had when we'd guests, so I think—" she stopped abruptly—"aye, there was *one* guest. I remember now. 'Twas Adam Campbell. But he didna stay over. After the big row in the garden with m'lord, the Campbell laird rode out posthaste."

Or so everyone but Ruarc thinks, at any rate, Killian added silently. Eliminating Adam totally from the scenario, however, as well as the other, apparently nonexistent guests, who else was about that night?

"Did Ruarc have guards posted in those days? Guards who would've been aware of the comings and goings of everyone, intruders included?"

Bessie nodded. "Aye. Rannoch has always been well guarded. Many a reiver covets m'lord's fine cattle, ye know."

So, it was unlikely some intruder—even Adam if he had decided to return—would've found his way into Rannoch and its grounds without being noticed. But that left only the castle dwellers. Had Sheila another, perhaps jealous, lover in Rannoch? Or did someone else— be that man or woman—in the castle hate her enough to kill her?

Killian's mind raced with all the possibilities. "Did you know the Lady Sheila very well, Bessie?"

The woman shrugged. "Nay, I wouldna say so. Lady Sheila didn't oft involve herself with the kitchen or its staff. 'Twasn't where her interests lay."

"And what exactly did Sheila like to do?"

"She fancied her parties, entertaining, and the such. She liked to pay long visits to her friends, Adam Campbell included. It got so Lady Sheila was gone from Rannoch more than she lived here."

Killian stooped, sloshed her rag in the water bucket, then moved to wipe one of the lower shelves. "And why was that, do you think, Bessie? That Sheila avoided Rannoch so much, I mean?"

"She was verra unhappy, m'lady. Everyone could see that, even m'lord. And he tried aught he could think of to please her."

"But nothing worked?"

"Nay, naught worked, it seemed." Cook sighed. "'Twas so verra sad, though, her dying as she did. Poor, poor lass."

"Yes, it was indeed very sad," Killian said by way of agreement. The saddest part of all, though, was the long-standing damage her mysterious death had wrought.

She only wondered if Sheila's killer had ever, for even a moment, regretted the sequence of events the barbarous act had set into motion.

†

GLYNNIS found Killian in the pantry, helping Cook load the last of the food supplies back onto the shelves. She eyed the younger woman and grimaced.

Didn't the lass yet know her place? A place that was hardly in a pantry, covered in dust and cobwebs, helping mop out the corners and sort the dry goods. But then, what purpose would it serve to chide her?

Ruarc was hardly any better, as oft as he rode out to lend an extra hand with the haying or to help herd the cows back down the mountains from the summer shielings. If the truth were told, she'd wager

Rannoch's laird had ordered the poor lass to work herself near to exhaustion. He had always been so single-minded, after all, when it came to placing Rannoch's welfare over everything and everyone else.

Killian did, however, have a way with the servants even Sheila had lacked. Why, she had never seen Bessie look quite so animated or at ease, her thin face flushed and bright with cheer. Killian appeared equally happy as she stepped up on a lower shelf edge to reach a bag of flour.

"Er, m'lady," Glynnis said, choosing that moment to move forward, "if ye would, I'd like a word with ye."

Killian grabbed the flour bag, clasped it to her, and climbed down. The cloth bag had several holes in it, most likely left by hungry mice, and the white powder puffed through the cavities, leaving floury splotches on her gown. She gingerly offered the bag to Cook, then turned to Glynnis.

"I'm rather busy at this moment." She glanced down, noted the flour marks, and tried to dust them away with the side of her hand. "Will this take very long? If so, perhaps I could meet you in the library in a half hour's time?"

The implication that housekeeping was more important than a visit with one's peers irked Glynnis. She hid her irritation, though, beneath a sweet smile. "It won't take long, m'lady, but I'd be happy to meet ye later in the library. I can see that, at present, ye're quite enthralled with cleaning the pantry."

Killian grinned, apparently choosing not to take offense at Glynnis's snide observation. "Well, I wouldn't quite call it enthralled, but this kitchen does need a long-overdue cleaning before the fall harvest of flour is loaded in here. It'd do no good to put new bags in a filthy spot."

"Nay, I suppose not, m'lady." Glynnis gathered her skirts and stepped back. "Shall we plan to meet in the library in a half hour then?"

"Yes. In a half hour."

†

A HALF hour later, Glynnis nervously paced the library, all the while fingering the letter in her pocket. Was it truly wise, she asked herself yet again, to give the young Colonial Adam's missive?

She could only imagine what the handsome Campbell laird had said. She hadn't dared open and read it, fearing she wouldn't be able to hide the evidence of her tampering. One way or another, though, none of it would surely bode well—for either Killian or Ruarc.

Not that Glynnis cared for whatever pain or damage it might cause her despicable stepson. But Killian's heart, though mayhap extremely gullible, was good. Glynnis hated even the consideration of doing the lass harm. Still, Killian had apparently made her choice for her husband and must bear the consequences. Sooner or later, the lass *must* face the truth about Ruarc MacDonald.

True to her word, Killian arrived on the half-hour stroke of the big library floor clock. She hadn't bothered to remove her flour-dusted apron or head scarf, and the hem of her gown and sleeves were smudged with dirt. Striding up to where Glynnis now sat at the table, Killian halted.

"Well, what is it, Glynnis? We've had a small emergency in the kitchen—one of the serving maids not only spilled hot grease all over the floor, but also burned her arm—and I promised I'd return and help deal with the mess. So, if you don't mind getting to the point . . ."

"Bessie can handle the emergency for a time more, m'lady. What I have for ye will mayhap present an even greater problem." Glynnis withdrew the letter and handed it over. "It's from Adam Campbell."

At mention of Adam's name, Killian promptly withdrew the hand she had extended for the letter. "Adam sent me a letter? Why?"

Glynnis continued to offer the letter. "I can't say, m'lady. He didn't choose to confide in me, only to use me as his go-between." Her hand fell back to her side. "But if accepting it makes ye uncomfortable, I well understand. I can't say I feel verra comfortable myself, delivering this to ye."

"Then why did you do so?" Killian's eyes narrowed with suspicion. "I thought you'd finally learned your lesson, in helping Adam set that trap for Ruarc."

Glynnis laid the letter on the table and rose. "I only accepted this from his messenger because I thought it'd be of import to ye. But if it isn't, then mayhap it's best ye toss it into the hearth fire and be done with it. It matters not to me."

With that, she gathered her skirts and headed for the door. Just as her hand reached out to slip the door latch, however, Glynnis paused and shot a quick look over her shoulder. Killian stood there still, her arms clasped tightly to her, staring at the letter lying on the table.

A grim satisfaction filled Glynnis. The lass was sorely tempted, that she was. Adam's ploy, whatever it now was, might work after all. She could only pray its ultimate success would finally ensure Ruarc's downfall.

But what if, in the doing, irreparable harm was also done to Killian? Glynnis's hand tightened on the door handle. *Fool,* she scolded herself, *never forget the silly wench has chosen Ruarc. She must suffer the consequences.*

Indeed, hadn't they all, in some way or another, suffered because of Ruarc? It only remained to hold fast to her resolve to see him destroyed.

Then none of them, Killian included, would ever have to suffer again.

†

Dearest Cousin,

Forgive my audacity in penning this missive to you. Some time has passed, though, since you left so unexpectedly, and my concern for you has grown apace with my puzzlement. Why did you depart from me? What did I do to offend or frighten you? Tell me, I pray, so I can make amends.

I find it impossible to understand why you left with Ruarc MacDonald, or why you remain with him. Has he in some way bewitched you? Does he hold you under duress? Pray, tell me how you're faring, dear cousin. Tell me how I may be of assistance, if you truly do need assistance.

We are kin, you and I, even if only by marriage. My feelings for you, however, extend far past those of blood and law. Be assured that they always will.

Devotedly yours,
Adam

Killian folded the letter closed and shoved it into her apron pocket. She walked to the tall library window, drew back the curtains, and looked outside.

It had turned into a typical, thoroughly bleak, chilly Highland day. In the hours she and Bessie had worked in the kitchen, clouds had blown in. Rain now sleeted from the heavens, clattering on the roof, drenching the land. A gloomy pall hung over the scene of frost-killed garden; black, skeletal trees dripping with icicles; and distant, mist-shrouded mountains. Winter would surely follow soon on the heels of such miserable weather.

There was something almost sinister about a day like today. People crept about, clutching at their woolen shawls and cloaks, their faces taut and strained. They jumped at the slightest noise, were distracted by the most minor of things. They fully expected disaster, and soon found it.

Was she, too, courting disaster? Were Adam's motives in writing her sinister, or were they motivated only by a sincere concern and affection? It was impossible to know, leastwise with only one letter and without meeting with him.

One thing was certain. Her first loyalty now lay with her husband, and she wouldn't do anything to jeopardize their budding relationship. *Nothing* was more important than that.

She didn't dare risk a face-to-face encounter with Adam. He could still mean to use her to trap Ruarc. Indeed, perhaps this letter was yet another of his devious attempts to discover and use some other chink in Ruarc's armor. A chink that could well involve her.

With a shiver, Killian turned from the window and hurried to stand before the fire. The flames leaped high in the big, stone hearth, bright red-and-yellow tongues licking hungrily upward as they devoured the wood that was their meal. The fire's voracious glee, however, offered little comfort. It reminded her too forcefully of Ruarc's enemies and how eagerly they sought his destruction.

She pulled the letter from her pocket, opened it once more, and reread the bold script. Adam had always been kind to her. Up until that night he had refused to help her return home, he had treated her with the utmost courtesy and concern. Save for his obsessive hatred for Ruarc and its cause, he had always seemed a good, honorable man.

Was there no way to bring these two men together, to make peace between them? Ruarc wasn't a wife killer. If there was only some way to convince Adam of that, perhaps this bitter feud between them could end.

As she had begun to work daily with Francis on the castle accounts, gently instructing him about the myriad tasks required for proper bookkeeping, the young man had mentioned one day that Ruarc and Adam had once been friends, joined by their common dedication to the cause of the then Prince William of Orange and his defense of Holland. It had been Sheila, Francis had scathingly informed her, who had irretrievably destroyed the friendship, first in agreeing to wed Ruarc, then compounding it later in her adulterous relationship with her foster brother.

"She was naught more than a harlot," Francis spat, throwing down his quill pen in disgust. "Petty and self-serving to her dying day, she toyed with the feelings of everyone. I took her measure shortly after she arrived at Rannoch, lad though I was, and soon ascertained the paucity of her love for m'lord. Always, always, did I strive to mitigate her destructive influence on Rannoch and m'lord. There was naught I could do, though, for the pain she wrought upon his heart."

It was strange, Killian mused, thinking back to that day and Francis's impassioned revelation, how one woman could affect different people in such different ways. Was Sheila truly such a fatally complex woman, or were her actions but interpreted differently by everyone she touched, strained as they were through the filter of each person's expectations and perceptions? It was hard to know, for which one fully understood the person Sheila really was?

How had Adam viewed his foster sister? Perhaps if Killian began better to understand his view of what had happened to her, she might finally find some common ground wherein he and Ruarc might be able to make peace. But how could that ever come about with Adam so far away and with no possible chance now of bringing him to Rannoch?

Killian held up the letter. Was it worth the risk? She answered her own question by tossing it into the fire. In a explosion of flame, the paper curled, blackened, then was gone.

No, it wasn't worth the risk of hurting Ruarc. Nothing was anymore. All Killian wanted was to help him in every way she could. The problem was, the path to that end was becoming increasingly convoluted and far, far more precarious.

†

AS FATHER Kenneth gave the benediction signaling the end of that Sunday's Mass, Killian glanced at Ruarc kneeling in the pew beside her. Though he dutifully made the sign of the cross in response to the priest's corresponding actions, his face was expressionless, his movements automatic. He went through the motions because it was expected, not because he truly believed.

She wondered when Ruarc had lost his love for God. Perhaps it had happened when his mother died. Such heart-wrenching losses were enough to test the faith of grown men, much less that of a boy. And, from what Ruarc had told her of his father . . . well, Killian now knew his sire had been of little support or comfort when Ruarc needed it most.

They filed from the chapel together, Gavin skipping ahead of them down the pew-lined aisle. As soon as they were outside, however, the little boy wheeled about and ran back to Ruarc.

"Can we go for a walk?" Gavin gazed up at the big Highlander with pleading eyes. "Just you, me, and our dogs?"

Ruarc chuckled and looked to Killian. "Would ye mind? We've another two hours before the midday meal, and it *is* a fine day."

Shading her eyes, she glanced at the sky. She wouldn't go so far as to agree it was a fine day, noting the hazy glow of the sun behind the light overcast and the sharp, cold bite of the air, but Killian also knew a brisk walk wouldn't do any harm, either. Ruarc would see to it Gavin stayed warm and turn back at the first sign of inclement weather.

She smiled. "No, I wouldn't mind. I've a few things I'd like to discuss with Father Kenneth at any rate."

"Do ye now?" Her husband grinned down at her. "Ye two seem to be becoming fast friends. I'm glad. After the rocky start ye had with Father, I wondered if ye ever would."

"Did you now?" Killian eyed him mischievously. "Then it must come as some relief that I find Father Kenneth a very wise, if unusual, man." She gave Ruarc a playful shove. "Now, away with you, or you and Gavin will never make it back in time. I know how you two get when you go out with those dogs."

"Och, we do tend to wander a bit, don't we?" Ruarc laughed. "Mayhap it's time I take ye out with me for a wee ride. Then ye'll understand why we're gone for such a long while."

She never thought she'd ever admit to it, much less want it, but Killian nodded in eager agreement. "I'd like that. I haven't seen all that much of MacDonald lands, you know. Assuming, of course," she added with a grin, "there's much worth seeing?"

"Ye know there is, ye saucy wench."

Ruarc made a move to take her by the arm and pull her to him but, with a laugh, Killian nimbly eluded him. "Get on with you. There's time aplenty for that tonight, and well you know it."

"Aye, there is indeed," Father Kenneth agreed, walking up to join Killian. He turned to her. "I overheard ye saying ye wished to speak with me."

"Yes, I do, if you've the time."

He offered her his arm, which she immediately accepted. "Aye, that I do. It's past time, at any rate, Ruarc share ye a bit. He's been verra selfish, near to keeping ye all to himself, this past month."

"Och, and that's a gross and unfair exaggeration if ever I heard one," Ruarc cried over his shoulder as he began to lead Gavin away. "I can hardly find the lass most days, so busy has she been with all her duties."

"Pay him no heed, lass." Father Kenneth tipped his shaggy head toward her as they turned and walked off. "Besides, it'll do the lad good to fret a bit. He'll only savor the time ye spend together all the more."

Killian shook her head in fond exasperation. The priest, it appeared, couldn't help but play the matchmaker at every opportunity. "And what if I fret equally as much when I'm apart from Ruarc? What would you advise then, Father?"

He shrugged. "Och, I wouldn't presume to advise aught. I'm just verra pleased yer heart longs after yer husband. That has always been my fondest wish for ye and Ruarc."

They walked for a time in silence. Finally, Father Kenneth glanced at her. "What, then, did ye wish to speak with me about? There's naught amiss, is there, lass?"

Killian hesitated. Two weeks had passed since that dreary day Glynnis had first delivered Adam's letter. Though Killian had decided against sending any reply, that reminder of the two men's long-standing animosity had intensified her mission to discover Sheila's true killer.

"There are no pressing problems between Ruarc and me, if that's what you mean," she replied finally. "I'm very happy with how well our marriage is going."

"Then what distresses ye, lass?"

"Ruarc's problems with Adam. Francis told me they used to be friends, but ever since Sheila . . . well, you know more about that than even I, I suppose."

The priest scratched his beard. "And why should ye worry? Clan feuds are common enough in the Highlands. As long as Ruarc has a care to take his men with him whenever he goes off MacDonald lands, he should be safe enough."

"Ruarc's my husband now and Adam's my cousin. I care about the both of them."

"Yer concern is quite commendable, but what if it came down to choosing between the two? Who would ye choose?"

Puzzlement filled her. Father Kenneth must be searching for something here, as he was hardly a heartless or suspicious man.

"I'd choose Ruarc, of course," she said. "But don't you see? I want to prevent that from ever happening. I want to make peace between them."

"And exactly how," he asked, fixing her now with a piercing stare, "do ye propose to do that? Any meeting between the two of them would be foolish, not to mention likely fatal for at least one if not for both of them."

Killian shook her head. "I realize the futility of their meeting right now. Rather, I'd prefer to get to the bottom of who killed Sheila."

"I gather ye don't think Adam did it, do ye?"

"No, I don't. Do you?"

Father Kenneth stroked his beard thoughtfully. "Nay, I suppose I don't. Adam wouldn't be so set on revenge otherwise."

"Then who?" Killian cried in frustration. "Who *did* do it, and why?"

"I truly don't know, lass." Father Kenneth eyed her for a long, considering moment. "I see ye've yet to hear the full tale of that night." He gestured back toward the chapel. "Come. These days the cold doesn't set well with my bones. Let us adjourn to a warmer spot."

She complied silently, well knowing once they were back inside, the little priest meant to share his view of the story surrounding Sheila's death. And, just as soon as they were seated in the pew before the altar, he did just that.

"Though Ruarc was well aware, by the time he'd been wed to Sheila all those years, of the rumors of her infidelities, he chose not to pay them heed," Father Kenneth began. "But then Ruarc, when it came to Sheila, had always turned a deaf ear and blind eye to anything less than complimentary about her."

"And why was that, do you think?"

"Why else?" The priest shrugged and smiled apologetically. "For a long while, he loved her almost past the point of reason. He gave her everything she ever wanted and tolerated her failings, which over time grew to considerable proportions. I even think if Sheila hadn't finally confronted him that night, after Ruarc found her and Adam embracing in the garden, he might have even forgiven her that, too."

Killian's clenched hands grew clammy. She opened them, surprised that she had grown so tense. "What did Sheila say to Ruarc?"

A pensive look settled over his face. "Mayhap I've overstepped myself, in even telling ye this much, lass. The rest, at any rate, should come from Ruarc, if he's ever of a mind to tell ye."

"But I need to know, to understand! How else am I to get Ruarc and Adam to make peace? How else am I to save our marriage, before it becomes irrevocably entwined in the self-destructive morass that was Sheila's life?"

"Suffice it to say, Ruarc has even more of a reason to hate Adam than Adam has to hate Ruarc."

"If it's because Adam and Sheila lay together, I already know that. Glynnis told me."

"Aye," Father Kenneth muttered, "and why doesn't that surprise me? Glynnis cannot tell ye, though, what Sheila's relationship with Adam did to Ruarc, can she? Nor would she care at any rate."

"But you can," Killian persisted. "You know, don't you?"

He nodded. "Aye, I know. But it's still best ye hear the rest from yer husband. He's what matters, the pain he suffered and how it has affected him, and how it might yet affect yer marriage. If ye wish to help him, and even someday heal the wounds that poor, lost lass wrought on him—and mayhap even upon Adam, too—ye must start with Ruarc." He cocked his head. "Do ye understand me, lass?"

The old priest was right. Though she and Ruarc had come far in the past weeks, there was still more that needed to be shared, more that must be understood. Not only about Ruarc and Sheila, but perhaps about Adam, too.

"Yes, I suppose I do understand," she said. "I just wish I could finally come to the end of all the mystery and pain."

"Ye will in time, lass," Father Kenneth assured her, smiling at last. "Ye will, in God's own good time."

NOVEMBER eased into a frosty December. One day early in the month Killian decided to resume her ongoing inquiry about Sheila's death by paying Glynnis a visit. She found her warming herself against the bitter winds blowing in from the north at her bedchamber hearth fire. As Finola let Killian into the room, Ruarc's stepmother glanced up from some finely wrought piece of embroidery she was working.

"Welcome, m'lady." The older woman set aside her needlework and rose from the padded bench to greet her. "Whatever brings ye here on such a cold, miserable day?"

Killian glanced at the serving maid. "I've a private matter to discuss, if you've the time."

Glynnis's gaze turned in the same direction as Killian's, and she nodded. "Of course I've the time. Finola—" she looked directly at the girl—"would ye mind fetching two mugs of mulled cider from the kitchen? I could do with something warm in my belly, as I'm certain could Lady MacDonald as well."

"Aye, mistress." Finola curtsied and immediately departed.

"Come, sit yerself here beside me at the hearth," Glynnis next said. "On days such as this ye cannot help but feel the cold deep in yer bones, unless ye're fast up by a fire." She shivered delicately. "I keep urging Ruarc to close off this older part of the castle and build on a new, more tightly constructed addition, but he insists on squandering any profit we turn each year from land rent to improving the fields and repairing the crofts."

Harking back to the sad state of the castle accounts, Killian imagined there was never as much profit realized each year as Glynnis may have thought. In time, though, that might well change. Then she, too, would raise her voice for improvements at Rannoch. Anything, after all, that would lead to increased efficiency would save money in the end.

"I'll talk to Ruarc about your concerns," she said, seating herself on the bench next to Glynnis. "In the meanwhile, I've given a great deal of thought to the issue of Ruarc and Adam's enmity, and its cause."

A sudden gleam of interest flared in her ebony-haired companion's eyes. "Indeed? And do ye now wish to send a reply to Adam's letter?"

Killian shook her head. "Most certainly not. No purpose would be served in responding to Adam behind Ruarc's back. Though I dearly wish them to reconcile, it can't be effected in such a manner."

Glynnis frowned. "Then how may I be of help, m'lady?"

"Putting aside your feelings for Ruarc for just a moment," Killian said, leaning toward her now, "if Ruarc didn't kill Sheila, and neither did Adam, who else would've had cause to do so?"

Ruarc's stepmother pursed her lips and shot her a jaundiced look. "Why, I wouldn't know, m'lady. I never considered anyone other than Ruarc."

Killian sighed. "But if you *did*, Glynnis, who else would be a likely suspect, and why?"

"Well, since ye insist on playing this guessing game, I suppose Francis comes to mind. His hatred of Sheila was always but thinly veiled behind a simpering mask of courtesy."

"Francis?" Killian couldn't help but laugh. "He's never impressed me as a very physical person, much less a violent one."

"Mayhap not." Glynnis shrugged, took up her needlework, and began to stitch. "But ye did ask me to play the guessing game, did ye not? And, in all truth, I cannot imagine who else would've held a grudge against Sheila strong enough to wish to kill her. Leastwise, no one else but Ruarc."

"You said she'd had several lovers besides Adam. What about them?"

"None were at Rannoch that night, or even nearby. One was a soldier, who had been reassigned to Fort William a year earlier. Two others were noblemen who lived outside the glen. And the rest—" Glynnis smiled sadly—"well, suffice it to say, they've disappeared into the Highland mists long ago."

"Sheila did indeed confide everything to you, didn't she?"

With an effort, Killian clamped down hard on a note of sarcasm. What manner of wife would so wantonly bed so many men and still wish to remain wed to her husband? If the respect and love were gone, what was left?

But then, *she* had remained with Alexander for years after any real respect or love was long dead. She had done so, though, because of her wedding vows and because she had mistakenly clung to her false dreams. What, then, were Sheila's reasons for staying so long with Ruarc?

"Aye, the wee lass opened her heart to me," Glynnis replied, a faraway look in her eyes. "I was both mither and friend to her. Her foster mither—Adam's mither—the scheming, greedy witch that she was, never considered Sheila as aught more than a bargaining piece in her relentless quest to further her family's wealth and position. It was why she all but pushed Sheila on Ruarc, then refused to listen when Sheila came to her and begged to back out of the marriage."

"Still, Sheila could've told Ruarc herself," Killian said. "He wouldn't have married her if she'd been unwilling."

Glynnis shook her head. "The tale's far more complicated than what ye might first imagine. Just a few months before Adam and Ruarc returned to Scotland after their battle victories for William in Holland, Adam's elder brother died. As the only other son, Adam automatically became Achallader's next heir. And, for all Sheila's willfulness, when it came to Adam, she would've never done aught to harm him. That's precisely what she feared would happen, however, if she revealed her true feelings.

"Adam's mither wanted a better marriage for her son than that of one with Sheila, the daughter of a lesser clansman. She convinced the lass that Adam would be disinherited if he wed her. The woman

221

proceeded to point out what a splendid opportunity for social advancement wedding Ruarc MacDonald was."

Glynnis's lips curled into a sneer. "Sheila never had a chance. Adam's mither enlisted her husband's aid in hounding the poor lass until Sheila didn't know which way to turn. And then there was the strong social taboo associated with marriage of fosterlings to those in the family in which they were fostered. Though not condemned by law or Kirk, most still considered it nigh onto incest anyways."

"So Sheila never told Adam, did she?" Killian asked. "And Ruarc, as well as Adam, never knew what had transpired until long after."

"Nay, they didn't. To be sure, Adam was the first to hear Sheila's tale, but she didn't tell him until two years later, when Adam's father died and he inherited Achallader. It was far too late by then, though. She was carrying Ruarc's first bairn at that time, and she felt committed to the marriage for the sake of the child, if for naught else. And, by the time she'd lost all her other wee ones in succeeding years, I think she'd given up hope of ever being happy again. When Adam's mither died, six years after she and Ruarc had wed, Sheila was but a dried shell of the woman she'd once been. The day after they buried Adam's mither, Sheila took her first lover."

"There was no one to judge or constrain her anymore after that, was there?" Killian offered softly, as understanding began to dawn. "And no reason to keep her vows to Ruarc, vows she'd really only made because of that woman, after all."

"Aye, I suppose that's as good an explanation as any." Glynnis laid aside her embroidery, leaned back in her chair, and closed her eyes. "I didn't like what she became after that. In truth, I knew in my heart Ruarc had never been to blame, save for his arrogance in refusing to believe Sheila had never loved him. But I stood by her, nonetheless, to the verra end. Sheila needed me, and I so wanted to be needed by someone."

"She was fortunate to have had you as a friend, Glynnis."

"Aye, she was." Glynnis opened her eyes and turned to Killian. "She'd few friends in Rannoch, ye know, especially after Adam's mither died and she found little reason anymore to pretend to a happy marriage. She turned peevish, demanding, and all but relinquished her duties as Rannoch's lady. She discharged servants for the most minimal of reasons. She alienated several noblemen and their wives, including the clan chief, Alasdair MacDonald. There were more than a few dry eyes at her funeral, ye can be sure."

"So there *is* the possibility someone outside Rannoch wished her ill and might've somehow sought to harm her."

The older woman studied her for a long moment, then nodded. "Aye, I suppose there is. Sheila's been dead three years now, however. If someone outside Rannoch truly did kill her, that trail's all but vanished by now."

"Perhaps it has." Gooseflesh rose on Killian's skin as a sudden, chill wind briefly but most effectively found its way into the bedchamber. "I refuse to give up on this, though. Sheila's specter must be laid to rest, or I fear her tragic life—and death—will always come between Ruarc and me. She isn't truly dead and buried until her killer is found.

"And I'll not," Killian added with grim determination, "stand helplessly by and watch yet another husband spiral slowly downward into self-destruction."

†

TWO DAYS later while Adam was at his evening meal, Lachlan, a small leather-wrapped parcel in hand, joined him at table. Achallader's laird shot the package his cousin laid beside him a cursory glance, then returned to his plate of roast venison and potatoes.

"Does that require my immediate attention?" he asked around a mouthful of savory deer meat.

The red-haired young man leaned close. "The letter's from Rannoch, m'lord. Ye must be the one to decide its urgency or no."

Adam's pulse quickened with a thrill of excitement. Mayhap fate had finally smiled on him, and the letter was from Killian. Even so, it could wait a few moments more. This was the best piece of venison he'd had in a long while, and he intended on enjoying every bite. Her letter, however, might well be a fitting end to what had already been a profitable and highly informative day.

Only two hours ago, he had returned from a brief meeting with the Earl of Breadalbane. His uncle, Adam had been informed, had been in frequent correspondence with Sir John Dalrymple, Master of Stair. As leader of the first Scottish parliament with King William often abroad at the wars, and virtual ruler of Scotland, the Master of Stair was claimed to be coconspirator with Breadalbane in a plan to punish any and all who failed to sign the king's oath. A Lowlander, Stair was well known to be intolerant of the Highlands, viewing its peoples as barbarous and brutal and the last refuge of the Jacobites loyal to King James.

Though Adam hardly shared the Master of Stair's scathing assessment of his beloved Highlands, the highly placed Stair's influence and part in the plot could only help open the door to Adam's intent to finally lay hold of Ruarc MacDonald. Breadalbane had given Adam a moment of pause today, however, when he had loudly claimed that the recalcitrant chiefs must be so handsomely mauled that their will to resist would be crushed forever. *All* the rebels, he had added with a wild light in his eyes, but if not, a selected few like MacDonald of Glencoe and Keppoch would do.

That moment of pause, though, had quickly faded, as Adam recalled the wording of the King's demand. "The utmost extremity of the law" was generally taken to mean extirpation, or to make a clan landless and chiefless. At worst, the MacDonald chief would be imprisoned and the clan driven from their lands. If that happened, Ruarc, as one of the Glencoe MacDonalds, would lose Rannoch. Once cast from the safety of his castle, it would, Adam hoped, make it an easy task to soon capture and imprison his enemy.

Aye, he thought, as he finally shoved back his plate and took up the letter, it had indeed been a good day. And if Killian had chosen to respond to his first correspondence to her, the rest of the eve would be spent in an equally pleasant endeavor, devising a way to draw her yet more deeply into his confidences.

†

THANKS to Killian's untiring and creative efforts, Yuletide came early to Rannoch Castle. Evergreens, particularly holly, festooned the banisters, above the doors, and over the fireplace mantels. Candles were set in the windows to light the way of a stranger—as well as for that of the Holy Family on Christmas Eve.

A holiday pudding, rich with raisins, spices, and candied cherries and oranges, was prepared well in advance, everyone making a wish, then taking a turn stirring the pudding from east to west in remembrance of the Three Wise Men's journey. And, finally, plans were made for a big feast, replete with a savory lamb stew, shortbread, and the by then well-aged pudding, after Midnight Mass on Christmas Eve.

Ruarc watched all the preparations with a wondering eye. In the span of three and a half months, Killian had effected an amazing transformation at Rannoch. The floors and furniture were clean, the windows sparkled, the meals were hot and delicious, and the servants unusually happy and energetic.

The physical improvements in the castle, however, paled in comparison to the amazing transformation she had wrought within him. Ruarc found that he laughed and smiled more. He rode home eagerly now after each day's hard work. And his anticipation of each night to come was as ardent as some lad afire with his first love.

And it was more than physical. He equally craved the tender emotional intimacy and sense of safe haven he always found with Killian.

If he'd had his way, he would've gladly gone on for the entire winter, ensconced in his happy contentment, aglow in his love. The outside world and increasingly gloomy political fortunes of the Highland clans still stubbornly holding out against signing the oath of fealty, however, wouldn't long allow him such continued peace. On the twentieth of December, just eleven days before the signing deadline, Ruarc decided to try one last time to convince his clan chief the time for waiting on James II was over.

He found Killian that morning sitting before the Great Hall's hearth fire, stitching furiously away at something that, at his approach, she hurriedly shoved into her sewing bag. Standing, she smoothed the wrinkles from her open skirt of rose-colored silk looped at both sides and the matching embroidered underskirt. The color, Ruarc noted, suited her well, nicely accenting her pale hair, softly glowing cheeks, and smooth, ivory-hued skin.

For a fleeting instant, his glance dropped to the boned bodice decorated with ivory- and mauve-colored ribbons. It still fit her small waist snugly. Disappointment stabbed at him, then was gone.

If she were already carrying his child, it had yet to show. Most likely, if she were already carrying his child, Killian had yet even to realize it herself.

There was time. He and Killian were still young. Besides, if the truth were told, he cherished these special days and weeks of getting to know each other. A bairn, when it finally came, would place demands on Killian that would, understandably, cut short their own time together. Aye, Ruarc consoled himself yet again. There was indeed plenty of time.

"You wish something of me, husband?" Killian's sweet voice intruded into his avid contemplation of her. "Or did you come just to stare and devour me with those glorious green eyes of yours?"

Hot blood filled his cheeks. "And would ye protest all that loudly if I did devour ye? Ye *are* quite a delectable sight, ye know, in that bonny gown of yers."

She laughed then, and the sound sent a most pleasurable shiver down Ruarc's spine.

"Then it was well worth the time spent altering it," she said. "Glynnis offered it to me, claiming it'd always been too tight for her anyways."

At mention of his stepmother, Ruarc scowled. "Aye, I'd imagine it was too tight. But then, everything Glynnis wears is far too tight and too revealing, if ye ask my opinion."

"Well, perhaps I won't then," she replied, shooting him a wry look. "Now, I say again—do you wish something of me?"

He knew his scathing comment about Glynnis had dampened the happiness of the moment, and he sorely regretted his uncharitable tongue. Try as he might, though, Glynnis and Thomas remained a burr that rubbed him hard and deeply. He couldn't say he liked the thought of Killian getting too close to Glynnis, either. Despite his wife's efforts to the contrary, Ruarc wasn't so sure that particular sentiment of his would ever change.

"Aye, I do wish something of ye," he replied finally. "I've decided to pay the MacDonald clan chief a wee visit. Would ye like to come along and meet him? He's verra partial to lovely young lasses, and I think ye'll find him equally as magnificent, for our braw Alasdair is a huge man by anyone's reckoning."

"Even larger than you, husband?"

As he watched, her gaze ran up and down his six-foot-plus length.

Ruarc grinned and nodded. "Aye, even larger than me by a good five or six inches, I'd wager. He isn't called 'MacIain of the gigantic mould' for naught."

"Well, I'd like very much to meet your chief." She gave a resolute nod. "When do you wish to depart?"

"In an hour's time, if ye can prepare yerself by then. We'll stay overnight at Alasdair's house in Carnoch, then return on the morrow."

"And what's the reason for this sudden visit?"

"Mainly social—to introduce my new wife to the clan—but also to discuss a few issues that have yet to be resolved. I promise, though, not to spend the entire time engaged in deep political discussions."

"I should hope not," Killian agreed fervently. "What exactly would those political discussions be about?"

He opened his mouth to inform her, then thought better of it. "Mayhap that'd best be explained on our ride to Carnoch. Get on with ye now," Ruarc urged, taking her by the arm and turning her in the direction of the stairs. "We'll have plenty of time to talk on the way."

Killian shot him an arch look, walked to her chair, picked up her sewing bag, and set out. Ruarc watched until she reached the top of the staircase and, with a quick smile over her shoulder, disappeared down the hallway leading to their bedchamber. With a grin, he turned and headed off to complete his own preparations for the journey.

†

IT WAS a bitterly cold day. The sun barely glowed behind a thick shroud of haze. The snow lay deep on the land. Periodically a sharp breeze would stir, setting the somber, naked tree branches to clacking and an icy blast to numbing cheeks and noses.

Still, Killian mused as she pulled the hood of her thick woolen cloak more closely to her and glanced around at the stark winter landscape, there was something beautiful and majestic about this land. As they rode out from Rannoch, the bleak, flat bogs of Rannoch Moor soon faded from view. They followed the River Coupall down the glen to its joining with the River Etive. As the mountains began to rise on either side, the glen gradually became little more than a sunless rent, a gorge slashed at its base by sluggish, ice-choked waters.

They saw several ptarmigan dressed in their winter plumage, their white bodies blending well into the snow-covered land, and a herd of red deer. Frost-killed bell heather and gentians, which had only weeks before bloomed, now poked their bent, brown heads from the protective shield of gullies cleaving to the mountainsides. High overhead, a golden eagle soared then dove, followed several minutes later by two squawking ravens beating frantically downward in its wake.

"That towering mountain there on yer left is Buachaille Etive Mor, affectionately known as the Great Herdsman of Etive," Ruarc offered as they guided their mounts along the river's edge. "The next one past the Great Herdsman on the left will be the Buachaille Etive Beag, or the Small Herdsman. They're called the herdsmen because their lower slopes provide rich grazing for our black cattle. On yer right is Beinn a' Chrulaiste. Together with the Great Herdsman, that mountainous slump guards the entrance to the glen and helps funnel the unhindered winds and weathers off Rannoch Moor."

Killian peered down the curving length of the glen, or leastwise as far as the jutting rocks allowed her to see. "The glen is ringed by all sorts of mountains, isn't it? That's why it's so easy to defend, or so I've heard."

"Aye. In all of the Highlands, there isn't a more well-defensible sanctuary. Otherwise, Adam Campbell and his ilk would have attempted a direct attack on Rannoch and the rest of the homes along the glen long ago. There are only two easy—if ye care to call aught here easy—entrances to Glencoe: Rannoch Moor to the east and Loch Levenside in the west. The mountains to the north and south of the glen only lead men to higher and higher passes."

Ruarc smiled grimly. "We MacDonalds live in a special place, and few outside the clan are foolhardy enough to venture here with thoughts of war or plunder on their minds. However, that said, with the right planning and leadership, it'd also be an easy matter to block both ends of the glen with but a small force of men, then send the rest in to wreak great destruction."

He pointed to a rippling, saw-toothed escarpment far down the glen. "That's Aonach Eagach, the Notched Ridge. It runs on for eight miles or so and marks the middle of the glen. At its eastern end is the Devil's Staircase, a narrow, crooked trail that climbs from the head of Loch Leven, flanks Aonach Eagach's escarpment for five miles, then comes down at last to Rannoch. It's the only path into Glencoe from the north, if ye care to risk it."

Killian shivered and shook her head. "I'd rather not risk anything here without you at my side. Only someone who truly knows this glen should be venturing out into it."

Ruarc chuckled. "Glencoe *can* be intimidating for those unfamiliar with it. In time, though, it becomes a place of wild, fierce beauty. Ye'll see it better when spring gives way to the lush loveliness of summer. Yet still, to my mind," he added with a soft, wistful smile, "the quiet days of early winter are the best."

"You can be quite the poet when you set your mind to it." She cocked her head and studied him with wondering delight. "Just when I begin to imagine I've discovered all your secrets, you reveal yet another."

"It's believed in the Highlands, and particularly by the MacDonalds, that all men of Glencoe are poets from birth. Indeed," he added with a grin, "it's said any man who lives in the glen, and cannot readily put his tongue to verse when invited, will soon have his paternity brought to question."

"Is your chief a poet then, as well?"

"Och, he's not only a poet, but a man much loved by his neighbors, blameless in conduct, and a person of great integrity, honor, good nature, and courage."

"Then what can be of such political importance that you feel compelled to visit him in such cold weather, and so close to Christmas?"

Ruarc's smile faded. "There are problems afoot, if Alasdair refuses to sign the oath of fealty demanded by King William. . . ."

As Killian listened to her husband's explanation of the King's intent to subdue the Highland chiefs and garner their loyalty from that of the deposed James II, her concern grew apace with his tale.

Finally, when Ruarc paused to concentrate on guiding his horse around a large boulder, she could contain herself no longer. "What will happen if your chief refuses to sign?" she asked. "And what effect will it have on you, and on Rannoch?"

"We are one clan. We must support our chief in all that he does. Even if," Ruarc added darkly, "he appears intent on destroying us all in his futile, unswerving loyalty to James."

Unease rippled through Killian. "What do you think the King will do if Alasdair refuses to sign? Surely it'd be little more than a fine, or a few months' imprisonment?"

Ruarc reined in his horse. With a rising sense of foreboding, Killian did the same.

"If it were solely up to William," he replied, not meeting her anxious gaze, "your supposition might well be correct. But there are many in the English Court who hate all Highlanders, and some in the Highlands who especially hate the MacDonalds. Unfortunately for us, those particular Scotsmen are also some of the most powerful voices at Court."

"Like the Campbells, you mean?"

"Aye." He nodded. "That was the reason I was so near Achallader that night I found ye in the forest. I was hoping to spy on that grand meeting of Campbell nobles gathered there. Unfortunately, thanks to my unexpected meeting with ye in the forest and a search party sent out to pursue me soon thereafter, I never had the chance to complete my mission."

"Ah, that explains why you disappeared and left Gavin and me that night."

"I'd no choice. Besides, I assumed my pursuers would soon find ye. They didn't, though, did they?"

"No, they didn't." Killian frowned in thought. "I remember a few names at the ball—a Captain Robert Campbell of Glenlyon and a Sir John Campbell, Earl of Breadalbane. And Adam said something curious when he gave the toast that night. Something about the night drawing clan Campbell yet closer to the seat of British power. That it was a night that'd grant us all our heart's desires."

"Breadalbane!" Ruarc cursed softly. "I don't like this. Breadalbane's the most distrusted man in all of Scotland. There are things afoot here that don't bode well for clan MacDonald. If Alasdair, in refusing to sign on time, unwittingly plays into Campbell hands . . ." He expelled a deep, frustrated breath. "Well, even more the reason for this journey, I'd say."

"You never told me what you thought the King might do if your chief failed to sign." Killian twisted in the saddle to more fully meet his gaze. "Tell me the truth, Ruarc. As your wife, I've the right to know."

His eyes narrowed. His mouth went hard. "The King could send troops from Fort William to punish us. He could seize our lands, order us imprisoned, or even deported to the Colonies. But, worst of all, if the Campbells and their ilk have a say in it, the orders might turn even more deadly. We could be put to the sword."

Killian's mouth went dry. "But surely the King wouldn't allow that—"

"He might not know until it was too late, lass," Ruarc interjected hoarsely. "Too late for us, at any rate."

"Then *why* won't your chief sign the oath? Surely he must realize the danger involved in refusing?"

"Alasdair is first and foremost James's man. Two years ago he swore an oath, along with many other Jacobite chiefs, to mutually protect each other and support James. Alasdair is a man of his word. Until James releases him from that bond, Alasdair will not sign for William."

Frustration, mixed with a growing fear, filled her. "Then perhaps it'd be best to try a different tack. Why not seek out the King in London and beg him to reconsider?"

"I've already written him several letters. William views Clan MacDonald as little more than a den of robbers, has no love for Scotland, and feels he has greater issues at present to deal with than the seemingly endless squabbling among the clans. He remains adamant. The Highland chiefs must submit or pay the price."

A grim determination flooded Killian. She nudged her horse in its side, urging it forward. "Then come. There's no time to waste. We must reach Carnoch as soon as possible and convince your chief to sign for William. If James won't consider the plight of his people, then it's up to us to do so."

18

RUARC had not exaggerated in calling his clan chief a man of gigantic mould. As Killian pulled her horse up before a two-story, lime-washed house with a blue slate-covered roof, a very tall, massively built old man with a mane of white hair almost to his shoulders strode out. He had dark, wild eyes and a fierce beak of a nose. A long, white mustache graced his face, giving him the appearance of some Viking warrior. At the very least, he looked well into his sixties, though his stride was long and strong, and he carried himself like a much younger man.

Dressed in trews of dark tartan and a doublet of bull's hide, Alasdair MacDonald hurried up, clapped Ruarc soundly on the back, and turned to Killian. "Ye'll be Ruarc's new wife, will ye not?" he demanded and, without a moment's pause, lifted his arms to help her dismount.

As soon as Killian's feet touched ground, she found herself all but smothered in an enormous embrace, then shoved back for a thorough inspection. "Ye're a wee one, that ye are," he pronounced at long last, "but ye've a look of spirit about ye. I think ye'll do well by my kinsman, that I do."

With that, Alasdair released her and turned back to Ruarc. "I can't for the life of me fathom how the likes of ye managed to win such a bonny lassie for yer own. And she's from the Colonies, is she?"

By then Killian, growing weary of being discussed as if she wasn't included in the conversation, had had enough. "Yes, I'm from the

Colonies. And, before you hear it from someone else, you should know my first husband was a Campbell. So if you've any qualms about that, let's get it out right here and now."

She had to admit she had never seen Ruarc look quite so stunned before, but it was Alasdair's stern look and arch of a thick white brow that made her take a step back and rethink her hastily uttered words. Still, all she had spoken *was* truth, and wasn't it best to reveal that from the start?

"And why would I be having any qualms, lassie?" the big man demanded softly. "Don't ye love yer husband?"

His question took her by surprise. No admission of love had been shared as yet by either she or Ruarc. Warmth flooded Killian's cheeks. This was hardly a topic she wished to discuss just now, standing out here in the cold, an eagle-eyed old man and her husband watching her every thought and move.

"I . . . I hardly think that has any bearing on my being formerly wed to a Campbell," she said, prevaricating. "I only wished not to hide anything that might upset you, or lessen Ruarc's credibility in your eyes."

"And what of yer credibility as a Campbell, if ye don't love yer husband?" Alasdair countered, apparently refusing to give ground. "How can we MacDonalds trust ye if yer loyalty to the clan is suspect?"

"Killian's loyalty's unquestioned." Ruarc chose that moment to walk up and slip an arm about her waist. She shot him a quick, grateful look.

"But she doesn't love ye, is that what ye're saying?"

"I never said I didn't love him!" Anger swelled, then exploded within Killian. How dare he goad Ruarc like that, and all but humiliate him! "He's my husband. Of course I love him!"

"Ye do?" With a swift motion, Ruarc turned her to face him. "Truly, ye do, lass?"

If her own sudden recognition of the depth of her feelings for him hadn't been enough, the wild, joyous look in his eyes surely confirmed it. She did indeed love him, Killian realized, and loved him deeply and well.

"Of course I love you, you silly man. Didn't you know? Couldn't you tell?"

"I'd hoped ye'd come to love me, but was afraid to expect . . ."

"And do you love me then, as well?" If Ruarc had been afraid to hope, so had she. "Tell me true."

"Aye, I love ye verra, verra much, sweet lass." He took her into his arms. "And that, I vow, is God's truth."

"Well, now that that's all said and sealed," Alasdair offered with a laugh, "why don't we hie ourselves into my house? As fine as all this love talk is on the ear and heart, it's becoming exceedingly cold standing out here."

From the warm haven of Ruarc's embrace, Killian shot him a scathing glance. "You've no one to blame for that but yourself. Let that be a lesson to you."

"Och, that it will, lassie," the MacDonald chief agreed with a good-natured chuckle. "That it will indeed."

†

AFTER a hearty meal of fish, leek, and potato pie followed by a dessert of *cranachan,* a special treat of lightly whipped cream, toasted oatmeal, honey, and whiskey, Alasdair, Ruarc, and Killian retired to the council room. The clan chief immediately filled a large, two-handled silver cup called a *quaich* with more whiskey and, after a deep draught, offered it to Ruarc.

With some amusement, Killian watched her husband take a polite swallow, knowing he rarely imbibed of the traditional Scots' brew.

When Alasdair next offered her a drink, she smiled and waved it away. "I've yet to acquire a fancy for the drink. The one time I tasted whiskey, it near to took my breath away."

"As well it should," the big man agreed with a huge grin. "Any *usquebaugh* worth its salt *should* be fiery and heartwarming. Our 'water of life' is a most pleasing union of cereals and spirits, both of which have always held the secret to a long life. We but simplified the recipe by combining the two in whiskey."

He took another swallow, seemingly savoring the malt brew, and closed his eyes. "A fine Ferintosh, to be sure," Alasdair murmured, a touch of reverence in his voice. "Its quality is undisputed."

Then, as if finally remembering his guests, he opened his eyes, set the quaich aside, and looked to Ruarc. "So, apart from yer need to introduce yer bonny wife to me at long last, what else brings ye to Carnoch at such a bitter time of year?"

Ruarc gestured to the chairs set around a long table strewn with papers. "Can we sit? After such a grand meal, I feel a need to take a wee bit of weight off my feet, as I'm quite certain, does my wife."

"Och, aye." Alasdair pulled out a chair. "Here, Lady MacDonald. Have a seat. I must be forgetting what little manners I ever had."

Killian walked over and sat in the chair the MacDonald chief offered. "Thank you, m'lord."

Alasdair then took his own chair, Ruarc quickly following. The white-haired old Highlander rested his arms on the scarred table and met Ruarc's steady gaze. "Well, what's it to be then, laddie? Not yer usual tirade against Jamie and for William, I hope?"

For a fleeting instant, Ruarc's gaze skittered off Killian's, then locked again with his chief's. "Ye've only eleven days remaining to sign the oath of fealty. At this late a date, I fear James intends never to release ye and the other chiefs from yer vow to him."

"Aye, so it'd seem," Alasdair agreed with a solemn nod. "And what of it? James still hopes to regain the throne. Who can fault him if he wishes to retain the loyalty of the Highland chiefs who first signed for him?"

"*I* can fault him if he persists in a hopeless, doomed quest," Ruarc ground out tersely, "and in the bargain, seals yer and our people's death warrant because of his foolish, self-serving behavior. James will remain safe and sound this winter at Saint-Germain under the protection of the French king, while ye and yers might well be evicted from yer homes and land. And that'll be the best ye can hope for, if ye refuse to sign the oath."

"Do ye think I don't realize the potential consequences?" His face mottling, Alasdair leaned toward Ruarc.

Killian's hands clenched in her lap. For all his charming demeanor, she sensed Alasdair MacDonald wasn't a man to be goaded into anything or lectured to like some schoolboy.

"Aye, I'm certain ye realize the potential consequences," her husband replied as evenly as he could. "And I admire ye greatly for yer sense of honor, and for the fact ye're a man of yer word. I'm just not so sure ye fully realize all the forces gathering against ye.

"Killian here—" Ruarc gestured toward her—"was at a Campbell clan gathering in September at Achallader. Among many others, Breadalbane was present. After the falling-out ye had with him this past June at the meeting with the other chiefs, I doubt he feels any too kindly toward ye. He'd be verra pleased, I'd wager, if ye failed to sign the oath in time."

"The treacherous, blackmailing, murdering swine!" Alasdair swore. "That meeting at Achallader was a farce! Well ye know Breadalbane all but tried to bribe us into signing that truce, in order to garner favor with the king. As I said it then, I'll say it now. I've no trust in someone who's Willie's man in Edinburgh and Jamie's in the Highlands!"

"Neither do I. But sometimes being right isn't enough. Sometimes a man must think past his personal honor to the welfare of others. And the welfare of the MacDonalds now lies with King William, not James."

"Or so *ye* think." Alasdair scowled now at Ruarc. "I, though, am not so certain. As much as I loathe to say it, mayhap yer perspective is a wee bit muddied by yer close association with the King, now these many years past. There are some of yer clan, ye know, who think ye naught more than the king's man, set upon procuring his will in the Highlands."

Ruarc's hands fisted before him, but he never once broke eye contact with his chief. "And do they also say I hold the king in higher regard than my own people? Do they, Alasdair?"

The old man glanced away. "Aye, there are a few."

"Who?" Ruarc's voice went low and hoarse. "Who dares impugn my honor? I've the right to know!"

With rising consternation, Killian looked from one man to the other. She had been in the Highlands long enough now to know how fiercely proud a Scotsman was of his honor, and that he'd fight to the death to defend it. If Alasdair mentioned any names . . .

"Och, so that's how it's to be, is it?" The MacDonald chief scraped back his chair and rose. "If ye cannot convince us by dint of fine words to sign for yer precious Willie, then ye're determined to call out each and every one of yer kinsmen who questions yer motives? Nay—" he shook his head so fiercely it reminded Killian of some great lion—"I won't allow ye to cause any more havoc within the clan. I'm yer chief and have made up my mind. The matter is closed. Until I hear from Jamie, I *will not* sign the oath!"

"And if, by some miracle, ye do hear from him in the next week or so, what will ye do then?" His eyes smoldering pits of fury and frustration, Ruarc stared up at his chief. "Will ye sign? For the sake of the clan, will ye, Alasdair?"

The seconds ticked by and the old warrior glared down at Ruarc. Then, as if he had fought some savage battle within himself and lost, his shoulders slumped and his head lowered. "Aye," he muttered. "Though it may be the hardest thing I'll ever do, I'll sign for Willie. But only for the sake of my clan, and never, ever because I bear the king any affection or goodwill."

†

BREAKFAST the next morning was a hot bowl of porridge and milk. The farewells between Ruarc and his chief were cool and restrained, but it was evident, at least to Killian, the pain her husband felt at the less-than-warm parting. For a time, as they headed eastward back down the glen, Killian and Ruarc rode in silence.

Finally, though, as if compelled to explain himself and expunge his guilt, Ruarc glanced over at her. "I'm not the king's man. I'd never put the well-being of my clan in jeopardy just to curry William's favor. But I'm also a realist, and I think I see Scotland's future far more clearly than most."

"And what *is* Scotland's future?"

"It's not and never again will be with Jamie—or any other Stuart—no matter how dearly we wish it to be so. England's far too powerful, wealthy, and entrenched here for us ever again to conclusively defeat them. Not to mention," he added dryly, "we pose too great a threat, if we ally with their enemies, to allow us self-rule. And William most certainly has enemies. He knows he must obtain our allegiance, no matter the cost."

"And the cost will be paid by those Highland chiefs foolish enough to defy him," Killian finished for him.

"Aye. Ye can be certain of that."

Despite her short time in Scotland, Killian knew Ruarc's fears were far from groundless. It was the way of things the world over.

The strong had no choice but endlessly to grow stronger or risk losing their power, annihilating all who stood in their way. There was no room for compassion, for personal choice, for trust or love. There was only that insatiable, and frequently brutal, quest for power.

It was, however, always the innocent who seemed to suffer for it—the simple folk who wished nothing more than to live their lives, raise their children, and find their happiness where they may. It was also, Killian realized with a shiver of premonition, the good men who saw what was to come and tried as best they could to halt the senseless destruction who also stood in danger of losing everything.

"What more can we do, Ruarc?" Suddenly, Killian was overcome with the chill and gloom of the new day. "It's so unfair you and the people of Rannoch suffer because of Alasdair's stubborn pride!"

"It's even more unfair that James withholds his leave to release the chiefs of their vow to him," he cried in despair. "Even more than Alasdair, I blame that cowardly, indecisive old fool!"

"Then we must prepare for the worst." Killian nodded in conviction. "We must be ready to fight, if need be."

Ruarc sighed and shook his head. "Aye, we may well have to fight. In the end, though, England will still prevail."

A sudden idea seized her. "We could go to Virginia." The longer she thought about it, the more the consideration excited her. "The tobacco plantation Alexander and I started is now solely mine. My overseer has sent word it continues to profit nicely. We could start over in Virginia!"

"And what would become of my people if I deserted them?" He turned to her, his face a tortured mask of anguish. "I couldn't do that, lass, no matter the cost."

Killian stared back at him, not knowing what more to say, only knowing Ruarc had become her whole life and she didn't want to lose him.

"Would ye leave me for Virginia," he asked, "if disaster struck? If I felt it necessary to stay here? Would ye?"

All she wanted was to be with him. That, and to live out a long, happy life at his side. Still, Killian was forced to admit, if the long life at Ruarc's side wasn't to be, she'd take whatever happiness she could steal with him, for as long as she could.

"No," Killian whispered, her whole heart and soul in that single word. "I won't leave you. We made holy vows to cling fast to each other through good times and bad. I'll keep those vows to my dying day. And not just because I made those vows before God," she added, a tiny smile twitching at the corner of her mouth, "but because I also made them to you, and I love you."

A fierce burning fire exploded in his eyes. Ruarc took her hand. Leaning toward her, he lifted it to his lips. "And I love ye, and thank ye for yer loyalty to me. I never thought to gain such devotion from a woman again, much less allow myself to want it. I certainly don't deserve it."

"And why wouldn't you deserve loyalty and devotion from your own wife?" Killian cocked her head, knowing full well of whom he spoke. "Whatever happened between you and Sheila to make you feel you didn't deserve it from her?"

He was silent for a long while, so long Killian began to think he didn't intend to answer. But, finally, he expelled a deep breath and looked away. "How did I *not* fail Sheila as her husband? She came to me, full of hopes and dreams, wanting only for me to cherish and adore her, to make everything right, and I could never seem to be what she so dearly desired. It was almost . . . almost as if I couldn't quite give myself completely to her."

"And why would you have withheld yourself, unless she'd somehow given you cause to do so?"

"I don't know." He looked away and shrugged. "Mayhap the fault always lay with me rather than with her. Mayhap I thought too much of my own needs and too little of hers, imagining I could make all come right in the end."

"Then why did you wed her?"

"Why?" Ruarc shrugged again. "Because when I first met her she was beautiful and full of life, and I fancied her the perfect woman for me. And because, arrogant fool that I was, I felt I could soon and easily make her come to love me."

"But you couldn't?"

"Nay, I couldn't, though I tried my verra best. I fought hard for our marriage because I believed in those vows I made, but also because I refused to give up my dream of having the same happiness my parents had."

He sighed and shook his head. "Mayhap if I *had* given up and let Sheila go, she might still be alive today."

"Did she ever ask you to let her go?"

"Nay, she never did. Finally, though, Sheila seemed to abandon all pretense of a happy marriage. She turned me from our bed. Flamboyant and flirtatious in the best of times, she began enticing other men. At first I pretended not to notice, feeling I was somehow to blame for her behavior, hoping she'd eventually return to me. Soon, however, it was all I could do to keep her in check and from creating one scandal after another."

Ruarc reined in his horse. "Then one night during yet another of Adam Campbell's increasingly frequent visits, I found her in the gardens in his arms. I nearly killed Adam before Sheila could pull me off him. And, when he slunk away, I turned on her."

His voice grew hoarse with anguish. "Though she protested at first their embrace wasn't what it seemed, I knew better. I could see the guilt as clearly in her eyes as I'd seen it in Adam's. I called her all sorts of vile names until I had her weeping. Then I turned and walked away. I had to. If I'd stayed a moment longer, I might have done her harm."

He glanced at her, his eyes now bright with tears. "So I left Sheila there in the gardens that night, left her to her murderer, and I never saw her alive again."

"You couldn't have known what was to come, Ruarc."

"Nay, I couldn't. I suspect Adam crept back after I left. Crept back to ask her to run away with him and, when Sheila refused, he killed her. Adam was always in love with her, ye know, and Sheila, with him. She finally admitted that to me that night, taunting me with the fact she had never, ever, loved me. Instead, it'd always been Adam."

Sympathy welled in Killian. No wonder Ruarc had always withheld a part of himself from Sheila. Deep down somewhere, he must have sensed the truth. "That was cruel of her. After all, she was the one who wed you under false pretenses. No matter her feelings for Adam, Sheila owed you better than that."

"Did she?" Ruarc expelled a deep breath, the sound soft and bewildered. "Mayhap she did. I'm not so certain of aught anymore."

"Well, one thing *is* certain. You can't go on hating yourself, or

Adam, for this. You both may have made mistakes, and you both had the misfortune of wanting the wrong woman, but it's past time to forgive and get on with your lives."

"Aye," her husband agreed grimly, "Adam and I both indeed made mistakes and shared the misfortune of wanting the wrong woman. But I didn't kill Sheila. Adam did. And he still has yet to pay for that."

"You can't be certain Adam killed her, Ruarc," Killian cried, rising to her kinsman's defense. "From what you've told me about Sheila, and from what I've been able to piece together about her so far from others, she surely had enemies at Rannoch. Indeed, who's to say one of her other lovers might not have overheard Sheila telling you she'd always loved Adam, then come up after you left and killed her in a jealous rage? After all, Adam had loved Sheila all those years and never once harmed her. Why would he suddenly choose to do so that night?"

"I don't know why he killed her," he said between gritted teeth. "I just know he did."

"And Adam knows what he knows, too. That's why he's persisted in trying to avenge Sheila by killing you." A rising frustration tautened her voice. "Yet if you both allow things to take their course, this won't be over until one or both of you are dead. And neither of you killed Sheila!" Killian shook her head. "Hasn't she caused enough harm by her living? Must she now continue to destroy lives even in death?"

"That's *not* what I want!" Ruarc bent his head, clenching shut his eyes. "But don't ye see I *must* avenge her? In a way I'm as guilty as her killer, for I refused to listen to or believe her. I was the one who turned my back on her that night and walked away, leaving her alone and defenseless in the gardens. And mayhap I even killed her a little bit every day of our marriage, by failing to be the husband she needed."

With his words, the full weight of Ruarc's guilt and pain settled over Killian. How had he gone on as well as he had, carrying such a horrendous burden? And how had he ever found the courage to dare to love again, in coming to love her?

Yet he had, and she was a woman blessed to know and love him.

Her heart swelled with a fierce resolve. Somehow, some way, she would help Ruarc heal these terrible wounds still tormenting him.

"Ruarc," Killian offered gently, "the only way you could've ever been the husband Sheila thought she needed was to become Adam. Still, I wonder if anyone could've ever truly fulfilled her. She reminds me a lot of myself, how I used to be, clinging to unrealistic dreams for far too long. I tried to help Alexander, endured his abuse, blaming myself for much of what tortured him. I told myself if only I could become a better wife, he'd be happy. But he never was, Ruarc. And I finally had to face the truth about myself and our marriage. You helped me, you know, to do that."

He opened his eyes at last, frowning in puzzlement. "I did? How?"

A smile lifted her lips. "By showing me what a real marriage between a man and a woman should be like. I'd given up on love before I met you, relegating it to some corner of my silly, hopeless dreams."

"Ye did the same for me, too."

"Then I think we must try not to let our pasts tarnish our future. Father Kenneth was right, you know, in calling Sheila a lost soul. She was lost in the darkness, grasping after impossible dreams, all the while failing to see the happiness right in front of her. But she was lost long before she met and wed you, Ruarc. Perhaps even before Adam came to love her, too."

"Mayhap she was. But she *was* once my wife. Before I can truly set aside all the guilt and pain over Sheila, I owe her at least the final honor of laying her soul to rest by punishing her murderer."

"And what if, in the doing, you destroy what *we* have? Can any retribution be worth such a price?"

Ruarc nudged his horse once more, urging it forward. "That won't happen," he muttered over his shoulder. "I won't let it happen. But it *is* my right to avenge Sheila."

Killian watched him head down a rocky embankment, then signaled her horse to follow. "And when has vengeance," she asked softly, engulfed in a sudden swell of despair, "ever rightfully belonged to anyone but God?"

19

CHRISTMAS passed with laughter and song and sumptuous meals. On Christmas Day, Killian rode out with Ruarc to visit the crofters, gifting them each with a bag of fruit from the orchards and a sack of barley flour. Rannoch's laird quickly saw how much she enjoyed the contact with his people—and how quickly they warmed to her—and vowed to involve her more with them as her duties at the castle permitted.

Between Christmas and December thirty-first, the weather remained relatively mild but cold. Ruarc tried as best as he could to stay busy, but time and again his thoughts strayed to his chief and what, if anything, he had done about signing the oath of fealty. Isolated as they were at the far end of the glen, news came only sporadically. Indeed, since Christmas, no messengers whatsoever had made their way to the castle. And no news, Ruarc feared, meant Alasdair had chosen to do nothing.

On the thirty-first, strong northwesterly winds roared in, carrying with them fresh snow. Nearly the full daylong the winds blew and the snow fell until, finally, at sunset, they slackened.

Sometime past midnight, however, when Ruarc woke from a fitful sleep, he found the snow had begun again with an even greater intensity, drifting and swirling with the force of the wind. From between the thick curtains of their bedchamber window, he watched the somber scene of falling snow against a setting of blackened mountains. With a weary sigh, Ruarc stepped back into the room and was soon snuggling against Killian's warm body.

Dawn of January first brought even more furious winds and solid, driving snow, conditions that only worsened as the day drew on. Though Ruarc tried to bury his increasingly tumultuous concerns in his paperwork, he soon found himself up and about, restlessly pacing the halls and growling at any and everyone foolish enough to draw near.

The blizzard continued into the next day, when it finally abated. Ruarc was sorely tempted to ride out to Carnoch, but knew travel would be nigh impossible for at least several days. Besides, he reminded himself, either Alasdair had signed in time or not. If he hadn't, there was little danger of troops soon marching into Glencoe after such a storm.

A week later, Ruarc finally had his answer. James's permission for the chiefs to do as they thought best hadn't reached Carnoch until the twenty-ninth of December. The very next day, Alasdair had ridden out to Inverlochy to swear his oath to the British governor, John Hill. Hill, however, had no such power to administer the oath and soon sent the MacDonald chief on his way to Campbell of Ardkinglas in Inveraray.

Thanks to the fierce storm, Alasdair hadn't reached the Campbell capital until the second of January. There he discovered that Sir Colin Campbell of Ardkinglas was away. Impotently fuming, the MacDonald chief had no choice but to find shelter in a local inn and await Ardkinglas's return.

On January fifth, Sir Colin returned from his New Year's holiday and summoned Alasdair to the Courthouse. He roundly scolded the old chief, refusing to accept his excuses for missing the deadline or to administer the oath. At that, Alasdair broke down and wept, knowing full well the likely consequences for his failure to sign in time.

Apparently moved by the MacDonald's show of naked fear, Ardkinglas finally relented. The next day he permitted Alasdair to sign and swear the oath of fealty to King William and Queen Mary. A few days after the chief's return home, messengers were sent throughout the glen, confirming that Alasdair, as clan chief, had taken the oath in their name as well as in his own, and ordering the clan to live peaceably under King William's protection. If the oath was kept, he assured them, there was nothing to fear.

Ruarc, however, continued to worry that all of Alasdair's efforts might yet be for naught. Days passed. He didn't sleep well. He became increasingly irritable and sharp-tongued. At long last, one afternoon in the middle of January, Killian finally sought him out.

Hard at work in the library, Ruarc chose not to acknowledge the opening of the door or the sound of soft footsteps moving across the wooden floor. It was supremely difficult, however, to continue long to ignore the beguiling scent of flowers and fresh air that wafted to him as Killian drew near. He refused, though, to look up. Better for her if she kept her distance until he came to terms with his concerns.

Killian, however, seemed undaunted by his lack of welcome and surly demeanor. She halted at his side and patiently waited, until Ruarc could no longer pretend ignorance of her presence.

From beneath dark, scowling brows, he glanced up at her. "Aye, and what would ye be needing, lass?" He shuttered his gaze back to his papers. "I'm verra busy just now and don't wish to be disturbed."

"You haven't wished to be disturbed for the past two weeks," she countered tartly, standing her ground. "That's precisely *why* I've come to talk."

"Och, ye have, have ye?" Half irritated and half pleased by her courage in bearding him in his den, Ruarc set aside his pen and lifted his gaze once more. "And what exactly would ye like to talk about?"

"What else?" Killian's hands rose to fist on her hips. "Your disagreeable mood of late, of course."

"I've had a lot on my mind. Surely ye can understand why."

"Yes, I understand. But nothing has happened, and it appears nothing will. You yourself admitted the chances were good that Alasdair's oath was accepted."

"Aye, that I did. Still—" Ruarc paused to scratch his jaw, which, he suddenly realized, was in dire need of a shave—"I won't rest easy until I receive answer from William to the letter I sent three days ago. Only when I hear from the king himself that he has accepted Alasdair's oath will I know we're safe."

"Well, that reply might be a long time in coming. What are we at Rannoch to do in the meanwhile, with you snorting, snuffling, and lumbering about like some old bear?"

He shrugged, fighting to hide a smile. "I can't say what the others might do, but I'll gladly offer some suggestions as to what ye can do."

She grinned then. "And what exactly did you have in mind?"

"A hot bath with a bonny lassie to scrub my back," Ruarc offered with a hopeful look, "would surely go a long way to lightening my mood. Do ye think ye might be willing—"

A brisk rapping sounded at the door. Ruarc's glance locked with Killian's. "Were ye expecting someone?"

She shook her head.

He frowned. "Well, I gave strict orders not to be disturbed."

"So I was informed," his wife said dryly. "I'll see who it is."

Davie MacDonald stood there, a grim look in his eyes. Ruarc heard Killian say something to him, then receive a mumbled answer. In the next instant, she had wheeled around and, with Davie at her side, marched back to the library table.

The younger man nodded curtly to Ruarc. "I've news for ye, m'lord. Verra important news."

Ruarc's heart gave a great lurch. Had what he had so long feared finally come to pass? "What is it, Davie? Are there soldiers marching on Glencoe?"

"Nay, m'lord." Davie hesitated and sent Killian, who had drawn up beside him, a slanting glance. "No soldiers, but something of a more private nature, if ye will."

Apparently taking the hint, Killian looked to her husband. "I've work with Francis that needs doing. I'll leave you men to your business."

"As ye wish, lass."

With some regret, Ruarc watched her depart. If it hadn't been for the strange look in Davie's eyes, he would've insisted Killian stay and hear his captain's news with him. But something was amiss here. Something that boded ill. Mayhap it was better Killian not be a party to it.

When the library door had shut firmly behind her, Rannoch's laird riveted his full attention on the man standing before him. "Well, spit it out, lad. What was of such pressing import that ye felt it necessary to interrupt us?"

"It seems there's been more passing of letters between Achallader and Rannoch." Davie pulled a sealed package from inside the voluminous folds of his belted plaid and handed it to Ruarc. "As ye suspected, yer stepmither continues to be involved. With but a wee bit of encouragement, the Campbell messenger we found skulking about today admitted he was to deliver that into the hands of either the Lady Glynnis or Thomas."

Ruarc's blood went cold. After the failed attempt to send him riding into a trap when Killian tried to leave Rannoch, Ruarc had set Davie and his men to watch Glynnis and her son's every move. It seemed his patience—and vigilance—had been finally rewarded.

"It was but a matter of time, I see, until Glynnis felt safe to resume her plotting with Adam."

Ruarc opened the package and withdrew a letter sealed in wax with Achallader's crest. He broke the seal and spread out the letter before him on the table. As Ruarc read the familiar masculine script, horror rose. Adam wasn't addressing Glynnis, but Killian. What made it all the worse, however, was the quite evident mention Adam made in this letter to a previous letter Killian had written him.

"I read your kind words," the letter went, "assuring me of your continued affection with great relief, and not without considerable joy. I, too, look forward eagerly to the day we can once more embrace as kin."

Adam went on to express doubt that any peaceable resolution could ever be found between him and Ruarc, but that he was open, for Killian's sake, to any suggestions she might have, knowing, as she did "her husband's heart far better than he."

Adam closed by wishing her well in her marriage, hoping it would remain a safe and happy one, and asking her to tender his fondest greeting to his dear little cousin, Gavin, whom he hoped he'd soon be able to see.

Fury swelled in Ruarc. With the greatest difficulty, he controlled the impulse to crumple the letter in his hand, then hurl it across the room into the fire. Indeed, it was far too valuable to destroy.

The letter was proof of Glynnis's continued perfidy, and it was something more. It was also a razor-sharp sword that had pierced his heart. For some unknown reason, his wife had entered into a secret dialogue with his enemy.

But why? His emotions reeled crazily from a pained sense of betrayal to anger to utter confusion. In the past few months, Killian had seemed so happy here. She had told him she loved him. So why would she begin a clandestine correspondence with a man she knew sought to end his life?

There was no way to know, save to ask her. *If* he could dare risk believing her answer.

"Are ye all right, m'lord?" Davie's voice came from some place far away. "Ye look verra ill. Shall I send for m'lady?"

"Nay." With an effort, Ruarc met his cousin's gaze. "Not just yet. I need a time to mull over this letter and devise some response to it."

He nodded toward the door. "Ye may leave, Davie. And my thanks for yer fine work in capturing this messenger. Detain him for a time more, will ye, where neither Glynnis nor my inquisitive half brother can find him?"

"As ye wish, m'lord." His cousin bowed, then turned on his heel and strode from the room.

†

KILLIAN closed the castle ledger with a satisfied sigh. "You've done a fine job with the accounts these past two months, Francis. But then, I always sensed you'd an agile mind and would learn quickly."

"Och, my thanks, m'lady," the young clerk said with a laugh. "But my agile mind first needed a teacher, and that ye were."

She laid the ledger aside on the desk and stood. "Another month or so, I believe, and we'll have everything completely balanced. After that, Rannoch should be debt-free."

Francis looked up at her. "M'lady, I must confess I didn't verra much like ye when ye first came to Rannoch. But I was wrong about ye. For that I'm verra sorry."

"I know. Those were difficult times for us all."

"M'lord had been hurt enough by women," he continued, as if feeling the need to explain. "Sheila betrayed him in so verra many ways. She wasn't verra kind to me, either, belittling everything I did. I can't say I cared much for her, and I was glad when she was finally gone."

Her woman's instincts stirred. *Careful*, Killian cautioned herself. *Be careful what you say.* "Were you, Francis? Glad that she died?"

As if realizing his slip of the tongue too late, the blood drained from the clerk's face. "Och, I didn't mean it like it sounded, m'lady. Though as cruel as she was to m'lord, especially in those last years . . . well, be that as it may, she didn't deserve to die like that."

"Where were you that night? And did you note any strangers about, or any suspicious activity?"

"I worked late on the ledgers that night, as I always do, then retired to my bed. If there were strangers about or suspicious activity, I wasn't aware of it." Francis met her gaze. "Why do ye ask? The Lady Sheila's been dead more than three years now. Surely ye can't mean to reopen an investigation after all this time? It'd only cause m'lord further pain."

"Would it cause more pain than what he already suffers in never having found Sheila's killer? in living constantly with the threat of Adam Campbell's vengeance hanging over his head?"

Francis looked away. "Nay, I suppose not, m'lady."

"Help me then, Francis," Killian urged. "I can't do this by myself. Anything you can uncover, even the smallest detail, might fit as some piece in the puzzle."

"Aye, I'll help ye, m'lady. Because I know now ye've truly m'lord's best interests at heart. Just as ye made yer vows, so have I, to devote my life to m'lord."

She relaxed then, and eyed him with a teasing grin. "That vow doesn't preclude you taking a wife and starting a family someday, does it? If it did, I'd be forced to have a talk with Ruarc about releasing you from it."

The clerk flushed crimson to the roots of his dark blond hair. "I suppose it wouldn't. Not that I've been all that interested in such matters, mind ye. I've just never had much time, or knew how to act around the lasses."

"Well, if you ever desire a few suggestions, let me know." She laid a hand on Francis' shoulder. "I'm sure I can suggest several young ladies who find you quite fetching."

He blushed again. "Och, get on with ye!"

"Which is exactly what I plan to do," Killian said, heading for the door. "Gavin needs his hair trimmed, and I promised to play some games with him. I'll see you at supper then, I'd imagine?"

"Aye, m'lady, that ye will."

Once out in the hall, Killian made a beeline for Gavin's bed-chamber, where she found him playing with Eilidh before the hearth fire. She joined in for a while, before setting to the task of cutting the hair of an incessantly squirming little boy. By the time the mouthwatering aromas of the supper meal being set out reached her nose, Killian was more than happy to lead her son downstairs.

Ruarc wasn't at table. She was tempted to seek him out and remind him it was time to eat, but finally decided against it. Her husband was never one to miss a meal unless there was pressing business, and then nothing—even food—deterred him from completing it.

She harked back to Davie's visit in the library, wondering if that was the matter still keeping Ruarc from his supper. It worried her that, whatever it was, it had required a private conversation between the two men. She didn't want any harm to come to Ruarc or Rannoch.

He never made it to table. By and by, Killian had a plate of food prepared and kept covered in a warm spot by the kitchen fire. After a time of visiting with Glynnis and Thomas in the Great Hall, she finally retired to her bedchamber. Several more hours spent in embroidery work passed before, just as she decided to prepare for bed, Ruarc at last walked in.

One look at his set jaw and mouth drawn into an angry, forbid-ding line, and Killian knew there was trouble afoot. She hurried to him. "Ruarc, whatever is the matter?" She reached up to touch his cheek. "Tell me, I beg—"

He caught her hand in midair, halting it. "Don't." His voice was little more than a rough, rusty growl. "Don't ye dare touch me."

Killian froze. Her hand, still in Ruarc's iron clasp, fell to her side. "What . . . what do you mean? Why can't I touch you?"

"Why?" Releasing her hand, he withdrew a carelessly folded letter from his plaid and, taking her hand, thrust the letter into it. "Here. Read this. Then mayhap ye'll understand."

With rising anxiety, Killian unfolded the paper. Her heart sank. It was from Adam, apparently replying to her letter. Save for one thing. She had never written him.

Overtly, he had said little that was inflammatory, but there were disturbing implications there nonetheless. Implications Ruarc could only perceive in a negative fashion. An easy camaraderie. An almost conspiratorial tone. And, worst of all, a privileged intimacy with Killian predating Ruarc's.

"How . . . how did you get this?" She looked up at him.

He shrugged, his mouth twisting sardonically. "Ever since Glynnis's last attempt to deliver me into Adam's hand, I've secretly had her and Thomas's comings and goings watched."

At her look of surprise, he gave a harsh laugh. "Did ye truly imagine, just because I agreed to allow her to remain at Rannoch, that I ever began to trust her? I'm not that big a fool, though it now appears Glynnis wasn't the only one still trying to play me for one."

Killian's hands fisted, unconsciously crushing the letter. "I never played you for a fool! I give you my word. I never wrote Adam, and I don't know why he replies as if I did." She handed the paper back to him.

"This letter gives the lie to yer words." Briefly, Ruarc held it up, then tossed it onto the table. "Why, madam? Why would ye purposely choose to jeopardize what we had, if indeed ye truly valued it to begin with?"

His continued needling and suspicious demeanor angered her. "Of course I value what we have, you great, lumbering lummox! That's exactly *why* I didn't write Adam. I love you. I wouldn't risk our marriage by going behind your back like this. True, I want there to be peace between you and Adam. I want this festering animosity to end. But I'd never go about it in such a manner. Never!"

"Fine words," he spat out in reply, "now that ye've been caught in the act. But I'm not so certain I believe them, or can now trust ye ever again."

She stared up at him in stunned disbelief. "After all we've been to each other, after how hard I've tried to be a good wife to you, *you don't know if you can ever trust me again?*"

When he didn't answer, Killian forged on, a sickening realization that Ruarc was once again pulling back behind his high-walled defenses filling her. "And why are *you* always so willing, the first chance you get, to doubt me? Do you know how that makes me—"

Her throat constricted on such a savage swell of emotion that, for a moment, Killian couldn't go on. "Do you know how that makes me feel?" she finished finally. "Like there's no chance for us. Like I have to tiptoe about on tenterhooks with you, second-guessing everything I do for fear of stirring yet again your innate mistrust."

"Ye knew before ye wed me that I was this way. Ye should've taken greater care not to risk so much for so little."

"But that's exactly *why* I didn't risk it!" Killian cried, her anger growing apace now with her anguish. "Instead, I've been gradually questioning everyone at Rannoch about the night Sheila died. Until you find a final resolution and acceptance of Sheila's death, you might well always remain this way, imprisoned in your narrow, suspicious, unloving little world. And I didn't want that for you, Ruarc."

In the heat of the moment, Killian finally forgot herself and grabbed his arm. "In coming to know and love you, I could see you've so much more than that to give. And I wanted you safe from that horrible, dangerous vendetta against Adam."

Ever so deliberately, Ruarc took her hand and pulled it free. "Mayhap ye did. Or mayhap ye didn't. For the present, however, I don't know what to think about ye or that letter."

He stepped back, his eyes cold, his features glacial. "The fact that Glynnis is yet involved in another sorry mess also concerns me, almost as much as the fact ye cannot seem to separate yerself from her and her nefarious deeds. Are ye, I wonder, so supremely naïve ye cannot learn from yer mistakes, or do yer motives spring from more sinister reasons?"

"If I'm naïve," she countered hotly, her temper finally getting the best of her, "it's more likely in hoping I can ever have a mature, reasonable relationship with you! Are you blind as well as pigheaded? Are you?"

Fury blazed then in Ruarc's eyes. "Have a care, madam, with that sharp tongue of yers. And recall, if ye will, who's first and foremost at fault here."

"Think what you will, then. I've told you the truth. I can do no more. If you can't trust me enough to believe me, well, you're soon going to be one very lonely man."

"Mayhap," he snarled back, "but at least I'll be alive."

Killian gave a disbelieving snort. "There are some things in life, husband dear, far more important than mere survival. But unless you're willing to risk not always being right, unless you can finally see past that stubborn pride to what really matters, you'll never know that, will you?"

Then, before she lost control of the tears welling in her eyes and the remaining remnants of her pride, Killian turned and stalked from the room.

20

"THERE wasna aught I could do, m'lord," the messenger offered in his own defense two days later. "'Twas almost as if they were watching for me. I couldna escape them."

Adam eyed his man closely. Always before, Angus had been a dependable, resourceful servant. There was no reason to doubt the veracity of his claims now.

"Then it seems our little ploy's outlived its usefulness," he said with a sigh. "It was bound to happen. We were fortunate, I suppose, to slip as many letters past Ruarc MacDonald as we did." Adam made a dismissing motion. "My thanks to ye, Angus. Best ye return to yer usual duties."

"Aye, m'lord." The man bowed and departed.

Curse Ruarc, Adam thought, turning his gaze out the window overlooking Achallader's courtyard. The letters to Killian had shown great promise. He'd had hopes of someday even arranging a meeting with the lass.

Fleetingly, his thoughts turned to what might now happen to Killian. His last letter had left no doubt as to whom he had been writing. At the very least Ruarc would be angry, feeling that in daring to correspond with an enemy his wife had betrayed him. Adam only hoped the lass was safe, and that Ruarc had yet to do her any harm.

If she could only endure a short time longer, he might yet be able to rescue her. Once Ruarc was forced from Glencoe along with the rest of his brutish clan, the odds were good not only would Adam be able to lay hands on him, but mayhap even convince Killian, in the bargain, to return to Achallader.

It was a pity she had wed Ruarc. She was the first woman since Sheila he had given even a passing thought to taking as wife. One way or another, he supposed he must soon. Achallader needed a legitimate heir as much as Rannoch did.

Aye, Adam thought, gazing out on the scene of snow-shrouded hills and ice-clogged burns, *one way or another, it won't be long now.*

†

IT TOOK until late afternoon of the next day for Killian to compose herself adequately to confront Glynnis. She found her at a small table in the Great Hall, working intently over her endless bits of embroidery. She was not alone, however. Ruarc and his cousin stood nearby before the hearth, talking quietly. Killian, however, didn't care. She drew up before Glynnis.

The older woman lifted her gaze, recognized Killian, and smiled. "M'lady. What a pleasant surprise." She indicated the other chair at the table. "Come, sit. I haven't seen ye most of the day, and sorely missed yer company."

"I don't wish to sit, Glynnis. I want to talk with you, and I want to do so in private. Come away with me, please."

Ruarc's stepmother's brow furrowed in puzzlement. "What is it, m'lady? Ye look distressed."

Glynnis cut a glance toward the fire. At Killian's arrival, both men had stopped talking and had turned to watch them. She looked back to Killian. "Aye, mayhap it'd be best if we adjourned to a more private place," she said, laying her embroidery aside. "There are too many curious spectators here, to be sure."

Not venturing further comment for fear of what she might say, Killian spun on her heel and strode away. Only when they reached the library did Killian pause. She opened the door. "Inside, please." She followed as Glynnis entered the room.

One glance around was enough to assure her they were alone. Killian closed the door firmly behind them and turned the lock. Then she wheeled about.

"Ruarc presented me with a letter yestereve," she began without preamble. "A letter written to me by Adam Campbell. A letter in response to a letter I'd apparently written to him. Do you happen to know anything about such a letter?"

Glynnis went pale. Her hand rose to her throat. "I . . . I . . ." She swallowed hard and nodded. "Aye, m'lady, I do know about that letter. I wrote it to Adam in yer name."

Outrage swelled in Killian. She could barely force words past her suddenly constricted throat. "*You* wrote Adam in *my* name? Why? I never gave you leave to do so. Never!"

"I meant to h-help, m'lady. Help ye effect a reconciliation between Ruarc and Adam. It's what ye wanted, isn't it? To get them to make peace?"

"Yes, I want them to make peace, but not in such a manner. Not behind Ruarc's back. I told you that before, Glynnis. Not at the risk of my marriage!"

Killian began to pace, her hands clenching and unclenching as she walked. "And that's exactly what's happened. It's put my marriage at risk."

"Och, m'lady, m'lady. What have I done?" The ebony-haired woman glanced distractedly around until she spied a chair. She hurried over, flung herself into it, and buried her face in her hands. "I didn't think Ruarc would catch my messenger," she said, her voice now muffled. "I thought I'd taken all necessary precautions. I'm so sorry. So verra, verra sorry!"

"Don't tell *me*, Glynnis," Killian said through gritted teeth, not feeling particularly sympathetic. "Tell Ruarc."

Glynnis's head jerked up. She stared at Killian with wide, terror-stricken eyes. "Och, he won't believe me, that my intentions this time were well meant, m'lady. He'll banish me for certain, and most likely Thomas, too."

"Yes, he probably will. But if you don't go to him and tell him, Ruarc may never forgive *me*, much less trust me again. Indeed, I might well have to join you and Thomas, and leave Rannoch, too."

"Did ye tell him ye'd no part in the letters?"

"Yes, but understandably so, he'd difficulty believing me, considering Adam addressed me directly in his letter."

"Ye could go to Ruarc. Blame Adam for trying to cause problems between ye and him by pretending ye'd written that letter." For the first time since they had entered the library, a ray of hope gleamed in Glynnis's eyes. "Aye, that might work. Ruarc mistrusts Adam enough to consider him capable of any and all sorts of deceit."

"I'll not compound this sorry mess by lying to Ruarc."

"But I didn't mean to hurt either ye or Ruarc. Not this time. Not ever again. I've learned my lesson. I just want to help."

Killian dearly wanted to believe otherwise, if for no other reason than she could then go to Ruarc and accuse Glynnis. But the look on Glynnis's face told the real truth. Whatever her motives had initially been in writing Adam, at long last Glynnis truly did seem sincere.

"Well, you didn't help, Glynnis. And, as much as I'd like to believe this time your efforts were well meant, it doesn't matter. If I protect you, I may threaten my marriage. I don't want to do that."

"And what sort of marriage is it," Glynnis spat out sullenly, "if Ruarc cannot bring himself to trust ye? Think on that if ye will, m'lady. Ye told him the truth. Why won't he believe ye?"

"I-I don't know." And Killian didn't.

"Well, I'll tell ye why. Ruarc is still the same man he always was. Still self-righteous, rigid, and not inclined to trust or forgive. In his heart, he still can't believe any good, decent woman would love him. All along, he's been waiting for ye to betray him. If it hadn't happened because of this letter, it would've happened in some other way at another time. More than anything, Ruarc always, always has to be right."

Killian opened her mouth to protest, to refute Glynnis's accusations. The words, however, wouldn't come. How could they? Glynnis had spoken true.

The tiny ember of fear that Ruarc would turn on her someday flared now to a roaring conflagration. He *did* put great store on being right and attacking first, before anyone had the chance to take him by surprise. Sadly enough, he was rarely disappointed in his estimation of the danger others presented him.

But was his outlook perhaps part of the problem? In his swift response to any perceived threat, did he not inadvertently engender what he so much feared?

Killian was too weary to deal with all the chaotic emotions just now. All she knew was, after her disastrous first marriage, trust was of the utmost importance. If Ruarc couldn't find it within himself to trust her, Killian held out just as little hope for *their* marriage.

†

"YE CAN'T go on like this, lad." On a blustery fifth of February, Father Kenneth set aside his mug of mulled cider and turned to Rannoch's laird. "It's been over two weeks now, and it's eating ye alive, this anger ye carry in yer heart. Ye must make yer peace with the lass, and do so posthaste."

"Must I now?" Ruarc rose from his seat by the Great Hall's huge hearth and strode over to stare into the fiercely burning fire. "And pray, what has changed between Killian and me to warrant my making peace? I'm still angry with her. And I don't trust her." He wheeled about, freshened pain welling within. "She was in correspondence with my direst of enemies. She was *conspiring* with him, no less!"

"I've talked with the lass. She swears she didn't write Adam. And I believe her."

"Well, I don't," Ruarc muttered, his confused emotions roiling so wildly he was hard put to sort one from the other. "Killian refuses to venture any other reason for that letter. She says all that matters is she didn't write it. But it isn't all that matters. Adam won't stop until he sees me dead."

"Aye, it'd take a wee miracle, I'm thinking, ever to heal that lad's anger against ye. Still—" Father Kenneth cocked his head, a wry grin on his face—"the good Lord's been known to work far greater miracles than a mere reconciliation between ye and Adam."

Ruarc made a disgusted sound. "Och, aye, and I'd be daft to risk my life on such a feeble premise as that. The good Lord will have to make His will a lot more clear if He wishes for me to believe His hand's in this sorry situation."

"Well, I say, give Him time. Just give Him time." Once again, the priest took up his mug and drank from it. "In the meanwhile, what do ye plan to do about Killian? Ye refuse to speak with her. And all the servants are chattering away about how ye now keep separate bedchambers. This isn't right, lad. Ye swore to honor and cleave to her through good times and bad. Have ye suddenly ceased to be a man of yer word?"

Ruarc sent the old man a seething look. "I'm still wed to her, aren't I? I haven't tossed her and those two vile compatriots of hers out into the snow yet, have I? Though, come spring," he added with a hard twist of his mouth, "I may well send Glynnis and Thomas on their way. It's long overdue, ye know."

"Come, come, lad." Father Kenneth waved him back over. "Come, sit again with me. I can't say I care much for all this shouting back and forth."

With an exasperated shake of his head, Ruarc rejoined the priest, taking a seat across from him. Immediately, Father Kenneth scooted his chair closer until their knees almost touched.

Bending toward Ruarc, he clasped his hands before him. "She claims she's tried several times now to ask yer forgiveness and ye won't give it. Yet how can ye now turn yer back on the lass, deny the love ye've still burning for her in yer heart?"

"How?" Ruarc gave a harsh laugh. "Ye forget, Father. Sheila taught me all too well. And now, the irony of it is both of my wives have, in some way or another, ended up betraying me with Adam. Fool that I may be, even I learn my lesson in time."

"If ye're a fool," Father Kenneth countered, meeting him eye to eye, "it's in yer absurd attempt to protect yerself by pushing anyone away who dares make an honest, human mistake. It's in yer blind determination never to forgive. And it's in yer fear of the pain that comes from risking yer heart, of beginning anew."

"But I *did* risk my heart with Killian. I *did* try to begin anew. And this is all I got for my efforts."

"Aye, I'll give ye that. Ye did try for a short while. At the first sign of trouble, though, ye were also verra quick to scamper back to the safety of old ways."

Scalding rage, mixed with a freshened sense of betrayal, engulfed Ruarc. Had it come to this, then, that even his beloved confessor turned now on him? "Have a care, Father, in daring to impugn my courage," he said with a snarl. "As highly as I honor ye as holy priest and friend, I'll not tolerate hearing that from any man."

"And would ye, then, tolerate hearing it from God?"

Ruarc frowned. "What does God have to do with this?"

"Am I not His consecrated servant? And am I not sanctioned to speak for Him to His children?"

"Aye," Ruarc replied carefully, wondering where this was leading, "I suppose so. But then, ye well know I gave up hope long ago of ever expecting to hear from God."

"Nay, lad," the old priest corrected him sadly, "ye gave up listening to Him. Ye gave up trusting in and loving Him. And now ye've such a stiff-necked pride ye cannot long bear anyone too close to ye or yer heart. Not the Lord—or a woman who truly and deeply loves ye."

"And when has either God or any woman ever been there when I truly needed them? When, Father? When?"

Overcome with a sudden, overwhelming sense of despair, Ruarc lowered his head and leaned his arms on his knees. "I just don't know what else to do, save what has always worked before. Above everything else, I must think first and foremost of Rannoch and its people. And Adam threatens them as much as does Glynnis and all the rest. In the end, I'm all they have to depend upon."

"Nay, lad. In that ye're so verra, verra mistaken." Father Kenneth laid a hand gently upon Ruarc's head. "There are times in our lives when the Lord calls us to seize the opportunities presented us. When we must, no matter how hard or fearful, summon the courage to step out into the unknown, brave the darkness, and embrace the dawn. With the Lord's help, though, such seemingly impossible feats become not only attainable, but essential.

"The Lord has always been yer friend—the verra finest friend ye could ever hope to have—and has guided yer path all the days of yer life. Guided ye to the wee lass, who is also yer friend, though ye refuse just now to see it. She's a blessing for ye, a precious gift from God. As ye are to her, I might add."

"I'm not so sure I trust aught anymore that comes from God, Father. All I see is how harshly He treated me in taking my mither from me, bringing Glynnis into my life, and in gifting me with Sheila, and all the pain and destruction she wrought."

"Even Sheila was a blessing, though ye've yet to fully appreciate or fathom her special gift to ye. But that's the Lord's way, ye know, lad. Only in the fullness of His time does He reveal His plans for us. Ye must but wait on Him in all patience and humility. Ye must trust."

"Patience? Humility? Trust?" Ruarc gave a shaky laugh. "And

when, Father, have any of those virtues been my strengths? God asks far too much of me."

"He only asks ye to surrender what is keeping ye from Him." Father Kenneth's mouth lifted in a pensive little smile. "Strangely enough, these are the same virtues ye'll need to mend yer now torn and tattered marriage. If only," he added, steadily meeting Ruarc's gaze, "ye've the courage."

"Och, ye never let up, do ye? Neither in the Lord's cause nor Killian's, either."

"How can I, lad? Even as the lass battles for yer heart, I fight a battle for yer soul. Ye're like a son to me, ye know, the kind of man any father would be proud to call his own. Yet, in the end, I'm but a dim image of yer true Father in heaven. Think on that, if ye will, lad. Think on that, and mayhap ye'll finally begin to understand."

Across the Great Hall, the main door swung open, sending a turbulent blast of cold air into the room. In its wake strode Davie. At his side walked another man bundled in the warm folds of his plaid. Something plucked at Ruarc, something rife with unease. He stood to await them.

"M'lord," Davie was quick to say just as soon as they drew up before Ruarc, "this is Hugh MacDonald, a messenger from our chief. He has news of verra great import."

Ruarc offered Hugh his hand. "Ye're welcome here. The hospitality of Rannoch is yers for as long as ye wish to stay."

Hugh accepted Ruarc's hand with a hearty shake, then released it. "A hot meal and a warm bed for the night will suffice, m'lord. In the meanwhile, I've a letter from the MacDonald. He said ye're to read it posthaste."

"And how are things with our chief?" Ruarc asked as he accepted the leather parcel, opened it, and withdrew the letter. "Is his health still good and his larders full?"

"For a time more, mayhap, if the soldiers who've taken up lodging with us dinna tarry overlong. But read the letter, m'lord. 'Twill explain everything, that 'twill."

Ruarc's gaze lowered to the paper he held in his hand.

Three days ago a force of one hundred and twenty redcoats of the Argyll regiment, led by Robert Campbell of Glenlyon, arrived at Carnoch. They are, Campbell claims, but passing through. Due to the chancy weather, however, they have begged quarters and food for a week or two.

We have offered them Highland hospitality, quartering them among the cottages. All is well, or at least for the time being as they enjoy our meat and fires. I advise ye, however, to take every precaution to protect yerself until their true intent is discovered, or they depart Glencoe for other places.

It was dated the fourth of February.

Ruarc glanced up. "And how did ye find the situation, lad? Is it truly as peaceable as our chief claims?"

The big MacDonald shrugged. "So far I'd say aye. The soldiers are mannerly, working their drills during the morn, running and wrestling in the afternoon, then feasting with us at night. They're mostly High-landers and Campbells, with a few Lowlanders thrown in. Our chief has taken Glenlyon's measure and feels there's no guile in him."

"And what of Alasdair's two sons? How do they feel?"

"John's in agreement with his father, but the younger one, Alasdair Og, still has his doubts. He claims Glenlyon appears nervous about something, and his wife, who ye know is Glenlyon's niece, claims to a woman's foreboding."

Ruarc nodded. "I must admit to a similar foreboding."

His first impulse was to gather all the able-bodied men he could, from his own people as well as from other villages as they headed down the glen, and fall upon the soldiers with all force and fury. But then there was the sticky matter of Highland hospitality. Alasdair had offered it, Glenlyon had accepted, and woe to any Highlander who dared dishonor it. Unless expressly requested by his chief to bring fighting men to his aid, Ruarc's hands were tied.

"Well, mayhap Glenlyon and his men will be gone in a week or so," Ruarc said. "I must admit, however, they'll be foremost in my mind until they do."

"As they will in mine, m'lord." Hugh licked his lips and glanced around then. "Would ye be having a wee dram of whiskey or some other warming drink? The ride here was verra cold, what with the wind blowing so fiercely today."

"Och, aye." Ruarc forced a laugh and clapped him on the back. "Here, seat yerself by the fire while I call over a servant. We'll have ye right as rain in no time."

Soon Hugh was well warmed and happy by the fire, talking with Father Kenneth while he quickly downed a cup of whiskey, then a large mug of mulled wine. Ruarc, however, when hospitality finally permitted, excused himself. Alasdair's letter in hand, he headed for the privacy of the library to think further on the strange and disturbing turn of events.

†

THE WINDS blew through all day but, by the next morning, the sun began to pierce the clouds churning above the peaks of the Two Herdsmen. By late morning, it felt positively balmy. Killian, feeling hemmed in and full of growing tension, decided she needed a nice, long walk.

The past two and a half weeks had been some of the most miserable days of her life. Alexander had always taken his anger out on her in a painfully physical manner. But Ruarc's cold, distant, and most intimidating demeanor, though it didn't inflict bodily damage, was just as torturous. Their seemingly ever-widening emotional chasm, especially after the happiness they had so recently known, was becoming increasingly harder to bear.

The snow had melted here in the valley bottom. The pastures showed now, winter-bleached and sodden with moisture. It was indeed a soft, mild day, and many of the crofters and servants had taken outdoors to do their work. As Killian walked along, she saw young men heading out to the hills to hunt the red deer and older ones take to their stools to mend their small, flat-bottomed boats used in summer to fish the lochs. Women brought out huge iron pots and built fires beneath them to make dyes of lichen and heather for the wools they had spun and would soon weave into plaid.

All was well in the hearts and homes of the simple folk. Not so, though, with their laird.

Would Ruarc ever believe her, much less forgive her? Killian had never seen him so angry. Yet he kept his anger under tight control, a simmering volcano that threatened dire consequences to any who dared approach. Even Gavin had noticed and commented upon it, informing her Ruarc was no longer much fun to be around.

Tears stung Killian's eyes. She'd had such high hopes for the success of this, her second marriage. She had thought she had finally found the man of her heart, her dreams.

But now . . . now Killian questioned the wisdom of her earlier convictions. Now she began to doubt, once again, the wisdom of remaining long at Rannoch. Thank the Lord she hadn't yet written that letter to her overseer, instructing him to sell the plantation.

As Killian passed one of the crofts situated not far from the stables, the sound of a weaver at her loom drifted through an open window. She paused to look inside.

Mary MacDonald, the wife of Davie, Ruarc's captain of the guard, glanced up just then to catch Killian staring in at her. A plump, pretty young woman in her early twenties, she always seemed happy and content. She smiled now with such a warm, open countenance it made Killian's heart twist within her breast.

"Is there aught I can do for ye, m'lady?" the fair, auburn-haired woman asked.

Her eyes were so bright with welcome and a sincere interest that Killian couldn't help herself. Just for a short time, she'd like to forget the pain and rejection. Just for a short time, she'd like to talk with someone content with her life.

"Would you mind if I came in and watched you weave? I've always had a fascination with the art of weaving and how one uses the loom to create such beautiful, soft woolens."

"Och, aye, m'lady." Mary motioned her inside. "I'd be happy to show ye the use of the loom." She waited until Killian next stood beside her before continuing with her weaving.

"This is a floor loom," Mary began. "After ye dress the loom with the warp threads—all those threads running lengthwise there," she added, pointing to them, "ye push down on the foot treadle. That raises the harnesses attached to the warp threads. Then ye throw the shuttle between the two rows formed of threads."

Killian leaned over to take a closer look. "And that thread attached to the shuttle on that bobbin is called a weft thread, correct?"

"Aye, that 'tis," the other woman agreed. "Next ye pull the beater back toward ye sharply to pack the weft tightly together. Then ye press a different treadle and throw the shuttle in the opposite direction. That's pretty much how ye weave, save that, for a particular tartan pattern I have to vary the order, number, and color of warp threads the weft skips under, as the shuttle is passed across the loom."

"Would you mind . . ." Killian hesitated for an instant, then forged on. "Would you mind if I gave it a try?"

Laughing in delight, Mary slid from behind her loom. "Och, aye, m'lady. I'd be verra happy to teach ye. And mayhap, in time, ye might even weave our laird a fine, warm plaid. I dinna know of any man who doesna cherish one made by his woman."

The consideration heartened Killian. Indeed, wouldn't Ruarc be proud of her if she learned such a fine skill? With that hopeful image in mind, she took her seat at the loom.

"Mary, if you wouldn't mind, I've one thing more to ask you," Killian said as a sudden thought assailed her.

Perhaps the only way to regain Ruarc's trust was to renew her efforts to discover Sheila's killer. Mary might have heard talk among the other crofters about the night of Sheila's death. Even if all her earlier efforts had failed to produce any viable leads, Killian was determined not to give up. Once Ruarc and Adam were finally convinced neither of the other was a murderer, perhaps they'd talk. And, perhaps then, Ruarc would at last believe her.

"Aye, m'lady," Mary asked, pausing beside the loom, "and what might yer question be?"

"The Lady Sheila. Did she have any enemies, anyone who bore her a grudge, among the crofters?"

Mary pursed her lips in thought, then shook her head. "Nay, not to speak of. Lady Sheila rarely visited even us, and Davie's m'lord's cousin and all. She didna care to associate much with the more common folk, I suppose."

"Was there any talk, any speculation, of what really happened that night?"

"Well, no one ever thought for a moment that m'lord had done his wife any harm. Leastwise, none of us crofters."

"Then who did they suspect?"

"Adam Campbell, of course." Suddenly, Mary couldn't quite meet her gaze. "And there was some brief talk that mayhap 'twas Thomas MacDonald. Davie and a few others saw him and Lady Sheila arguing a few days earlier."

Excitement swelled in Killian. *Thomas.* She had given him only passing consideration. But on second thought, Sheila's death might have well served his and his mother's needs. Even if Killian found it improbable that Glynnis would've sought Sheila's death, there was no reason Thomas might not have taken matters into his own hands.

Killian nodded, then turned her attention back to the loom. "My thanks, Mary. You've been most helpful. Now, is this the proper way to do this?"

After a time of more careful supervision, Mary finally left her for a few minutes to see to her baby. The weaving went smoothly. Soon, Killian had a rhythmic flow going. Her thoughts began to journey, naturally returning to what had been uppermost in her mind—the problem of what to do about Ruarc.

He was such a proud, stubborn man. And his fears of betrayal were understandable, after what Sheila had done to him. He also had good reason to distrust anything involving Adam. But if Sheila's true killer was never discovered and the problems with Adam were never resolved, would she ever be able to feel secure in his love? Would she never, then, find the stable home and happy family she had always sought?

The full enormity of her situation struck Killian once more, burying her beneath a crushing weight of hopelessness. Suddenly, the shuttle caught in the warp threads, slipped through, and fell to the floor. Flustered and upset, Killian scooted back her stool, bent and, in the process of trying to retrieve the shuttle, inadvertently banged her forehead hard on the loom's frame.

Tears of pain filled her eyes. Frustration flooded her anew. In a rush of long pent-up emotion, Killian began to weep. Strangely, once she allowed the floodgates finally to open, a torrent gushed forth. A most disconcerting, uncontrollable torrent.

Mary returned, her babe in her arms, to find her mistress sobbing as if her heart would break. She hurried over. "M'lady? Whatever's the matter? Is there aught I can do to help ye?"

"N-no," Killian replied, choking out the word. "It'll . . . it'll be a-all right. It *has* to be all r-right."

There was nothing, however, either Killian or Mary could seem to do to staunch the fitful, body-wracking sobs. Finally, with a soft cry of distress, Davie's wife ran from the cottage.

†

"HE MEANS to see us gone from here, Mither," Thomas observed glumly as they walked along. "Mark my words. Before summer, Ruarc will have us banished from Rannoch."

"Aye, it's likely indeed." To warm her hands, Glynnis slid them into the folds of her woolen cloak. "But we've still time, though I cannot think what our recourse might be."

"Short of murdering him in his bed—which I'll tell ye now I've no stomach for—I can't imagine what's left us. I greatly fear—"

From around the front of the stable just then, a frantic Mary MacDonald, her infant clasped to her chest, ran out. At sight of Glynnis and her son, her eyes lit with hope. "Och, m'lady, come quick! M'lady Killian's in our cottage, weeping as if her heart's nigh unto breaking."

Glynnis and Thomas exchanged a puzzled glance.

"The heartless swine," her son snarled, apparently the first to piece together all the likely possibilities for Killian's strange behavior. "It's Ruarc's fault. I just know it!"

"Have a care for yer idle tongue." Glynnis cast a slanting look in Mary's direction. She turned then to her. "Take me to m'lady. Thomas—" she glanced over her shoulder—"why don't ye help Mary here and carry her wee bairn for her?"

With an uncertain look, Thomas awkwardly complied, and they headed for Mary's cottage. As they drew up outside, Glynnis turned once more to the young mother. "Would ye mind terribly, lass, staying out here with my son while I talk with Killian? I'm thinking it'd go better if we all didn't rush in at once and started milling about and gaping at the poor lass."

"Och, aye, m'lady." Mary's head bobbed in eager—and probably relieved, Glynnis imagined—assent. "I'll be most happy to wait out here."

Gathering her skirts, Glynnis then entered the cottage. Killian sat on the floor by the loom, her head buried in her hands, still weeping piteously.

Staring down at the young Colonial, Glynnis's heart swelled with compassion and a motherly concern. Killian didn't deserve the cruel treatment Ruarc was dealing out to her. Even if *he* still doubted his wife's innocence, Glynnis knew the truth. And that knowledge filled her with guilt.

She knelt beside her, touching her on the shoulder. "Killian? Come, lass. Tell me what I can do to help."

"H-help?" The younger woman lifted a tear-ravaged face to her. "H-help me win back Ruarc's l-love. Th-that's all I w-want."

"Ye could do better than the likes of him." All the old bitterness swelled once again. "Mayhap it'd be wiser to leave him to his own self-destruction."

Killian stared up at her for a long, bewildered moment, then commenced to bawl all the louder. Glynnis rolled her eyes. Well, now she had really gone and done it. Whenever would she learn to curb her unkind tongue?

"Och, lass, lass," Glynnis crooned, leaning down to pull Killian into her arms. "Forgive me. Ye well know how I feel about Ruarc, but this also isn't the time for such matters. What ye need is my support, not endless criticisms of yer husband. "What ye need," she added, her resolve finally made, "is for me to go to Ruarc and tell him the truth."

"N-no," Killian protested between shuddering hiccups. "At f-first I thought that would s-solve everything. But n-now I know the real problem is Ruarc's trust in me. Either it's there or it isn't."

Frustration tautened Glynnis's voice. "Then what do ye want from me? Tell me, whatever it is, and I'll do it."

"I n-need someone to t-tell me what to d-do." She gazed up at Glynnis. "It's n-not too l-late, is it? Oh, please, d-don't tell me it's t-too late!"

"I don't know, lass." Ever so gently, she began to stroke Killian's hair. "I'm hardly the one, after all, to tell ye what's in my stepson's heart."

Glynnis paused, thinking back to her own life and the things she had always regretted not doing. If only she hadn't given up quite so quickly on Robert and Ruarc. If only she had tried to be a friend and help the grieving father and son come to terms with their loss, perhaps they might have yet grown into a happy family. But she had been so young, so unsure of what to do. If only she'd had someone older, more experienced to talk to . . .

Glynnis grasped Killian by the shoulders and pushed her back. "Do ye really want my advice? Woman to woman, I mean?"

The young Colonial gazed up at her, her tears ceasing as a sudden look of hope flared in her eyes. "Yes. More than anything, I need your advice."

A warm surety flooded Glynnis. "Ye must fight for yer husband, fight for him tooth and nail. And if words fail in convincing him ye have and will always love him, then convince him with deeds, over and over and over. Don't let him intimidate ye or push ye aside. Be there for him in all things."

"Truly, Glynnis? Do you think that might work?"

"Ruarc's a pigheadedly stubborn man. Beat him at his own game. Be even more stubborn in yer quest to win back his love. If he loved ye once, he may come to love ye again."

A resolute light gleamed in Killian's eyes. Her chin lifted; her shoulders squared. "Yes. You're right. If Ruarc thinks he's won this little battle, he's mistaken. This time I'll not stand passively by and hope things will mend all on their own. I'll not deny the truth and keep the peace at all costs. When it comes to a fight for his heart and soul, to win back the man I know he can truly be, my husband's in for a surprise." She nodded in grim determination. "A *verra* big surprise."

21

On THE tenth of February, Hugh, another letter in hand, arrived once more. Ruarc quickly read his chief's reply to his last letter, informing Rannoch's laird that Glenlyon and his men were still quartered at Carnoch with no apparent intent to leave.

For the rest of the day Ruarc fumed and paced, wondering what, if anything, could be done about the increasingly unsettling situation. At long last, he decided no plan would be worthwhile until he knew more. On the morrow, he resolved to pay Alasdair and his guests a visit.

Out of courtesy to Killian as Lady of Rannoch, Ruarc joined her at supper to inform her of his departure the next morning. At her reaction, he heartily regretted telling her at all.

"So, you're planning a trip to Carnoch, are you?" his wife asked as she cut a small piece of salted herring, then carefully scraped the skin and bones from it. "That's a wonderful idea. I'm sorely weary of this castle and would love a change of scenery. When will we depart on the morrow?"

For an instant, Ruarc wasn't certain what he had said that had given Killian the impression she had been invited. Then, with an angry mental shake, he cast the question aside. One way or another, she wasn't going with him.

"This isn't a social visit, madam. Indeed, it's likely verra dangerous, what with Robert Campbell and his men quartered in Carnoch."

"You suspect something's afoot, do you?"

"Aye, that I do, though I dare not reveal those suspicions."

As she chewed her herring, Killian's brow furrowed in thought. "Well then," she said finally, "it seems that's yet another reason for me to accompany you. Your visit will appear all the more innocent with me along. The appearance of a social visit is indeed the best plan."

She had a point. Still, he couldn't say it made the consideration of spending so much private time with her any more palatable. Despite the nights he lay awake in his lonely bed aching for Killian or the days bereft of her sprightly company, Ruarc was no more ready to talk or work on a reconciliation than he had been before. His heart seemed frozen in a perpetual state of limbo. Though he knew he must free it sooner or later, somehow the time still didn't seem right.

"Nonetheless," he said, "yer proper place is here. I'll go alone."

Killian set down her knife and fork, and turned to him. "I want to go, Ruarc. Please, take me with you."

His breath caught in his throat. Och, but it was hard to refuse her aught when she looked at him like that. It had been so long . . .

With a jerk, he recalled himself. This was *exactly* why he didn't want to spend any time with Killian right now. In his current state of mind, she'd most certainly beguile him into seeing things her way. Sheila had managed to do so for many years, until he had finally hardened himself to her feminine wiles. And Killian's allure was even more potent.

"Nay." With more vehemence than was perhaps necessary, Ruarc shook his head. "My mind is made. I'll go to Carnoch alone."

"Fine. As you wish." Killian returned her attention to her plate.

He eyed her warily, surprised at such ready acceptance. Then Ruarc shrugged and bent to his own meal, telling himself to savor whatever blessings were lucky enough to come his way.

†

AT DAWN the next morning, Ruarc set out for Carnoch. The sun rose, taking its sweet time angling its way into the glen.

When it finally did, however, the rocky walls' upper reaches were bathed in a luminous radiance. There was little snow present here, deep in the glen. The frosts on the floor, however, would linger until well past noon in an area that, this time of year, saw little more than five or six hours of daylight.

As he rode along, Ruarc marveled at the beauty of his home. The loftier echelons of Glencoe with its ridges, rock faces, and craggy summits always called to him. They tugged at his spirit to come and soar high above the towering peaks, like the eagles that danced and whirled in those unfettered regions of air and light.

Yet he always found an equal joy and sense of peace gazing at the mountain bases with their deep, basin-shaped corries, crashing waterfalls and icy burns, and the myriad passes that led to high, verdant summer pastures. Aye, he knew Glencoe like the back of his hand and loved every bit of it.

He loved the deep silence of the glen, too. One could hear for miles. Few who lived elsewhere were ever stealthy enough to sneak up on a Glencoe MacDonald. And certainly not the person riding not far behind him this morn, Ruarc thought, catching the intermittent sound of hooves striking stone. But who else would be making a similar trip west this morn?

With a curse, he wheeled about on his horse. Not a half mile back, and just disappearing behind a flank of mountainside, was a lone figure swathed in a dark plaid. Was it a rider sent from Rannoch to carry a message to him? Or was it a stranger with mayhap more sinister motives?

One could never be too careful in times such as these. Ruarc pulled his pistol from his belt, then backed his horse behind a pile of scree and waited.

The mysterious rider, his plaid shielding his face, soon rode into view. As soon as the rider saw Ruarc, pistol drawn and pointed at him, he halted his horse.

"So, has it come to this then," a familiar voice asked dryly, "that you now take to threatening your own wife?"

"And what, by mountain and sea, are *ye* doing here?" Ruarc demanded angrily. "Ye know better than to ride out alone, yet I see no escort."

"I don't need one now, do I? After all, I've got you."

His eyes narrowed. "As ye well know, I'm on my way to Carnoch. I don't have the time to take ye back—" An unpleasant realization dawned. "Curse ye, woman! I told ye yestreen ye couldna come with me."

She shrugged. "Well, I'm here and don't mean to go back. You can either take me with you, or I'll just go on by myself."

Ruarc shoved his pistol into his belt, then urged his mount forward until it drew alongside Killian's. "Why are ye doing this?" With difficulty, he contained the urge to reach over and throttle her. "I don't want ye with me. Indeed, I don't want ye near me."

Killian's mouth set in a stubborn line. "I don't care. From here on, wherever you are, there will I be. Sooner or later, we're going to talk this problem out and settle it. And we certainly can't do that if we're not together."

"So, ye think to force me, do ye?"

She gave a curt nod. "If that's what it takes. Nothing else has worked so far, not pleading with you, or giving you time to yourself to sort things through on your own. At this point, husband dear, I'd say I've got nothing to lose."

He couldn't help it. Angry as he was with Killian, Ruarc also found himself mightily impressed with her tenacity. He was, as well, more than a wee bit flattered she'd go to such lengths for him. Mayhap, just mayhap, there was a chance for them after all.

Ruarc had no intention, however, of letting Killian know how deeply this little escapade of hers had affected him. She was fast becoming as headstrong as any Scotswoman. He'd be a fool to encourage it any more than was necessary.

"Have it yer way, then." He reined his horse around to head back down the glen. "Not that ye've won aught, mind ye. I'd just lose valuable time if I took ye back to Rannoch this day."

"True enough." His wife nudged her mount to fall in alongside his. "If nothing else, you've always been a practical man."

"Aye, if naught else," Ruarc agreed, then set his gaze firmly away from hers.

†

As RUARC and Killian entered Carnoch, the soldiers had just finished a footrace with some of the villagers. There was so much shouting, clapping, and pandemonium they were able to reach the chief's house without anyone questioning them, or calling for them to halt. A servant soon ran out to inform them his master was in conference with Robert Campbell, but his mistress would meet with them shortly.

Ruarc saw to their horses, then brought in their bags. Killian warmed herself by the hearth fire in the great room. She had to admit she was glad to be finished with the ride. Though a pleasant day overall, as the shadows fell in the valley it had become quite cold.

Despite the warm plaid slung over her cloak, Killian felt frozen to the bone. She would've fain died of frostbite, however, before admitting that to Ruarc. It had been her idea, after all, to force herself onto this trip.

Alasdair's wife, a kindly older woman, soon arrived with hot, mulled cider. "Ye'll stay the night, won't ye?" she asked as she handed out the mugs of fragrant spiced, steaming liquid. "It's far too late to head back to Rannoch. Besides, I'm certain Alasdair will value yer insights regarding—" she shot a worried look in the direction of the council room—"the problem of our guests."

Ruarc smiled thinly. "And I'd like to speak with him about that verra same thing." He paused to take a sip of his cider. "To my mind, Campbell's visit here has dragged on overlong."

Once more, the old woman glanced in the direction of the closed door. "There's been talk, rumors of danger, growing in the glen. For some days the Bean Nighe has been seen by the waterfalls of the River Coe," she offered, lowering her voice, "cleansing a shroud again and again. None were brave enough, though, to approach and ask that ghostly washerwoman whose shroud it might be. And for several nights the Caoineag has been heard, keening for someone's death."

"Och, dinna fash yerself," Ruarc said with a laugh, meeting Killian's questioning gaze with a twinkle in his eye. "They're but old, superstitious tales and mean naught. Indeed, if he were to hear of them, yer priest would soon chastise ye for paying credence to such silly mutterings."

"Mayhap," Alasdair's wife agreed. "Nonetheless, I'll sleep easier once these redcoats are gone."

"As will we all in Glencoe, if for somewhat different reasons."

The door to the council room opened just then. Out walked Alasdair followed by Robert Campbell of Glenlyon. Seeing him now,

Killian recognized the man from the gathering Adam had held at Achallader that night of the storm. He was one of the guests Alexander had put such store in introducing her to, and was at least part of the reason he had become so murderously angry.

Glenlyon was a tall man with a long, thin face and a hooked nose. Though she knew him to be in his sixties, his complexion was still youthful and his long, flaxen hair was scarcely tinged with gray. It was his eyes, though, that unsettled Killian. They were nervous and shifting, and had the glazed look of a drinker. He seemed, at least to Killian's mind, a man ravaged by time, personal weakness, and indulgence.

"Och, and what do we owe the pleasure of such an unexpected visit?" Alasdair's face lit with delight as he caught sight of Ruarc and Killian. He turned to Glenlyon. "Come, Robbie. Meet my kinsman Ruarc MacDonald of Rannoch, and his bonny wife, the Lady Killian."

At mention of their names, Robert Campbell's gaze flickered momentarily. Then he moved to join the MacDonald chief. "So ye're the man who has managed to keep Adam Campbell fuming and foaming at the mouth all these years." He eyed Ruarc up and down, then held out his hand. "I'm honored to make yer acquaintance."

Ruarc took his hand for a brief, curt shake, then released it. "And I've heard much about ye, as well, m'lord. Are ye finding MacDonald hospitality to yer liking then?"

"Verra much so," the older man said. "There's none so generous and welcoming as yer chief."

"So, lad," Alasdair cut in. "Will ye and yer lady be wanting to stay the night at Carnoch? We'd be honored to have ye here."

"Ye've got guests aplenty, what with Sir Robert visiting and all. We can find lodging elsewhere."

"Nay, nay." His chief held up his hand. "Robbie has chosen to make his bed at Inverrigan near Alasdair Og and his wife, Sarah. We've room aplenty for ye here."

Ruarc looked to Killian, who nodded perhaps a bit too readily. "It seems—" he turned back to Alasdair with a wry twist to his mouth— "m'lady is most amenable to sharing yer hospitality this eve."

"Fine, fine," the older MacDonald said. "My wife will show ye to yer usual bedchamber then, where ye can freshen up and rest until the supper meal. In the meanwhile, I'll see Robbie out, for he's of a mind to head back to Inverrigan before dark."

Robert Campbell bowed first to Alasdair's wife, then to Killian. "It was most pleasant finally making yer acquaintance. We're kin of a sort, I'd imagine, through yer first husband."

Killian returned the man's speculative gaze with what she hoped was a calm, steady one of her own. "Yes, I suppose we are, though I feel far more a MacDonald now than I ever did a Campbell."

Glenlyon's prim mouth flattened into a tight line. "Do ye now? Well, I suppose, being a Colonial and all, ye cannot fully appreciate the love a Highlander has for his own clan."

With only the greatest difficulty, Killian squelched the impulse to inform him what she thought of ever belonging to the Campbells. But no good would be served in rudeness. "I suppose I can't, m'lord."

With that, Alasdair led Robert Campbell from the house. Killian watched the two men depart before turning to her husband. He eyed her with quizzical amusement.

"What? What did I do wrong now?"

Ruarc smiled and shook his head. "Naught, lass. Ye must have a care, though, to hide yer true emotions better. Though yer words were measured and courteous, yer face betrayed yer utter contempt for the man."

"Did it now?" Heat flooded her face. "Well, for that I'm sorry. I don't wish to cause you or your chief any additional problems."

"Och, dinna fash yerself, lassie," Alasdair's wife interjected laughingly. "It's past time, it is, that Robbie Campbell realize he's long outstayed his welcome."

"Aye," Ruarc muttered as he stooped to pick up their bags. "Only I'd say he outstayed it long before he ever came to Glencoe."

†

AFTER A hearty meal and a long talk with Alasdair, who couldn't be persuaded that he or any of the clan were in danger from Glenlyon and his men, Ruarc and Killian bade him good night. As they headed upstairs to their bedchamber, though Ruarc's mind remained seemingly on the frustrating discussion they had just finished, Killian's was already flitting ahead to the night to come. Would they reconcile and talk through all their problems? Would Ruarc, at long last, again share her bed?

Save for his reluctantly allowing her to journey with him to Carnoch, nothing really had changed between them. He was still distant, his thoughts shuttered from her. And nothing she seemed to do to win back his love had borne any fruit.

Talking with Thomas about the night of Sheila's death hadn't uncovered any new clues. He had been most forthright in revealing the cause of his argument with Sheila. She had tried to seduce him, and he had flatly rebuffed her. Though he and his older brother had never been on the best of terms, Thomas refused to cuckold Ruarc.

Perhaps she was too trusting, Killian thought as she and Ruarc drew up before their bedchamber, but she believed Thomas. Problem was, once again the trail had slammed into yet another dead end. She was no closer to discovering the truth than she had been to begin with.

"I don't care what Alasdair said," Ruarc muttered as he finally shut the door behind them. "He's deluding himself if he for one moment imagines just because the redcoats have eaten his meat and he, thanks to Governor Hill's letter, has procured the government's protection, we're now all doubly secure.

"I'm thinking we'll depart on the morrow," he continued as he began to undress for bed. "Once home, I'll raise as many men as I can, then march back to Carnoch."

"That does seem, by far, the wisest course. I know I'll be glad to leave. There's just something about this place right now that makes me uneasy." At the consideration, Killian shivered, then, to distract herself, pulled her nightdress from her bag. "But if you bring back men to guard Carnoch, won't that be in direct opposition to what Alasdair wishes? Won't you risk offending him?"

"Aye, I most likely *will* anger Alasdair. But I can't sit idly by and wait anymore. I'll tell ye true, lass. Though I don't give much credence to all those tales the Lady MacDonald told me, I'm with ye in believing they stem from some instinctive sense of danger. Many a time when people see things they don't comprehend, those nameless fears resurface in some symbolic way."

"And you think that's what's happening here?"

He nodded. "Verra much so. One thing more I noted today. Those soldiers. They're Breadalbane's men. That's no coincidence."

A chill washed over Killian. Suddenly, more than anything she had ever wanted, she wanted to get back to Rannoch. "Then we must hurry home posthaste. I only pray we've enough time left."

"So do I." Her husband wrapped himself in his plaid and lay down by the hearth fire. "So do I."

She stared at him, stung that, even now, sharing the same bedchamber after so many weeks apart and bound again by a common cause, Ruarc still chose not to come to her as a husband. Frustration welled. For an instant, Killian wanted to give up.

Then freshened resolve filled her. Heartened by the thought they were at least talking and spending time together, she snuffed out the candle and undressed in the dim light of the fire.

†

THE MORNING of the twelfth of February, the weather changed for the worse. The winds shifted to the northeast, began to whine through the valley and up the steep-walled corries. All afternoon as they rode along, headed back down the glen toward Rannoch, the sky loomed heavy and black with the threat of snow.

The waters of Loch Achtriochtan, as the couple passed the village situated there, churned restlessly, portentously.

A short ways beyond the high, narrow corrie called Coire Gabhail, where stolen cattle were frequently hidden, a flock of ptarmigan bolted suddenly from a stand of scrub. In a melee of feathers and flapping wings, the stout little birds scattered before Ruarc's horse, spooking it. The animal reared, lost its footing on the slippery ground, and fell.

Thrown clear, Ruarc climbed quickly to his feet. Not so for his unfortunate mount. His right front leg was broken clean through.

Killian, her own horse's reins firmly in hand, dismounted and joined her husband, who stood beside his now thrashing steed. "Is there anything that can be done?"

He shot her an anguished look. "Nay, naught." Ruarc withdrew his pistol and cocked it. "If ye can't stand to watch, turn yer head."

She was barely able to glance away as he took aim and fired. With a grunt, the horse stilled. Killian looked back to see an expression of bitter regret etched on Ruarc's face. "Was he a prized animal then?"

"Aye. I raised him from a foal, and he was but six years old." Then, as if to forestall further commentary, Ruarc shoved his pistol back into his belt and proceeded to remove his dead mount's saddle, bridle, and other gear. Finding a low overhang of stone, he stashed the tack beneath it.

"I'll come back for that later. In the meanwhile, we'll have to double up on yer horse," he said, finally turning back to Killian. "I'm not so certain, though, how much farther we'll be riding this day."

He glanced at the sky, which was darkening ominously even as the first, fat flakes floated down. "From the looks of it, I'm thinking we'll soon be in for a verra fierce storm."

"Perhaps there's some crofter along the way who'll give us shelter."

"Mayhap. The next several miles, however, are virtually uninhabited. Pray we make good time, or we risk being caught out in the snow."

With that, Ruarc took the reins from Killian, lifted her back on her horse, then climbed on behind her. She signaled the animal forward, heading it straight into the now driving wind.

Two hours passed at little more than a walk, with the overburdened horse fighting against a strong head wind and increasingly heavy snowdrifts. Finally, though, they came to what appeared to be a deserted crofter's hut. Ruarc jumped down, strode over to thrust open a rickety door that almost fell from its rotting leather hinges, and peered inside the little building of stone and thatch. Numb from the bitter winds, Killian could do little more than sit there in the rapidly approaching darkness, hoping he'd find the hut suitable.

Apparently he did. A few minutes later, Ruarc returned and lifted his arms to her. "Come down, lass. The dwelling's filthy and dank, but a fire should warm it soon enough."

Killian all but fell from her horse into her husband's arms, where she clasped him tightly until the circulation began at last to return to her legs. Surprisingly, Ruarc didn't immediately push her back from him. Indeed, when she did finally step back, only to find her legs still lifeless and weak, he quickly swung her up into his arms.

"Why didn't ye tell me sooner ye were all but frozen from the cold?" he demanded angrily as he carried Killian into the crofter's hut. "Did ye mean to kill yerself then?"

"And wh-what g-good would it have d-done?" she asked through chattering teeth. "You c-couldn't do a-anything about it until you f-found us sh-shelter."

"Aye, mayhap not." He set her down in the dimly lit enclosure. "But if I'd known ye were so cold, I could've held ye closer and wrapped my plaid about ye."

She reached up and touched his face. "I'll b-be all r-right. Even being out of the w-wind is already helping."

He took her hand and shoved it back inside her cloak. "Give me a few minutes, and I'll have some wood gathered and a fire started. Then ye'll be feeling even better."

"I can help—"

"Nay. Stay here. I don't want ye back outside in that wind. I'm far more used to this kind of weather than ye are."

There was nothing more to be done after that but to comply. In time, Ruarc returned with an armload of wood. He dumped it inside a circle of stones. With some rooting around in the hut, he found bits of old cloth and balls of dust, which he added to the wood. Then, using a small tinderbox drawn from the bag he had brought along, Ruarc struck a flame.

It took repeated efforts to get the damp wood to catch fire. At long last, though, Ruarc succeeded.

"Keep an eye on it, will ye," he asked, "while I see to the horse? There's a byre at the back of the hut. From the looks of things outside, the horse'll need shelter this coming night as much as we."

"I'll see to it." Killian bent low to blow gently on the fire. "Just hurry back as soon as you can. I don't care how hardened you are to this weather. You don't need to be spending any more time out there than you have to, either."

Ruarc turned and headed for the door. "Ah, at long last. Some wifely concern."

Killian made a face at his retreating back. "As if you'd be noticing anything of the sort of late."

He halted and glanced back at her. "Did you really mean what ye said yestreen? When ye told Glenlyon ye felt far more a MacDonald than ye ever had a Campbell?"

Her heart skipped a beat. "Yes, I meant it."

Something smoldered deep in the measureless depths of Ruarc's eyes. "Well, ye made me proud when ye said that. Verra proud."

Then, before the dumbfounded Killian could find words to utter in reply, Ruarc strode out into the storm.

22

FROM FAR down the glen a man's voice shouting something wild and unintelligible woke Killian from a deep slumber. Her eyes opened to a shadowy room thick with woodsmoke and the sight of blackened rafters festooned with long, tangled cobwebs. Killian blinked in momentary confusion, then finally recalled where she was and why.

The hand and arm she had used to pillow her head on all night were asleep. She dragged the limp, seemingly lifeless limb out and tried to shake some blood back into it. In her movement, someone behind her stirred. He grunted in displeasure, then scooted all the more closer. Snuggling up along her backside, he flung an arm across her.

Ruarc. When, sometime in the night, had he moved so near? She smiled, leaning back into him. It felt good to have her husband close again. She savored his warmth, the long, lean muscles pressed against her. She inhaled his heady, masculine scent. Oh, how she had missed him, missed this!

The cry came again, closer now. Killian lifted her head. The sound had risen from down the valley, in the direction of Carnoch and the other villages. Who was it? What did it mean?

Behind her, Ruarc snored softly. No sense waking him any sooner than need be. She'd just get up and peek outside to see who might be coming. If there appeared to be any danger, it'd be an easy thing to rouse Ruarc.

The plan to extricate herself from her husband's clasp without waking him, however, wasn't as simple as she had first imagined. In time, though, Killian was able to slip away.

It was still early, perhaps seven at best, she realized as she stepped outside. The blizzard had ended. Thick drifts of snow filled the glen and covered the mountains. From somewhere, a faint whiff of smoke wafted by. Killian frowned. Their own fire had died hours ago. Perhaps they weren't as far from an inhabited croft as they had thought.

Again the cry came. This time it was accompanied by the appearance of a man riding a small, Highland pony. Pistol in hand, he waved frantically to her.

Killian clutched her warm cloak and stepped out toward him. He was dressed in tartan colors she had seen many MacDonalds wear, so her apprehension abated somewhat. His face, however, was smudged with soot and what appeared to be blood. His expression was one of utter horror.

At the belated realization there was indeed danger, if not specifically from this poor man, Killian wheeled about to fetch Ruarc. She didn't have far to go. Her husband was standing behind her. After slamming into him, she staggered back only to slip and lose her balance. Immediately, he reached out and gripped her arms to steady her.

"Ruarc," she said, gasping in relief, "something's very wrong."

"Aye, lass, it appears so." He looked down at her. "Go inside. I'll talk with the lad, whoever he is."

Though he released her, shoving her gently in the direction of the hut, for some reason Killian's legs refused to carry her far. The Highlander rode up, leaped from his mount, and staggered over to Ruarc. She turned, her heart in her throat.

"Glenlyon!" The man reached out to Ruarc. "Glenlyon's killed us! He's k-killed us!"

Ruarc grabbed the man to keep him on his feet. "What are ye talking about, lad? Slow down. Tell me what's happened."

"Carnoch. Inverrigan. Achnacone. Achtriochtan," the man cried, almost sobbing now. "All the folk have been murdered or sent running for their lives into the snow, their houses set afire, their livestock confiscated. 'Tis Glenlyon's work, the filthy swine, and those of the other redcoats and officers who've joined him."

"Our chief," Killian heard her husband demand hoarsely. "What of him and his sons?"

"Alasdair was one of the first to die. I don't know what became of his sons." The man began to weep. "Och, what will we do? What *can* we do?"

"Ye can come with me and my wife, if ye will, to Rannoch. I'm laird there. I'll protect ye the same as my own."

"N-nay. Nay." The man twisted free of Ruarc's hold. "First, I must warn the others down the glen. Then I mean to sneak back and see what's become of my kin."

"Have at it then, lad." Ruarc nodded his assent. "And we must hie ourselves to Rannoch posthaste. There's no telling if more soldiers will come, and from where."

"Aye, have a care for that," the man said, backing now to his horse. "I believe Glenlyon has joined with another troop of soldiers. As I hid for my life beneath a bridge, I heard them speak of yet another company who was still to come over the Devil's Staircase to join them."

The Devil's Staircase. Killian remembered Ruarc telling her about the treacherous trail through the mountains near Aonach Eagach. From the end of the mountainous trail, it'd be a short march to Rannoch Castle.

Terror swamping her now, Killian ran back into the croft house and packed their bags. What if something happened to Gavin? The man had said the soldiers were slaughtering indiscriminately, including children. Whatever would she do if Gavin was—

Before the rising hysteria could gain the upper hand, Killian clamped down savagely on her gruesome thoughts. Nothing was served in surrendering to mindless panic. All that mattered now was getting back to Rannoch as quickly as possible.

Grabbing up the bags, Killian ran from the hut. Even then, Ruarc was bringing the horse around.

He took the bags from her, slung them over the saddle, then motioned for her to mount. "Come, lass. There's no time to spare. If luck's with us, that company coming over the Devil's Staircase should've been slowed by last night's blizzard. We may just be able to make it to Rannoch before them."

Killian climbed onto the horse. As Ruarc began to lead the animal down the hill, she leaned over and grabbed his plaid. "Aren't you going to ride?"

"Nay." He shook his head. "The snow's too deep for the horse to carry both of us. We'll make better time if I walk."

"But you'll wear yourself out, not to mention get wet and cold trudging through it."

"Dinna fash yerself." He pulled forward on the reins. "All that matters is we reach Rannoch before the soldiers do."

†

AN HOUR passed with frustratingly slow progress. Still Ruarc trudged on, fighting the deep drifts with a savage intensity and an ever-mounting fear. What if he didn't reach Rannoch in time? What would happen to his people?

No one would be on the lookout for soldiers coming down through the Devil's Staircase, especially not after such a storm. The crofters would be defenseless in their homes, with little warning of approaching danger. Indeed, Davie lived in one of those crofts. He might well be cut down before he could reach the castle and raise an alarm. And there was no one living within Rannoch with sufficient skill to defend it. Certainly not Thomas or Francis at any rate.

In time, however, Ruarc's thoughts turned to what had already happened. Glenlyon had betrayed the most sacred Highland code, and he as much a Highlander as any MacDonald. He had eaten Alasdair's meat, lived under his protection for nearly two weeks, and then repaid the old man's trust and hospitality by killing him.

One thing was certain. As one of His Majesty's officers, Glenlyon wouldn't have acted thusly, no matter the long-standing grudges he held against the MacDonalds for past raids on his livestock and other possessions, unless his orders came from a higher command. At the very least, Ruarc wagered that Breadalbane was involved. At the very worst, the treachery reached all the way to London—to William and Mary's throne.

A sharp pain lanced through him. Was it possible this terrible atrocity began and ended with William? Or were there other hands stretched between him and Glencoe, stirring the pot, spreading falsehoods, plotting revenge against a proud old man who had clung overlong to his honor and a useless vow to a dissolute former king?

Ruarc aimed to find out, but first he had more pressing matters to attend to. He must see to his people's protection, then offer whatever aid he could to the rest of his clan spread out down the glen. *If* he had aught left of his own to give. *If* Rannoch was indeed fortunate enough to escape attack.

It was a miracle as it was that he and Killian had evaded the slaughter themselves. If they had remained at Carnoch just one night more, they might well have been murdered along with Alasdair. Just one night more . . .

The acrid tang of something burning reached him, borne on a wind blowing from the east now. Haze filled the air. Ruarc looked over his shoulder at Killian. Her eyes were wide, her countenance waxen and, from the higher vantage of the horse's back, she seemed to stare at some object far away.

"What is it, lass?" he asked, fearing the worst. "What do ye see?"

"Fire. Black smoke and flames. And men on horseback riding south and west, toward us, from Rannoch. Riding fast."

"Och!" Ruarc groaned. "Are we too late then?"

Tears in her eyes, she met his agonized gaze. "I don't know, Ruarc. I hope not, but I fear . . . I fear we may be."

He swiftly scanned the area. Not far away was a deep corrie swathed in shadow. "Come, we need to hide, and fast, before those soldiers find us. They'll not treat us any more mercifully than they've treated any other MacDonald."

Killian nodded and urged her horse in the direction Ruarc had indicated. They reached the corrie only a few minutes before a troop of soldiers came into view. Their faces grim, their fine uniforms bloodstained and smoke blackened, they soon rode past.

It was all Ruarc could do not to leap out from his hiding place and kill every last one of them. Save for Killian—and the fact his people were in dire need of him—he would've done so even if it had cost him his life. But he *was* needed so, instead, he ground his teeth and held back.

At long last it was safe to come out. Glancing down the glen toward Rannoch, Ruarc wanted nothing more than to take Killian from her horse, mount it, and ride out as fast as he could. But he couldn't leave her here in the cold and snow, defenseless. It tore at him, this obligation to keep Killian safe, yet wanting at the same time and with all his heart to get to Rannoch. He didn't know when before his emotions had been so crazily divided.

Still, there was nothing to be done for it. Ruarc clutched his pain tightly to him, trudging on as fast as he could. And the closer he drew to home, the more the knowledge grew to a sickening certainty. The carnage wrought this day had touched him and his, just as cruelly as it had the rest of his clan.

†

BLOOD.

Everywhere Killian looked there was blood.

Bodies lay strewn on the snow-covered ground. The thatched roofs of the croft houses burned hot and bright, the smoke-tinged flames leaping hungrily to the heavens. Sheep, freed from their broken pens, milled about, bleating piteously. What few cattle that remained lowed in confusion as they wandered out into the snowy fields. And the people, bewildered and dazed, stumbled about purposelessly among the fallen bodies and ruined homes.

Ruarc soon found Davie, seriously wounded with a musket ball in his chest, lying in Mary's arms outside their burning house. "Let me have him, lass," he urged gently, taking his cousin and slinging him over his shoulder. "Let's get Davie into Rannoch where we can care for him better."

Killian swung down from her horse and hurried to the young woman. "Your baby. Where's your baby, Mary?"

For an instant, Mary glanced around frantically. Then she caught sight of her babe, wrapped in a plaid, lying in a nearby wooden feeding trough. She rose, took up her child, then turned back to Killian.

"They left but a half hour ago," she said. "Redcoats came from the north and, later, some Campbells from the south. The soldiers descended like a pack of wolves, shooting us as they could, using their bayonets when they finally tired of reloading. 'Twas hellish, 'twas, m'lady. Davie tried to stop them, to reason with them, but the redcoats wouldna listen. They shot him first of all."

"Come, Mary." Fighting to contain her own horror, Killian tried to pull her along. "You're shaking from the cold. Come with me into Rannoch. I'm sure there's a nice big fire in the Great Hall where you can warm yourself and your baby."

The young woman began to weep. "Wh-what's to become of us, m'lady? Why would they do this to us? We've done no wrong, meant no one any harm. Wh-why did this happen?"

Killian slipped an arm around Mary's shoulders. "I don't know, Mary. We'll find all that out later. First, though, we need to get you and your baby inside where it's warm."

She looked around her as they walked along. "Come. All of you," she said to the people milling about. "Come with us."

Some stared dumbly at her, apparently so aggrieved they didn't know how to respond. Then a few old women and children began to follow, clinging to each other for support. Killian nodded at them in encouragement, then turned toward the castle.

Though the door to the main hall was flung wide open and showed signs of severe damage, otherwise the castle looked virtually unscathed. Killian's hopes lifted. Perhaps, just perhaps, the soldiers had cut short their killing spree before they could wreak much havoc within the castle. Perhaps everyone who had taken shelter there was safe and sound.

Everyone . . . and most especially Gavin.

The cruel sight that greeted her as she entered Rannoch, however, dashed her hopes as swiftly as they had risen. Paintings still hanging on the walls were slashed. Furniture was overturned and broken. The draperies at the tall windows on either side of the main door were torn down. The scent of smoke tinged the air and, glancing up the staircase, Killian could see servants dashing about upstairs with buckets of water.

A shrill keening rose from the direction of the Great Hall. Killian righted a chair and pushed Mary into it. "Sit," she ordered the young woman. "Wait here while I see what has happened in the Great Hall."

Mary took her hand. "Dinna leave me too long, I beg ye. I-I

dinna know what to do." Panic-stricken, she looked wildly around. "Where's Davie? Och, what's become of my husband?"

Her arms full of sheets, Finola dashed by just then. Killian halted her. "Do you know where Ruarc took Davie?"

The maidservant nodded. "Aye. They're in the kitchen. We've set up a surgery there. I was sent to fetch sheets for bandages."

"Take Mary with you then." Killian pulled Davie's wife to her feet. "She needs to be with her husband. She can help tear bandages or the like, too."

Finola nodded and, grasping Mary by the arm, led her away. Killian watched them for a moment, then gathered her skirts and headed resolutely toward the Great Hall.

The huge room was in as terrible disarray as the entry area. Tapestries had been ripped down, and those that hadn't been had been mutilated beyond repair. The long dining table was broken in two, as if someone had ridden a horse atop it until it had collapsed beneath the weight.

For an instant Killian closed her eyes, unable to bear the horrible, senseless destruction. Then the wailing began again.

She wheeled about to find Glynnis, the bloodied, lifeless body of Thomas in her arms, kneeling in the alcove beneath the upstairs balcony. Her always perfectly dressed hair in disarray, her immaculate gown bloodstained and torn, the older woman clutched her son to her, shrieking out her pain.

Killian hurried to her. "Glynnis, what happened?" She knelt before the sorrowing woman. "Is there anything I can do? Is Thomas—"

"A-aye." Glynnis threw back her head and groaned. "My dear lad is dead. They killed him right before my eyes, they did, the heartless dogs!"

Fleetingly, Killian's thoughts turned to her own son. Gavin was nowhere to be seen. She could only hope he was tucked away somewhere—

"Adam Campbell came," Glynnis offered of a sudden. "He meant to find Ruarc and kill him."

She smiled bitterly. "Mayhap Thomas would live still if Ruarc had been here to assuage Adam's anger. But he wasn't, so Adam took yer wee lad. When Thomas tried to stop him, one of the soldiers shot him. Shot him—unarmed as he was—cold-bloodedly in the back."

Dazed, Killian struggled to make sense of Glynnis's words. "Gavin's gone?" She gripped her by the arm. "Adam took him?"

"Aye. Didn't I just say so?"

"But why?" Hysteria, so long kept in check, rose to engulf her. "Wh-why would Adam take Gavin?"

"Why else, lass?" Father Kenneth, with Ruarc at his side, drew up just then. "When he couldn't have Ruarc, he took the next best thing. Adam means to hold the lad hostage."

Tears of despair welled, then coursed down Killian's cheeks. It was too much. She couldn't bear anymore. "N-no. I c-can't believe Adam would be so cruel."

"Nay, I suppose ye can't, considering how fond ye are of the man," her husband ground out savagely. "But it's the truth. Father Kenneth just informed me that's exactly what Adam wants. He wants me in exchange for Gavin."

Killian pushed to her feet. "I-I want my son back." She grabbed at Ruarc, her only thoughts now of Gavin. "Get me my son back!"

"And how do ye suggest I do that, madam?" was his icy reply as he stood there, arms at his side in what appeared rigid self-control. "Ride to Achallader and give myself up?"

"No." She clasped his plaid and lowered her head to rest it on his chest. Sheer, black hopelessness overwhelmed her. "I don't want that. All I know is I want Gavin back."

"Your desires for Gavin aren't the most pressing issues." Ever so carefully, Ruarc freed his plaid from her grasp. "Besides, the lad's too valuable to risk harming, and well Adam knows it. As much as I detest leaving him in Adam's clutches a moment longer than necessary, right now I must.

"We've people here who are dead or dying. Most of those still alive no longer have shelter from the bitter cold and snow. And then there's the verra real danger the soldiers might return at any time and finish what they so ignobly began."

As much as Killian hated to admit it, Ruarc was right. The immediate needs were right here and now. Odds were that Adam would guard Gavin with his life. After all, the boy was blood kin.

Killian stepped back and wiped away her tears. "What do you

propose then, to protect us all in case of another attack?" she asked, looking directly at him.

"We cannot defend Rannoch against so large a force as Davie informed me descended on us today. We have to leave, find a safer place until all this can be resolved. The summer shielings on Black Mount seem the best choice."

"But that'll put ye even closer to Achallader," Father Kenneth protested. "Is that wise?"

"As wise as any other plan. Besides, it isn't likely the redcoats would think to find us there, and that's what matters most right now. That, and the fact the shieling huts offer shelter, which," he added as he glanced at the smoke wafting down yet more thickly from upstairs, "is more than we may soon have left here."

"But how can we move so many people in such frigid weather?" Killian's horror rose anew. "Especially with so many wounded and weak, all the livestock scattered, and most of the carts destroyed?"

"It doesn't matter." A hard, determined light flared in his eyes. "What we must do, we'll do."

"But first we'll bury our dead," the old priest interjected. "It's the only decent thing to do."

"Then do it fast, Father," Rannoch's laird warned. "And cover them with stones, for we cannot hack out graves in frozen ground. Decent or not, we haven't the time right now to squander on the dead. Not, at any rate," he added grimly, "when the living are in such dire straits."

23

BY MIDDAY the bodies were gathered. Rannoch's piper, a black flag tied to his bagpipes, led the procession to the burial grounds out near the edge of Rannoch Moor. Behind him came the old women, crying the coronach. And finally, when the last notes of the traditional funeral dirge faded, beneath the imposing height of Buachaille Etive Mor the massacre's innocent victims were laid to rest.

Though he stood with the others as Father Kenneth spoke the prayers, Ruarc felt somehow removed from it all. His heart was numb, his mind roiling with a crazed jumble of anger, despair, and disbelief. It all seemed some horrific nightmare, a nightmare from which he wished desperately to awaken.

A frigid wind blew off the moors, and he watched his people shiver and draw their plaids about their pale, suffering faces. They were ill prepared for the journey to come, yet to remain here even one more night was to risk another attack. An attack, Ruarc well knew, most likely none of them would survive.

As the old priest reached the rocky cairn now covering Thomas's body, Glynnis began to sob loudly. Killian, standing beside her, wrapped her arms about the weeping mother. Like a child seeking comfort, Glynnis instinctively turned to her, laying her head on Killian's breast.

Thomas had been the only joy in Glynnis's life. Mayhap she had pampered him overmuch and contributed to the young man's indulgent lifestyle, but Ruarc knew she had loved him, and deeply so. No matter how much Ruarc may have suspected her actions in the past, his stepmother's display of abject grief was very real.

Father Kenneth had claimed that Thomas died trying to protect Gavin. Though he didn't doubt the priest's words, Ruarc couldn't help but find that revelation surprising. He hadn't thought his half brother cared for anyone or anything more than he did himself. But, for the sake of another, Thomas had dared stand up to Adam Campbell and his men.

Mayhap, just mayhap, he had never known Thomas half as well as he had imagined.

An odd, unfamiliar sense of regret tugged at Ruarc's heart. Thomas was dead and he had lost his only brother. Lost him before he had taken the time ever to know him. Lost him, and mayhap even a family, he had all but thrown away.

The thought, however fraught as it was with guilt and pain, was more than Ruarc could face just now. Such emotions would serve only to weaken him at a time when he needed all the strength he possessed. What was past was past. He didn't dare look behind, but only ahead.

Then the blessings said over Thomas's grave were done. Father Kenneth moved onto the next cairn, followed by all the other mourners save Glynnis and Killian. His stepmother could barely stand, so powerful were the sobs wracking her body. Killian whispered something to her. The two women started back for the carts.

Though he had yet to confirm it, Ruarc couldn't fathom any justification—save the failure to meet the oath of fealty's deadline—for the heinous attack. Watching Killian and Glynnis, he wondered if either of them had foreknowledge of the plan to punish Glencoe. Perhaps it was wrong to think such evil, but both women had, at one time or another, been in direct contact with Adam Campbell. And Adam had been a willing, informed participant in today's events.

Now that Ruarc thought on it, Killian had been very eager to return to Rannoch as soon as possible. Perhaps it was also why she had insisted on going with him to Carnoch—to hurry him along so he'd be back at Rannoch before Adam and the soldiers arrived. Still, she hadn't seemed overly anxious when his horse had broken his leg. Or when they'd had to take shelter in that hut.

He shook his head in frustration. There were too many contradictions in her behavior. He didn't know what to think anymore.

Killian's guilt or innocence didn't matter right now at any rate. One way or another, she must come with him and the others to Black Mount. And, once there, there'd be little opportunity for her to get another message to Adam. He'd see to that.

As Father Kenneth finished the final blessing, Ruarc turned and stalked to his horse. Time to head back to Rannoch and pack up what little was left them after all the burning and looting. Time to gather his people for the journey to Black Mount.

Though the distance was a mere seven miles, it'd be one through deep snow and ever-increasing elevation. What was an easy, delightful trek to the shielings in summer would now be an arduous, miserable one for people wounded and weak. There was no help for it, though. One way or another, they must all reach Black Mount before dark.

Once all the upstairs fires in the castle were extinguished, Ruarc had sent an advance party of young men ahead to prepare the huts and gather whatever wood they could find for fuel. Even more importantly, they were also to scout the area and ascertain if any redcoats or Adam's men lay in wait. Everything rested on what news the return rider brought back. Though Ruarc's other options were few and far less appealing, he refused to lead his people into an ambush. He just hoped he'd have his answer when they returned to Rannoch.

There wasn't any time left to spare.

†

IT WAS necessary to use all the remaining serviceable carts to carry what food stores and useful household items they could scavenge from the ruined croft houses and Rannoch. As a result, there were few spots left for the old and infirm to ride along. Most would be forced to walk all the way to Black Mount.

As everyone made ready to depart, Ruarc led his horse over to Killian. She had just finished buttoning Gavin's coat onto a boy about her son's age and size.

"There you go, sweeting," she said, a catch in her voice. "Keep that fastened nice and snug, and it'll keep you warm." She gave him a little shove. "Now, get on with you. Go find your mother. It's almost time to leave."

"That was kind of ye." Ruarc drew up before her as the boy hurried off. "Just be sure and have the coat returned."

"I'll do that if I ever get Gavin back." His wife straightened to meet his gaze.

At mention of that sore point, something in Ruarc hardened. "This isn't the time to speak of that, and well ye know it."

"Perhaps it isn't." She looked away. "You'll have to forgive me, though, if Gavin's not ever far from my thoughts."

"I don't blame ye for that," Ruarc offered more gently then. "I just can't deal with Gavin's plight right now."

Killian released a deep breath. "I know, Ruarc." She glanced back at him. "Isn't it time we were leaving?"

"Aye." He handed the horse's reins to her. "Here, ye ride. I'll walk with my people."

She studied him for a long moment. "And if Rannoch's laird chooses to walk, shouldn't also his lady?"

"The journey will be hard. Ride the horse."

"No—" Killian gave a shake of her head—"I think not." She handed the reins back to him, then headed toward an old woman sitting on a stool outside her ruined croft house, her face in her hands. "Come along—" Killian took her by the arm—"I want you to ride this horse."

Leading the old woman back, she assisted Ruarc in helping her to mount. Then Killian grabbed a young girl who was just then passing by with her mother, and lifted her onto the back of the horse behind the old woman. "Hold her tight about the waist," she instructed the girl before walking up to take the reins back from Ruarc.

As he looked down at his wife, myriad emotions assailed him. "Ye're a hardheaded one, that ye are." He held out his hand to her. "Come then, let's be off."

Killian smiled wanly and nodded. "Yes, let's be off."

As one they strode to the front of the gathering. Neither glanced back, but only ahead. Indeed, there was nothing left to look back for, Ruarc thought. Someday, they might all return to Rannoch, but when that day might be, he didn't know.

For the time being the future lay over the next hill, and then the next, no matter what the future might hold. The best anyone could do after a day such as this was just put one foot after another and trudge doggedly on.

†

THANKS to the fierce winds and snow, the fragile summer shielings on Black Mount were in a state of disrepair. Though the advance party had worked as hard and fast as they could before Ruarc and the others arrived, they were only able to make four larger huts and two smaller ones weather-fast. With the addition of a fire in each to warm the dwelling, this night's accommodations would be adequate if cramped.

"It matters not," Ruarc said to Father Kenneth that evening as dusk—and with it more wind and snow—settled over the land. "What with the potential danger of another attack, I need to set a goodly number of guards out and about. And with the cold, they'll need frequent relief to rewarm themselves in the shielings. We'll manage for the night. On the morrow, we'll ready yet more huts."

"I'll take a turn at guard," the little priest said. "It's only fair, what with the shortage of able-bodied men."

Though he hated to use the old priest in such a fashion, Father Kenneth was right. Their losses had been great. Including Thomas, fourteen men were dead, twelve were injured badly enough that it'd be impossible for them to be out in tonight's rising storm, and of the twenty remaining, Ruarc needed to post half of them at a time to cover all possible points of entry. Any extra help would be greatly appreciated.

Ruarc nodded. "As ye wish. Best I pair up with ye, though. That way if we're attacked ye can hold them off with prayers, while I run back to warn everyone."

"Aye, now that's a braw plan," Father Kenneth agreed with a halfhearted chuckle. "Especially considering I can hardly run nowadays, what with my rheumatism and all."

"Well, then, hie yerself to one of the shielings, warm yerself, and get a meal into yer belly. It's just now sunset. We're to take the next watch in two hours' time."

"And what of ye, lad? Mayhap ye should be joining me for that warming and meal?"

Ruarc shook his head. "I'm fine. And I've no appetite. Get on with ye. I may yet join ye for a warming, but first I've a need to check all the guard posts. We can't risk any surprises this night."

"Are ye still worried then, that Adam may return?"

Freshened anger flared in Ruarc. "I wouldn't put aught past that murdering swine."

"He didn't kill anyone, lad." Father Kenneth laid a hand on Ruarc's arm. "He didn't allow any of his men to do so, either. Adam arrived a short while after the redcoats came down the Devil's Staircase. It was the redcoats who did the slaughtering in the village and the hacking at Rannoch's door. Then Adam rode in. Immediately, he made the officer put a halt to the killing."

"Then how did Thomas die? If Adam had such control over everyone, how did Thomas come to be shot?"

"The officer accompanied Adam into Rannoch with some of his men. He told Adam he'd orders to put all the dwellings, the castle included, to the torch." The priest withdrew his hand and shrugged. "I suppose Adam thought he had to allow the soldiers something in order to prevent further bloodshed. So he let them come in and set fire to the castle."

"How magnanimous."

"By then, I think Adam realized ye weren't at Rannoch, knowing the castle wouldn't have been so easily taken if ye'd been there. So when he entered and saw Gavin huddling behind Glynnis's skirts, he must have changed his plan. As he began to drag Gavin away, Thomas suddenly leaped from out of nowhere, a dirk in his hand."

Father Kenneth sighed. "The officer shot him before he could harm Adam."

"It's a pity Thomas wasn't able to finish what he began."

"Aye, mayhap," the priest agreed. "But the Lord had His reasons, as He always does. Still, to Adam's credit, he saved whom he could. If he hadn't arrived when he did, I fear ye might have come home to all of us murdered."

"When this is all over, I'll have to remember to write him a fine thank-ye note." Rage settled over Ruarc like some heavy, smothering weight. He had to take several long, deep breaths to ease the band of tension constricting his chest.

The old cleric must have noted his distress. "It'll all work out in the end, lad. All things do for those who love the Lord."

Ruarc turned away to hide the sudden sting of tears. "More importantly, did the *Lord* ever love Glencoe? Where was God when Alasdair was being slaughtered by a man to whom he'd shown hospitality, a man who was even his kinsman by marriage? Once again, I see little evidence of a loving, merciful God."

"Aye, in times such as these, it's indeed difficult to fathom how a loving Creator could allow such things to happen. In times such as these, it's verra human to question God, to rage at Him, to beg Him for answers." Father Kenneth smiled sadly. "But, as Christians, we're also called to believe one day that all things will be perfect in Christ. We're called to believe that no matter the pain and horror of life at times, we must strive to continue loving, knowing that nothing with God is ultimately lost or wasted."

"Well, that kind of faith has always seemed a bit one-sided to me," Rannoch's laird muttered in frustration. "God asks for everything from us, yet what does He give us in return?"

"He gave us the greatest proof of love that anyone—even God—can give, lad. He gave us His perfect, innocent Son as a sacrificial offering to save us, as a ransom for many. What greater proof do ye need of His love?"

"I need to see some compassion and mercy in this life!" Ruarc cried, wheeling about. "I need to see an end to this ceaseless violence, this consuming, brutish thirst for vengeance!"

"Then begin with yerself." Father Kenneth stared up at him with a burning look. "All any of us can do is begin with ourselves. In losing our lives for the Lord's sake, we shall save them and find life everlasting. In losing our lives, we also begin to touch the lives of others."

"Braw words, but none that give me the answers I crave, or the consolation necessary to heal the pain this slaughter has wreaked on me and my people."

"Nay, I suppose they don't. The time isn't yet right for ye to hear them at any rate. And the sad truth is, ye have to *want* to listen before ye can begin to hear. The Lord'll never force aught on ye. He loves ye too much ever to do that."

Once more despair engulfed Ruarc, and he had to fight mightily to contain it. He shook his head, flinging more than just the snow from his eyes. "Let us speak no more of God this day, priest. I cannot bear yer preaching, atop of all else I must endure."

"As ye wish, lad." Father Kenneth paused. "What will ye do then? About getting the wee laddie back, I mean? It wouldn't be kind to long keep him from his mither."

Ruarc was silent as, to the northwest over the Great Herdsman, the clouds momentarily parted to reveal the sun setting in a blaze of bloodred sky. A fitting end, he thought bitterly. A bloody sky for a bloody, incomprehensible day.

"What *can* I do?" he replied finally. "To march up to Achallader and rescue Gavin, I'd need the fighting strength of the entire clan. And, after what has transpired today, what fighting men who still live are most likely scattered from Appin to Lochaber. Nay—" Ruarc shook his head—"there's naught that can be done for a time. We must bide awhile."

"Aye, most likely ye're right. For yer lady's sake, though, if for naught else, don't bide too long."

At mention of her, Ruarc's thoughts turned briefly to Killian. She was holding up surprisingly well, considering all that had transpired. It had to be hard for her, though, even knowing Adam was most likely treating Gavin well. He wished he could give her back her son this very night.

But he couldn't—and wouldn't. Just now, the plight of many was more important than the well-being of one small lad, even as much as he loved that little boy. Hard decisions had to be made. Killian might not like it, but Ruarc would do what needed to be done.

He was laird after all. His honor would bear no less.

†

"THIRTY-EIGHT dead in Glencoe, including two women and two children," Francis muttered as he stood beside Killian one rainy, cloud-shrouded day two weeks later, gazing from the heights of Black Mount down onto Rannoch Moor. "And that's not counting the poor folk who escaped into the blizzard that horrid morn and, ill prepared as they were, perished in the snow. Och, curse Glenlyon and his ilk. Curse those foul-hearted, murdering dogs!"

Killian sighed. Isolated as they were here on Black Mount, details of the massacre had reached them sporadically, and in bits and pieces. Only a few days ago, they had at last heard the final numbers, and how the MacDonald clan chief and his wife had died.

Alasdair had been awakened about five in the morning by a servant informing him the Campbell soldiers were leaving for Glengarry's country, and one of the officers, a Lieutenant John Lindsay, wished to personally thank him for his kindness.

No sooner had the old chief slipped from bed and begun to dress, shouting for a dram of whiskey to be taken to his guest, when Lindsay came in and shot him twice, once in the back and the other through the back of his head.

The MacDonald chief had fallen across the bed, dead, his face blown away from the force of the exiting ball. Though Lady MacDonald had immediately thrown herself on his body, the soldiers who had entered with Lindsay soon pulled her away. They tore the clothes from her body, leaving her naked, then proceeded to rip the rings from her fingers with their teeth. Though they didn't kill her, they threw her outside in the blizzard while they next set fire to her house. She died the following day of shock and exposure.

Even now, the memory of that terrible morn filled Killian with an anguished despair. So many innocent people slaughtered, and all because a proud old man had signed some pointless oath a few days too late. Not being a Highlander born and bred, she supposed she couldn't fully appreciate Glenlyon's treachery in his blatant desecration of the inviolable code of hospitality.

Still, Killian knew a coward's dastardly act when she saw it. The name of Robert Campbell of Glenlyon was certain to remain forever one of infamy.

She gazed out onto the brown, desolate moor. Encompassing over fifty square miles of peat bog and bare rock, peppered with a multitude of small lochans, Rannoch Moor was virtually impassable to any who hadn't grown up in its vicinity. In the distance, she could barely make out the lower slopes of Buachaille Etive Mor. Its peak swathed in thick, gray clouds, what little remained appeared scant more than a lumpy hillock.

A thin, frigid rain slanted down in successive, windy sheets. Wild gusts tore about, slamming repeatedly into the little stand of scrawny, leafless birches they stood beneath, shaking the branches until they scraped against each other, sending bits of bark and dead twigs careening down on them.

It was a dismal, forlorn, tearful day. It mirrored well the sorrowing mood of the people who had most unwillingly found refuge here.

Killian turned back to Francis. The young man looked as doleful as the day. His fair hair was drenched and hung in wet tendrils, plastered to his face. Dark shadows circled his eyes. His plaid was tattered and torn.

When the soldiers had attacked, Francis had sought first to protect the castle accounts. The two deerhounds at his heels, he had slipped down the back stairs to the larder to hide the ledgers. As he hurried from the cellar, however, someone—perhaps meaning to protect the castle stores—had slammed shut and locked the cellar door, trapping Francis and the dogs behind it. That act may well have saved all of their lives.

"At least Alasdair's sons and their families escaped," Killian offered finally, desperate to find some spark of hope in the gloomy aftermath. "With John now as clan chief, the line of MacDonald succession remains unbroken. And there are still enough MacDonalds alive to someday repopulate Glencoe. Whatever was intended, the villains failed to exterminate us."

"Aye, they surely did fail." As he suddenly appeared to change tack, Francis's mouth twitched sadly. "Ye make me feel verra proud, ye know. That ye finally and fully see yerself as a MacDonald. Despite all that's happened of late, m'lord's still most assuredly blessed to have taken ye to wife."

"Is he indeed?" Once again, Killian sighed, then averted her gaze. "I'll tell you true, Francis. I'm not so certain he'll ever again be happy with me."

The young clerk moved closer. From the corner of her eye, she saw him reach toward her, hesitate, then pull back his hand. The action, nonetheless, gladdened her heart. Though it must be apparent how estranged she and Ruarc had become, Francis still continued to offer his friendship. There were at least a few things she had managed to get right.

"Ye must be patient with m'lord. He loves ye; I'm certain of it. Just now, what with all the struggling to see his people housed and fed and safe, he doesn't have time to consider the more husbandly acts." A bright, hopeful look on his face, Francis angled his head into her vision. "Ye understand, don't ye, m'lady?"

"Yes, I understand." She shivered and pulled the hood of her cloak around her face. "But it's more than just that."

"More, m'lady?"

Killian hesitated. It most likely wasn't proper to be sharing even what she had already shared with a servant, but there was no one else she could talk to. Ruarc, devastated by the slaughter and continued suffering of his people, was all but unapproachable. She couldn't bear to add even one more worry to his already overburdened shoulders.

Glynnis, since Thomas's death, would hardly speak, spending her days wrapped in one of her son's plaids, huddled in a corner. It was all Killian could do to get the sorrowing woman to eat and drink, and occasionally wash and change her clothes. And Father Kenneth, it seemed, was ever at Ruarc's side, ministering to those far more bereft than she.

Though her concerns about her son grew with each passing day, Killian didn't feel it was fair to continually bemoan her fate. As a mother, though, she also couldn't *not* do something about Gavin. She just couldn't.

"Yes, Francis," Killian replied at long last, meeting his gaze with a firm one of her own. "It's more than just the difficulties between Ruarc and me. I'm deeply worried about my son, and yet I know the consequences to Ruarc if he tries to rescue him. On the other hand, I cannot bear to leave Gavin in Adam's clutches much longer."

She managed a weak smile. "So, do you begin to see my dilemma—and my pain?"

"Aye, that I do, m'lady." Francis's eyes warmed in sympathy. "But what other choice have ye, save to wait until m'lord deems it wise to go after the lad?"

"What choice, indeed?" She glanced down to hide the tears filling her eyes. "I just know Gavin needs to come home."

"If there was some way, I'd help ye. It near to breaks my heart to see ye in such distress. Indeed, I hate to think, as well, of the wee lad taken from his mither."

Killian wiped away an errant tear. "I thank you for that, Francis. I couldn't ask you, though, to go behind Ruarc's back. If I come up with some plan, I'll see to it myself."

"Och, m'lady," he said with a wry chuckle, "if I was to help ye, as long as I didn't endanger m'lord, how could I be harming him? Wouldn't I be, instead, helping to keep him alive, safe from Adam Campbell's murderous clutches?"

A faint ray of hope pierced the darkness of her despair. Perhaps there *was* a way, if she had help . . . "It's the same for me," she admitted. "No matter what happens, I don't want Ruarc endangered."

Francis nodded. "So what can we do? A direct attack on Achallader would be ludicrous, with just ye and me as the army."

"Yes, it would indeed." Killian's brow furrowed, and she released a long, slow breath. "I've considered many options, and the only one that has the slightest chance of success is to slip into Achallader unnoticed, find Gavin, and take him before an alarm is raised. I've stayed there long enough to know the castle environs and the servants' routines."

"It'd have to be done at night. Not the getting into Achallader necessarily, but the rescuing and escape." The clerk scratched his jaw. "But I'm also certain they lock all the doors at night. How would we get out without someone seeing us?"

She chewed on her lower lip. "We might be able to use the door in the chapel's courtyard. Or the sally port. The one Ruarc, Gavin, and I escaped from that night I freed Ruarc from Achallader's dungeon. Considering its continuing usefulness, I doubt they've boarded it up." Slowly, Killian nodded. "It worked once. It might work again."

"Aye, it might work indeed. We'd do well, though, to have an alternate plan or two, just in case."

She eyed Francis closely. He'd help her. That much was apparent. But how much help, in the end, would he really be? He wasn't overly large; he didn't appear to know much about the handling of weapons. Still, he was clever and devoted. If it came to it, Killian felt certain, as Rannoch's lady and Ruarc's wife, he'd risk his life for her.

But was it fair to endanger Francis in such a perilous undertaking? She didn't know what Adam would do to him if they were captured. Yet could she manage such an endeavor by herself? She truly doubted it.

"Ruarc said we're not all that far from Achallader."

Francis nodded. "No more than five miles over a few hills and through a large forest."

They'd come this way, Killian realized, that night she and Ruarc had escaped. A heady thrill raced through her. Even allowing for time it'd take to get there, slip into the castle, wait for nightfall, then extricate Gavin and escape, it might require only a day. If they left tonight, before Ruarc had a chance to guess their intent and stop them, she could well be holding Gavin in her arms, snug, safe, and warm in but another day or so.

"Are you certain, Francis?" Killian asked, gripping his arm. "Certain you want to help me? You know I'd never ask you to go against your first loyalty to Ruarc."

"And am I not being loyal to m'lord," the young man asked, his eyes glowing with determination and no small amount of excitement, "in seeing to his lady's protection and rescue of his stepson?"

"Some might see it that way. I'm not so certain, though, how Ruarc might ultimately see it."

"It doesn't matter," Francis declared stoutly. "I owe him more than even he realizes. And this, if only in some small way, might begin to repay that debt."

She gave a sharp, quick nod. "Then we'll do it. Tonight." Killian laughed. "Oh, Francis! I can't believe I'll soon have Gavin back. I just can't believe it!"

"Believe it, m'lady," he urged with a bright smile. "For in the believing, the task ahead is already half done."

24

IT HAD been the most miserable, exhausting of days, Ruarc thought as he trudged back to the tiny hut he and Killian shared with Glynnis. The rain had never ceased. The cold and damp seemed to have lodged permanently in his bones. He was ravenous, filthy, and desperately in need of a hot bath.

Perhaps, if he was very lucky, Killian might have anticipated his needs and have a bath waiting. Though it wasn't as easy as it had been at Rannoch to procure enough hot water to fill the whiskey barrel, which now served as a rudimentary bathing tub, from time to time they had managed the feat. With a blanket hung from the low-lying rafters for privacy and a peat fire going in the center of the single-roomed hut, Killian could create a most favorable bathing environment.

To Ruarc's immense disappointment, however, as he stepped into the hut and closed the door, there was no tub of steaming water awaiting him. Indeed, save for Glynnis, who was huddling in her usual corner, the room was deserted.

He met his stepmother's steely gaze. "Where's Killian?"

"And what's it to ye?" came the snarled reply. "If she isn't here to wait on ye when ye finally deign to drag yerself home every night, only then do ye demand to know her whereabouts. Otherwise, ye can't find the time or interest even to speak with her."

Ruarc scowled at the haggard woman glaring at him from the

corner. Why, after over two weeks of barely a word uttered between them, did Glynnis now have to choose to spew all her pent-up venom? Couldn't she see how tired and wet he was? A drowned rat right now would've surely looked better than he.

"Hold yer tongue, woman," Ruarc all but spat back at her. "I asked but a simple question. And a simple answer was all I required in return."

"Well, why don't ye, then—" with a stabbing gesture, Glynnis indicated the folded piece of paper sitting on the rustic tabletop—"read that? Killian left it for ye several hours ago. I haven't seen her since."

His irritation beginning to warm toward anger, Ruarc strode to the table. As he drew near, he saw the letter had his name on it, written in Killian's delicate script. He picked it up. The paper was sealed with a bit of candle wax.

Tearing open the note, Ruarc quickly scanned the message:

Beloved husband,

I have gone to bring back Gavin. Francis is with me, and it's really but a short journey after all, so we won't be away long. Don't worry about us. I'm quite familiar with Achallader. With a bit of care and some patience, I should be able to locate Gavin and rescue him.

Don't, I pray, be angry with me. I just couldn't bear to be separated from my son a moment longer. It's better this way. I'd have never forgiven myself if something had happened to you in attempting Gavin's rescue. You're needed far more where you are.

Your devoted wife,
Killian

For a long, disbelieving moment, Ruarc couldn't quite comprehend what he was reading. Killian . . . gone to rescue Gavin? With only Francis as her escort? Was the woman daft? Indeed, whatever was his clerk thinking, to strike out with a woman in such hostile times? The lad knew next to naught about weapons or how to defend himself.

He crumpled the note in his hand, then turned and hurled it into the peat fire.

"So, what did the lass say to anger ye so?" Glynnis shoved to her feet. "That she can't abide yer foul mood a moment longer, and has left ye?"

Ruarc leveled a furious gaze on her. "On the contrary. She's attempting Gavin's rescue, with but Francis as her escort."

Her eyes went wide. "Nay, she didn't!"

"Aye, she did."

Glynnis began to rub her arms and pace. "They'll be fortunate if they even get to Achallader alive, they will." She halted and stared up at Ruarc. "Ye must go after them. Now. Posthaste. Ye must!"

"Must I?" Ruarc turned and walked to the other side of the room, trying to sort the emotions raging through him. He glanced back at Glynnis.

She stood there, both hands perched on her hips, glowering at him. "Aye, ye must, Ruarc MacDonald. Even if they get to Achallader safely, do ye imagine Adam isn't watching and waiting for something like that? Ye know Adam far better than I. Did ye ever, even for a moment, imagine him a stupid man?"

Ruarc's hands fisted at his sides. "Nay, I don't take Adam for a stupid man. But *I'm* also not a stupid man, madam. And I'll not be pushed into approaching Achallader until I'm ready to do so. Not by him, not by Killian, and most certainly not by ye."

"So ye'll just let yer wife go it alone, will ye?" Glynnis's voice took on a shrill tone. "Are ye daft, man? Do ye truly have any idea what ye're chancing, in so willingly risking her loss? Killian's the finest gift that's ever come yer way. Are ye so blind ye can't see that? Sheila, bless her dear departed soul, never held a candle to Killian. It'll be the worst mistake ye ever make if ye now turn yer back on her."

"Fine words," Ruarc said, his fury rising, "from a woman who'd like naught better than to see me dead. It'd set verra well with ye, I'd wager, for me to go after Killian and ride into yet another of Adam's traps. Then, at long last, ye'd have what ye've so long dreamt of— Rannoch."

A look of stunned incredulity slackened her features. She took a faltering step back. "And what's Rannoch to me anymore?" Glynnis whispered in a husky, ravaged voice. "I only wanted it for Thomas to ensure his future. Rannoch was never for me. Never."

"And why don't I believe ye? Tell me that, Glynnis!"

She shrugged. "Ye don't have to believe me. After all the years of enmity between us, I wouldn't expect ye to. But there's one thing ye must believe. Killian loves ye. She did this as much to spare ye the danger as to rescue Gavin. Don't turn yer back on her, Ruarc. Not now. Not when ye need her more than ever."

Glynnis had never spoken truer words. Ruarc knew that, no matter how hard he fought to deny it. But to ride off after Killian now was more than foolhardy. It could well jeopardize the lives of his people.

The danger was yet too great to leave them to their own devices. The new clan chief had sent word not to yet come out from the hiding places, for fear of further reprisals. And, though Ruarc had taken it upon himself to send a secret letter to King William demanding an explanation and a justice that included Robert Glenlyon's punishment, it'd be a time, he well knew, before he heard anything.

If he ever heard anything. Like a pebble in a shoe, the nagging question of what part the king might have played in this debacle gouged at and abraded Ruarc's heart. Had he been wrong, then, in placing such hopes in William? Had William, whom he had trusted, loved as a brother, betrayed him?

And now, to heap yet more worry and burden upon him, Killian had gone off on a foolhardy, hopeless quest. Frustrated anger swelled in Ruarc. *Why* couldn't she have waited a short while longer? It was bad enough Adam had Gavin. If he captured Killian, too, Ruarc didn't know what he'd do.

He *did* need her, even if, in the past days and weeks, he hadn't been the most pleasant or attentive of husbands. Most likely he had been wrong about Killian, too. In these heartrending times, she had stood by him. Amidst all the turmoil and anguish, it had been enough just to know she was there. It had been enough to give him hope for the future, however grim the present might currently seem.

A strength-sapping weariness engulfed him. Ruarc walked back to the table, pulled out a chair, and sat. For a moment, he stared into the fire. If he were a weaker man, he might mute his anguish in the sharply seductive depths of strong drink, as did so many of his clansmen. But he knew there was no lasting solace found in such temporal things. There was no solace left anywhere, it seemed, save in the meager comfort found in the knowledge of what an honorable man must do.

But where was there any honor left him in this life? Had everything he had ever chosen to do, in the end, been wrong? And what was a man, torn between duty to his people and what might well be a doomed love for his wife, to do?

Biting back a savage curse, Ruarc leaped to his feet and stalked from the hut.

†

IT WAS slow going through the black, cloud-covered night. Many were the times Killian doubted the wisdom of her plan and almost turned to Francis to tell him they should go back.

But then Gavin's sweet face would rise anew in her mind's eye. She'd see his tears. She'd hear him calling for her, know his confusion and sense of abandonment. Then freshened determination—and a mother's love—would again drive her on.

At dawn, they reached Achallader. Damp and chilled from the night's journey, Killian and Francis huddled together for warmth behind some rocks that afforded a clear view of the back of the castle. After a time the sun finally poked through a rent in the clouds, and it didn't seem quite so cold anymore.

Killian withdrew a parcel of pickled herring and day-old bannocks from a sack. "Here, eat this." She handed Francis several herrings rolled in the flat, circular, oatmeal bread. "We need to keep up our strength."

Francis took the proffered food, then paused to eye her up and down and grin.

"What's so funny?" Killian demanded, as she prepared her own meal.

"Yer legs. What with the long skirts ye always wear, I never before realized how shapely yer limbs are."

She glanced at the pair of trews she had borrowed from Francis. "And did you also forget I'm now disguised as a boy, so how else was I to dress?" To add further emphasis to her comment, she gave a sharp tug on the Highland bonnet she wore cocked on the side of her head to hide her long hair.

"Och, I'm not complaining, m'lady," the clerk hurried to explain. "It's but passing strange, ye looking so much like a lad, and I knowing ye aren't."

Killian took a large bite of her herring and bannock. The fish juices oozed out and ran down her chin. She wiped them away with the back of her hand. Then she pulled out a flask of cider and took a long swig.

"So, was that ladylike enough for you, Francis?" She stoppered the flask and tossed it to him. "Or do you wish further demonstration?"

He caught the flask. "Nay, that won't be necessary. Ye make a braw lad when ye put yer mind to it. That ye do."

They proceeded to pass the next hour watching as Achallader came alive with activity, awaiting the first and best opportunity to find some unobtrusive way into the castle. Finally, a man headed from one of the nearby crofts to a long shed behind the stone fortress. He took up a peat barrow, placed it before the shed's doorway, and walked inside. He soon returned with an armload of dried peat, which he loaded onto the barrow. After several more trips inside, the man wheeled the laden barrow through an open door in the surrounding castle wall. From her vantage, Killian could see him knock on another door, which promptly opened, and then begin to carry the peat inside.

Killian grabbed Francis's arm. "Let's see if he needs help. You do the talking, though, as I'm not sure I can convincingly pretend an authentic Scots' accent."

The young man arched a brow, then shrugged. "If ye wish, m'lady. Carrying peat's hard, dirty work. Are ye certain ye want to do this?"

"We can't wait about all day, and it's almost midday as it is. Just let the man think we're looking for work, and try as best you can to wrangle some pay from him. It'll make us seem more credible."

Francis wiped his greasy fingers on his plaid, rose, and offered her his hand. "Aye, that'll do the trick, and no mistake," he muttered, pulling Killian to her feet.

The laborer was more than willing to accept their help, and soon put them to work. The kitchen stores of peat were low. Killian and Francis worked until supper stacking the dried, partially decomposed turf in a room off the kitchen. For their efforts, instead of money they were fed a hearty meal.

In the resulting confusion of the kitchen staff hurrying to serve supper upstairs, Killian and Francis were able to slip away. Once out in a corridor, she turned to him.

"I know a hiding place, a room that's used for storing some unused furniture and portraits of certain family members Adam was less than fond of. You can stay there until I return."

His eyes narrowed in suspicion. "And what do ye plan to do in the meanwhile?"

"Search out where they've put Gavin, of course."

"Well, mayhap I should be going with—"

"No, you shouldn't. One of us walking about might not attract much notice. But two strange faces . . . well, it's too great a chance to risk. Besides, I know this place and can more easily hide if need be, not to mention find my way around."

Killian led him to a door down the hall, then opened it. "In you go," she said, shoving Francis into the room. "If all goes well, I shouldn't be long. Then we can both hide here until the castle goes to bed."

Though he looked as if he wanted to say more, the clerk did as he was told. After depositing her plaid and satchel with Francis, Killian was soon on her way. Filled with a renewed sense of purpose, she set out down the long, stone corridor.

So far, everything had turned out pretty well, even if the peat loading had been backbreaking. No one had commented on their unfamiliar faces or questioned them. Now, if only she could find Gavin's room as easily, the quest would soon be completed. Luckily, she had a few ideas where Adam might be keeping her son.

†

AS KILLIAN slipped up the stairs and down the corridor to the bedchambers, the sound of two female voices coming from the far end of the hall reached her. She ducked into a shadowed doorway and waited.

"Och, but ye wouldna believe the trouble such a wee lad can cause," came a familiar feminine voice. "He weeps if I but look at him askance, throws all sorts of things at me, and I even once caught him trying to climb through the iron window bars."

"Imagine that," the other feminine voice said. "If the lad had managed to get through the bars, he might've fallen to his death."

"Aye," the woman Killian now recognized as Janet agreed with a chuckle, as she finally came into view. "But the wee Gavin's a resourceful one, if naught else. He'd knotted his bedsheets together, then tied the end to the bars. He was of a mind, I suppose, to climb down them and make his way home."

"Well, dinna let it be said he's lacking in Campbell courage." The other woman laughed. "'Tis a shame his mither has acted such a fool, in wedding that vile MacDonald. 'Twould serve her right if m'lord never returned her son."

Janet drew up before a door not far from where Killian stood, pulled a key from her pocket, and unlocked it. "Mayhap 'twould. 'Tis none of our concern, though. M'lord will do what he sees fit." She took a step inside the room.

"Och, look what ye've gone and done this time, Gavin!" she immediately cried in frustration. "Smearing the walls with fireplace soot isna the proper way for a lad of yer age to be acting. Ye'll be helping me clean it all up, ye will—"

The door closed behind her. With a muffled giggle, the other servant continued down the corridor and disappeared.

For a fleeting instant, a wild impulse to dash across the hall and retrieve her son filled Killian. Only the sternest self-discipline kept her from doing so. *No*, she told herself, *wait. Wait just a while longer. If you take chances now, you might jeopardize everything.*

She'd need that key of Janet's, though. There was no getting around that, unless they chose to hack through the door with an ax or use gunpowder to blow it open, neither of which would make for a quiet, inconspicuous rescue. Better to bide her time, wait until Janet came out again, then follow her until the young maidservant returned the key to wherever it went. Hopefully, it'd then be a simple matter to retrieve the key.

The wait for Janet, however, required nearly an hour. Finally, she opened the door, stepped out, then closed and locked it behind her. Killian watched until the servant neared the end of the hall and turned the corner. Once more, she checked in both directions to assure herself no one else was about, then ran after Janet. As she neared the corner, Killian slowed. She halted too late, however.

Just then a man rounded the corner, slamming into her. The impact flung her backward. Killian lost her balance and fell, landing hard on her bottom. Her bonnet flew off. Her hair tumbled down.

Even as she reacted, twisting about to grab for the bonnet, a heart-stoppingly familiar male voice rumbled above her.

"So, what have we here?" Adam Campbell asked with a mix of amused satisfaction. "Is it possible, sweet cousin, ye've finally seen fit to accept my invitation for a wee visit?" He leaned down, offering her his hand. "If ye have, ye know ye're verra much welcome. Welcome to stay on as long as ye—or I—see fit."

Choking back a cry of frustrated rage, Killian wheeled around. She glared up at him, all the while her mind racing with possible avenues of escape.

"Don't even try," Adam drawled silkily. "I can call the guards out on ye before ye're ten feet from Achallader, if ye even manage to get past me. Better to admit defeat, and be done with it." He shoved his hand even closer.

"I've come for Gavin, and I mean to have him." Ignoring his outstretched hand, Killian climbed to her feet.

"And have him ye shall, lass." Adam took her firmly by the arm. "I was never one to separate a mither from her child. It's been heart-breaking, to say the verra least."

"Yes, I'm sure it was."

He arched a dark brow. "So, did ye bring any accomplices with ye? I hardly think ye came alone."

Killian froze. Francis was downstairs, still hidden. There was a chance he might be able to slip out tonight and make his way back to Black Mount. But that'd only be possible if Adam didn't find him.

"I left them in the forest. I was the only one who knew her way in Achallader. I told them to await me there."

"Did ye now?" Adam smiled thinly. "Then I'm correct in assuming Ruarc didn't accompany ye? He would've never allowed ye to come here by yerself, would he?"

"No," Killian said with a shake of her head, "of course Ruarc didn't come with me. I'd no intention of endangering him when I thought I could do this myself."

"To be sure, yer devotion to yer husband is most commendable." He began to guide her back down the hall. "Not that he's at all deserving of it, but then Ruarc has never deserved either of his bonny wives."

They halted at the door to Gavin's room. Adam extracted a key from his belt, unlocked the door, and opened it.

"I need to send some men out to see if yer friends are still about. In the meanwhile, I think it best ye be kept safe in here. Ye'll want to reacquaint yerself with yer son, I'd imagine."

Killian jerked her arm free of his hold. It was over then. She had done her best to save Gavin and spare Ruarc. The rest was now in the hands of the Lord.

"Yes, I'd like to see my son." With that, Killian walked into the bedchamber.

"Mama! Mama!" Catching sight of her, Gavin jumped off the bed and ran to her, throwing himself into her arms.

Behind her Killian heard the door close and the key turn in the lock.

†

MID AFTERNOON the next day, Ruarc was up on the stone wall of a shieling, helping repair a hole in the roof thatching, when the guards brought in Francis. As soon as he saw the exhausted, bedraggled young man, he handed over the armload of barley straw he was holding, scrambled down, and hurried to him.

"Where's Killian?" Rannoch's laird demanded, noting Francis was alone. His heart began to hammer in his chest. If something had happened to Killian . . .

"Adam has her," Francis gasped, still out of breath. He hung his head. "I'm sorry, m'lord, but I failed ye." He sank to the ground at Ruarc's feet. "Punish me as ye see fit. I deserve all ye may wish to do to me."

His worst imaginings had come true. Ruarc groaned aloud. "Och, curse ye, Francis, for leading Killian on this misguided quest! And then ye left her? Ye left her behind?"

"I-I had no choice, m'lord," the young man cried. "M'lady bade me hide while she went to spy where Gavin was kept. She was only to do that, then return to me. After the castle slept, we were to strike out again to free the lad."

"Then what happened?" Ruarc bent, grabbed Francis by both arms, and dragged him to his feet. *"What happened?"*

"I-I don't know. She never came back. After a time, I heard men searching outside. I-I think m'lady led them to believe her escort awaited her in the forest, for they never found me in my hiding place in Achallader. Finally, in the wee hours of the night, I slipped from the room, made my way to the kitchen, and hid in the storage area where we'd worked to stack the peat yesterday. Just before dawn, I left through the kitchen door and ran for the forest. I returned as quickly as I could, to apprise ye of what had happened."

He lifted hopeful eyes to Ruarc. Though his anger had not abated, Ruarc knew Francis was hardly to blame. The fault lay with Killian. *She* had been the one to plan this misbegotten scheme, then convince Francis to go along with it. *She* would have most likely gone off to Achallader all by herself if no one else had been willing to accompany her.

"Go." Ruarc released him, then made a sharp, dismissing motion. "Ye look worn out. Get a hot meal in yer belly, some dry clothes, and then hie yerself to bed. There's naught more ye can do."

"I'll ride with ye, m'lord, when ye go to fetch yer wife," Francis offered eagerly, clasping his hands before him. "I'm ready to go now, if that's yer intention. I didn't willingly desert m'lady. I swear it!"

From the edge of his vision, Ruarc saw Father Kenneth hurrying toward them. Good. He needed some advice, and desperately so.

He turned back to his clerk. "There'll be no riding anywhere today. The reasons I chose not to go to Achallader in the first place haven't changed."

"But m'lady's in the gravest danger!"

"On the contrary. She's in verra little danger," Ruarc snapped, at the end of his patience. "Adam will now use her to draw me to him, just as he'd hoped to do with Gavin. Ye and Killian have only raised the stakes."

"But m'lord—"

"Francis, I bade ye go and I meant it. No more of it now. Do ye hear me? No more!"

Tears welled, coursing down the young man's cheeks. He nodded mutely, then turned and walked away. In his wake, however, came Father Kenneth.

"I heard. Killian's in Adam's clutches now, isn't she?"

A despair Ruarc had managed to keep at bay until now all but squeezed the breath from his body. "Aye, that she is."

The priest took one look at him and grabbed his arm, tugging on it. "Come, let's hie ourselves to a more private place. What we must speak of, no one else should overhear."

Numbly, Ruarc strode out with Father Kenneth. They soon came to a jumbled stand of boulders, a good distance from the shielings, overlooking the moor. The priest bade Ruarc sit, then took up a spot beside him.

"So, lad," he began, "it seems the fat's now in the fire. What will ye do?"

Ruarc leaned back and rested his head against a boulder. The rocky face was hard and rough. He welcomed the discomfort. More than anything he had ever needed, he needed right now to keep himself grounded in reality.

"What will I do?" he repeated thoughtfully. "I don't know. What's the more honorable thing to do? Ride out and attempt to rescue my wife, most likely in the bargain causing the deaths of countless more of my men whom I can hardly spare? Or do I instead see to my people's needs, and leave Killian and her son at Achallader, hoping in time Adam tires of his cruel game?"

"It's a difficult choice either way, isn't it?"

"Och, I'm so verra weary of this vendetta! Why, oh why, is Sheila's murderer so bent on my destruction?" Ruarc buried his face in his hands. "*I* should be the one seeking *his* death, not he, mine."

"Do ye really think, lad," the old priest offered gently, "that Adam wouldn't hate ye so if he wasn't convinced *ye'd* killed Sheila? Yet a man driven by such undying vengeance must surely also be innocent. He hates ye, I'd wager, *because* he loved Sheila so."

Ruarc lifted his head. "But if Adam didn't kill Sheila, and I didn't, who did?"

Father Kenneth shrugged. "I don't know. What I do know is it's past time ye and Adam cease this pointless feud. Ye're both trying to kill each other over something neither of ye did."

"Och, aye." Rannoch's laird gave a sarcastic laugh. "I'm not the one ye should be convincing. It's Adam."

"I'm thinking that's a better task for ye than for me."

Puzzlement filled Ruarc. "What do ye mean? Are ye suggesting

I ride up to Achallader and demand a truce? Adam would laugh himself senseless over my folly, then proceed to throw me into his dungeon, most likely never to be seen again."

"Aye, he might well do that. But somewhere one of ye must finally find the courage to break this succession of increasingly cruel reprisals. Only the strongest, most courageous of men, after all, can stand up to the fate the Lord has chosen for him. And this strength, this courage, reveals itself in uncompromising truth. Truth about himself. Truth about all that has heretofore been but self-deception and false illusions. And truth that the only surrender, in the end, that can ever really matter is attained by self-sacrifice, by the acceptance of the cross he's called to bear."

"So that's my fate, is it? The one the Lord demands of me?" Ruarc asked bitterly. "To surrender myself to Adam, to all but commit suicide?"

"Nay, lad. Not suicide, but the first step toward rebirth. Toward yer new life. Salvation, after all, is finally attained by surrender, but a surrender freely given, knowing it's the best of all possible choices. A surrender willingly, lovingly, joyfully embraced. The forgiveness must begin, lad, and begin now, if either of ye are ever to heal from that tragic night in Rannoch's gardens."

It was too much to absorb, much less comprehend. Ruarc slid from the boulder. Many were the times Father Kenneth had spoken strangely. This time, however, his words did more than confuse and unsettle. This time, they terrified him.

"Forgiveness?" Ruarc managed finally to choke out. "Are ye daft? Adam doesn't want my forgiveness!"

"Doesn't he, lad? But without it, how can he ever begin to forgive himself?"

"And what do I care if Adam ever forgives himself for his adulterous liaison with my wife? I'm not responsible for that, for him, or for his happiness!"

The old priest studied him sadly. "And are we all not our brothers' keepers, lad? Especially ye for Adam who, for a time, was almost as close as any brother?"

"Aye, as was William," Ruarc cried in anguish, "and look what he has done to me and mine! The more I think on it, the more I realize he's betrayed me as cravenly as James has betrayed his own people."

He shook his head in fierce denial. "Nay. I'm not, and never will be, Adam's keeper if it requires the sacrifice of my life, or the lives of those I love, in the doing."

"Och, lad, I don't think it'll come to that. Go to him in peace. And remember, Adam's no more a murderer than are ye."

What Father Kenneth proposed was so radical—and dangerous—if he hadn't long been convinced of the old priest's love and devotion, Ruarc would've suspected his motives. But he did trust Father Kenneth. Trusted him implicitly.

With a sigh, Ruarc stepped away. He had to go somewhere, by himself, to think.

"Mayhap ye're correct, and Adam's not a murderer," he said. "Even so, I'm not certain I care ever to put that to the test."

"Yet ye cannot long remain in this disquieting state. Ye cannot long remain estranged from the Lord anymore, either, and well ye know it. It'll soon tear ye apart."

"Mayhap it will, Father." Ruarc turned, then stopped and glanced over his shoulder. "I'm just not so certain I know how to find my way back. And, I'll tell ye true. That frightens me most of all."

25

"WHY ARE you doing this, Adam? And don't try to justify it by claiming it's to avenge Sheila," Killian demanded the next day when Adam paid her and Gavin a visit. "Ruarc didn't kill her. If you'd use even half of that fine brain of yours, you'd realize that, too!"

Adam turned from the bedchamber window overlooking the front of Achallader and smiled thinly. He glanced at Janet, who was teaching Gavin a game of draughts. "It's a fine day outside. Why don't ye take the lad out for a walk about the castle?"

The maidservant immediately climbed to her feet and curtseyed. "Aye, m'lord." She glanced down at Gavin. "Come along, laddie. Let's go for a walk."

Gavin sent Killian an uncertain look.

She smiled her encouragement. "It's okay, sweeting. Go with Janet. I'll be here when you return."

"Promise, Mama?"

Killian nodded. "I promise."

With that, the boy took Janet's hand and skipped from the room.

"Well, answer me." Killian then turned again to confront Adam. "This is inhuman, what you're doing, first keeping Gavin from me, and now, keeping us from Ruarc. He doesn't deserve this, Adam. Ruarc's a good, decent man, and he *didn't* kill Sheila!"

"Mayhap he didn't." Adam shrugged. "Even if he didn't, it doesn't matter. What he did do to her—to us—is crime enough. I made a solemn vow upon her death to avenge her, no matter what it took or how long."

"If you're speaking of avenging her death, then if anyone has the right to avenge Sheila, it's not you, but Ruarc. He was, after all, her husband."

"Her husband, aye," Achallader's laird snarled all of a sudden, "but in name only. No matter what anyone, ye included, may think, I was the husband of her heart, always and forever!"

"Yes, so I've been told. Even Ruarc finally admitted to that." Killian walked to a chair placed before the hearth and sat. "I don't say any of this to judge either you or Sheila. I just want to understand why two good, honorable men can be so at each other's throats like you and Ruarc are with each other."

She put her hand on the arm of the chair beside her. "Come, sit, Adam, and tell me it all. I've learned much about Sheila from others who knew her. Now I want to see her through your eyes."

His gray eyes narrowed. "And why would ye care? Sheila's naught to ye."

"On the contrary," Killian countered with a wry laugh, "Sheila's everything. In one way or another, she has touched the lives of everyone here who has come to mean anything to me. The more I understand her, the better I can perhaps see a way through this terrible tragedy. A tragedy that has unfortunately become her legacy."

"What's between Ruarc and me wasn't her fault. She was but an innocent pawn in the battle between us."

"I want to understand, Adam." Frustration filled her. Killian looked up at him beseechingly. "Won't you please tell me about her? Please?"

"I suppose it's only fair, considering how caught up ye are between us." He eyed her for a long moment more, then with a sigh of resignation walked to the other chair and seated himself. "Sheila was always," Adam then began, "for all her great beauty, a vulnerable, insecure, submissive lass, endlessly searching for the love that'd compensate for the sadness of her life as a girl. Though she fostered with us, ye see, it was always against my mither's wishes, and she frequently took out her frustration on Sheila. I was ten when Sheila came to us as a wee lass of five. My older brother would have naught to do with her, so she latched herself on to me."

"I tried to treat her the best I could, and we became fast friends."
A pensive look on his face, Adam glanced into the fire. "Unfortunately, my father, thinking to get me with a good trade since my older
brother stood to inherit Achallader, soon thereafter sent me to live
with my mither's brother, a wealthy merchant in Holland."

His mouth twitched humorously. "My uncle thought to train me
to be a ship's captain who could sail his ships to the Indies and make
him an even wealthier man, but the seafaring life wasn't for me.
Finally, at age twenty, I'd had my fill of all the ships and seaports,
and took it upon myself to return to Scotland."

Suddenly restless, Adam rose from his chair, strode to the hearth,
and turned. "Sheila was fifteen that summer," he said with such a
tone of tenderness Killian knew his memories had surely flown back
to that special time, "and never was there a more bonny lass to be
found. Her hair was the deepest, richest shade of auburn, like that of
some fine red horse, her skin milk white and soft as a rose petal. She
was slender and lithe, and when she laughed, it was like a babbling
brook or the trill of birdsong."

"And you fell in love with Sheila that summer," Killian finished
for him, her heart swelling in compassion for the lonely young man
and the pretty, laughing girl.

"Aye, that I did." His smile of wonderment darkened slowly to
one of sadness. "We didn't feel like foster brother and sister. She'd
been such a wee lass when I left for Holland and claimed hardly even
to remember me."

"But in the growing closeness that summer," Killian supplied,
knowing this tale's inevitable conclusion, "you eventually became
aware of other, more physical feelings."

He made a sound deep in his throat. "I should've known, ye being
a woman and all, ye'd understand how it all came to be. We fought
those feelings for a long while, though, knowing in our minds if not
our hearts that our love was seen as a forbidden thing."

Killian sighed and leaned forward, steepling her fingers and rest-
ing her elbows on her knees. "How did your mother perceive this
budding relationship?"

"Verra poorly, of course." Adam's mouth tightened. "She
forbade us to be alone together. Sheila was constantly chaperoned
by the most insufferable, domineering woman ye could ever hope

to meet. Finally, there seemed naught left us but to run away together, find some minister to wed us, and then return to Holland. I'd many contacts there and felt certain we could make a good life."

"Then what happened?" Killian looked up at him.

"Holland had been at war with France for several years. The conflict began to near its end. I felt I owed it to all my Dutch comrades to return and help them. But only for a time, I promised Sheila, and then I'd return for her."

Adam shook his head ruefully. "Despite the danger, I should've taken her with me. But I, young fool that I was, thought the potential advantages gained in joining the then William of Orange's army and garnering his favor would only further secure our eventual future in Holland."

"One can't blame you for such considerations," Killian said. "It would've been very difficult, if not impossible, ever to return to Achallader after wedding Sheila against your parents' wishes. Assuring a secure start in a new country was indeed a wise decision."

"Aye, so I thought. But during that final year of war against France, I met Ruarc MacDonald, who had joined the Prince of Orange's military staff."

He gave a disparaging laugh. "Indeed, Ruarc, William, and I became so close I imagined them both my dearest of friends, almost brothers, even. I should've seen the warning signs, though. Ruarc always seemed to find ways I couldn't to ingratiate himself into William's closest confidences—confidences from which I seemed to stand apart. But, fool that I was, I turned a blind eye to Ruarc's maneuverings. When the final victory was won at Mons in August of 1678, we both made plans to return home to Scotland together.

"I even, in my excitement at returning finally to Sheila, invited Ruarc to visit for a time at Achallader. Ruarc, however, revealed the full depths of his self-serving arrogance as soon as he first caught sight of her. He decided he must have her. Imagining there was naught between Sheila and me, considering our bond of fosterage and the social strictures it seemingly placed on us, he wasted no time in approaching my mither to ask for Sheila's hand."

"You can't blame Ruarc for never suspecting you'd take offense at his offering for Sheila. You were the best of friends, after all."

"Aye, he didn't know the truth," Adam admitted. "That much

I'll give him. And I didn't know how to tell him. I trusted, instead, that Sheila would refuse him and that'd be the end of it."

"But Sheila didn't refuse him."

Adam bit his lip, then shook his head. "Nay, she didn't. I didn't discover this until much later but, between my mither's constant haranguing and Sheila's fear of ruining my opportunity to inherit Achallader, she allowed herself seriously to consider Ruarc's court-ship. At any rate, it all held Sheila in thrall just long enough for her to give him her consent.

"She was young, just sixteen after all, and easily swayed by a handsome stranger fresh from a victorious war. I hoped, to the moment she pledged her troth to Ruarc, Sheila would come to her senses and refuse to wed him. But, yet again, I was the fool, and lost her once and for all as my wife."

"I'm sorry, Adam."

Killian didn't know what else to say. Knowing how unhappy Ruarc and Sheila's marriage had ultimately been, she wished things had turned out differently for all of them. But it hadn't, because all of them had made mistakes, however unintentional they were. It was tragedy of the cruelest kind, though, for Ruarc and Adam to continue paying for those mistakes the rest of their lives.

"Aye, but not as sorry as I. I should've swallowed my pride and stepped forward at the marriage when the minister asked if any man had an objection. I should've braved it for my bonny lassie, but I didn't."

His eyes smoldered with a deep-seated anguish. "I didn't, and Sheila and I suffered for it. Indeed, I suffer still. She's the only one who's finally at peace."

"Ruarc suffers, too."

"Only because I make it so! Only because I hound him inces-santly with the reminder of his selfishness and the truth of how my wee, bonny Sheila died!"

"He'd suffer even if you weren't hounding him, Adam. Ruarc knows he failed in so many ways as her husband. He regrets the harsh things he said to Sheila that night in the gardens, though who can blame him after all she put him through with her infidelities? Infideli-ties that encompassed far more than just her couplings with you."

"She couldn't help it," he cried. "After the death of her last bairn and then that of my mither, something changed in her. Something shattered deep inside her that no amount of love, either from Ruarc or me or any of her other lovers, could ever hope to repair. Sheila was a broken woman. There was naught left her, or so she thought, but to seek the reassurance of her worth and womanhood from any man who cast her even a sideways glance."

"Was that when you finally came to her bed?"

Adam closed his eyes briefly, then nodded. "Aye, but not right away. At first I tried as best as I could to honor her marriage. I sought only to counsel her, to listen, to offer her consolation and comfort. But naught seemed to help. Bit by bit, I saw Sheila slide slowly into the pit of despair—and madness."

He turned his tortured gaze to her. "What was I supposed to do? I loved her more than life itself. I wanted her. And I feared . . ." For a moment his voice faltered. "I feared if I failed Sheila yet again when she needed me most, that it'd be the end of her.

"I couldn't do it. Indeed, I didn't even want to." He raised his chin defiantly, like a small child who knows he has done wrong and doesn't care. "So now ye have it all, sweet cousin. Ye know to what depths I've fallen in my unholy love for Ruarc's first wife."

Killian stared up at him for a long moment, pondering what she could say that would ease Adam's pain and put an end to his need to redeem his failures by killing her husband. It wasn't only Ruarc who so desperately needed healing, but Adam, too.

"You did the best you could," she said finally. "No man of compassion would fault you for that. And, I think, neither will God."

"God!" He gave a sharp, brittle laugh. "And when did God ever enter into this? I've broken so many of His laws since I came to know and love Sheila, that finishing this sorry mess by seeing Ruarc dead won't add verra much to my eternal punishment."

"You're a far harsher and more unforgiving judge of yourself than the Lord will ever be."

Adam walked to stand before her. He touched her face, running a finger down her cheek. "And *I* think, cousin, that ye're an innocent when it comes to man—and God."

"Perhaps I am, but one thing I do know. It's never too late to turn back to the Lord and ask His forgiveness. It's never too late, Adam, until you finally forfeit your soul."

He smiled then, but the action never reached his eyes. "And that forfeiture will finally and irrevocably occur when I see Ruarc Mac-Donald dead. That's what ye're saying, isn't it, lass?"

"You can't continue on this self-destructive course, Adam. And with Ruarc's death, how much more of you will die, too?"

"It doesn't matter." He shrugged. "I'm lost, one way or another. I've little more to lose."

†

A FINE, gentle rain drizzled on the thatched roofs and sodden ground, leaving little pools of shimmering, shifting water dotting the land. Occasionally in the distance thunder rumbled and dark clouds roiled, but Black Mount this day was calm if a wee bit cool.

Ruarc could see his breath as he walked along, his thick plaid flung over his head. A biting wind stung the bare legs below his kilt, but it didn't matter. The tang of spring was in the air. For that, above all, he was thankful.

Soon the weather would warm. The earth would thaw, and the planting could begin. Soon the grass would green, and the few cattle they had managed to scrounge running loose on the moor would begin to fatten. Rich milk would flow for the bairns.

Fresh cheese and greens would enliven their meager diet. They could cut and begin drying peat to warm themselves on cold nights. Hope, with the coming long, warm days of summer, would flare anew.

Soon, verra soon, Ruarc mused as he walked along, Clan MacDonald could turn once more to simple, happy things and leave behind the harrowing memories of what they had suffered in the past weeks and months since the massacre. Aye, by dint of daunting sacrifice and hard work, he had almost succeeded in leading his people safely through the winter.

His personal life, however, was in a shambles. Killian and Gavin were gone, prisoners of a man who still sought to see him dead. He missed his wife terribly, realizing, however belatedly, how thoroughly she had insinuated herself into his heart. The days—and nights—spent without her were becoming more than he could bear.

It had been two weeks now since Killian had left. Two, long, agonizing weeks. It grated on Ruarc that he must stand by and continue to let Adam keep her. It chafed at his soul, leaving his heart raw, his pride—his honor—hanging in tatters.

The disquieting admission of his part in this woeful mess was fast reaching a point beyond endurance. Had it all sprung then, those many years ago, from his single-minded intent to have Sheila for his own even when many had advised against it? Why, oh why, hadn't he listened then to Father Kenneth's gentle admonitions? The priest had warned him, when it came to Sheila, all was not as it seemed. If only Ruarc had been able to see past his youthful vainglory to the truth. If only he had examined more closely the ever-widening divide between him and Adam, once Ruarc had set his mind for Sheila.

But he hadn't. He hadn't listened. He hadn't paused to ponder aught. Indeed, he hadn't even concerned himself much over the haste he had taken in offering for Sheila's hand. But then, neither had Adam's mother. The very next Sunday after he had broached the subject of marriage with the woman, the first banns had been announced in Achallader's church.

Moisture saturated his plaid and beaded in his hair, where it began a steady drip down to his nose. With a distracted motion, Ruarc wiped it away. He glanced up, taking in the wide expanse of mountain and moor unfolding suddenly before him. His mouth quirked. Absorbed in his thoughts, he had scarcely noticed where his legs had carried him.

He stood on the hill overlooking Rannoch Moor. To his right was the tumbled stand of boulders where he had talked with Father Kenneth that day Francis had returned from Achallader. To his left, a small burn wound its tortuous way down to a silver lochan shrouded in mist far out on the moor.

With a weary sigh, Ruarc strode to the boulders and leaned against one. He was in no mood just now to return to the shielings. He didn't care to endure Glynnis's reproachful looks or further counsel from the priest. Yet the boisterous camaraderie of the larger cottages would, he knew, grate on him as well. It was best for all he keep himself, and his foul humors, private.

Och, but he was past weary of the guilt and shame he bore. If only it was such a simple thing as Father Kenneth advised, to ride to

Achallader, swallow his pride, and make amends. But Adam's anger ran deep. It wouldn't be easily appeased, if indeed it ever could be.

Yet he might never get Killian and her son back unless he took the risk. And it was past time he cease dragging his people into this sordid feud. It wasn't their fault his arrogant thoughtlessness had gotten him into this fix. If there was punishment due, it was his alone, not theirs.

Still, the consideration of riding meekly to his death held little appeal. Ruarc would willingly die fighting, if need be, to defend his life or the lives of those dear to him. But to all but surrender without a whimper made his gut clench in disgust. Especially when Adam meant to kill him for something he hadn't done.

"It's past time ye and Adam cease this pointless feud," Father Kenneth's words drifted back to him just then. *"One of ye must finally find the courage. . . . The forgiveness must begin, and begin now, if either of ye are ever to heal."*

"But I don't *want* to forgive," Ruarc muttered angrily. "I haven't the time nor the inclination. Let Adam wallow in his pit of anger and vengeance if he wishes. I've found a new chance at happiness with Killian, and that's all that matters."

"And are we all not our brothers' keepers? Especially ye for Adam who, for a time, was almost as close as any brother?"

Ruarc groaned aloud and closed his eyes. Memories long buried assaulted him. Of Adam and him racing their horses on the seashore. Of the long talks they had shared some nights around the campfire before a battle, trying as best they could to understand the men who had been their fathers. Of drinking and singing together until dawn.

And then one memory more pierced Ruarc's haze of anguish, shining bright and clear as that sunny day at Mons, when Adam had blocked with his own body a pistol shot meant for Ruarc. A shot aimed straight at his heart.

Aye, he had well and long buried that respect, that gratitude for his friend. Somehow, along the way, he had also forgotten the debt of life he still owed him. Instead, he had repaid Adam in pain and suffering, by stealing the woman his friend loved.

It didn't matter that Sheila, as Adam's foster sister, was all but forbidden him. The decision to keep them apart had never been Ruarc's to make. All that mattered was how badly he had repaid his debt and lost a good friend, a brother, in the bargain.

"Begin with yerself, lad. All any of us can do is begin with ourselves."

Ruarc pushed from the boulder and stood there as the rain came down, his shoulders rigid, his legs taut, his hands fisted.

It might well be too late ever to regain Adam's trust and friendship, or even his forgiveness, but he had to try. For the sake of what they had once shared, for the sake of what was still owed. For the sake of his honor.

And mayhap, Ruarc added with a sad, wondering smile, for the sake of their immortal souls, too. God, after all, was surely in this somewhere. Indeed, He had been there all along, even as Ruarc had striven so mightily to deny it.

According to Father Kenneth, with God nothing ultimately would be lost or wasted. And, though he feared what his eventual fate might be, Ruarc knew it was past time he began to listen, to turn back to his Lord and Savior, to surrender. Indeed, there'd never be a better time.

Father Kenneth's words came back to him again, filling Ruarc with a curious, and strangely satisfying, sense of peace. *"A surrender freely given, knowing it's the best of all possible choices . . . a surrender willing, lovingly, joyfully embraced."*

†

"YE'RE going after Killian and Gavin, aren't ye?"

Perhaps her blunt approach left a little to be desired, but Glynnis had to know. She met her stepson's scowling stare with an unwavering one of her own. "Well, are ye or aren't ye?"

"And what's it to ye, if I am? Do ye hope to get word to Adam that I'm coming? Is that it?"

Glynnis sighed. Would the man never come to his senses then? Their own, long-standing feud was over. Indeed, why should it continue? Neither of them had Rannoch now, and she, at any rate, no longer wanted it.

Gazing up at Ruarc, however, Glynnis could see the old wounds still ran deep. He was yet so wary, so on edge and angry. If there was to be any chance of healing, she supposed she must be the one to offer the balm.

"Nay." She gave a shake of her head. "What purpose would it serve to betray ye to Adam when yer people need ye and I want Killian back? Ye're all the kin I've left now. Ye, Killian, and wee Gavin. I've lost enough to last me a lifetime. I don't wish to lose ye, too."

Ruarc scratched his unshaven jaw, eyeing her. "And why the sudden concern for me? Yer interest in Killian's welfare I can understand, but not my own. Nay, not after all the years of our mutual antipathy."

"It's so verra strange, how ye can see a person so differently through one person's eyes than through another's. But since Killian has come to Rannoch, I've gradually begun to see ye in a new light." For a moment, Glynnis found she couldn't go on.

"Then," she finally continued, "after the massacre, after Thomas's death, it was as if the veil was finally and fully lifted. I saw how deeply ye loved our people. How tirelessly ye worked—aye, had always worked—in their behalf. And I finally allowed myself to acknowledge yer love for Killian and Gavin. Only then did I face myself and my hatred for ye. Only then did I finally admit I had wronged ye as deeply as ye had wronged me."

Glynnis paused, not sure how to put words to what she would next say. Leastwise, not in a manner Ruarc might take well. Still, if they were ever to have hope of forming any sort of fruitful relationship in the future, the truth must be told. All the pain and deception must be brought out into the light so it could be someday accepted and forgiven.

"I knew all those years that Sheila wronged ye," Glynnis finally forced out the humiliating admission. "I knew all about her infidelities. Part of me condoned her actions, because I well knew how tormented she was. But another part, a part I'm ashamed to own, was just as pleased that, in her adultery, she sinned against ye and yer wedding vows. Indeed, I felt Sheila was justified in doing so, wed as she was to a wretch such as ye."

"Do ye think I didn't know?" Ruarc's eyes went dark with some painful emotion. "Do ye think I wasn't aware ye gloated over it as well?"

"Aye, I suppose I did know. But still I fed Sheila's foolish convictions. I confirmed her belief she deserved aught she could seize in her futile search for happiness. And, mayhap in the doing, I contributed to her death as much as anyone else."

"As much as I did in killing her?"

Glynnis shook her head. "Ye didn't kill her, lad. I know that now. Indeed, I think I always, deep down, knew that."

His mouth tightened. "Am I to take that as some backhanded apology, then, for all those years ye spread such lies and slander about me? For how hard and long ye tried even to poison what Killian and I had?"

At the disparagement in his voice, a small spark of anger flared in Glynnis. She choked back a sharp reply. In those matters, at the very least, she was indeed at fault. And she *had* been the one who sought to begin this healing.

"Aye, I do ask yer forgiveness. For all of it." She lifted her chin and met his gaze. "For *all* I did to cause ye pain or harm. I was the one who betrayed ye to Adam when ye planned to spy on his meeting at Achallader. I was the one who revealed to Adam Killian's intent to escape Rannoch. And I was the one who wrote the letter in Killian's name—the one ye refused to believe she didn't write herself. That one time, however, I finally did what I did to effect a reconciliation between ye and Adam, not to betray ye to him."

"And why would ye care if Adam and I ever made peace?"

"Because it meant so much to Killian. Did ye know she'd been questioning everyone at Rannoch about the night Sheila died, determined to uncover Sheila's true killer? Did ye?"

Ruarc lowered his gaze. "Nay, I didn't. It was pointless at any rate, after so many years."

"Mayhap, but Killian couldn't leave it be without trying. She loved ye too much *not* to try."

"Why do ye tell me all this now? Why confess to deeds that could result in yer banishment?"

"Why?" Glynnis smiled sadly. "Because it doesn't matter anymore what becomes of me. I've lost Thomas. I may well have also lost Killian and Gavin, if ye refuse to rescue them. And, without her at yer side, I hold out little hope ye and I will ever reconcile."

"They matter that much to ye, do they?"

"Aye, they do. As do ye, though I know after how poorly I've treated ye and how cruelly I've failed ye, ye hardly care."

Ruarc looked away and closed his eyes. His hands fisted at his sides. He fought a fierce inner battle with himself. That much was evident even to Glynnis. But how to aid him in attaining the only victory worth achieving?

"I failed yer father as well," she whispered. "He rejected me, my love, and I was too young to understand why. Too inexperienced in the ways of the heart to step back from my pain, to understand his, and give him the time he needed. Mayhap, if I had—"

The admission was suddenly too bitter to speak, much less face. Och, if *only* she had given Robbie the time he had needed! But she hadn't. She had been too proud, too devastated by what she had viewed as his rejection of her. Yet all he had been doing was protecting what remained of his shattered heart.

"I failed ye and yer father as much as I failed Sheila," Glynnis said softly. "I thought I knew better. I thought vengeance was all that was left me. But all my lust for revenge did was harm me as badly as it did my intended victims."

"And now? What do ye know now?"

A wondering smile curved Glynnis's lips. "I know there's naught in life worth more than love. And I'm determined to spend the rest of my days in atonement for what I failed to do for those I should've loved better, by loving those I still *can* love."

"My father failed ye too," Ruarc offered of a sudden. "Mayhap even more so, for he was a seasoned man, and ye were little more than a girl yerself. He could've been more patient, more gentle with ye. And I," he added ruefully, "could've been kinder, though I tell ye true, Glynnis, I couldn't see much further than my own pain and confusion at the time."

He shook his head. "We all made terrible mistakes, didn't we? Mistakes that tainted our lives and the lives of those around us for a verra, verra long time."

"Aye, that we did." A fierce, sweet joy welled within Glynnis. "But ye and I, at least, have been blessed with a second chance. We dare not squander it again."

"Nay, we dare not," her stepson concurred, smiling at long last. "And, God willing, some good may still come of it all. For ye, Killian, Gavin, and me. Aye, and even for Adam, too.

"Aye," he said, a faraway look burning in his eyes, "some good may still come of it all. Even now, when things appear their verra bleakest, in the deep darkness just before the dawn."

26

"AT LONG last," Adam whispered in triumph a week later as he closed the letter set with the royal seal. "Ruarc has fallen from favor. At long last, William sees him for the self-serving opportunist he has always been. Whether he ever comes now for Killian, whether or not I ever have the personal pleasure of killing him, Ruarc MacDonald's fate is irrevocably sealed."

This was a moment to be savored. Adam walked to one of the tall, library windows and gazed out onto the inner courtyard. A gentle breeze wafted by, bringing with it the pungent scent of rich earth, freshly turned. Spring was in the air, a spring that, this year, would finally see the end to his long-standing feud with Ruarc MacDonald.

Once again, Adam opened the letter from the king. The missive required any and all who had knowledge of one Ruarc MacDonald's whereabouts to deliver such information to the closest constable. A reward of a considerable sum, Adam also noted, had been placed upon Ruarc's head for his alleged complicity in urging Alasdair MacDonald so long to deny his fealty to the king. Ruarc was ordered bound over to Edinburgh's Tollbooth until his trial.

In the weeks since the Glencoe massacre, when blame was being bandied about between one political faction and the other, it was inevitable many names would rise to the forefront. Already, Glenlyon's reputation had been irretrievably ruined. Breadalbane's, thanks to Glenlyon's drunken speeches to anyone who cared listen, was being periodically dragged through the mud as well.

But the accusations went even higher still—to John Dalrymple, Master of Stair, and King William himself. The king had, after all, been the one to sign the royal warrant for the extirpation of the MacDonalds when they had failed to render the oath of fealty in time.

It only made sense now that all of these men would scrabble about, trying to find other scapegoats to deflect the attention—and suspicion—from them. Soon after the massacre, Ruarc had been rumored to have sent a letter directly to William, demanding an immediate commission of inquiry into the matter, as well as Glenlyon's punishment. If he had stopped there, Adam suspected the matter might have met with William's favor. But Ruarc had also made certain allegations against the king. Somehow, news of that had leaked out as well. When it did, William had no other choice but to bring Ruarc to heel.

Adam couldn't really blame Rannoch's laird for his high emotions, considering the craven acts wrought upon his people. And William's willing, if disinterested, compliance in the plot *was* a distinct possibility. Still, Adam found the current situation a most pleasant contemplation. The proud, overbearing Ruarc MacDonald brought low at last. Och, but it was more than he had ever dared hope!

From across the courtyard, a commotion at the front gate caught his attention. The guards on the parapet walk hurried over to lean toward someone on the other side. Shouts were traded back and forth.

Frowning, Adam turned from the window, shoved the royal missive inside his coat, and headed from the room. Just as he reached the entry hall at the foot of the stairs, Lachlan, a look of excitement in his eyes, burst through the door.

"M'lord," the young man cried, "I've wonderful news! Ruarc MacDonald awaits outside the gates, asking to speak with ye."

"Call out all the men." Adam's mind raced with plans to withstand a siege. "Cover the wells, barricade the main gate with a stout log, and—"

"He comes alone, m'lord."

For a fleeting instant, Adam thought he had misheard his cousin. "Alone, ye say?" His gaze narrowed. "Surely ye're mistaken. Why would Ruarc MacDonald do such a daft thing?"

"Truly, I don't know, m'lord."

"I must see this for myself."

Adam pushed past Lachlan and stalked from the Lion's Hall. True to Lachlan's words, however, when Achallader's laird finally gained the parapet walk no army greeted him, only Ruarc Mac-Donald, seated on his horse.

At Adam's arrival, Ruarc lifted his gaze. "Yer promptness in coming out to greet me is most commendable. I thank ye for the courtesy."

"It's hardly a courtesy," Adam shouted down to him. "I just wanted to see if it was true ye came here without escort." He paused to scan the forest and countryside around them. "And it seems that ye have. Why is that, Ruarc?"

"I came in peace, Adam. I wish to talk with ye, man to man. That doesn't require an army."

"Ye can talk with me, man to man, if ye will." Adam straightened, his hands fisting on his hips. "Don't expect me to offer ye the safety of Highland hospitality, though. I'm in no mood to grant it to ye, if ye'd even believe it of a Campbell anyway, after all that's transpired of late."

Some dark emotion passed swiftly across Ruarc's face, then was gone. "I won't ask it, though I'm thinking ye're more honorable a man than yer kinsman, Glenlyon."

"Aye, that I am, to any man save the likes of ye."

Ruarc gestured toward the gate. "May I enter then?"

Adam turned and nodded to Lachlan, who now stood down by the front gate. "Let the laird of Rannoch in, will ye, lad? Only have a care to see him immediately disarmed once he's inside."

The gates slammed shut as soon as Ruarc rode through. He dismounted, permitted his person to be searched, then glanced up at Adam. "Are ye satisfied now I came in peace? As ye can see, I brought only a dirk and pistol for my personal protection on the journey."

Lachlan held up the pistol and dirk they had confiscated.

"So it seems." Adam made his way down the parapet stairs, then motioned over two guards. "Ye won't mind then, will ye, if I further assuage my suspicions by also having yer hands bound? To truly convince me ye come in peace?"

Ruarc's mouth tightened, but he nodded. "As ye wish." He stood calmly as the guards tied his hands behind his back.

When they were done, Adam stepped forward. "So, what is it ye want, Ruarc?"

"What else? I want my wife and her son back. I want this feud between us to end. It's gone on far too long."

"Indeed?" Hands clasped behind him, Adam began to circle Ruarc. "Well, I can easily understand why ye'd want such a bonny lass back, but I cannot fathom why ye'd care at such a late date whether our feud ends or not. As ye continue to suspect me of killing Sheila, I continue to suspect ye."

Ruarc turned his head to keep Adam in view. "I don't believe ye killed Sheila. Ye're not that sort of man, not to mention ye loved her more than life itself."

Anger swelled in Adam. "Then what sort of man am I? I bedded yer wife, didn't I? I laid with my own foster sister. If I could do those things, why wouldn't I be capable of murdering her too?" Adam came to stand before him, meeting Ruarc eye to eye. "Answer me that, if ye will."

"Because," his enemy replied, "I lived with ye for a year. Because I fought side by side with ye. Because we shared much, including our secret yearnings, our hearts. And because I'm weary of all the hatred and anger, all the unspoken pain we've caused each other over the years."

"Well, *I* know ye, too, Ruarc MacDonald," Adam all but spat back, his ire rising as fast as the memories assaulted him. "And I do think ye capable of murder. I do think ye capable of every lie and deceit known to man, just so ye get what ye want. Indeed, ye haven't changed a whit since those days in Holland. And ye never will."

For a long moment, Ruarc met Adam's furious gaze. Gradually, his eyes warmed with an emotion Adam thought curiously akin to compassion. Or was it pity?

Either way, Adam would have none of it. He grabbed the front of Ruarc's shirt and jerked him to himself. "As much as I hate ye, I'm a fair man. Ye want yer wife back. Well, I won't keep Killian against her will a day longer. I don't need to. I've what I want. I have ye, Ruarc MacDonald."

"Killing me won't ease that gaping hole in yer heart, Adam," Ruarc said softly.

"Then pray, what will?"

"Forgiveness and then, if not a renewed friendship between us, at least a peace and mutual respect."

With an oath, Adam shoved him back. "Are ye daft, man? I'll never forgive ye for what ye did to me, to Sheila. Never!"

A fierce burning light flared in Ruarc's eyes. "But I forgive ye, Adam. For what ye did to me."

This was all so unreal. Had Ruarc finally taken leave of his senses? Or did he yet seek to play some game?

"Take him to the dungeon." With a sharp, angry motion, Adam signaled his guards. "I've better things to do than stand here arguing with some madman. Take him to the dungeon. He can keep company with the rats and argue with them to his heart's content."

The guards strode up and grasped Ruarc by each arm. As they began to drag him away, however, Rannoch's laird dug in his heels. "Open yer ears, yer heart, man! If ye don't, this feud will destroy us both. And ye know as well as I, Sheila would've never wished that for either of us."

Once more the guards tugged on Ruarc's arms. This time, he let them lead him away.

†

KILLIAN gripped the iron bars that caged her window, the tears streaming down her face. Below her in the courtyard, she watched as Ruarc was bound and, after a brief discussion with an obviously angry Adam, led off by the guards. A sense of deep, anguished futility engulfed her.

For some reason Killian couldn't fathom, her husband had willingly surrendered himself to Adam. Surrendered himself to rescue her and Gavin, but at what cost? His life was far too great a price to pay, even for their freedom.

"Why, Ruarc? Why?" Killian whispered, her hoarse, tear-choked voice a grating sound in the room's stillness. "Why would you do it this way?"

Anger filled her. She wanted to break down the door to her

bedchamber, find Adam, and beat him until he finally listened. Nothing else in the past weeks spent at Achallader had seemed to work. Despite their talks, despite her most eloquent arguments, he remained adamantly locked in his narrow view of things. He wouldn't, Killian well knew, show Ruarc any mercy.

And here she stood, helpless, mired in her impotent misery, while her husband was led down to the dungeon to suffer untold torment. Her husband, the man she loved as she had never loved another. If she lost him, Killian didn't know what she'd do, how she'd survive.

She leaned her forehead against the iron bars. "Dear God, don't let my husband die. Not for this. Not for something he didn't do." Her voice broke on a sob. "And touch Adam's heart, I pray. Not only for Ruarc's sake, but for his as well."

A violent wind whipped down into the courtyard just then, sending the Campbell clan banners flapping wildly and dust spiraling into the air. The sun ducked behind the clouds. Far in the distance, thunder rumbled.

Killian lifted her gaze heavenward, then sighed. The sudden change in weather wasn't God sending down a reply. It was but another spring rain in the making. Still, she felt certain her prayers had been heard and heeded.

The only question remaining was how and when the Lord would choose to answer them.

†

THOUGH she begged Janet every time the maidservant visited that day to ask Adam to come to her, he never did. Killian spent an increasingly tense evening waiting, never touching her meal, pacing the floor in restless agitation.

Even Gavin began to note her strange mood. "Mama, what's wrong?" he asked finally, when Killian's supper meal sat uneaten long after he had wolfed his down. "Don't you like your food? Mine tasted good."

"I'm sure it was very good, sweeting," she replied as she prepared him for bed. "It's just that, sometimes, I'm not all that hungry." Killian bent, tucked the covers in around him, then kissed her son on the forehead. "Now, to sleep with you. The morrow will be upon us soon enough."

As Gavin obediently lay down and promptly fell asleep, Killian pulled a chair over and sat by the window. The spring storm had passed a few hours ago. The clouds had disappeared. A full moon shone, bathing the castle and its surrounding lands in silver. Everything was quiet, at peace.

Everything, that is, but her heart. Where was Ruarc now? Had he been fed? Was he in pain? Indeed, was he even still alive?

Her anger at Adam swelled anew. How could the man be so cruel? Surely he realized by now she knew of Ruarc's arrival. If he hadn't suspected she had seen the meeting in the courtyard, most assuredly her increasingly insistent requests that he visit her would have convinced him.

Killian clenched shut her eyes and slammed tightly fisted hands down hard on her knees. This suspense, the not knowing what had become of her husband, was eating her alive. To be so near Ruarc after all these weeks, and now not be able to get to him, was beyond bearing.

Behind her, a scrabbling sound rose from beyond the door. Killian wheeled around. A key slid into the lock, turned. Then, ever so quietly, the door swung open.

Adam stood there. His glance met hers, then moved to Gavin, sound asleep in the tester bed. He motioned for her to come to him.

Her heart hammering beneath her breast, Killian leaped to her feet and rushed over. "I must talk with you. Please, Adam."

He pushed the door open a bit farther. "Aye. And I must speak with ye."

She slipped from the room. Adam closed the door and locked it, securing the key beneath the waistband of his trews. He took her arm. "Come. Ruarc has been asking for ye. It's past time we settle this matter."

"Is he all right?" she asked as they walked down the corridor leading to the main stairs. "You haven't harmed him, have you?"

Adam shrugged indolently. "Nay, no more than chaining him hand and foot to a dungeon wall might harm him. I chose not to give either of ye the chance, this time, so easily to escape. The one key to Ruarc's chains, ye see, will remain at all times in my possession."

"Why did he come alone?" Killian glanced up at Adam. "Knowing how you feel about him, it doesn't make sense."

He shrugged again. "I can't say really. He began babbling about making amends, asking my forgiveness, but such are the ravings of a madman. Mayhap ye'll have greater success understanding him than I did."

Making amends . . . asking forgiveness . . . Killian shook her head in bewilderment. Knowing Ruarc's feelings for Adam, such words did indeed sound strange. True, her husband had been under intense stress in these past weeks since the massacre, and she was well aware how deeply Ruarc mourned the loss of Alasdair and all his kin, but surely he hadn't gone mad. He was a strong man in every way.

Had, then, something else touched his life, changed him so dramatically he truly meant the words Adam had repeated? She had cautioned him, that night he had confronted her about Adam's letter, that this feud could destroy them both. Was he, at long last, heeding her admonitions?

Even so, his change of heart may well have come too late, and in the wrong place. It was one thing to offer reconciliation from a position of strength, or at least from one between equals. It was quite another to make such an overture when one stood helpless in the clutches of one's enemy. Such behavior was indeed the act of a madman—or of one of immense courage.

They made their way down the stairs, crossed the entry hall, then took another corridor leading to the soldiers' quarters and the stairs to the dungeon. It was bitterly cold and damp, Killian noted as she followed Adam down into the dungeon. Chained to a wall as Adam claimed Ruarc was, he must be half frozen by now.

Achallader's laird led her past the guard post in the main room, took down a ring of keys on the wall, then headed toward a cell barred by a stout wooden door. As he paused to unlock it, Killian's hands went clammy with nervous anticipation. She wanted so to see Ruarc, to hold him, to speak with him, but she suddenly feared her reception. What if he was still angry with her or blamed her for the situation he was now in?

Then, as Adam pushed open the door and she saw Ruarc in the dim torchlight, all but hanging from the opposite wall, nothing else mattered but him. With a cry, Killian rushed past Adam and ran to her husband. She drew to a halt, however, just before she reached him. "Ruarc," she breathed, gazing up at him. "Oh, Ruarc, why did you come? I *told* you not to come."

"Ye're my wife, lass," he said thickly, as if he hadn't had cause to use his voice for a while. "Did ye think I'd not come, sooner or later?"

"But not like this." Killian made a shaky motion that encompassed him, his chains, and the dungeon. "If you had to come, why didn't you bring men with you? But, Ruarc, not like this!"

He shifted uncomfortably in his shackles. For the first time, she noted his abraded, bloody wrists. His arms outstretched above his head, his feet barely touching the floor, dressed only in trews, a pair of soft brogues, and a thin shirt that gaped open to expose his chest, Ruarc was nearly blue from the cold. Uttering a soft sound of compassion, Killian closed the remaining distance between them. Wrapping her arms about his lower body, she clutched him close.

As she began to sob, he made soft, crooning sounds. "Hush, hush, lass. It isn't as bad as all that. We're together at last, and that counts for a lot."

"Wh-why?" Killian lifted her gaze to him. "Why?"

He must have guessed her true meaning. He smiled sadly. "Because I wanted to make peace with Adam. Because what we shared in loving Sheila shouldn't become the death of us both. And how was I to convince him of my sincerity if I'd come with fighting men?"

"But he doesn't b-believe you, Ruarc!"

"Nay, he doesn't, but I've hope he will eventually."

As hard as she tried to warm him with her own body, his chilled flesh didn't seem to lose its icy feel. Rage filled her. Ruarc would never have his chance to convince Adam of anything. The cold would kill him long before Adam ever relinquished his pigheaded vendetta!

She swung about to find Achallader's laird still standing in the open doorway, watching them. "This is no way to treat another human being! Take Ruarc down now before he dies from the cold."

"Dying from the cold would be a far more merciful end than what else I could do to him," Adam said in reply. "But if ye prefer I throw him back into that dank pit where ye first found him all those months ago, I suppose that could be arranged."

"He came to you unarmed, in peace! Doesn't that count for something?"

For a moment, Adam appeared to consider her question. Then he shook his head. "Nay, not especially. He still murdered Sheila."

"But he *didn't* murder Sheila," Killian screamed, teetering now on the edge of hysteria. "How many times—"

"Killian. Lass. He won't believe ye. Yer judgment is clouded by yer love for me. Besides, ye weren't even there."

She spun around, the tears coursing down her cheeks. "Yes, I *do* love you, but my judgment isn't clouded. I saw the kind of man you were *before* I fell in love with you. I wouldn't have let myself love you if you'd been—"

"Ye fell in love with Alexander, didn't ye," Adam taunted softly as he came up behind her, "and he was a brutal man."

At Killian's swift look of surprise, he nodded. "Aye, later, after ye'd run away with Ruarc, I began to hear tales from the servants who'd seen the cruel ways Alexander treated ye, grabbing ye, twisting yer arm when he thought no one was looking. Pushing ye about, and once even slapping ye full across the face. It all made sense then, ye asking me that night to help ye return to the Colonies. For failing ye in yer hour of need, I'm verra sorry. It doesn't, however, speak well of yer judgment in men."

Killian met his pitying gaze. "Or perhaps it does," she countered with a squaring of her shoulders. "Perhaps it says a lot for what I learned with Alexander, that I chose Ruarc for my next husband. A man unjustly accused of murdering his first wife, a woman many lesser men would've killed years before Sheila actually died and, in the bargain, then been acquitted by their peers for the deed. Yet all Ruarc ever did was forgive her, then blame himself for her behavior. Like you, Adam, he tried the best he knew how to help Sheila. But, like you, he couldn't. No one could, Adam. No one."

Adam's face twisted in anguish. "Nay, ye're wrong. *I* could've helped her. I understood Sheila like no one else ever could. I could've saved her, if only she had gone away with me, become my wife. But he—" Adam pointed to Ruarc—"he stole her from me. Stole the woman I loved, without a by-yer-leave or second thought."

"I didn't know, Adam," Ruarc said. "How could I know? Ye never told me, and Sheila didn't, either. If I'd known she loved ye, I never would've married her, no matter how enamored I was with my foolish dreams. I didn't wed her to hurt ye. *But I didn't know!*"

His captor gave a harsh, unsteady laugh. "Aye, mayhap ye didn't at first, but eventually ye had to suspect. That night ye found us together in Rannoch's gardens, ye couldn't deny the truth any longer, could ye? And Sheila, my bonny Sheila, died because of that."

"She may well have died because of that," Ruarc agreed, "but it wasn't because I killed her. Someone else must have heard us. Someone else must have come to her after I left her. But I swear to ye, Adam, on all that is holy, when I left Sheila that night *she was still alive!*"

For a fleeting instant, Adam's resolve seemed finally to waver. His mouth opened, moved silently, then snapped shut again. His shoulders went rigid. He shook his head.

"It doesn't matter, in the end, what the truth may have been," he said hoarsely. "Ye're most likely a dead man anyway." He pulled a folded piece of paper, marked by a broken red seal, from his coat. "This is a warrant for yer arrest, signed by no less than the king himself. Ye're to be bound over to Edinburgh's Tollbooth and held there until ye can be tried."

Killian shot Ruarc a horrified look.

"On what grounds?" Rannoch's laird demanded. "What have I done?"

Once again, Adam laughed. "Seems ye urged Alasdair MacDonald not to sign the oath of fealty. Seems ye're as guilty of the Glencoe slaughter as was Glenlyon. But he acted under orders. Ye didn't. And that, as ye well know, is treason."

27

ON THE last day of March, a troop of redcoats moved down the road, following the serpentine path with rigid, military precision. A mounted officer led the procession, attended by ten armed foot soldiers, then another mounted soldier dragging behind him a bound man tied to a rope. The prisoner, from all appearances, was near exhaustion. He staggered along, his head down, his shoulders slumped.

Just then, the enlisted man's horse shied. The rope tied to Ruarc's hands jerked hard, pulling him off balance. He stumbled, fell to his knees. Before he could regain his footing, however, the mounted redcoat glanced back, grinned wolfishly, then urged his horse forward.

From their hiding place in the pines on a hill overlooking the road, Killian, Davie, and eight other men watched.

"The heartless dog," she muttered, eyeing the pistol she carried. Killian was sorely tempted to shoot the man off his horse. It was too soon, though, to risk alerting the soldiers to their presence.

"Hold on, Ruarc," she whispered instead. "Hold on."

In but a few minutes more, the officer and the first of his men would enter the narrowest part of the road, little more than the width of a cattle path, running beside a chasm slashed by a deep, fast-flowing river. The plan, though risky considering the redcoats' superior firepower, was to rush them before they had a chance to shoot, drive some off into the river, and dispense with the rest however necessary. While Davie and the other men were so engaged, Killian was to sneak down, free Ruarc, and help him to safety. Afterwards, they'd all join up again and head for the safety of the mountains.

Still, as the seconds ticked by, it became more and more painful to watch Ruarc being dragged along that rocky road. Killian's breath caught in her throat. Her hands fisted knuckle white, her nails digging into her palms.

"Bear with it a wee bit longer, m'lady," Davie said, shooting her a worried glance. "M'lord can take it. And, soon enough, the redcoats will pay." He eyed her an instant more. "Are ye quite certain ye wish to involve yerself in this? I'd greatly prefer ye waited up here until the fighting's done."

Killian shook her head. "You'll need every man you have to fight the redcoats. And while you do, someone's got to get Ruarc away."

"Aye, but ye're such a wee slip of a thing. And m'lord's weak. That much is more than evident."

"I'll get him to safety, Davie," she said with grim determination, "if I have to drag him all the way myself."

He grinned. "Aye, I do believe ye could." He turned his gaze back to the scene below them. The officer was, even then, riding onto the narrow stretch of road.

Davie took aim with his musket and fired. In rapid succession, the others followed. Five soldiers fell.

Shouting the MacDonald battle cry, Davie and his men leaped to their feet. Leather targes held high to shield them, swords in their hands, they charged down the hillside. The soldiers, still reeling from the unexpected attack, could barely get their own muskets up, much less fire. With a clash of weapons and thud of body slamming into body, the two sides met in desperate battle.

Through the chaos of clanging arms, rearing horses, and gunpowder smoke thick on the air, Killian searched for Ruarc. When she found him, she jumped up and ran down the hill. Even as she did, the enlisted man who had dragged Ruarc behind his horse drew his sword and maneuvered his mount to strike at him.

Ruarc jerked back hard on the rope. The horse shied. Killian lifted her pistol, took aim, and fired.

The ball flew straight at the redcoat. As he raised his sword high for the killing blow, the shot struck him in the arm. He screamed, dropped his sword, and tumbled from his horse.

Then Killian was at Ruarc's side, the spent pistol tossed away, a dirk in her hand. "Give me your hands. Now!"

For a fleeting instant, Ruarc stared up at her in stunned disbelief. Then he lifted his hands. With a few quick slashes, the ropes fell away.

She grabbed him by the wrist, tugging on him. "Get up! We've got to get away while we can!"

Ruarc struggled to his feet, staggered, and almost fell again. Killian grasped him about the waist and began to all but drag her husband away.

"Y-ye wee fool," he gasped, as he lurched along with her. "If we g-get out of this alive—"

"Save your strength." Already, Killian was tiring with the burden of his additional weight. "And save mine too!"

Behind them, the sounds of fighting raged on. Cries of anger mingled with those of pain. Steel rang against steel.

She didn't dare look back. She didn't dare squander the energy. Ruarc tried as best he could to keep up, but it was evident he was weakening rapidly. Killian's lungs burned now, felt as if they'd burst, but she forced herself to go on. She had Ruarc. She wasn't about to lose him now.

He fell just as they topped the hill. Grasping him beneath his arms, Killian dragged him out of sight of the battle below. Then, at long last, she turned. The officer still fought on, hacking away at two MacDonalds with targes held up to deflect his blows. Two other redcoats, three additional MacDonalds in hot pursuit, fled back down the road where they had first come. The rest of the soldiers lay lifeless on the ground or floundered helplessly down in the river.

One MacDonald sprawled nearby, and two others staggered about, grasping bleeding wounds. Davie paused, glanced up to Killian. She waved back, the signal she had Ruarc. Then he aimed his pistol at the officer. "Cease," he roared, "or I'll shoot ye dead!"

Catching sight of the pistol, the officer froze.

"Drop yer weapon," Davie next ordered.

The redcoat did as he was told. His two attackers then proceeded to pull him from his horse and bind his arms behind his back.

After that, Killian didn't watch anymore. She turned to Ruarc, who had finally managed to lever himself back to a sitting position. He looked a sorry sight, his clothes torn and filthy, his face, arms, and chest bruised and scraped. But he was alive. And he was once again free.

She hurried to her horse and retrieved a water flask. Returning to Ruarc, Killian unstopped the flask then handed it to him. "Drink. Then we need to get you up on my horse. We dare not linger here overlong."

Ruarc gulped down the water eagerly. Finally, realizing how thirsty he really was, Killian pulled the flask away. "Wait a bit, then you can have more. You don't want to make yourself sick, do you?"

He managed a lopsided grin, which tugged at his split lip, making him wince. "Nay, I suppose not." As his glance looked her up and down, taking in, Killian well knew, her mannish appearance dressed as she was in trews, shirt, jacket, brogues, and bonnet, his smile faded into a frown. "I don't like it at all that ye risked yer life. This sort of thing is men's work."

Killian laughed. "And who do you think planned this rescue? I wasn't about to let Adam send you to the Tollbooth. We'd never have been able to get you out of there."

"Aye, ye most certainly wouldn't have. Still, what would've been the point of rescuing me if I was to lose ye in the process? Do ye think I would've wished to go on without ye? Do ye, lass?"

His words gladdened her heart. "And what of me, Ruarc MacDonald? It was hard enough to leave you at Achallader and return to Black Mount, when Adam gave me the choice. But I knew if I'd stayed, I'd little chance of freeing you. Indeed, the sooner I left, the sooner Adam would unchain you from that frigid dungeon wall."

Ruarc nodded. "And that he did, though I can't say I particularly enjoyed returning to that miserable pit. Since the last time I'd been there, I swear the rats had doubled in size."

She squatted before him. "It doesn't matter anymore. Nothing will ever separate us again. Nothing!"

A remorseful light flared in his eyes. "I'm sorry I doubted ye all those times, lass. I was so verra wrong to do so. Can ye ever forgive me?"

Killian reached down to tenderly brush the hair from his face.

"I love you, husband. It'll take more than a few misunderstandings to frighten me off."

He took her hand and kissed the palm, then pressed it to his heart. "And I love ye. Always and forever."

Davie's voice, shouting a joyous welcome, carried to them as he and the other men topped the hill. Killian and Ruarc glanced toward them, then back at each other.

"Here," she said huskily, handing him back the flask. "One more drink, and then we must be on our way."

"But not back to Black Mount." He took the flask from her.

"No." Killian pushed to her feet. "To somewhere a lot more safe and hidden. To Coire Gabhail."

†

APRIL flowed effortlessly into May as Killian nursed Ruarc back to health. Summer began with the Feast of Beltane on the first of May. Under Ruarc's patient tutelage Killian learned to make the traditional Beltane bannock, which was broken into pieces and offered to the wild beasts of the glen to propitiate them, forestalling their raiding of domesticated stock. Then, left relatively alone for weeks on end, save for monthly visits from Davie and others who brought supplies, Killian, Ruarc, and Gavin enjoyed a peace and simplicity that had been lacking since even before the massacre.

Full-blown summer, with all the fanfare of fresh green grass, ice-cold rushing burns, and a riotous display of wildflowers, commenced in June. The milk cow Davie had brought them thrived on the lush grazing, producing copious amounts of milk that kept Killian busy learning how to make cheese and butter. The wild strawberries grew until, near the end of the month, they were ruby-ripe and succulent.

Finally, early one afternoon as Ruarc was immersed in writing yet another letter to their new chief, Killian walked in and thrust a basket before him. Puzzled, he looked up at her and was immediately struck by the sheer beauty of her rosy cheeks, dancing eyes, and windblown hair.

"And how may I help ye, lass?" he asked, wondering even as he spoke if any man alive was as fortunate as he. "Does yer basket need repairing or such?"

"No," she said with an impish grin, "it needs filling. It's time to pick the strawberries."

Ruarc shoved back his chair. "And must this picking of berries include me?"

"Of course. We're all going—you, me, Gavin, Fionn, and Eilidh."

He considered that pronouncement for a moment, then shrugged. "As ye wish. I suppose this letter can wait a wee bit longer."

"It most certainly can. It's not as if John MacDonald can't manage a day or two without another set of instructions from you."

"They aren't 'instructions,' only suggestions, and a few questions thrown in to sweeten the pot."

She took his hand and pulled him from the chair. "Come along, m'lord. I'm thinking a nice bowl of strawberries and thick cream this eve will sweeten both our dispositions far better than that letter."

Ruarc laughed, grabbed the basket, and followed her from the snug little bothy that was now their home. After the hut's relative dimness, the bright sunlight momentarily blinded him. He shaded his eyes, marveling at how vibrant the colors could be in the mountains this time of year.

On the open slopes, purple bell heather and yellow gentians sparkled like jewels. In shady nooks beneath rocky overhangs, sprawling masses of white-flowered, alpine lady's mantle and buttery-hued saxifrage brightened the gloom. Intermittent stands of pine mingled with birch and holly. The grassy turf looked as smooth as emerald velvet, and most beckoning.

Killian, however, would have none of his whispered suggestions that they leave the berry picking to Gavin and the snuggling beside some mossy boulder to them.

"You're most incorrigible, you know," she said, tossing a gay laugh over her shoulder as she skipped away, headed to another—and probably far safer—patch of strawberries. As the minutes passed, Ruarc did his best to gather as many of the sweet, crimson fruit as fast as he could. Still, from time to time, his gaze couldn't help but stray toward Killian.

She looked so very much the Scottish lassie, she did, dressed now in the simple garb of a peasant woman. The dark plaid skirt and matching long, plaid shawl, fastened over her breast with a circular silver brooch and belted at her waist, contrasted strikingly with her snowy white blouse and long, golden hair. Though most married women wore their hair twisted up on their heads and covered by a white cap or kerchief, Ruarc far preferred Killian's hair down and tumbling about her shoulders and back.

A beauty on the mountain, she looked as if she fit here, high in this rocky fastness among the heather, stones, and turf. He loved her so intensely, sometimes he thought his heart might burst with emotion. She was the part of him that had always been missing. It had been a long time in coming, but Ruarc felt finally, blessedly, complete.

"And what are *you* looking at?" Killian demanded of a sudden.

"Ye, lass," he boldly replied, showing his teeth in a wide, unrepentant grin. "I'm looking at my bonny wife."

With a long-suffering roll of her eyes and a smile twitching at the edge of her mouth, Killian bent again to her task. "You're incorrigible, you are, Ruarc MacDonald."

†

AN HOUR later, lulled by the sound of Gavin down the hill near the bothy tossing sticks for the two deerhounds to fetch, Killian rested contentedly in Ruarc's arms. "You know," she murmured, lifting her head to gaze at his roughly chiseled face, "if I had to change a thing about you—" she paused long enough for Ruarc to open his eyes and arch a dark brow—"I wouldn't change a thing."

He smiled. "Well, that's verra reassuring to hear. Seeing as how I wouldn't change aught about ye, either."

She sighed and settled back onto the warm expanse of his chest. "It's funny, though, isn't it, how things can change in such a short time, and just from coming to love someone?"

"Can it now?" His voice rumbled against her ear, tickling it.

"Yes. When I first came to Scotland, I didn't really want to be here. And I soon realized this was a most peculiar, uncivilized country. Well—" Killian gave a short laugh—"or leastwise I thought it so, what with all the differences in culture and weather and food. And you all spoke rather strangely, too."

"If ye recall, I also thought ye spoke strangely at first."

"Be that as it may," she continued as she began to draw imaginary circles on his chest, "now, I find everyone speaks most delightfully. I love the food—well, most of it anyway—and I feel like I belong here."

Ruarc chuckled. "Ye wouldn't be speaking about our beloved haggis, now would ye?"

She smiled. "I might be."

"Well, after what ye've done for me and my people, I suppose I can forgive that one wee failing. Indeed, if anyone deserves to belong here, to be called a Scotswoman, I'd wager it's ye, lass."

"That's very kind of you to say that."

He gave a snort of disgust. "Kindness has naught to do with it. Ye've earned my respect, as well as the respect of the clan. Ye're a braw lass. I'm so verra proud ye're mine."

She pushed to one elbow. "Do you know when, among all the other wonderful things you've done, I felt most proud of you?"

Ruarc appeared to consider her question for a moment, then shook his head. "Nay, lass, I don't. Among so many other wonderful things that I do, it'd be hard to pick just one."

"And aren't you the cocky one!" Killian gave him a playful slap on his arm. "Not that it isn't well deserved, mind you, but I did have one particular instance in mind nonetheless."

"And that was?"

Her smile faded. "When you came for me at Achallader. I saw you ride up and face Adam. Alone. Unarmed. I still think about that sometimes and wonder why you did what you did."

"Do ye mean it wasn't sufficient I loved ye enough to risk my life to get ye back?" A teasing note threaded the deep timbre of his voice.

This time, however, Killian wasn't about to be deterred. "Of course it was enough. But there was more, wasn't there, Ruarc? Another reason you came to Adam as you did."

He sighed and looked away. "Aye, there was. I was past weary of our feuding and all the damage it had done to the both of us. I suppose I finally accepted what ye'd told me, that it would destroy us both.

"And then I also felt the weight of my own guilt for the part I'd played in bringing about all the anger and pain." Ruarc turned back to meet her gaze. "I suppose I imagined if I went to Adam in all sincerity, unarmed and in peace, he'd see past all the hatred, the hurt, and forgive me."

"But he didn't, did he?" A deep sadness filled Killian. Ruarc had risked so much, and it hadn't helped.

"Nay, Adam didn't." He smiled, then, and touched her face. "But mayhap, just mayhap, I planted a seed. A seed that'll bear fruit someday," he whispered, lightly stroking his way from her cheek to the corner of her mouth. "Just as the seeds ye've planted in me—regarding Glynnis and, aye, even regarding the Lord—are beginning to bear fruit." Ruarc laughed. "Well, mayhap I should give Father Kenneth a wee bit of credit, too, when it comes to God."

Surprisingly—or perhaps not so surprisingly—tears stung her eyes. It might sound strange, foolish even, what she was next to tell him, but Killian needed him to know. Know how much he meant to her, and why.

"Do you realize, Ruarc MacDonald, that you're the bravest, finest man I've ever known?" she asked through an emotion-choked voice. "And that you're the embodiment of all my dreams? Dreams I came to despair ever of seeing fulfilled."

She smiled in wonderment. "That night I ran out into the storm and away from Alexander, I begged God to save me. And He answered me. Somehow I suddenly knew that what I'd asked for, been always seeking, awaited me in the forest."

"And what had ye been seeking, lass?"

Killian swiped at her tears, then gave it up as a futile endeavor. "I was seeking freedom from all the pain and abuse, but something more, too. It was as if . . . as if I sensed you—and all you represented—out there that night. Sensed that the fulfillment of my dreams, my heart's desires lay just beyond those castle walls, awaiting me, beckoning to me, if only I'd the courage to take the first step."

"And ye did, lass." Ruarc levered himself up to kiss her temple. "As wondrously strange as it seemed, I *was* there for ye, at the right time and place."

"It wasn't strange. It was the Lord Jesus. He answered my prayers."

Rannoch's laird lay back and sighed. "Aye. He also answered mine, even if I'd long ago given up any hope in Him. But now I have ye, and I'm content."

"Is that the only prayer you had? That you might someday find a good wife?"

For a fleeting instant, sadness crept into Ruarc's eyes, then was gone. "I also wished someday to have a child. And now I have one, in Gavin."

"Well, I'm thinking Gavin needs a little playmate."

Killian cocked her head in mock contemplation. "Which would you prefer, husband? Another boy or a bonny little lassie?"

He stared at her in confusion. "But I already told ye Gavin was—" His eyes narrowed. "What are ye trying to tell me, lass? If ye're playing some game—"

"The only game I'm playing is the counting game. Counting how long before our wee bairn arrives."

Grabbing her arms, Ruarc pulled her with him to a sitting position. "Are ye—" he swallowed convulsively—"are ye . . . ?"

Smiling broadly, Killian nodded. "Yes. I'm with child."

"When? When's the babe to come?"

She shrugged. "Sometime next February."

He laughed in joyous relief. "A father. I'm to be a father!"

"Well, actually, you already are a father," she corrected him gently. "You're Gavin's stepfather."

"Och, aye." Ruarc nodded vigorously. "But now I'll be doubly a father, with a child from my loins. An heir for Rannoch."

"Yes, an heir for Rannoch. For the day the king finally pardons you, and you can return home."

His smile faded. "Aye, if that day ever comes. Still, even if I never regain Rannoch for myself, I might be able to secure it for the child."

"And would that be enough for you? If our child someday called Rannoch his own?"

"It'd suffice." He pulled her close to him. "As long as I had ye at my side, it'd suffice."

†

As June eased into a lush, warm July, Killian's pregnancy progressed uneventfully if happily. The people at Black Mount soon heard the good news and rejoiced in turn. Promises of knit caps, warm baby blankets, and carved toys soon reached Coire Gabhail. And, with them, also came news of the world outside Glencoe.

"Copies of the *Paris Gazette* containing an account of the massacre reached London and Edinburgh in April," Father Kenneth reported, having newly arrived with Davie and Francis the last week of July. "Rumors still abound, though, that the only mercy left the MacDonalds is transportation as bonded servants or slaves to the Colonial plantations. And the Master of Stair now shares a joint secretariat with James Johnston of Warriston who, it's rumored, doesn't see eye to eye with Dalrymple on most things and seeks even to have him removed from office."

"Aye," Ruarc said, as he worked to sharpen his sword on a whetstone, "but what of William? Has he commenced any sort of inquiry into the massacre or had anyone brought to trial?"

The priest sighed and shook his head. "Nay. The King remains conspicuously silent on the matter. I fear it'll take a great hue and cry to move him to any action. Whether from shame that he signed the warrant in the first place or because he's reluctant to implicate men who were but serving him, I cannot say. Either way, though, his inaction gives me a verra bad feeling, lad. A verra bad feeling."

"As it does me." Ruarc laid aside his now sharpened sword and took up his pistol. Poking a rag attached to a ramrod down the barrel, he proceeded to clean the weapon.

It was as he had feared, even as he had written that first letter to the king after the massacre. In retrospect, it would've been wiser never to have sent it. At the worst, he might not now be an outlaw.

News of his daring rescue had soon reached London. The king had reportedly been livid, declared Ruarc a man outside the law, and doubled the reward for his capture. If it hadn't been for the current reluctance of neighboring clans to involve themselves in aught that smacked of the king and his toadies, Ruarc knew he would've been in danger of his life.

But then, all MacDonalds were essentially still hunted men, threatened with deportation if not death. No pardon had been offered as yet to anyone, though John MacDonald, through Governor Hill, was said to be working tirelessly on the matter. Until that day came—if it ever did—Ruarc knew he was as safe as any of them were.

"So, how are the people faring on Black Mount?" he asked,

deciding a more pleasant change of subject was needed. "Did Flora ever have her first bairn? And how goes the farming?"

Father Kenneth laughed. "Och, she delivered of a braw, squalling lad two weeks ago. And the oats and barley have been planted, as have the cabbage, curly kail, and potatoes."

Ruarc set aside his pistol and rags. "I miss them all—my people—as I do Rannoch. It's past time we face the reality of my situation, though. I may well never be permitted to return to Rannoch. Mayhap it's time I appoint Davie as interim laird for my wee bairn to come."

"By right, Rannoch is first Glynnis's," Father Kenneth said. "After ye, I mean, as yer father's wife."

"And has she begun making noise again, since I've left, that she wants it?"

"Nay, she hasn't said one word. But the lady has taken a firm hand with the organization of the women's daily tasks, and I've seen great progress in many areas because of it. Indeed, Glynnis doesn't seem to find even the humblest duties beneath her anymore. It's quite a surprising transformation, it is."

"Well, mayhap it is. I cannot fault her for her kindness to Killian. She's sent many things to us since we came to Coire Gabhail. And, from the letters Glynnis sends her, Killian claims the woman is greatly pleased about the bairn to come."

"Ye're all she has left in this world. I think she wishes to be a true grandmither to the babe."

"We'll see," Ruarc said. "We'll—"

Killian rushed in, breathless and flushed. "There are riders heading up the ravine. Davie wants you to come quickly."

Ruarc loaded his pistol, then shoved it into his belt. He grabbed up his sword. "Ye stay here with Father Kenneth," he ordered Killian, "until we ascertain who the riders might be. If someone has discovered our hiding place, Davie, Francis, and I can hold off quite a force for a time. Time enough for ye, Gavin, and Father Kenneth to take safe shelter higher up the mountain."

She clutched his arm. "I don't want to leave you, Ruarc. Your fate is mine."

He glanced down at her belly. "Any other time I might let ye fight at my side. But not now. Not when ye're carrying our child. Yer first concern must now be for it."

Killian locked gazes with him and, for a moment, Ruarc thought she might offer further protest. Then she nodded. "Because this child means so much to you, I'll do as you ask. But only because of this child—and because of Gavin."

"I know, lass." He touched a finger to her lips. "I know."

Ruarc turned then to Father Kenneth. "Watch and wait up here. Ye'll know soon enough what ye must do."

The priest nodded. "I'll be praying verra hard I won't need to do aught, lad."

"Aye, ye do that, Father." Then, in a flurry of kilt and legs, Ruarc was gone.

†

KILLIAN shot Father Kenneth an anguished glance. "I hate living like this, knowing each day with Ruarc might be our last together. I wish I could convince him to leave Scotland and come with me to Virginia. We'd be safe there."

"But he doesn't want to go, does he?"

"No, and I won't ask him to. No matter what happens, I won't ask him."

"Because if ye did, especially now with the bairn growing within ye, he'd go if ye asked."

"Yes, I think he would. But we both know it'd tear out his heart to leave these mountains and Glencoe."

"My dearest prayer for ye and him is that it never comes to that." He smiled. "If, of course, that's the Lord's will."

"Whatever God may have planned for us, I'm thankful for what I've had with Ruarc. It's been hard at times, but it's all been worth it. Ruarc's been worth it."

"As I knew he'd be for ye." Father Kenneth grinned, mischief dancing in his eyes. "Not that ye believed me at first, if I do recall."

Killian managed a weak smile. "No, I most certainly didn't. It's a good thing you saw everything far more clearly than either Ruarc or I did. I thank you for that."

"It was my pleasure." Father Kenneth rose. "Now, I'm thinking I should go out and see what I can see. I haven't heard any sounds of shooting or battle, so I'm hoping the riders are friendly."

"Yes, I was beginning to hope for the same thing."

She walked to the door and opened it. Two riders had dismounted and were talking to Ruarc, Davie, and Francis. Ruarc was smiling. Relief filled Killian.

Finally, the two riders climbed back on their horses. They didn't ride off, however, but appeared to be waiting for something. Ruarc spoke a few more words to Davie and Francis, then turned and strode back to the bothy.

"Who were the men, and what did they want?" Killian was quick to ask as he drew up before them.

"The King has agreed to allow John, in the name of all the Glencoe MacDonalds, to swear fealty at Inveraray before Campbell of Ardkinglas," her husband informed her. "Once he does, John can take his people home."

"And does the king's generosity extend to you as well?"

Ruarc's mouth quirked grimly. "I doubt it. John, however, has summoned me to a private meeting, where I'm certain I'll learn more."

"When will you meet with him?"

"I've been asked to ride out with those two lads," he said, pointing to the mounted horsemen. "They'll take me to a secret place where I'll speak with John."

Ruarc paused, eyeing her closely. "It'll only be for a few days. In the meantime, I want to send Father Kenneth and Davie to Black Mount to begin preparing for the move back to Rannoch. Francis can remain here with ye, though, until I return."

She saw the concern in his eyes and knew he wouldn't go to John if she didn't want him to. But if John had some news from the King, some plan for how Ruarc could clear his name and be exonerated of the false charges against him, Killian wanted her husband to know as soon as possible.

"I'll be fine." She gave him a reassuring smile. "As you said, it'll only be for a few days. I've much to do in the meantime, and Francis will be here. Besides, what could possibly happen in a place as secret and safe as Coire Gabhail?"

28

IT WAS a beautiful, golden day for the first of August. A frolicsome breeze blew down from the mountain peaks. Eagles soared high overhead, dipping then rising on the air currents. The sky was a clear, seamless blue, with only a few scattered wisps of clouds to mar its cerulean purity.

A good day to wash, Killian thought, glancing down at the pile of soiled clothing in the woven willow basket. Sunny days, as always, were rare jewels to be cherished. They were also something of which to take full advantage.

She dragged the basket outside, then returned to the hut for the cast-iron pot and the soap. After starting a hot fire, she hung the pot over the flames from a tripod frame and filled it with water. As Killian sat down to wait for the water to heat, Francis and Gavin, accompanied by the ever faithful Fionn and Eilidh, came bounding over the hill.

"Mama! Mama!" her son cried in excitement. "We've been having so much fun. Francis and I've climbed rocks and explored caves. And look what I found."

He handed her a dirt-encrusted wooden figure that, on closer inspection, Killian realized was a carved horse. Though primitive in design and darkened with age, the animal appeared to have been created by someone with a decided talent. She handed it back to Gavin.

"What a wonderful discovery." Killian glanced up to Francis. "And have you been having as much fun as Gavin? You certainly look as if he's been keeping you running about a lot," she added with a smile, noting the clerk's flushed face, tousled hair, and dirty hands and knees.

"Och, aye," Francis replied with a laugh. "I haven't had so much fun since I was a lad. We only returned because we thought it might be time for the midday meal."

She shot a look at the pot of water. It'd be a while yet before it was hot enough for the wash. Killian stood. "It'll be simple fare, just some bannocks and cheese, with what's left of the cider to wash it down. I promise, though, to make a nice venison stew tonight."

"That'll do us, won't it, lad?" Francis ruffled Gavin's blond mop of hair. "Then, afterwards, we'll see to a wee bit more exploring, if that's all right with yer mither."

"That'll be fine. Just have a care on those rocks. I don't want any accidents."

They followed Killian into the bothy. "Do you think—" she shot a glance back at Francis—"Ruarc will be home soon? He's been gone two days now. Whatever could John MacDonald have to say that'd require more than a two-day visit?"

Francis shrugged. "I wouldn't know. Mayhap m'lord and he have plans to make, in case the King's pardon is less than constant. Considering no one's been charged in the massacre and it's going on six months now, I can't say I'd be verra inclined to trust William, either."

"Neither would I." She took down the freshly baked bannocks and laid them on a clean cloth on the makeshift little table. After slicing some thick slabs of cheese and putting out a crock of sweet butter, Killian poured them each a mug of cider. They ate in silence, the males apparently too ravenous for talk, and she thoroughly content just to watch them.

Gavin had grown a good two inches in the past year. As of May he was six years old now and had definitely lost all the solid chubbiness of toddlerhood. He looked, she realized with a small jolt of surprise, like a boy now. A boy, lean and hard and summer browned. He wasn't her baby anymore.

Her hand slipped to her belly. Another baby was on the way, so perhaps it was best Gavin was growing up. He'd be a big help to her when the baby came. A baby, he had firmly insisted, that must be a brother. A brother to play with, and not some silly sister.

As she watched, awash with happy memories, Gavin popped the last bite of bannock into his mouth, finished off his cider, then wiped his mouth with the back of his hand. "Well, I'm ready," he announced, climbing to his feet. "How about you, Francis?"

The clerk grinned. "Well, I don't know, lad. After such a fine meal, I'm thinking I'm now in need of a wee nap. What do ye think about that?"

Gavin groaned. "But you promised, Francis. You promised!"

With a laugh, Francis leaped to his feet. "Och, I was only teasing ye, lad. Let's be off."

Whooping with joy, Gavin darted from the bothy, the clerk close on his heels. Killian watched until they disappeared over the closest hill, then went to check the water. It was simmering nicely.

An hour later, the wash was done and hanging out to dry. Killian dumped the now soiled water, then settled down once again, this time with her Bible. By some miracle, she had managed to find it the day of the massacre in the chaos and upheaval of their bedchamber at Rannoch. Aside from Gavin and Ruarc, the holy book was now her most prized possession, and she cherished the time she made each day to read it.

Killian had just begun her study of Proverbs, and a particularly beautiful verse in chapter three soon caught her eye: "'Trust in the Lord with all thine heart,'" she read the line out loud, "'and lean not unto thine own understanding.'"

She closed the Bible and shut her eyes, turning the words over and over in her mind, marveling at their deep richness and truth. How often that particular line had touched her life, especially in the year since she had first come to Scotland. God had led her on paths strange and even fearsome at times, yet He had always—always, Killian realized now—led her true.

As He would lead her and Ruarc through these difficult times, too, if only they trusted in the Lord with all their hearts.

Carried on the gusting breeze, a faint cry reached her. She opened her eyes and looked up, trying to ascertain from where it had come. Then the cry came again, closer now. A man appeared over the hill—Francis—staggering and carrying something in his arms, a deerhound on either side.

Killian set aside her Bible and stood. Her gaze narrowed, straining against the brightness of the sun to make out what Francis carried. Then, as the object took form in limp legs and arms, and a small head lolling back, her heart gave a great lurch.

"Gavin!" She gathered her skirts, raced up the hill.

A stricken look on his pale face, Francis hurried to meet her. "I'm s-sorry," he gasped. "I t-told him to go sl-slowly up on the boulders, but . . . but he was like some m-mountain goat, scrabbling ever h-higher without a care for the d-danger. Och, I'm s-so verra s-sorry!"

Killian slid to a halt before him. Gavin lay in Francis's arms, motionless and white save for the huge, purpling knot forming on the side of his head. His left cheek was badly scraped, as were his hands and knees, and there was blood in his hair. Blessedly, though, he still breathed.

Sheer terror and an almost overwhelming urge to throw back her head and wail out her anguish to the skies filled Killian. *Not now, God. Don't turn your back on us when we've finally, found happiness!*

"Give him to me." Killian held out her hands.

Francis passed Gavin over. Immediately, she wheeled about and headed down the hill to the bothy as fast as she safely could.

"How far?" she bit out as she hurried along. "How far did he fall?"

"A-about t-ten feet or so, I'd say," Francis stammered. "I sh-shouldn't have let him get so f-far ahead of me."

"No, you shouldn't have."

Killian strode into the bothy and laid her son on his little pallet against the far wall. He didn't move. "Gavin?" she called to him. "Can you hear me, sweeting?"

The boy remained motionless and unresponsive. Killian turned to Francis. "Bring me water and rags."

As the young man hurried to do her bidding, she carefully felt Gavin's body for signs of other injuries. Thankfully, nothing appeared broken. She examined his bloody scalp and found the wound near the big knot nothing but a shallow if long gash. There was no blood in his nose, mouth, or ears, however, and that heartened her.

Francis returned with the water and rags. "Will . . . will he be all right? I . . . I don't know what I'll do if he isn't all right."

She shot him a quelling glance. "I don't know. Nothing appears broken, at least not outwardly. Perhaps the fall but knocked him unconscious. Only time will tell."

Tearing off a large piece of rag, Killian dipped it into the water and began gently to cleanse the gash on the side of Gavin's head. "Could you bring me that jar over there on the shelf? It's the wound ointment Father Kenneth left for us."

He brought it to her, opened it, then knelt at her side. "What's in this?" He wrinkled his nose. "It smells strange."

"A combination of Saint-John's-wort, germander, speedwell, and goldenrod chopped and mixed in butter and grease." Killian took the jar, removed a large glob, and smoothed it into the wound she had just finished cleansing. "Father Kenneth says it's just about the best application for wounds there is."

"Well, he should know. There are few others who posses greater healing skills."

She proceeded to bandage her son's head, then added some ointment lightly to his scraped face. Next, Killian washed his abraded hands and knees. Finally, when ointment had been applied to every wound she could find, she covered Gavin tenderly with a blanket.

"What do we do now?" Francis asked, as she rose and pulled over a stool.

"We wait and watch and pray. If Gavin doesn't waken in the next hour or two—" she bit her lip and looked away—"well, then, I don't know what we'll do."

He stood and took her hand. "It's but a wee bump on the head, m'lady. Gavin will soon be fine. Ye just wait and see."

Killian turned to Francis. "Yes, I'm sure he will be. He has to be." She paused. "I'm sorry if I was short with you when you first brought Gavin to me. I know you'd never do anything to harm Gavin. As you said, it was an accident."

At her words, something must have finally let loose within Francis. His eyes filled with tears. "Och, m'lady, truly I curse the day I was ever born," he wailed, the tears falling. "Ye've never been aught but kind to me, and this is how I repay ye. It's almost as if . . . as if I cannot help but do harm to those I love most. First with m'lord, in the tragedy with Sheila, and now ye, with Gavin. Och, I don't deserve to live!"

Killian stared in shock. Whatever was he talking about? An uneasy presentiment filled her. She steered him to the stool. "Sit." She pushed him down onto it. "We must talk."

Pulling over the other stool, Killian took a seat close to Francis at Gavin's bedside. She grasped the young man's hand. "Now, tell me. Tell me all, Francis. About Ruarc and Sheila."

At first he barely made any sense, so fierce had become his weeping. Bit by bit, though, the words began to come together into a coherent form. "I didn't mean . . . to do it. But I was there . . . I saw it all. Sheila and Adam. M'lord finding them. The sharp words . . . the blows. Then Sheila screaming at them, hitting Ruarc, pulling Adam away."

"You were in the gardens that night? You saw who killed Sheila?"

"She didn't deserve him." The tears ceased as swiftly as they had begun. His face took on an angry, congested look. "She even laughed at him as m'lord finally left her and walked away. Laughed at her husband, the man who had forgiven her time and again for all her wanton behavior."

Francis wiped his nose on his sleeve, then met Killian's bewildered gaze. "I hated her. I couldn't stand watching how she treated m'lord, day in and day out. And she knew I despised her, and dealt with me accordingly.

"That night, though, something snapped in me. I forgot she was m'lord's lady. I forgot the courtesy I owed her, even if I'd long ago ceased rendering her respect. So I confronted her in the garden after m'lord left. Confronted her, telling her in the harshest terms exactly what I thought of her."

As Killian listened to Francis's impassioned tale, a growing disbelief plucked at the edges of her awareness. After all her efforts, had she carelessly dismissed Sheila's true killer? But surely mild-mannered, retiring Francis hadn't murdered her, then kept it secret all these years?

"Sheila, of course, was outraged at my audacity, but I didn't care," he continued. "I kept on, hammering away at her, until I finally ran out of breath. Then, to add yet further insult, I turned and walked away. She screamed at me to halt, not to leave until I was bidden, but I kept on walking. It was evil of me, I know, and totally discourteous, but I no longer cared. I hated her that much.

"Then, of a sudden, I heard her run up behind me." He shook his head in wonderment. "I don't know why I turned, but I did. That impulse saved my life. Even then, Sheila was lifting her arm to plunge her bodice knife into my back."

"She attacked you?" Killian stared in horror. "Sheila tried to kill you?"

"Aye, I believe that was her intent, as overwrought as she was. I tried to stop her, but she was strong. We struggled, fought, and finally tripped and fell." Francis inhaled a deep, ragged breath. "I landed atop her. When I climbed away, Sheila lay there, unmoving. I turned her over and found her bodice knife plunged to the hilt in her chest."

Killian reached out to him. "Oh, Francis. Oh, no!"

"A-aye," he said, his voice quavering once more. "If ye're looking for Sheila's murderer, ye haven't any further to look. Though I meant but to defend myself, in the doing I killed her."

How strikingly Francis's unwilling participation in Sheila's death mirrored hers in the killing of her husband. Neither had ever intended to take anyone's life. Both had acted on what they had believed was Ruarc's behalf. Yet though Killian had finally made her peace with what she had done, Francis's tragic deed—and his refusal to speak the truth about it—continued to have far-reaching repercussions. But how to help him bring an end to it?

She sighed. "You didn't kill her, Francis. It was an accident."

"Mayhap." His head dipped in shame. "But I hadn't the courage to tell anyone. Instead, I thought the blame would fall on one of her many lovers, mayhap even on Adam. It would've been only right if it had. But instead . . . instead . . ." He buried his face in his hands and began to sob.

"Instead," Killian said softly, "the blame fell on Ruarc, where it has remained until this very day."

"Och, m'lady," the young man said, weeping, "now ye see ye've even greater cause to hate and despise me. Not only have I failed ye and Gavin, but ye see what my cowardice has done to m'lord."

"Why didn't you ever tell Ruarc? He would've forgiven you. He would've understood."

"Mayhap if I'd told him right away, he might have forgiven me, but not later, after all the scandal, after all the years of feuding with Adam and the damage it had done." A wild look in his eyes, Francis gazed up at her. "Besides, I couldn't bear to risk losing his love, even from the beginning. M'lord has always been like a father to me. The only family I ever had who truly loved me. If he'd sent me away, it would've destroyed me. So I sought to make up for what I'd done—the only hurt I ever inflicted upon him—by striving to serve him, and only him, all the rest of the days of my life."

"And you have, Francis," she said soothingly, growing concerned over his rising agitation. "Save for that one mistake, you've served Ruarc and Rannoch to the very best of your ability. Even now, I think if you were to tell him the truth about that night, Ruarc would forgive you still."

Stark terror tightened his features. He grabbed her hands, clutching them tightly. "Ye won't tell him, will ye? Och, I beg of ye not to tell m'lord! I couldn't bear it. I swear I couldn't bear it!"

Though a part of her wanted desperately to tell Ruarc, to force Francis to confess before Adam as well, Killian knew this tale wasn't hers to tell. Francis must find the courage to do it himself, surrender to his fears and face them, or his healing would never begin. But to allow Ruarc undeservedly to suffer for this even an instant longer . . .

Killian sighed her acquiescence. "No, Francis, I won't tell Ruarc. But somehow, some way, *you* must find the courage to do so. As difficult as it is for Ruarc to bear, this tragic secret, if left secret much longer, will surely destroy you."

She managed a wan smile. "Just know, when the time comes, if you wish it, I'll be there for you. To give you strength. To give you courage. To give you love."

Eyes brimming with freshened tears, Francis nodded. "Thank ye, m'lady."

For a long moment, their gazes met and melded. Then, her smile fading, Killian turned back to sit vigil with her son.

†

TWO HOURS came and went, and still Gavin failed to regain consciousness. Killian's anxiety mounted until she thought she'd scream aloud from the fear. Finally, though, she knew it was time to seek outside help.

"We need to take Gavin to Father Kenneth." As she spoke, she began gathering things for the journey. "Get the horses saddled. There's not a moment to spare."

"Mayhap it'd be better if I went and fetched Father," Francis offered. "It can't be good for the lad to take such a long horseback ride."

"No, it won't be good," Killian admitted, "but I'm not certain we can spare the time it would require to bring Father Kenneth back here, either. Besides, if Gavin's condition worsens while you're gone, what will I do without your help? Either way, there are no easy answers. I can only make the best decision I can."

"As ye wish, m'lady." Francis hurried from the hut.

Killian pulled on her shoes, flung a shawl about her shoulders, then began to wrap Gavin in a blanket. As she worked, from some corner of her awareness she thought she heard voices, but discounted that as Francis most likely talking to the horses as he readied them. Then heavy footsteps sounded outside, the door swung open, and Ruarc stalked into the bothy.

She looked up, a joyous relief filling her. "Oh, Ruarc, thank the Lord you returned!" Killian flung herself into his arms. "I need you so badly."

He pressed her against the warm, familiar bulk of his body. "Aye, lass. Francis told me what happened. I only wish I'd been here for ye from the beginning."

Fighting her tears, Killian savored, for one instant more, his comforting strength. Then she leaned back to meet his gaze. "Gavin's no better, and I don't know what else to do. We must take him to Father Kenneth at Black Mount."

"Aye, that's likely the best plan. He isn't at Black Mount anymore, though. This morn, they all left for Rannoch."

Rannoch . . . Killian's thoughts raced. There had been talk that Rannoch was being watched by redcoats with orders to shoot Ruarc on sight. If the King's recent pardon of MacDonalds didn't extend to him, the danger to Ruarc in returning to Rannoch was great.

"What news from John?" She searched her husband's face for any favorable sign. "Will William's mercy fall on you as well as on the rest of the clan?"

A sad smile on his lips, he shook his head. "Not yet, it seems."

Killian's heart sank. "Then you cannot come with us. Surely the redcoats still await you there."

"Most likely. We'll deal with that wee problem, though, when we come to it."

"No, Ruarc." She pushed away. "I won't risk losing you too."

"And I, sweet lass, won't leave ye in yer hour of direst need. Gavin's as much my child now as yers. I won't desert him, either."

A fierce love welled in her heart for this brave, wonderful man. "Then come with us only part of the way. You can wait—"

Francis burst into the hut. "Riders! Ten or twenty of them, coming up the pass. And they don't look like MacDonalds!"

Ruarc turned to Killian. "Stay in here with Francis. I'll see who it is."

He took a step toward the door, hesitated, then unsheathed his sword and laid it on the table. Reaching behind his back, he next pulled free his pistol, adding it to the sword.

Killian grabbed his hand. "What are you doing? If they're enemy, how can you go out to them unarmed? You must protect yourself!"

"If they're enemy, and as large a force as Francis claims, I've no hope of prevailing. In the bargain, all I'll do is endanger ye." He shook his head. "Nay, what matters now is that ye get Gavin to Father Kenneth. If I go to these men in peace, mayhap they'll feel more favorable toward helping ye. And, if they're friends, I don't need the weapons."

With a clatter of hooves and harsh voices, the riders drew up outside the bothy. "Ruarc MacDonald," a familiar voice—Adam's voice—shouted. "If ye're in there, show yerself. And don't risk Killian and the lad's life by trying aught foolish. If ye do, it'll go verra badly for ye."

Once more, Killian and Ruarc exchanged glances. Her eyes filled with tears. Would they never be free of Adam and his hatred, or ever live again in peace?

"Ruarc." Her throat clogged with unshed tears. "Oh, Ruarc . . ."

His own eyes brimming, he smiled down at her. "It could be worse. At least Adam will help ye take Gavin to Rannoch. The lad's kin, after all."

"But what of y-you?" Despair and a bone-deep sense of futility swamped her. "What of you?"

"First, let's think of Gavin," he said lightly, lovingly touching her face. "Time enough later to consider me."

Ruarc turned then to Francis. "Keep her inside, if ye have to hold her. I don't know what awaits me out there."

His countenance waxen, it seemed all Francis could do even to nod. He moved to stand beside Killian, however, taking her hand.

With that, Rannoch's laird smiled, then wheeled about and strode out the door.

†

HIS PISTOL drawn, Adam sat his horse. A grim satisfaction filled him. No matter how many times Sheila's killer eluded him, he'd never give up until justice was finally served. If it took until the end of his days, he'd see Ruarc MacDonald hunted down like the mangy cur he was. He'd make his life a living torment.

With the generous price now on Ruarc's head, however, it had only been a matter of time before someone betrayed him. Luckily for Adam, one of the broken, clanless men at the meeting between Rannoch's laird and John MacDonald had seized the opportunity presented him, riding all night to Achallader to inform Adam. It had been a simple enough matter, after that, to post spies who soon notified him of Ruarc's departure.

And now, once again, Adam had Ruarc trapped.

The door to the bothy swung open. His hand gripping his pistol, Adam leaned forward in anticipation. Ruarc walked out, then closed the door behind him. His empty hands held open at his sides, he headed directly for Adam.

"I'm unarmed," Ruarc said. "Ye and yer men can all lower yer weapons."

"And what of those inside?" Adam demanded. "Can ye vouch for them as well?"

"Aye. There's just Killian, Francis, and Gavin. And Gavin's verra ill. We were just leaving to carry him to Rannoch and Father Kenneth. If ye'll not let me take him, then I beg ye to take the lad yerself."

Adam's eyes narrowed in suspicion. "So, Gavin's verra ill, is he?"

He shoved his pistol in his belt and swung off his horse. "Let me be the judge of that."

He shouldered past Ruarc, who followed him inside. As his vision adjusted to the dimmer light, Adam saw Killian kneeling by Gavin's side. Near a table, whereupon lay Ruarc's sword and pistol, Francis glowered back at him.

As he moved closer, Adam saw the bandage swathing the boy's head. The lad lay there, quiet and pale. Concern filled him. "What happened?" he asked hoarsely, squatting beside Killian.

She angled her head toward him. "He fell climbing on some rocks. He's been senseless now for about two and a half hours." Her expression turned bleak. "I fear for his life, Adam. Please help us."

He eyed the boy for a long moment more, then rose to face Ruarc. "I'll take the lad and his mither to Rannoch. Ye, however, will continue on to Edinburgh with my men. This time, I mean to see ye locked in the Tollbooth before any have a chance even to realize ye've been recaptured."

"No, Adam!" Killian cried from behind him, grabbing at his leg. "Don't do this. I beg of you. Don't do this!"

"Killian. Don't," Ruarc chided her gently. "It won't do any good. It's not just a matter of Adam's revenge anymore. He's now bound by the King's command, and cannot disobey."

She pushed to her feet. "Adam knows as well as I that the King is misinformed, that you're innocent of those accusations. And Adam's clever enough to find some excuse to set you free, if he's of a mind to do it."

"But I'm not—and never will be, lass," Adam chose at that moment to interject. He gestured toward Gavin. "Now, we can stand about and debate this issue further, but it looks to me like the lad needs immediate attention."

"Aye," Ruarc agreed, "we must see to Gavin."

Adam glanced at Ruarc. "Then ye consent to go peaceably with my men if I escort Killian and her son to Rannoch?"

"I've little choice."

From the corner of his vision, Adam saw Francis grab just then at something on the table. The weapons. He had forgotten the weapons!

Even as Francis lifted the pistol and fired, Adam leaped aside and sought his own pistol. A ball whizzed past Adam's head, widely missing him. His shot, however, struck true.

With a cry, Francis staggered backward. The pistol fell from his hand. A bewildered look in his eyes, he clutched at his chest. Then, as a red stain seeped slowly through his fingers, the clerk's knees buckled.

Killian screamed. Ruarc lurched forward, catching Francis as he fell. Ever so gently, he lowered him to the floor. "Why?" He pulled Francis close. "Why did ye try such a foolish thing?"

"I . . . I couldn't let him take ye, m'lord," Francis whispered. "I've done . . . done ye enough harm."

As several men rushed into the bothy and Adam motioned them immediately back out, Francis's head turned to find Killian, now kneeling on his other side. "Ye said, when the time came . . . that ye'd be . . . with me."

"Yes." Tears streamed down her face. "That I did."

He locked gazes with Ruarc once more. "I've something . . . something to tell ye, m'lord. The Lady Killian . . . knows already. But she said it . . . was my place to tell ye."

"Ye don't need to explain aught to me, lad. Best ye conserve yer strength. Now, we've two patients to take to Father Kenneth."

Francis waved weakly to Adam, signaling him over. Warily, Adam approached.

"Ye, too, need to . . . to hear this," the young man explained. "So ye'll also know the truth . . . and at last cease yer cruel persecution of m'lord."

Adam moved closer. "And what truth might that be?"

"That it was me who killed the Lady Sheila that night in the garden." Francis began to cough. Foamy blood spewed from his mouth. He lifted his arm and awkwardly wiped it away. "It was an accident. After ye and m'lord left, we . . . we got into an argument, the Lady Sheila and I. Then . . . then she attacked me . . . with her bodice knife. We struggled . . . fell. She stabbed herself . . . with her own knife."

It was too preposterous to accept. Adam swallowed hard, trying to make sense of it all. "And why should I believe ye? Mayhap this is but yer attempt to do yer laird one final service, by taking the blame onto yerself."

"It's true, Adam," Killian countered quietly. "Francis finally told me the tale earlier today, after Gavin had fallen and he was overcome with guilt. This isn't some contrived deathbed confession."

Adam looked up. Her gaze was clear, guileless. She was telling the truth. The enormity of what he had done, dwelt ceaselessly upon for the past four years, rose up to overwhelm him.

Suddenly, Adam felt sick to the marrow of his bones. He staggered backward, shaking his head. "It can't be. I don't believe it!"

"B-believe . . ." Francis breathed. "Believe . . . for it's God's truth." He turned back to Ruarc. "Forgive . . . I beg . . . of ye. I was so afraid of losing yer love. . . . Forgive me, m'lord."

Ruarc gathered him yet closer. "Ye know I forgive ye, lad. It wasn't yer fault. It wasn't anyone's fault. All of us made mistakes. *All.*"

Francis managed a wobbly smile. "Thank ye . . . m'lord."

"Ye did the right thing, lad," Ruarc said with a husky catch in his voice, as Francis began to cough now so hard he was soon choking. "Ye overcame yer greatest fear, risked all, and have attained yer victory."

As Killian and Ruarc moved close to hold him in his final moments, Adam fled the bothy. He staggered out into the sunlight, which suddenly seemed too bright, too revealing. There, as Killian's mournful wail rose in the air, Adam sank to his knees and retched.

29

A SHORT while later, Ruarc walked from the bothy. Adam, in the
interim, had sent his men off to water their mounts.

Ruarc turned and made his way to Adam. "Francis is dead."
Ruarc appeared to have been weeping.

"I'm verra sorry. However, I was only defending myself."

"I know." Rannoch's laird looked away. "He wasn't much good
with weapons. Though ye didn't realize it, ye were in little danger."

Adam turned his gaze in the direction Ruarc was staring. In the
distance, the sun was beginning to set in a blaze of crimson glory.
What a strange day it had been, he mused. So beautiful, yet so filled
with tragedy.

"About what Francis told us . . ." Adam exhaled a deep, considering breath. "Well, I don't know what to say."

"It'll take a time, I'd wager, for all of us to sort through it all."
Ruarc turned back to him. "What matters now is getting Gavin to
Rannoch. Are ye still willing to escort him and Killian there?"

"Aye. And, thinking on it a bit more, I believe ye should accompany us. At a time such as this, both Killian and Gavin will have great
need of ye."

Ruarc's eyes lit with a burning intensity. "I thank ye for that,
Adam." He paused. "I'd also like to bring Francis back with us, to be
buried with his kin."

"As ye wish." Adam gestured toward his men. "Even now they're watering their mounts in preparation for the ride. How soon can ye and Killian be ready?"

"Give me ten minutes to finish saddling our horses."

Ruarc spun about then and headed into the bothy. A few minutes later, he exited and walked around to the small horse pen behind the hut.

Adam's bout of vomiting had left a sour taste in his mouth. A cooling drink from the burn would do him good. He stared after Ruarc a moment more, then headed to the stream.

Was he a fool to take Ruarc with him to Rannoch rather than send him along with his men to Edinburgh? Ruarc was clever enough to seize any opportunity offered for escape. He was a desperate man for good reason. He'd most likely never leave the Tollbooth save to walk to the gallows.

Still, for all the torment he had heaped on him all these years, Adam felt he owed Rannoch's laird some small gesture of conciliation. Ruarc hadn't killed Sheila. No one had.

No one save mayhap Sheila herself. And her death that night in Rannoch's garden, Adam realized at long last, had been but the final culmination of a self-destruction begun many years before.

†

IN THE deepening twilight, Ruarc cradled Gavin in his arms and rode hard and fast down the glen. Surrounded by Adam and his men, the two deerhounds loping along behind, Killian guided her own horse alongside her. Yet, in the span of the hour and a half it took to reach the fork of the Rivers Coupall and Etive at the edge of the glen, the little boy never moved or stirred.

Finally, when the guard post campfires at Rannoch's outskirts were but distant beacons in the night, Adam halted their party. He spoke quietly to one man, his words unintelligible to Ruarc from his position farther back. Then, in a loud voice, the man Adam had spoken to called out seven names.

"Come, lads," he commanded. "'Tis back to Achallader we go."

In a flurry of hoofbeats and dust, they departed, leaving only Adam and his cousin Lachlan behind.

Ruarc exchanged a puzzled glance with Killian, then nudged his horse forward. "Why did ye send yer men away?"

"They were no longer needed. Lachlan's companion enough for me. After all, ye gave yer word ye'd go along to Edinburgh without problem, didn't ye, if I saw Gavin to Rannoch?"

Even Adam knew how fiercely he honored his word. Never before, though, had Ruarc viewed it as the trap he did just now. "Aye," he said, "that I did."

Adam shrugged. "Then we didn't need the extra men, did we?" He went silent, his gaze riveting now on the flickering campfires. "One problem remains, though. How to get ye past the guards and into Rannoch."

"Ye've already one dead man. I could play dead as well."

Achallader's laird appeared to consider that idea, then nodded. "Aye, that might work. Few would question my word at any rate."

Ruarc looked to Killian. "No matter what the soldiers do, if they feel a need to test how dead I really am, ye mustn't utter a sound. Do ye hear me, lass?"

Even in the dim light, he could see her eyes grow wide. "Whatever might they do to you?"

"It doesn't matter. It's our best hope of getting me into Rannoch. We haven't time to waste."

She sighed her acquiescence. "As you wish. Someday, though, I'd like very much not to worry from one minute to the next how much longer you'll be alive."

He managed a grin. "So would I, lass. Here—" he handed Gavin to her—"I don't think I can hold him and convincingly play dead at the same time."

Killian accepted her son, cradling him tenderly to her. For a moment more they gazed at each other. Then Ruarc signaled his horse forward, drawing alongside Adam.

"Take these." He tossed the reins to Adam, then swung his leg over his saddle and flipped onto his belly.

"If only ye knew how many times I'd dreamt of bringing ye back in such a state," Adam muttered dryly.

Ruarc lifted his head. "And if only *ye* knew how happy I am still to be alive to see yer dreams come true."

With a disgusted snort, Adam urged his horse forward. Lachlan followed, pulling the horse carrying Francis's body. Killian soon fell into place behind them.

From time to time, amidst the clip-clop of the horses' hooves, Ruarc caught snatches of songs and words she murmured to her son. It tugged at his heart, Killian's efforts to mother Gavin in what few ways still left her. It also strengthened his resolve to do whatever necessary to save the boy's life—even if it required the sacrifice of his own.

Not long thereafter, they reached the sentries and were ordered to halt. Once Adam made clear who he was and his purpose in wishing to reach Rannoch, they were allowed to pass. As they drew away from the soldiers, Ruarc heaved a deep sigh of relief. He hadn't particularly relished the state of his viability being tested with a dirk thrust or two into his body.

Once inside the relative privacy of Rannoch's grounds, Ruarc slid from his horse. After a few seconds spent massaging his now aching abdomen, he hurried to Killian. "Give me the lad." He lifted his arms to her.

She quickly handed Gavin down, dismounted, and took back her son. By then Father Kenneth, Davie, and Glynnis had hurried out to ascertain who their unexpected visitors were. Davie was the first to recognize Ruarc.

"M'lord," he said, "whatever are ye doing here? 'Tisn't safe for ye to be at Rannoch. Indeed, how did ye get past the soldiers?"

"By playing dead," Ruarc replied. "Which is exactly how they'd like to see me." He pointed back to the horse Lachlan led. "Francis, sadly, *is* dead. Will ye take him and see to his burial preparations? Father Kenneth can conduct his funeral on the morrow."

"Aye, m'lord." Davie strode out toward Francis's body.

"What's wrong, lad?" Father Kenneth then demanded, drawing up before Ruarc. "Ye wouldn't be here unless something was terribly wrong."

"It's Gavin. He's taken a bad fall and won't waken." Even as Ruarc spoke, Glynnis, who had hurried to greet Killian, gave a low cry. "Come," he urged, taking the priest by the arm, "have a look at the lad."

In the light of torches held aloft now by two servants, Ruarc took

Gavin from his wife. Father Kenneth quickly examined him. Finally, he looked up, a grim expression on his face.

"As ye say, the lad's in a stupor. Let's carry him inside where I can mayhap do more."

"He'll be all right, won't he, Father?" Killian asked anxiously. "If anyone can help Gavin, I know you can."

The little priest slipped an arm about Killian's shoulders. "I'll do all I can, lass, and no mistake." He began to walk her into the castle. "Ye know that, don't ye?"

"Yes, I know that. I just need . . . need for Gavin to get better. I don't know what I'll do if he doesn't."

The look on Father Kenneth's face wasn't any more hopeful, however, a half hour later after Gavin's wound had been inspected and redressed and the boy had been put to bed on a makeshift pallet in the library. Ruarc and Adam soon joined him in the hall, while Glynnis remained with Killian and her son.

"It doesn't bode well," the priest said, "that the lad's been unconscious for so many hours now. I fear he's suffered some sort of brain injury."

"Isn't there aught ye can give him, Father?" Ruarc asked. "Ye've always had some healing herb or concoction for almost every ailment."

"There's only one thing left that might save the lad."

Ruarc leaned forward with a savage determination. "Tell me what ye need, and I'll ride out this verra moment to obtain it."

Father Kenneth smiled sadly. "Ye don't have to ride any further than the chapel. It's prayer, lad. Prayer and the dear Lord's mercy are all that's left us."

For an instant, Ruarc felt as if the priest had plunged a fist deep into his gut. He couldn't speak. He couldn't breathe. And the pain. Och, the pain twisting his heart brought tears to his eyes.

"Nay," he groaned finally, shaking his head. "Don't say that. Don't tell me ye think it's hopeless. I won't stand for it. I won't!"

"Mayhap a physician might be of assistance," Adam offered. "I could ride to Inverarary and fetch one. There's a physician there who has treated the King at one time. He's said to be verra good."

The priest shook his head. "Truly, lad, if I thought someone with skill great enough to help Gavin lay as close as Inverarary, I'd be the first to fetch him myself. But even as fine a physician as ye claim this man to be cannot do aught more. The lad's life is now in the Lord's hands."

"He speaks true." Ruarc cut Adam off before he could voice the protest Ruarc saw forming on the other man's lips. "Father Kenneth is verra knowledgeable when it comes to healing. I've never seen anyone, even most physicians, who knows more."

"Aye, mayhap ye're right." Adam gave in with a sigh. "I just hate to see the wee lad die, that's all."

"Well, I don't aim to see him die, either," the priest said firmly. "Hence why I'm hieing myself straight off to the chapel." He glanced from Ruarc to Adam. "Are either of ye of a mind to join me?"

Ruarc locked gazes with Adam, who shook his head. "Mayhap later." He turned back to Father Kenneth. "Right now, though, I think I'm needed more at Killian's side."

Adam nodded his agreement. "Aye. That's where I intend to be too."

Father Kenneth shrugged. "Suit yerselves. If the lad takes a turn for the worse, ye know where to find me." He swung about and hobbled away.

"Mayhap ye'd like something to eat," Rannoch's laird offered, turning back to Adam. "I've already had a meal prepared for Lachlan in the kitchen. It'll be simple fare, considering my people just today returned to Rannoch, but all that we have is yers."

"Yer hospitality is most appreciated and speaks far better for MacDonalds than for Campbells of late." Adam's mouth tightened somberly. "I can't say, though, I've much of an appetite. I killed an all but defenseless man today, and now my wee cousin may well be dying." He lowered his head and massaged his eyes and temples. "To add insult to injury, I also just learned I've been wrongly accusing ye all these years for Sheila's death."

Adam looked up, his expression bleak. "That's not the worst of it, though. I thought I knew ye for the man ye truly were. I thought Sheila's death was but the final culmination of yer cruelty to her all those years. But then I also thought I knew her, understood her, and that none of her unhappiness was her fault, but yers, always yers."

"And now?" Ruarc asked with quiet intensity. "What do ye think now? And can one incident ye thought ye always knew the cause for, and now find that ye didn't, make such a difference?"

"Aye, it can." Adam's voice went hoarse with emotion. "For I see ye're not the same man I knew all those years ago in Holland. Ye've grown, changed. Only I've stayed the same, mired in my jealousy, self-pity, and hatred for ye. But ye were never at fault. *I* crippled *myself*. And that revelation today, above everything else, sickens me."

A peace, that strange peace he had first experienced the day he had decided to ride to Achallader and confront Adam, filled Ruarc once more. It had been long in coming, this consummation of their feud, the end to this festering enmity over Sheila, but it *had* come. All it had required was a willingness to take a risk, to grow past old disappointments, and to trust. Trust that the Lord would bring it to fruition in His own good time.

"Ye'd no reason to think otherwise of me, Adam," Ruarc replied. "When all was said and done, I took away the woman ye loved. I made some terrible mistakes, too, out of pride, selfishness, and sheer stupidity. Mistakes that caused others, including Sheila, great pain." He managed a wistful smile. "I'd say we just about balanced the scales in our blind foolishness."

Adam nodded, the tension finally seeming to ease from him. "Aye, mayhap we did. It all just seems so upside down and inside out now. For a time ye'd everything a man could desire, a beautiful wife in Sheila, the King's favor, and significant wealth, stature, and respect in yer clan. And now . . . now ye've lost it all to become an outlaw. Yet ye seem far happier than I, who may now stand to win William's favor at long last if I turn ye over to him and, with it, the possible reward of a prestigious position at Court."

Adam shook his head in seeming amazement. "Strange as it may sound, though, I'm no longer so certain, in light of William's alleged involvement in the massacre, I even want his favor anymore. I'm no longer certain I trust or even respect him. It'll be difficult enough to make peace with my clan's shameful involvement in the killings."

"We both see things far differently now than we saw them as young men in Holland." Ruarc smiled. "Yet it's good to know, isn't it, that there's always hope, even for the blindest, most pigheaded of men?"

"Aye." Adam hesitated for a long moment. "One thing more.

When Gavin's well again, ye need to escape. William will accept that I brought ye here as an act of humanity. Especially—" he shot Ruarc a sly look—"when I loudly publicize his most kind act of compassion toward ye in yer hour of need. But the King also knows what a wily fox ye can be, so he'll understand how ye managed yet again to hoodwink me."

A warm gratitude filled Ruarc. "Thank ye, Adam. I'll never forget this."

Achallader's laird gave a short, harsh laugh. "Best ye don't. If I know William, he'll soon enough have me hot on yer trail again."

†

RELIEF swept through Killian at the sight of Ruarc returning to the library. She hadn't realized, until just now, how much she had needed her husband. Somehow, with him at her side, it made the pain a bit easier to bear. He was strong, solid, and the fact that he had so willingly stood by her, even at the risk of his own life, was a comfort like no other.

Her joy, however, dimmed as Adam entered right behind Ruarc. The man represented such a continued threat that Killian had to fight back a surge of intense dislike. Why, oh why, couldn't he just leave them alone?

"How's the lad?" Ruarc asked as he came to stand beside her. His hand settled lightly on her shoulder.

She looked up, meeting his concerned gaze. "No change. Not a one."

Glynnis reached over and gave Killian's hand a reassuring pat. "Gavin's a braw, strong lad. Ye mustn't give up hope, m'lady." She then tilted her head back to stare at Adam. "Well, I never thought to see ye standing beside Ruarc MacDonald, in Rannoch Castle no less."

A smile glimmered on Adam's mouth. "And I never thought to see ye offering comfort to Ruarc and Killian. Strange how things change."

"Strange how life can bring enemies together and turn some so-called kin into enemies," Ruarc added.

Killian knew he was alluding to how Robert Campbell had turned on his own relations. But what did he mean about enemies being brought together?

Once more, she looked from Ruarc to Adam. Was it possible? Were he and Adam finally beginning a reconciliation? *Oh, dear Lord,* she prayed, noting how the two men stood side by side, apparently relaxed in each other's presence, *let it be so. Oh, please, let it be so!*

"Have ye seen Father Kenneth?" She glanced up at her husband. "He said he'd an important matter to address."

"He's gone to confer with the Lord." Ruarc laid his other hand on her shoulder and began gently to massage her neck and shoulders. "Ye're as tight as a bowstring, lass. Why don't ye and Glynnis take a wee walk to the kitchen and get yerselves something to eat? Adam and I can watch Gavin while ye're gone."

Stubbornly, Killian shook her head. "No. I'm not hungry."

"Then at least go and get something to drink. I know ye haven't had aught to drink for hours." He punctuated that suggestion by grasping her by her arms and pulling her to her feet. "Just a wee walk about Rannoch, and a drink. Cook's sure to have a store of cider hidden somewhere."

"Aye, m'lady," Glynnis urged, rising as well. "A short respite will do ye a world of good. Yer husband is quite capable of watching Gavin for a time. He's always had a way with the lad, after all."

To please Ruarc and Glynnis, who she knew were but concerned for her, Killian finally acceded. "Fine. A short respite couldn't hurt. But I won't be gone long. I don't know how much time I've left with Gavin. I don't dare squander it."

An infinitely tender look in his eyes, Ruarc crooked a finger beneath her chin and tipped it up. He leaned down and kissed her on the lips. "Ye'll have the rest of yer life, lass, if I have any say in the matter," he whispered as he pulled back at last.

She forced a tremulous smile. "Do you know how much I love you?"

"Aye, as a matter of fact, I do." His expressive, beautiful eyes warmed to deepest jade. "And that makes me the luckiest man alive."

Before he could see the moisture flooding her eyes, Killian turned away. She wanted to be strong for him. Indeed, she *needed* just as desperately to be strong, to stay in control for Gavin. She didn't dare allow the floodgates of her emotions to open right now. The sheer force of her anguish might carry her so far away, Killian feared she'd never find herself again.

"Would you like me to bring you and Adam something back from the kitchen?"

"A mug of mulled cider would be most welcome." Ruarc glanced at Adam. "Is there aught ye'd like?"

"The cider will do me as well."

Killian nodded, then turned to Glynnis. "Shall we be on our way?"

"Aye, m'lady," the older woman replied and, gathering her skirts, followed Killian from the room.

They walked in silence for a time. From some place far away, Killian noted the damage done to the castle. It'd take months to repair the destruction. But none of it mattered in light of the loss of human life, and the potential of losing Gavin. Homes could be rebuilt, furnishings restored. The death of even a single loved one, however, was the loss of a treasure beyond price. When that precious being was gone, it would never be again. Leastwise, never again in this life.

Bessie was just shooing Lachlan from the kitchen when Killian and Glynnis arrived. Killian greeted the young man. "Has anyone found you a place to sleep for the night?"

Lachlan shook his head. "It doesn't appear ye've much in the way of fine accommodations available, m'lady. Leastwise, not just now. It's not a problem, though. The night is mild, and I can sleep outdoors."

"We're not so destitute we must make our guests sleep on the hard ground." Killian turned to Bessie. "Can you find Lachlan some blankets and a pillow? We should at least be able to fix him a pallet of sorts."

"Aye, m'lady," the woman agreed with a curtsey. "'Twill be no problem at all." She eyed the red-haired young man. "Well, come along then, if ye will. I havena all night to tuck ye in all nice and cozy. I've still pots to scrub and bread to set to rising for the morrow."

Lachlan grinned and followed her from the kitchen. "Och, I feel right at home now," he exclaimed with a chuckle. "Ye sound just like my wee mither."

Glynnis found a jug of cider and two cups. She poured them both out some of the fermented juice, then took a seat at the big worktable.

Killian pulled out a stool on the opposite side. They sat there for a while, each sipping her cider.

Finally, when Bessie returned, Glynnis rose. "If ye wouldn't mind, m'lady, I'd like to help finish off those pots. Bessie's been working all day. She must be nigh unto exhausted."

With an effort, Killian pulled back from her morose thoughts. "Oh, yes, please do. In fact—" she shoved to her feet—"I could help, too. Then we'd be done even sooner."

"Nay, m'lady." Glynnis motioned her to sit back down. "Ye're not in much better condition than Cook. Just sit a spell and enjoy yer cider."

She was right, Killian admitted. She *was* tired. But so was everyone else. Her thoughts turned to Father Kenneth. How long had he been praying now? He shouldn't be the only one interceding before the Lord this night. After all, Gavin was her son.

Ah, Killian inwardly sighed as she turned and stared out the window into a black, starry night, if only this day hadn't turned out as it had. She was back home, where she belonged, at Rannoch. It had been her dream—to return to Rannoch—for the past six months of their exile, but now it didn't matter anymore. Her home had always been where her heart was—with Ruarc and Gavin.

If she lost Gavin, would she ever feel at home anywhere again? She'd give anything to go back to earlier today and change what had happened. If only she hadn't let him go off after the midday meal. If only she had gone with him. Perhaps, if she closed her eyes and wished it with all her might, she could make it all happen differently.

And, if that didn't work, why, oh why, couldn't God just take her life in exchange for Gavin's? Her son was innocent. *She* was the one to blame. She had failed him as his mother. She was the one who deserved to die, not Gavin.

Killian's eyes stung with unshed tears. No matter how desperately she wished it, the reality was still the same. She couldn't trade places with her son. Somehow, she must find the strength to accept that. She had others who depended on her just as deeply now. Ruarc, Glynnis, their people, and her and Ruarc's unborn child.

At long last she had found the family she had always sought, even as she might well soon lose a part of it.

She couldn't go in Gavin's place—if it was indeed his time to go—no matter how torn her mother's heart might be. She might rail and curse, but in the end she must still accept that.

Trust in the Lord with all thine heart . . . accept . . . surrender . . . and find the strength to go on. Surrender . . . and bear the burden of her loss to the end of her days.

Father Kenneth had once said submission to God's will was both the hardest and yet the most precious duty a soul was ever called to perform. Finally, on this most heartrending of nights, Killian understood what he had meant.

She pushed to her feet and walked to Glynnis. "Would you mind very much if I asked you to return alone with Ruarc's and Adam's cider? I need . . . I need to spend a time in prayer."

Ruarc's stepmother nodded as she scrubbed vigorously on a pot. "Go where ye feel ye must, m'lady. I'll tell Ruarc."

Gratitude filled her. "You've been such a help and support, Glynnis. I don't know what I'd have done without you."

"Och, dinna fash yerself, m'lady. Weren't ye there for us all those many times before, defending Thomas and me when Ruarc sought to banish us? Ye've always been a good and true friend. I only aim to repay that favor."

"We *have* come a long way, you and I." Killian reached out and grasped the other woman's arm. "Indeed, we've *all* come a long way with each other."

At such a time as this, the realization was bittersweet, but Killian clutched it to herself nonetheless. It heartened her. If such kindness could still be found, if mercy and compassion and forgiveness still abounded even in such savage and heartless of times, surely there was hope of even greater miracles this night.

A miracle of healing, but only if God would grant it so. If only He wished it for His greater glory.

She clasped Glynnis's arm for a brief moment more, then turned and made her way to the chapel.

†

THE NIGHT wore on. Glynnis and Adam eventually fell asleep on pallets near the wall bookcases, as Ruarc sat all but immobile with Killian beside Gavin. And he watched, as the hours passed, dark circles smudged beneath her eyes. Her face became so tight and drawn from exhaustion, it finally became too painful for Ruarc even to look at her.

A knot formed and grew in the middle of his chest. Frustration simmered, threatening to explode. After a time, it took all of Ruarc's self-control not to leap to his feet and roar at the sheer unfairness of it all.

Just when he and Killian were finally coming to a deep and stable relationship, just when the child of his body was growing within the woman he loved, this terrible suffering, atop all the tragedies and misfortunes they had already endured, must now befall them. Was God just some trickster then, giving with one hand while He took away with the other?

He wanted to rail at the Almighty, shout until he was hoarse. Until he had nothing left to give. Only then would he finally be numb, and the aching, endless pain might cease. But he couldn't do that here. Killian couldn't bear much more, and especially not the sight of her husband falling to pieces before her. If for no one else, Ruarc knew he must be strong for her.

Still, a brief respite from the ever-spiraling tension at this heart-breaking bedside might be wise. And Ruarc knew exactly where to go to release his pent-up frustrations. He'd go to a sacred place where God was sure to hear him.

"Lass," he said softly, laying a hand on Killian's arm.

She lifted haunted eyes to him. "Yes?"

"I need a time to seek out Father Kenneth. Will ye be all right until I return?"

Killian nodded, then turned her gaze back to her son. "Yes. Take all the time you need."

He leaned over, kissed her on the cheek, then brushed aside a lock of hair that had fallen into her eyes. "When I return, might ye not take a wee nap? Ye look well past weary, ye do."

She managed a weak smile. "Perhaps."

For a fleeting instant, Ruarc almost decided against leaving her. Something, however, seemed to call him to the chapel. He stood, hesitated a moment more, then turned and strode from the library.

The night air was pleasantly mild, bracing after the stifling atmosphere in the library. Though the weight of their ordeal was in no way lifted from his shoulders, Ruarc was glad, nonetheless, he had decided to leave.

He found Father Kenneth kneeling up near the altar. A small, red votive candle burned there, casting its flickering light on the wooden crucifix, white altar linens, and a simple, etched brass tabernacle. An aura of deep, watchful holiness pervaded the little stone chapel. Ruarc almost turned and left.

Just then, however, the old priest saw him. He waved him forward. Ruarc squared his shoulders and headed up the aisle.

"Come, lad." Father Kenneth rose and limped to the nearest pew. He patted the spot beside him. "I've been hoping ye'd join me. Indeed, I've been praying for it nearly as hard as I've been praying for the wee Gavin."

Ruarc seated himself, leaned forward, and rested his forearms on his kilt-covered thighs. "Well, half of yer prayers have been answered. Not the most important half, though."

"Mayhap not." The priest shrugged. "But who's to say what comes first with the Lord? All I know is the lad needs everyone's prayers, and yers are as important as all the rest."

"Indeed?" Ruarc gave a disbelieving laugh. "I hardly think my prayers are of much value, especially when compared to ye, a man who has devoted his whole life to serving God."

"And do ye, then, imagine it's too late for ye to serve Him? Do ye, lad?"

Ruarc lowered his head. "For a time I thought the Lord must surely be guiding me to reconcile with Adam. I even began to see Him again as a merciful, loving God. But now . . . now I wonder if I wasn't but deluding myself."

"Did ye pray to the Lord to help ye with Adam?"

"Aye," Rannoch's laird responded slowly. "I did."

"And have ye also prayed to the Lord for Gavin?"

Ruarc's eyes began to burn, but whether from exhaustion or tears, he didn't know. "Nay, I haven't. I've been too angry. Too frightened of losing Gavin and what it might do to Killian. And I'll tell ye true, Father. I didn't know what to say."

"Then don't say aught, lad. The Lord Jesus, after all, knows what's in yer heart even before ye speak it, aye, even before ye know it yerself. Sit here for a time. Still yer mind and listen. Listen and love."

"But I don't know how—"

"Ye don't need to, lad. Let the Lord teach ye." Father Kenneth rose, traced the sign of the cross on Ruarc's forehead, then walked quietly from the chapel.

As soon as the chapel door closed behind the old priest, panic surged through Ruarc. What was he doing here?

Listen and love . . .

But he was a man of action, not one of forbearance. He was one to take charge, not wait in humble anticipation for what he knew not. He chose to rely on himself rather than risk trusting to another's mercy.

Yet all those traits—forbearance, humility, and trust—were what the Lord required of those who wished to follow Him.

With a swift intake of breath, Ruarc forced himself to stand and walk to the altar railing. He closed his eyes, sank to his knees, and folded his hands. And there, in the stillness of the night before dawn, he began to pray. Pray from his heart, plunging deeply into that well-spring of life he had allowed to all but dry up, watering it anew with his profound repentance and humble trust.

And, as the hours ticked by, Ruarc's petition that Gavin might live transformed to one for himself as well. After all, wasn't he as much in need of a rebirth? A rebirth into the light of God's love? Wasn't he as much in need of a rededication to a path he had long ago forsaken, yet a path to which he must finally return if he ever hoped to save his soul and win eternal life?

Indeed, a man of honor could do no less. He owed Killian, Gavin, and his unborn child far more than just a home and a devoted upbringing. He owed them the very best he could be.

The very best he could be—as a man with a heart full of trust, love, and fidelity to his Lord and Savior.

30

IN THE wee hours of the night, Killian finally lay down beside Gavin and fell into an exhausted sleep. Somewhere in that deep, dark land of her slumbering mind, she found Alexander. In her dream, he was happy, at peace, and Killian again recognized in him all the attributes that had first drawn her to him.

"I'm so verra glad ye've found the courage to pursue yer dreams." He walked up to take her hand. "I was never the man for ye, though I loved ye the best I could."

"I know, Alexander," Killian replied, her heart burning with the bittersweet realization. Somehow she had always known that, even as she had also come to realize his love wasn't enough to assuage all the pain.

"Ye've grown. Ye've been tested, found strong and good. There's naught left to fear."

"I still fear death, fear losing the ones I love." Killian's thoughts turned to Gavin. "Our son . . . he's dying."

"But as much as ye fear it, ye accept it, don't ye?" Alexander smiled. "Accept that our lives are but gifts the Lord gives, and that He will someday ask for them back."

"Yes, I accept that. I trust in Him."

"Aye, ye must, lass. The Lord asks much of us, but He gives even more in return. More than any of us can ever fully know or hope to realize."

Even in her dream, Killian was struck by the irony of such counsel, such wisdom, coming from Alexander. But then, in the early years of her life with him, he had been a different man.

"He has already given me so much, in giving me Ruarc, his child growing within me, and this land and its people."

"Aye, that He has, but He has yet more to give ye. So verra, verra much more. Just trust . . . trust and wait on Him . . ."

From someplace far away sounds . . . a voice . . . intruded. She tried to shut them out, tried to focus on Alexander and what he was saying. But the sounds . . . that strangely familiar voice . . . plucked at her.

"Mama? Mama," the sweet voice croaked. "Mama, wake up."

Killian jerked awake. A high ceiling of dark, massive beams filled her vision. The faint scent of woodsmoke permeated the air. The stone floor she had fallen asleep upon suddenly seemed unbearably hard.

"Mama?" A hand touched her cheek. "Are you all right?"

Gavin.

For an instant, panic surged through her, and Killian was afraid she was still dreaming. Her heart pounded in her chest. If this was a dream, she didn't want ever to wake up!

"Mama, I'm thirsty. Can I have a drink?"

At her child's plaintive cry, all her maternal instincts swelled, raging to the forefront. She turned. Dream or no, Gavin needed her.

A pair of bright blue eyes, topped by a tousled mop of pale blond hair, gazed solemnly back at her. "I'm thirsty, Mama. And why are we here, instead of back at the bothy? I want to go climb rocks again."

Killian shoved to a sitting position. She looked around. Through the rents in the curtains, sunlight streamed into the room. Voices, the sound of footsteps, rose from out in the corridor. Adam's and Glynnis's pallets near the bookcases were empty.

With a trembling hand, Killian reached out to Gavin. She touched silky hair, smooth skin, a soft, curved mouth. Her eyes filled with tears. "It's really you, isn't it? It's not a dream."

He frowned in childish annoyance. "Of course it's me, Mama. Why are you acting so silly?"

"Oh, no reason," Killian choked out. "I'm just being a mama, that's all." She scooted close and pulled her son into her arms. "Because you're my child and I love you so very, very much."

Gavin snuggled close for a long moment, then began to squirm in her arms. "You're holding me too tight," he complained. "And I'm thirsty, Mama. I'm really thirsty!"

"Yes." Killian released him and leaned back, reveling in the sight. "Yes, you are."

She looked around. A pottery pitcher and two cups sat on a nearby sidetable. The cider. Ruarc's and Adam's cider. Perhaps there was still a bit left from last night.

She rose, walked to the table, and checked the pitcher's contents. It was half full. Killian poured her son a cup, then turned to him. Gavin was already sitting up, a look of anticipation on his face. Killian hurried over and knelt beside him, offering him the cider. In one, long swallow, he drank the cup's contents.

"More, Mama." He held out the now empty cup. "Please."

He hadn't eaten since midday the day before. "Let's wait a short while, then you can have some more," she said, smiling down at him. "Too much cider on an empty stomach might—"

The library door opened. Father Kenneth walked in. His glance traveled across the room until it reached them, then widened in joyous surprise. "Is it possible?" He closed the door and hurried over. "Is our wee lad finally awake and feeling better?"

Gavin bobbed his head in reply, which evidenced a wince of pain. "I'm better, I suppose." Gingerly, he touched his bandages. "My head hurts, though, and Mama won't give me more cider. And I'm still *very* thirsty."

The little priest's gaze moved to Killian. "So, he's thirsty, is he? That's a verra good sign. When did he awaken?"

"Only ten minutes or so ago. He woke me."

Father Kenneth eyed Gavin, then grinned. "I must tell Ruarc. He's been praying all night in the chapel, ye know."

Killian stared up at him. "Ruarc? Praying in the chapel?"

"Aye, lass. Yer husband finally turned to the only One who could heal yer son." A soft, satisfied light glowed in his eyes. "To my mind, that's nearly as big a miracle as the wee Gavin's healing."

"And to my mind, too." Killian climbed to her feet. "Could you stay with Gavin while I go and tell Ruarc the good news?"

Father Kenneth nodded. "Aye. It's only right ye should be the one to tell him. After all, it was ye who helped bring him to such a place. If ye hadn't come into the lad's life, I don't know what would've happened to him. Truly, I don't."

"Ruarc has been my helpmate, as much as I've been his." Killian hesitated, then leaned over and kissed the old priest on the cheek. "And neither of us could've accomplished anything without you."

"Och, get on with ye!" Father Kenneth blushed. "If ye don't have a care, ye'll soon be filling my head with all sorts of wild fancies. And me, naught more than a humble priest."

"You may be humble, but you're also one of God's finest servants. I'm grateful to call you friend."

She glanced down at Gavin, marveling anew that he was alive and appeared at last on the road to recovery. "Mama will be back soon with Ruarc. Father Kenneth may give you some more cider in another ten minutes or so."

"Bring back Fionn and Eilidh, too, will you, Mama?" Gavin called after her as she set out across the library. "I want to play with them."

Killian chuckled as she closed the door and headed down the corridor to the entry hall. It was a very good sign indeed that Gavin was already thinking about playing. Those two huge dogs, however, wouldn't soon be included in any activities more strenuous than a quick, and very well controlled, visit.

The morning air was crisp and invigorating. Mists curled at the base of the Great Herdsman and far out on Rannoch Moor. The grass was damp with dew, the droplets sparkling wherever the sunlight touched them. Birds sang; she heard the laughter of children. Killian thought it the most perfect, most beautiful of morns.

Gavin had survived his terrible injury. A new babe grew within her and her husband, the man she loved like no other, had finally turned back to God.

Fleetingly, Killian's thoughts drifted once more to her dream. It had seemed so real— Alexander visiting her, bestowing his benediction on this new life. Most likely it was but the workings of her own mind, whispering words of acceptance and approbation, but it didn't matter. The sense of peace and soul-deep satisfaction remained. The realization of the dramatic change her life had taken—that *she* had taken— lingered.

She *had* grown. She had risked all—in daring to leave Alexander, love Ruarc, and build a new life in the renewed pursuit of her heart's desire. In the doing, Killian had learned so much about herself, about others and, most of all, about God. In the doing, she had risked so little to gain the whole world.

Now it was time to share her joy with her husband. To share with him her intent to sell the plantation in Virginia and, someday, when Ruarc would surely be pardoned, use the money to rebuild Rannoch and help its people. *Her* people now. Her home.

Killian drew up before the chapel, squared her shoulders, and inhaled a deep breath. The beauty of the world this glorious morn was almost more than her heart could hold. She laughed in sheer exultation, then pushed open the chapel door and walked in.

He was slumped over the altar rail, exhausted, stiff from the cold and the hours spent on his knees. For an instant, when Killian touched him, Ruarc didn't move or respond. Then, finally, he lifted a ravaged face to her.

"I tried, lass," he said, his voice rusty with pain. "I prayed to God in every way I knew how. But He just . . . just didn't seem to hear."

She knelt beside him at the altar, wrapped an arm about his shoulders, and bent her head to touch his. "But He *did* hear, husband," she said softly. "And the Lord was most pleased with your prayers. Gavin woke this morning. He's fine."

Ruarc lifted his head and stared at her. "Gavin? Gavin's fine?"

"Yes. He's already had a drink of cider and asked to play with Fionn and Eilidh."

It seemed to take a moment more before the import of her words permeated Ruarc's weary mind. Then, as realization appeared finally to dawn, joy exploded in his eyes. He gave a bark of laughter. He grabbed Killian, pulling her to him.

"I asked God for a miracle and He gave it to me!" Ruarc reared back to look at her, the tears welling and streaming down his face. "A miracle, lass! A miracle He wrought not only in the saving of Gavin's life, but in my own heart, too."

"Yes, my love," she whispered, tears misting her eyes. "As He has done with us all."

"Aye, as He has done with us all."

He gathered Killian back into the comforting haven of his arms. Then, before the Lord and all His saints, Ruarc MacDonald, laird of Rannoch Castle, kissed her.

ABOUT THE AUTHOR

KATHLEEN MORGAN is an award-winning, best-selling writer whose work includes twenty-six published novels. She lives in Colorado with her husband and son, and in her spare time she likes to quilt, garden, and play the folk harp.

Kathleen has received numerous awards for her work, including Romantic Times' Reviewer's Choice and Career Achievement awards, as well as The Literary Times award for Literary Excellence in the Field of Romantic Fiction. She was also a Romance Writers of America RITA finalist. Her previous books include the Brides of Culdee Creek series, *Child of the Mist, Wings of Morning,* and *Giver of Roses.*

For more information on Kathleen or her upcoming releases, visit her Web site at www.kathleenmorgan.com.

Best-selling Author

KATHLEEN MORGAN

If you missed Kathleen Morgan's *Consuming Fire*, turn the page for an exciting preview.

Flanders
AUGUST 1694

A SHOT rang out in the darkness. With a lethal sibilance, a lead ball whizzed past Adam Campbell's head. Instinctively, he dove from his horse's back, tucked, and rolled, slamming onto the damp muck of the forest floor. For the space of an inhaled breath, Adam lay there, listening, waiting.

Where were his unknown assailants? Indeed, who'd be attacking him so far from Scotland? Were they but common thugs, out to rob some unsuspecting—

A branch snapped somewhere close, to his right. Not more than ten feet behind him, someone splashed through a puddle. Adam pulled free his pistol, shoved to one knee, and twisted around.

In the faint light of a cloud-shrouded night, a man loomed over him. Adam aimed and fired. Once more lead, propelled by exploding gunpowder, sped through the darkness.

The man grunted, staggered back, and fell. Then, all was bedlam. A shout of rage. A fierce war cry. The rhythmic pounding of feet as another attacker came from the left, and yet another from the right.

No time to reload. Battle-honed reflexes held sway. Dirk in hand, Adam shoved to his feet. Simultaneously, another flash of fire, a loud blast. Pain ripped through his shoulder.

He stumbled, slipped in the mire of rotting leaves and vegetation, sank to his knees. The acrid stench of gunpowder filled his lungs, choking him. And the pain. It rolled through Adam in sickening waves, sending him to the very brink of oblivion.

Then voices, triumphantly muttering words that sounded like English, pierced his dizzying haze. They thought they had him. Thought they'd won.

Remorse swamped him. Lachlan . . . I'm sorry, lad. So verra, verra sorry . . .

His cousin's face rose before him. Adam ground his teeth against his frustration, his sense of failure. He had failed in his mission and now Lachlan would die. Die . . . and the lad innocent.

Innocent . . .

The thought infuriated Adam. Renewed rage sent the blood pulsing through his veins. His vision cleared. The mists dispersed and renewed strength flowed through him.

"Nay," he whispered through clenched teeth. "I'll not let ye die . . . for me."

A hand snagged in his hair, wrenched back his head. With a feral snarl, Adam lunged forward, slashing out in the darkness . A scream tore from his opponent's throat— then he went silent .

The grip on his hair relaxed, fell away. Adam leaped up and grasped the man as he fell, using him as a human shield. Just in time. The other assailant fired his pistol. The ball slammed into his companion's body, the impact nearly knocking Adam over before he could regain his footing.

He shoved his now limp burden at the other attacker. The man staggered backward, but quickly recovered himself and threw the body aside. Dirk held high, Adam flung himself at him. They fell to the ground, fighting, grunting, and grappling for the upper hand.

Fire slashed across Adam's left cheek. His opponent, he realized, was equally armed with a knife, and equally powerful. This'd be no easy kill.

Muscles strained against muscles. Legs entwined as they twisted and rolled back and forth across the damp, slimy ground. Breaths came now in sharp, tortured gasps, and still neither could seem to gain the advantage.

His shoulder burned fiercely. By sheer force of will, Adam shoved the pain into some distant corner of his mind. It wasn't so easy, though, to mitigate the damage the pistol shot had delivered to his body. He could feel himself weakening. Once more, the edges of his vision grayed, grew fuzzy.

Lachlan. A memory flashed through Adam's mind. Lachlan of the flaming red hair and laughing countenance. Lachlan, who was all but a brother to him. How could he fail him, heap yet one more tragedy upon the dung hill that had become his life?

With a savage growl, he summoned forth his remaining strength, managing a glancing slice to the side of the other man's neck. Hissing in pain, his opponent broke free of the grip Adam had on his knife hand. Before Adam could stop him, the man cut him deeply across the side. Adam struck him hard to the jaw.

His assailant's head jerked back . He arched stiffly , lifting Adam with him. His mouth opened in a soundless cry. Then he slumped and went still.

For long, pain-wracked minutes, Adam lay there atop the now lifeless body, panting, struggling desperately to catch his breath. From somewhere far away, he heard a crack of thunder. Lightning flashed high above the trees.

The sound of rain, pattering down through the leaves, filled the now silent forest. Drops of water touched Adam's cheek, rolled down his face. A sweet, savage joy filled him.

He was alive. He had prevailed. And so would Lachlan.

Adam pushed from the body he still laid upon, awkwardly climbing to his knees. His head swam. His body quivered with weakness.

The rain began to fall harder, pelting him now with large splats. Though the night had been warm, a chill coursed through him. His hand moved to his shoulder. His fingers came back slick and sticky with blood. He touched his side, and gasped at the searing pain. Fresh blood drenched his fingers yet again.

He must get to a town, or even some farmhouse, find help, or he might well bleed to death. He wasn't far from Cambrai, his destination. He had been a fool, though, to have pushed himself so hard and traveled into the night. In an attempt to reach Cambrai even a day earlier, he had almost not arrived there at all.

With a low whistle, Adam called for his horse. There was no answering movement, no soft nicker, no sound of approaching hooves. For the first time, despair filled him. As injured as he was, how would he ever make it on foot? Yet there appeared no other choice.

This night's battle for his life, Adam realized grimly, was far from over.

Somehow, he managed to get to his feet. Somehow—or so he hoped—he found his bearings and set out in the direction of Cambrai. And somehow, though he didn't know from whence the strength came, he walked on through the night.

At times, Adam wasn't certain if it was the loss of blood, or the chill his body took on in the endless rain, that contributed to the confusion and haunting scenes flashing endlessly through his mind. Yet, in a strange sense, they seemed almost a blessing, holding at bay his awareness of his agonizing wounds. The memories tormented him nonetheless, replaying again and again events that had brought him to this unfortunate place on an even more unfortunate quest . . .

But six weeks ago, reivers had made off with five of Adam's prize black cattle. Lachlan, visiting Castle Achallader, Adam's home deep in the Highlands, had been even more eager than his cousin to set off after the thieves. Their pursuit had eventually led them out of Campbell lands and into the territory of clan Robertson. Still, on that last night, they had finally caught up with the reivers.

Though Adam had offered to spare the lives of the cattle thieves, their leader had answered with a volley of lead that soon disintegrated into deadly, hand-to-hand combat . . .

"Lachlan!" In the ensuing chaos, Adam grabbed the arm of his captain and Lachlan's brother, Robert Campbell, jerking him to a halt. "Have ye seen Lachlan, lad?"

Robbie turned a face streaked with powder and blood to his laird. "Nay, m'lord. Not for a time. He set off after one of the reivers, and that's the last I've seen of him."

"The young fool!"

Adam choked back a curse. In the darkness and confusion, it was especially dangerous to separate oneself from the rest of one's clansmen. If Lachlan blundered onto several of the reivers who'd escaped into the hills . . .

"Which way did ye see him go, lad?"

Robbie pointed in the direction of a path leading up past a jagged outcropping of rocks. "That way, m'lord."

"Round up the reivers who still live and hold them until I

return." Adam glanced at the pistol Robbie held. "Is that primed and ready?"

"Aye." His cousin held out the pistol. "Take it. Ye may well need more than just yer own pistol."

"If we don't return in a half hour's time, send some men out on our trail." Adam took the pistol from Robbie and shoved it into his belt. Not awaiting a reply, he turned on his heel and set out.

As he drew away from the fighting the night fell silent, the stars piercing the ebony sky with millions of tiny, glinting lights. A fresh, soothing breeze blew down from the mountains, carrying with it the scent of green grass and wildflowers. If not for the grim purpose of this night's work, Adam could've almost imagined himself out for a fine summer's eve stroll.

But, this night, whether he wished it or not, the tang of death was also strong on the air. Adam prayed that his young, headstrong cousin wouldn't ultimately be numbered among those who died.

As he jogged along, following an ever upward climb, a faint shout caught his ear. Adam quickened his pace, traversing the narrow, twisting path as fast as he dared. Sounds of struggle reached him, of men grappling, of fists thudding repeatedly against flesh.

Climbing a steep rise, Adam topped the hill to stare down at a moonlight bathed plateau. There, sprawled at the edge of a precipice overlooking the valley below, was Lachlan. Towering over him, a sizeable rock held above his head, was Lachlan's opponent.

Adam fired his own pistol into the air. "Stand quiet now," he then shouted even as he tossed away the spent pistol, withdrew Robbie's weapon, and pointed it at the reiver. "Drop yer wee rock and surrender. Ye've lost. Give way."

The rock still held aloft, the man wheeled about to glare up at Adam. As he did, Lachlan apparently saw his opportunity. He lunged at the reiver, grabbing him about the legs. The man screamed in rage, turned back to Adam's cousin, and kneed him hard in the face. Then, with great force, he flung the rock at Lachlan.

Adam fired, aiming only to disable the reiver. The shot flew true, striking the man in the shoulder. It gave Lachlan the opportunity he needed. He managed to duck the rock and throw himself aside. At that instant, however, the ledge the reiver and Lachlan were on began to weaken and tear away from solid earth. The reiver staggered backward. Backward to the very edge of the cliff.

Adam raced down the trail toward them. "Lachlan!" he cried. "Come away, lad. Come away!"

Instantly, Lachlan reacted to his cousin's command. He climbed to his hands and knees and scooted back to solid ground. Adam reached him, pulled him farther back, then turned to the reiver—and hesitated. For a moment slowed in time, he stood there. Stood there as the ledge finally separated and fell away. Shrieking in terror the man tipped backward, teetered on the cliff's edge then, as if in slow motion, sailed out into black nothingness.